MARINOV BRATVA
BOOK TWO

ALEKSEI

LILIAN HARRIS

Editing/Interior Formatting: CPR Publishing Services

Proofreader: Judy's Proofreading

Cover Design: Wildheart Graphics

FOR THE GIRL WHO DARED TO BELIEVE SHE COULD AND REFUSED TO STOP UNTIL SHE DID.

HERE'S TO BOOK #20, AND I'M ONLY JUST GETTING STARTED.

TRANSLATIONS & PRONOUNCIATIONS

- Fionn – "Fee-yun"
- Eriu – "Air-ooh"
- Iseult – "Ee-salt"
- Tynan – "Tie-nan"
- Cillian – "KILL-ee-in"
- Dorogaya – dear
- Katyonak – kitten
- Moya ptichka – my little bird
- Moya okhotnitsa – my huntress
- Lyubov moya – my love
- Detka – baby
- Moya – mine
- Svolichy – bastards
- Blyat – fuck
- Slava Bogu – thank God
- Davay – let's go
- moy brat – my brother
- Porca miseria – for goodness' sake
- Ublyudok - scumbag
- Ya tvayu mamu yibal – Doesn't translate well into English, but it literally means, "I fucked your mother."

ONE

FIONA

I feel him before I see him.

That slow burn at the base of my spine. The hitch in my breath that I pretend is nothing. The way my fingers tighten around a drink I don't even like.

He's here. I know it.

The bass pulses low and heavy through the bar, chairs scraping across worn hardwood, while Dana's laughter cuts through it all. She's a fellow prosecutor, the kind of woman men orbit around. Blonde. Sunny. Unapologetically warm.

I'm the opposite. I like rules. Boundaries. Men in cages—preferably the kind that slam shut with a satisfying clank after a guilty verdict.

We won today. Put one of them away. Yet here I am scanning the room, pretending it's not for him.

Dana raises her glass of pinot noir. "You should be smiling after that win today."

My mouth quirks a fraction. "This *is* me smiling."

She rolls her eyes playfully and mutters something about my resting murder face, but I'm only half listening. My gaze drifts again, drawn like a tide.

Every shadow looks like him. Every dark corner promises the same devil. And I hate what it does to me.

It's been two months since the trial ended. Since I stood in court and laid out every ounce of evidence I had, certain I'd finally be the one to bring down Aleksei Marinov. But the bastard walked free.

Now, he's everywhere. On the street. Behind me in line for tea or coffee. Even in my damn dreams.

And the worst part? My body reacts before my mind catches up. My pulse stutters. My thighs press. A slow, traitorous ache coils deep.

It's instinctual. Primal. And utterly unforgivable. A man like him shouldn't make me feel anything but disgust. But whenever we lock eyes, I go still, needing to be near him, like a match to gasoline.

I take another sip, trying to calm the hurricane churning beneath my skin. I tell myself I'm imagining it. That I'm paranoid. That he has better things to do at night than stalk the woman who tried to destroy him. He has plenty willing to keep his bed warm, which would be a much better use of his time.

But I know better. A man like Aleksei doesn't let things go, and I got under his skin. I saw it. Felt it.

He should've forgotten me, but he watches me instead. Smirks like he knows how close I am to strangling him to death. And if I wasn't sure he'd kill me for it, I'd have filed the restraining order weeks ago.

But deep down? I think I like it. There's a twisted thrill in knowing I live in his head. That despite everything, he still can't stop watching me. That when he closes his eyes, he sees me. That I crawled so deep into his mind during that trial, he still hasn't figured out how to scrape me out. And if he's not careful, I'll do it again.

Because that's what you do with men like him: you ruin them.

I sip my drink and pretend not to sense the heat at the back of my neck. Pretend I don't know who it belongs to.

I pretend so hard, I almost believe it.

Until the crowd shifts and I see him.

Aleksei Marinov.

He appeared out of nowhere. Sitting in the corner like a goddamn king, one arm draped across the back of the booth, a glass of something dark and expensive in his hand. He doesn't blink. Doesn't bother smiling, either. He simply watches me with those deep brown eyes.

And I hate how fast my stomach drops. How my breath goes shallow. How I feel seen in a way that has nothing to do with admiration. My blood pumps louder as I remember the cocky grin he wore as they read the verdict, his dark irises zeroing in on me. Like he was taunting me.

I drop my gaze to my glass, wondering how it'd feel if I broke it into thick shards and stuck one in his neck.

I bet the sick bastard would like it.

My attention fastens to him again. That chestnut hair is slicked back, jaw cut sharp enough to draw blood, his black dress shirt undone just enough to reveal the ink crawling over sun-warmed skin. He looks like something ripped from a *GQ* spread…if *GQ* featured monsters.

And still, something raw and alive claws through my chest. It's repulsive how well-attuned I am to him. How easily my senses betray me. I shift in my seat as his mouth curls just slightly, as though he knows the affect he has on me.

When I glance away, a sense of relief hits me. But like a flame, I'm pulled back to him. Our eyes align, something intense and feral within his. I feel his gaze as though it's touching me, catching fire, and spreading inside me.

I hate that he can do this to me. Even after everything.

I remember standing in court, looking him straight in the eye, and presenting the murder charge with everything I had. Every word I spoke felt fueled, every point sharpened. I wanted the jury to see the monster I knew he was.

And still, even then, every time our eyes met, something inside me splintered.

It's the same look now. Dark. Ravenous.

I should have buried that feeling. Drowned it in every legal brief and piece of evidence I filed against him. But it survived. It grew. And when I lost the case and he walked out of that courtroom free and untouched, what cut deepest wasn't the failure. It was the way he looked back at me on his way out, like he owned me.

But *I'm* the one who owns *him*.

Obsession. Hatred. Lust. He feels it all…for me.

I'm no better, though. I feel it too. All these damn emotions tangled up in a man who should never make me feel this alive.

As I look away, I find two men approaching, clean-cut, not much older than us.

Oh, great…

"You ladies want another drink?"

Dana perks up immediately, smiling flirtatiously as they pull up two chairs.

"No, thanks." I stare indifferently, lifting my beverage that I've barely made a dent in.

The taller one eyes me intently. Sure, he's attractive, but I'm just over the whole male population.

"You celebrating something?"

"Yeah. Conviction," I say flatly.

He laughs like I'm joking.

I know men like him. So sure of themselves. Then they get in bed and last three minutes.

Or maybe it's just with me.

I can already see it. He'd get me naked and get turned off, but because he's such a nice guy, he'd switch off the lights and pity-fuck me, and then I'd never see him again.

Not because there's something wrong with my body. It's my skin that turns them off. Segmental vitiligo, something I've had since I was around fifteen. The faint marbled patch of skin crawls over my right hip and around to my back. I used to hate it, but not anymore. It's who I am, and if they don't like it, they can fuck right off.

But I don't even bother with dating anymore. It's not worth the effort. There aren't very many good guys left, and I seem to attract the shittiest of the pile.

My mother thinks I just haven't found the right man. That one day I'll find someone just like my dad. But I'm twenty-eight, and that still hasn't happened.

At that, I glance at Aleksei, and instead of being disgusted, I find myself wondering if he's the type of man who'd worship every inch of me.

Fuck, why am I even thinking that?

I turn away for just a second, and when I look back, his fingers trace the rim of his glass like he's already imagining my skin beneath them.

Heat crawls up my neck as the image sneaks in—his hands on me, his mouth grazing mine—and suddenly, it's impossible to sit still and act like my body isn't already affected.

It's dirty. Cruel. Torture.

He's all wrong. He's a criminal. But here I am consumed with the very idea of being his, even for the night.

He continues watching, but this time his focus is on the men at our table. His expression doesn't change, but something about the angle of his jaw, the tension in his posture…it shifts slightly. Like a storm rolling in.

Is he…jealous?

I guess we'll find out.

I lean in closer to the guy beside me, laughing at whatever lame joke he's telling and pretending it's funny. My hand brushes his arm, just enough to test a theory.

And when I glance back toward Aleksei…

He's gone.

A sharp exhale slips past my lips. Relief rushes in, cold and fleeting, followed by disappointment. They tear through me like rivals, clawing for dominance.

Clearly I've gone crazy. The last thing I need is more of his attention. I want him to leave me alone, not stalk me more than he already is.

I push back from the table, grab my peacoat, and slip into it as I rise.

Dana squints up at me. "You heading out?"

"Yeah." I force a smile. "Tired."

She stands to give me a quick hug. "See you at work."

My attention flicks to the two guys still at the table. One's droning on about something, and the other winks at me.

Seriously?

"You sure you want to stay?" I murmur. "One of them looks like he works in insurance, and the other just tried to flirt with his eyelid."

Dana snorts. "I'll manage."

"If you say so. Text me when you get home so I don't have to worry about dragging your body out of a ditch."

"I'll be fine." She laughs, settling back at the table.

I start toward the parking lot, already regretting every second I stayed. The night is different now. Darker, heavier. The kind that presses against your skin, slipping beneath your collar until it chokes you.

As I walk faster, my heels strike the pavement in loud clicks. Each step toward the back lot tightens something inside me. The breeze catches the hem of my dress and slides beneath my coat, and the sensation crawling up the back of my neck only grows more intense.

My body knows before my mind will admit it: he's here.

My keys are already in my hand, clenched between my fingers like a weapon I plan to use if I have to. When my car comes into view, I force myself forward, locking on to it like salvation.

Just get in. Just drive. Just breathe. You're fine.

I tell myself that, over and over.

"Running off so soon, Ms. Prosecutor?"

TWO

FIONA

My body locks the instant I register his voice.

It doesn't just reach me. It wraps tightly around me. Every cell reacts. Blood rushes like static in my ears, goosebumps rise along my arms, my thighs clench on instinct, and there's a flutter low in my belly, like prey sensing the predator.

Then, slowly, I pivot, already cursing the way my pulse stammers and the betrayal of that deep throbbing between my legs.

And there he is: Aleksei Marinov. Lust, danger, and everything I've tried to forget.

He towers over me, easily six-four to my five-six, standing just a few feet away like he owns the pavement. Like he owns *me*. A devil in all his glory.

One hand's tucked into the pocket of his tailored coat, posture deceptively relaxed. But those eyes, they're fire and violence and possession wrapped in ice. He rakes them over me, slow and unapologetic, carving himself into every inch of skin they touch like it's his right.

There's nothing gentle in it. No pretense of civility. Everything about him is raw and unrepentant, and it hits me like a match to dry kindling.

I should look away, give myself the illusion of distance, but my eyes stay locked on his.

I remember walking out of court near the end of the trial, hands shaking with adrenaline, furious I was losing and even more furious at the low curl in my gut every time Aleksei's gaze found me. And now he's like a shadow I can't outrun. A reminder. A threat. A temptation.

The man I tried to destroy…and the one who's still destroying me.

He takes one step toward me, and I take one back, caught between craving his touch and retreating from the threat he so clearly is.

"What the hell are you doing here, Marinov?"

I don't even know why I'm asking. It's obvious he's been following me, but the real question is how he's able to find me every time. I've had experts sweep my car, my house, my goddamn phone, and nothing.

He keeps closing the distance until the car meets my back and I have nowhere left to escape him or the way he affects me.

"That's obvious." His Russian accent trails over my skin like rope tightening around my throat. "I followed you to make sure you don't get mugged. I'm quite the gentleman."

When I scoff, the corner of his mouth lifts in that slow, cocky twist that should repulse me. Instead, it sends need licking down my spine. His presence devours space as he draws even closer, stealing breath, thought, and logic until there's barely a whisper between us.

"You look different." The heated pools of his eyes trail the length of my body like he's committing it to memory.

No, like he already owns it.

"I can't decide if I prefer picturing myself stripping you out of those uptight little suits you wore to court…" His finger lifts, skimming the edge of my neckline, just beneath the V of my dress. "Or tearing this tight little thing off you instead."

Every nerve ending lights up, my core tightening painfully. "Just because your brother and my best friend are married, it doesn't mean I'll let you fuck me. Now back off."

But I don't even convince myself, my voice giving out.

"You are right…" His fingers trace down between my breasts, each stroke unraveling another thread of resistance. "You're the last woman I should be anywhere near."

His breath grazes my cheek, while I can't seem to move.

"Yet here you are," I whisper. "Following me like a lost little puppy."

My palm hits his chest, hard muscle beneath cotton. He chuckles—low, dark, amused. I push again, but he doesn't budge.

"Get away from me." This time, I mean it.

Maybe.

Footsteps scuff the pavement behind him. Some stranger passing through, unaware of the war unfolding.

Aleksei doesn't turn. Doesn't even flinch. His body cages me, pressing into mine, while his gaze pins me just as tightly, like he's daring me to run. Like he already knows I won't.

"Ma'am, are you okay?"

Aleksei's jaw twitches as he cups my cheek, the sensation causing me to forget how bad this is. His mouth drops to my ear.

"Say one wrong thing and he will be dead before you can take your next breath."

And I know he means it.

"I'm fine."

The stranger nods. "Okay. Have a good night."

When he walks away, I breathe a sigh of relief. Only when his car drives off does Aleksei move, his fingers tightening around my jaw, thumb dragging lazily across my bottom lip.

A shiver skates down my spine.

"Good girl. I like it when you're obedient."

I despise how those words melt something inside me. "Don't ever call me that again."

His husky laugh sends liquid heat down my body. "But you like it, don't you, moya okhotnitsa? I bet if I dipped a finger inside that cunt, you'd soak it."

My core instantly clenches.

How the hell does he know? And what does that word mean?

"Listen to me, asshole. This ends now. You need to stop following me. Toying with me. Because if you don't, I will file a restraining order. And when you violate it, I'll bury you so deep in the system, they won't even find your teeth."

"You're very adorable, even when you play the frozen little ice princess. But I bet when I get you under me, you'll be soft, warm, and agreeable. And if not…" His knuckles softly graze my cheek. "I'll fuck the frost right out of you."

I slap him before I can stop myself. My eyes expand the moment it happens, and his smirk widens, a growl spilling from deep in his chest.

His grip finds my throat, squeezing tight, while his body pushes into mine until I can feel him thick and heavy against my stomach. "That was not very polite."

"Let me go."

He tsks. "Not until you apologize. Nicely."

I tip my chin up, needing to fight whatever is happening here. "Fuck you, Marinov. This isn't a game."

His mouth hovers near mine, so close I can taste the promise of a kiss in the air between us. "I beg to differ. Because I'm having a lot of fun."

His lips skim down the side of my throat, and the moment his mouth touches skin, my head tips back without permission, colliding with my car. A soft sound escapes me, and I immediately regret it when I see the smug expression on his gorgeous face. That same one he wore when he beat me in court.

Revulsion surges through my veins, colliding with the hunger I wish I could kill. I squeeze my eyes shut, and I'm back in the shower after court, fingers working between my thighs as I imagined all the filthy things he'd do if he ever got close enough.

And now here he is, touching me like he has the right.

Because who's going to stop him? Clearly not me.

"You should know, Ms. Prosecutor…" His words are a husky drag over my skin. "You're the one who came to my bar. Maybe I'm the one who needs a restraining order from you."

His bar? Oh God.

"I didn't know…" The confession slips out on a breath as his hand slides to my hip, then lower.

"Prove it."

My heartbeat stutters as his fingers slip under the hem of my dress, slow enough to make my lungs ache. He grazes bare skin, dragging upward, his touch a lazy threat that feels more like a promise. Inch by inch, higher and higher…until his knuckles ghost along the sensitive inside of my thigh.

A moan shivers out, my lips parting against my will. "Don't."

The word is both fragile and unconvincing. Because I don't even know what I mean.

Don't stop? Don't go further? Don't make me beg for something I swore I'd never want?

But he ignores me, fingers lingering, his body caging mine, his mouth so close I can almost taste him. Every second drags until my knees threaten to give. His erection digs even further into me, and it's obvious no matter what he thinks of me, no matter how much venom we've spat at each other, our bodies want. They crave. And there's not a damn thing either of us can do about it.

His mouth dips to the hollow beneath my ear, the warmth of his exhales wrapping around me, branding me. Fingertips trail up my leg, drawing fire over my skin until they pause just shy of the place that would strip me of whatever control I'm still pretending to have.

My fist finds his thick hair, gripping hard like it's the only thing keeping me upright. His hold around my throat clamps, cutting off just enough air that I'm dizzy, painfully aware of how close I am to coming from nothing but the power he's holding over me.

Why couldn't this be anyone else? Why does it have to be him?

But would it even be this good if it wasn't?

"How should I prove it?" The words come out low.

I'm desperate for a reprieve, some distraction from the madness clawing through me.

He eases back just an inch, enough to make the air rush between us, hitting me with a half-grin that makes my stomach twist. "You're the lawyer."

His mouth ghosts over mine, barely brushing my lips, making every nerve scream for more.

"Figure it out." His voice drops, rough and deep, stroking over the parts of me I've fought to keep buried from him.

His other hand toys with the strap of my thong, knowing exactly what he's doing. My eyes flutter shut, my body arching into his touch, craving what I swore was off-limits.

He's a murderer, Fiona. The kind of man you hate. Men like him destroy people.

And he will destroy you.

But my mind and my body are at war, and my body is winning.

When he slips my panties to the side and drags his fingertip over my clit, a broken whimper escapes. My clutch in his hair tightens, my teeth grinding as his eyes pin mine, watching me like this is the only thing keeping him alive.

"You like it, don't you?" He slides inside me slowly, barely breaching the entrance.

"No." The word catches in my throat, my walls squeezing him.

"You're not much of a liar, Ms. Clark."

Then he drives two fingers into me—hard, deep, stealing my breath.

Before I can scream, his palm clamps over my mouth, muffling the sound as he pounds into me faster, harder, forcing every ounce of control from my limbs. My nails dig into his hard biceps, needing something to hold on to, until it's like my body doesn't belong to me anymore.

The lot is silent except for my muted cries, the slick rhythm of my arousal, and the low, merciless cadence of his exhales while his gaze never leaves mine.

I'm so close. Too close. My eyes roll back, frantic to escape the intensity, but his head gives the smallest shake.

"You look at me. Only me. You will remember who made your cunt drip this good."

I force my vision back to his, and the flicker of satisfaction on his face makes my blood boil.

"That's it." Dark approval drips from each syllable. "You obey so well."

His words ignite something in me, fury tightening my jaw while need pools low, shameful and sweet.

I hate that I like it. Curse him for knowing it.

His mouth curves like he's reading my mind. "It's okay to lose control. Give it to me, okhotnitsa. Because it's already mine."

"I'll never give you anything."

A dark chuckle rolls out of him. "Except this." A hard thrust steals my breath. "Look at you, dripping down my fingers like a desperate whore. I bet you'd taste even sweeter begging for it."

My blood pumps louder in my ears, my core pulsing.

Another rough thrust and my body trembles on the edge. Just a little more and it'll be over. I can go home. Pretend this never happened.

"But you…" His tone dips lower, harsher. "You don't deserve it."

The next drive of his fingers is sharp enough to make my knees buckle. His nose drags up my throat, inhaling me like he's memorizing my scent.

"You don't deserve anything from me except the humiliation of knowing exactly what I can make you do…any time I want."

Then…he stops.

What?

The absence is violent. Every nerve in my body screams in protest, heat slamming into cold.

No. No, no, no. That son of a bitch.

He eases back, that haughty look etched into his face like it's been there his whole life as he slides one hand into his pocket as if none of this ever happened.

"Y-you…" My words fracture, too jagged to form anything coherent.

He tilts his head, studying me like I'm a puzzle he's already taken apart piece by piece.

"You should get home, Ms. Prosecutor." His voice turns low and deceptively gentle. "Late night. A lot of dangerous men out there."

Then he turns, strutting away like I'm already forgotten. While I'm still here, breathless and furious, shaking with something that has nothing to do with fear.

Desire. Loathing. Temptation. A tangle of contradictions, all tied up in the man I didn't want to be close to.

Yet his presence still clings to me—on my skin, in my breath— like he never left at all.

THREE

ALEKSEI

Three screens glow against the black marble of my kitchen island, surveillance feeds flipping like a roulette wheel of her life.

One shows the courthouse steps. Another, the street outside her office building. The last one, which is my personal favorite, stays trained on the alley facing into her office.

She doesn't know much about how I do what I do. How I can see her sitting at her desk right now, catching the side of her face as her brows tighten while she reads something on her computer.

Steam curls from the rim of my mug as I sip my coffee—black and scalding, just as I like it. No sugar. No cream. Nothing to soften the burn.

I watch her for a while, eyes locked on the flickering feed while she works, buried in files. Typing, pausing, brushing her hair behind her ear the way she always does when she's thinking hard. The way I crave to do it instead.

She picks up her cup of green tea, and I don't have to look at it closely to know I'm right. It's what she drinks every morning, while she prefers chamomile tea before bed. She only drinks coffee on occasion.

Fiona is predictable, and that makes it that much easier to know her every move without even needing these cameras.

I know her schedule better than she does. I know where she gets her tea, what time she takes her lunch, which streetlight she always speeds through when she's late.

So when she finally stands, smoothing down her suit jacket and reaching for her coat, I already know where she's heading.

My finger drags across the trackpad, and the camera angle slides to the next feed.

There she is, sauntering across the street, hips swaying like she forgets that the one she tried to bury has been watching her every move since the day she lost.

The day I won.

She does not know the extent of my depravity. What I did for her. The risk I took doing it. But now that I know everything, I would do it again, even knowing how much she enjoyed the thought of watching me rot in prison.

Blyat, she was beautiful that day when the jury read the verdict. That fire in her eyes. The way her mouth tightened like she was choking on glass. It lit something in me, something unnatural and possessive.

Not because I wanted her. Because I broke her.

And last night, I reminded her who's in control.

I can still see her in the rearview mirror as I drove away: green eyes blazing, fingers digging into the door like she couldn't decide whether to claw my face off or drag me back and make me finish what I'd started.

I would bet anything that she went home telling herself it was hate, contempt…every holy little word that makes her feel clean. But I know better. I felt the way her pulse jumped under my hand. I know how her body clamped around my fingers, greedy even when her mouth told me no.

Her body already understands what her mind refuses to admit: she'll bend for me. Completely.

She really thought she could take me down? Walk into a courtroom and strip a man like me to flesh and bone and I would just let her? Did she actually think the trial was the end of it, that I'd walk out and forget her name, her face, the way her lips curled when she thought she had won?

No.

Fiona has no idea what real power looks like.

Real power does not need a gavel or a badge. It watches. It waits. And when it strikes, it doesn't leave witnesses.

I switch to another feed. She's outside the courthouse talking to that other prosecutor, Dana. The one with the laugh too shrill to be tolerated. I nearly killed her just to shut her up, but I was trying to be civil.

Konstantin says I act too fast. That I should think things through before making them permanent. He might have a point. Not that I would ever admit that to my brother.

My jaw locks as Fiona brushes a hand through her hair, the same hand that slapped me last night. I felt that slap in my damn blood. She doesn't realize how close I came to kissing her until her lips bled.

Or maybe she does. Maybe she likes to pretend she'd turn me away, but I know better.

I could've killed her. Would've even made it painless because I'm such a nice guy. But where's the satisfaction in that?

What I have planned is going to be a lot more entertaining. It's what she likes, isn't it? Turning everything into a performance, just like in court.

She doesn't understand how badly she's infected me, how deeply she's lodged herself inside places I thought were dead. And now she's there, a slow poison I have no intention of curing.

Because she made it personal.

And I will make it worse. I'll hunt her in the dark, and I will be smiling when I take her apart. One nail at a time.

I'm going to take everything from her. Her freedom. Her body. Her damn soul.

She'll tell herself she has a choice. That she can fight me, that the law will save her. But I will close every door, burn every exit, until the only path left leads straight to me.

And when she finally comes, it won't be because she wants to. It will be because there's nowhere else to go. Not because I want her. But because I can. For the pleasure in her pain.

She has no idea what's coming. No idea how far I will go. But she will soon enough.

I stare at her again, my body pumping with adrenaline. She's wearing red today. The color of power. Of blood.

She's getting ready for another war, except she has no idea she's already in one. And I won't lose.

Her eyes flick to the streetlamp as she steps off the curb, like she senses me. She always does. A pull neither of us want to name.

But I don't need her. I just want to ruin her. Want her begging for mercy I will never give. Want her desperate for me until she hates herself.

And when she has nothing left, I'll make Fiona Clark look me in the eyes and thank me for the wreckage.

FOUR

ALEKSEI
FIVE MONTHS AGO

My lawyer said she wouldn't come. He begged me to let it go, muttering about ethics and appearances. About how no prosecutor would ever step foot into the holding block of the man she's trying to put away.

But he doesn't know her like I do. That woman needs to be close to me, even if it kills her.

Part hatred. Part fascination. And something far darker she will never confess, not even to her priest. If she was religious, that is.

I saw it the first day of trial when our eyes met across the courtroom. The way she sat too still, as if bracing for impact. How hard she fought not to look, and how much she failed. Her hands stayed steady, but her pulse told the truth. I could feel it, hear it, like my mouth was already at her throat.

Hers isn't the kind of hate you walk away from. It's the kind you get addicted to.

The door opens, and every part of me comes alive as soon as I see her face.

She walks in like she's in charge. Spine straight. Eyes sharp. Cream-colored suit hugging every curve like it was stitched straight onto her skin, making me picture things that would make her blush. Like the way my fingers would grip that tight ponytail while I forced her to her knees just so I could find out how well that mouth truly works.

She's like the angel of death. Or maybe the huntress. Both suit her.

If I didn't want to end her, I'd have Fiona bent over this table, taking me so deep she'd forget her own name.

Though fucking her and then killing her might actually be a better idea.

"Please, Ms. Clark, have a seat." I lean back in the cold metal chair, the cuffs biting into my wrists.

"I'll be right outside," the guard says before stepping out.

"Thanks," she tells him, her tone light, almost warm.

But the second she faces me, it's gone, wiped clean like it was never there. I smirk at the switch, at how quickly she can mask herself.

She narrows her eyes, pulling out the chair. "What do you want, Marinov? Your lawyer said you needed to discuss something."

My gaze drags over her, pausing in all the places I know she doesn't want me to look. "And you just came running? I'm touched, Ms. Clark. Spasebo." *Thank you.*

She scoffs. "Don't flatter yourself. Why the hell did you drag me out here? Please enlighten me." Her arms cross. "Then crawl back into whatever hole you slithered out of."

A low, rough chuckle escapes me. My eyes drop to her mouth, to the perfect slash of red lipstick I'd like to ruin with my teeth. My hands bend into fists beneath the table, cuffs digging deeper.

This attraction is nothing but a weapon. One I'll use when it suits me.

She thinks she's here on her own terms, free to walk away when she's done. She has no idea she's already stepped into my game. The pieces are in motion. The ending's already written. And when it comes, she won't be leaving the way she arrived.

"You look good." My smirk deepens when her eyes flare. "Ivory is definitely your color." My gaze drops, lingering on the rise and fall of her chest. "But I am thinking that suit would look much better crumpled on my floor."

A muscle tics in her cheek. "You dragged me down here to throw some prison fantasy at me? What's next? Are you going to recite poetry?"

I inhale slowly, savoring the scent of her, the crackle of tension between us. "No. I brought you here to remind you that monsters don't always live under the bed. Sometimes…" I lean in, close enough for her breath to catch. "Sometimes they stand right in front of you, and you never see them for what they are until it's too late."

"Is that some sort of threat?" she scoffs.

"Who said I was talking about myself?"

"What the hell does that even mean? Stop talking in riddles and tell me what you actually want to say."

"You're a smart girl." My eyes lock on hers. "I have faith you'll figure it out. And when I'm out of here, maybe we will even learn to tolerate each other."

Her laugh is cold, and she leans in like she's ready to cut me with it. "You're never getting out of here, Aleksei. Never."

"Mm." The chair scrapes as I pull in, her lips so close to mine I can almost taste it. "I like it when you say my name. Say it again, detka. Slower this time."

Disgust twists her face, and I drink it in.

"I will work night and day to make sure you rot in here. Every time you wake up, I want you to remember exactly why you're here, and exactly who put you inside. You understand me?" Her features turn with something that resembles victory, but it will unfortunately be short-lived.

"Da. I understand, my sweet Fiona. But I know one thing."

I reach out, dragging the pad of my finger across the top of her hand. She sucks in a sharp inhale, but doesn't pull away. My smile widens.

"And what's that?" Her voice is tighter now.

"That when you go to bed and close your eyes..." My gaze descends to her mouth. "It's me you see."

"I—"

"Don't deny it, Ms. Clark. It's beneath you." I meet her stare, and something sharp knots in my chest. "What do you see, hmm? What do I do to you? What do you want me to do? I bet you like it rough. You want a man who takes every inch of you without asking. Even now, I can tell from the way you press your thighs together, you want me to burn that fire right out of you. Isn't that right, Ms. Prosecutor?"

Her composure cracks—only for a second, but I catch it. The faint flush in her cheeks. The heat rising in her skin.

She hates me. But she wants me just as much.

"Fuck you," she snaps.

"Not yet. But we're getting there."

She rises in a rush, turning to leave, but I speak before she can take a step.

"You ever wonder why you came?"

Her body goes taut.

"You could've said no. Could've ignored my lawyer. But you didn't. You put on your tightest little suit, slicked your hair back, and walked right in." I let my smirk deepen. "You needed to see me up close, didn't you? Just once. Needed to know if I was real. If that look in my eyes was imagined."

She turns back, gaze molten, like she wants to burn me alive.

"You're done, Marinov." Her mouth presses into a hard line.

I rise slowly, letting her see how much control I still have, even here. The Marinov name carries a lot of weight, especially in prison.

"We'll see about that." My words are low, almost gentle.

Her hand lands on the door, and the guard buzzes it open.

"Run, Ms. Prosecutor," I call. "Because when I catch you…it won't be the law you're begging for."

The door shuts behind her, and I can almost feel the echo of her pulse in the air.

She's deeper in the game now, tangled with me in ways she won't admit. And that's exactly where I want her.

FIVE

FIONA
PRESENT DAY

The morning sun slips through my blinds, far too bright for the kind of thoughts I woke up with.

Two days. That's how long it's been since Aleksei Marinov pinned me against my car and reminded me exactly why I can't stand him and why I can't stop thinking about him either.

In his eyes—in the way he looked at me, touched me—it was as if he was reminding me that I was already his. As though it's been decided by some divine prophecy.

I'd laugh if it wasn't for this strange tingling in the back of my neck, like a warning of some kind.

I've replayed that night more times than I'll ever admit. The heat of his breath against my skin. The slow drag of his fingers over my thigh.

I tell myself it's over. That maybe he got whatever sick thrill he needed and now he'll vanish back into the darkness he crawled out of.

But I know better. He's not done with me. He never will be.

I pad across the hardwood floor, the familiar dread curling in my stomach as I near the front door, wondering if there will be another letter waiting for me in the mailbox. Sliding into my slippers, I walk out into the cool morning air, my fingers hovering over the latch to the mailbox just outside.

It's been like this since the middle of the trial. The anonymous letters that keep me on edge.

It has to be Aleksei messing with me. It would be like him. The psychological games. Shadow warfare. I've seen the way he and his family operate. Always two moves ahead. Always circling, never striking. Until they want you to bleed.

But the thing that keeps me awake at night is the gnawing possibility that it isn't him. That there's someone else out there. Someone far more dangerous.

And they're coming for me.

With my line of work, though, there's always a chance of that.

When I open the mailbox, a handful of envelopes waits inside, innocent at first glance. Snatching them up, I head back into the house, heart pounding as I sift through the stack.

I know it's here. I can just feel it.

Then I see it. There's no name. No postage. No return address. Just a plain white envelope with my name and address printed in big, blocky letters. Nothing to go on at all.

It sits heavy in my hands like something rotten, like it might bite.

I've gotten six others just like it, all meant to rattle me. The last one was the worst.

> Think you're safe? It's not over yet. Your time is coming.

And now, between Aleksei watching me and these anonymous threats, I can't even tell which monster to fear more.

If this is Aleksei's idea of a game, though, I swear to God, I'll kill him. Who the hell does he think he is?

With a sigh, I run a hand down my face. I probably need to tell my boss about this, though it's not like he'll do anything. No one's assigning me a bodyguard over some letters, and the cops won't have a damn thing to go on. This is on me to figure out.

I stare at the envelope again, hesitation thick in my chest, then tear it open before I can talk myself out of it, already bracing for whatever fresh hell waits inside.

> Do you know what happened the day you were attacked? Do you want to know why?

The words blur, a rush of fear spreading through my limbs. I haven't let myself think about that night in months. I buried it deep, so deep it almost stopped feeling real.

The fear. That cold, breathless certainty that I was about to die. Then…darkness.

Six months ago, I came home after a late court session. Just another ordinary day. The plan was to reheat some leftover pasta, maybe fall asleep on the couch with the TV still on.

I never made it that far.

I'm starving the moment I walk inside and lock up behind me. But as soon as the latch clicks, something pulls at my attention.

My vase in the foyer has been moved. Not by much, just a few inches to the left, but enough to make every instinct in me go on alert.

I reach for the knob again, ready to step back outside and call someone, anyone, but before I can turn it, a man steps out from behind the wall. Ski mask. Gloves. A gun held low.

My heart drops.

"Don't even think about it," he says, almost too calmly, while I'm

surrounded by pure panic.

My fingers hover over the handle, every part of me screaming to run out onto the porch and yell for help, but something tells me I won't make it three feet.

The moment his eyes bounce from the door back to me, I run toward the stairs, not even sure what the hell my plan is. I take off toward the bedroom because that's the only place that feels like an option.

But I only make it halfway up before he's behind me, his boots hitting the stairs with a pounding rhythm. I grab the banister and try to haul myself faster, but he catches my ankle and yanks.

I fall hard. My forehead smacks the step, and light bursts behind my eyes. My fingers scrape for something, anything, but he drags me down the stairs, my body slamming against each step, palms burning as I try to claw free. The gun clatters somewhere behind us when he switches his grip, his gloved hand fisting the back of my shirt.

I twist, shove, kick, but he's stronger. He pins me on the floor, one knee on the wood, the other pressing into my stomach while he reaches into his pocket and pulls out duct tape. The sight of it knocks the air out of my lungs.

If that tape touches my wrists, I'm not getting out of here alive.

Pure survival takes over. I dig my nails under the edge of his mask and find skin, clawing through as I let out a scream.

"Bitch!" He slaps me.

Instead of backing down when he draws closer, I lift up and bite the side of his cheek through the fabric, tasting blood. My legs kick wildly, and I knee him in the balls, slipping out from under him before rushing toward the front door like every inch of my life depends on it.

I get my hand on the knob, turning it halfway before he reaches me again. A scream sticks in my throat as his fist tangles in my hair, pain lancing through my scalp so fast my vision blurs.

The blow comes next. A hard, brutal crack to the side of my head that sends the world tilting away from me.

The door slips from my grip. The floor rushes up. Everything folds into spinning shapes and fading sound, darkness swallowing the hallway.

And the only thought that comes next is that I'm about to die.

But I didn't. I woke up on the floor, and he was gone. No sign of him either. No blood except my own. It was like someone had wiped the whole place clean.

The only proof left behind was the gash on my forehead and the terror still lodged in my throat.

When the cops arrived, they found nothing. No forced entry. No weapon or prints. They called it a failed robbery attempt, but I knew better.

Whoever he was, he didn't come for my things. He came for me. This wasn't random. It was personal.

The next day, I turned my home into a fortress. Alarms on every door and window. A camera by the entrance. Reinforced locks. Paranoia made tangible.

Then, several weeks later, the letters started coming. At first, I didn't think they were connected to the attack. But now? I'm certain.

The letter slips from my fingers and lands on the counter with a soft flutter, but the sound is deafening in the quiet. My nerves buzz as I pinch my temple and head toward the electric kettle to make some tea, needing something to calm me.

My cat winds between my legs, his soft meow tugging me from my thoughts. I scoop him up, burying my cheek in his black fur.

"I'm fine," I whisper.

He meows again, as if calling me a liar.

"It's really not cute being such a know-it-all, Poe."

He flicks his tail and jumps down just as the kettle clicks off behind me. I reach for a mug when my phone vibrates across the counter.

Emilia's name appears on the screen. Or should I call her Mrs. Marinova now, being that she's the wife of a Mob boss?

The thought alone makes me sick. My best friend married to a psychopath. Aleksei's whole family is crazy.

I swear, I think she lost her mind when she decided to stay with Konstantin. Every day, I worry that something will happen to her or she'll get caught up in whatever illegal dealings he's involved with.

She used to walk the straight and narrow, a damn good agent for the Bureau, until her brother got arrested and everything spiraled. It's hard for me to get over it all. I can only imagine how hard it's been for her.

But if she's truly happy with that crazy motherfucker, I *guess* I can be happy for her too.

Having Aleksei as a brother-in-law has to be hell, though. The man walks around with a permanent stick up his ass.

That is, unless he's busy tormenting me with mind games or filthy innuendos. Then, of course, he's smiling.

Smug, infuriating bastard.

"Hey, Em," I answer.

"Hey. How are you?"

Not well. I possibly have a second stalker. And the one you're related to, he's making it real hard not to commit murder.

"I'm good. Got a hair appointment in a bit, then stopping by my parents' later. What are you up to?"

She sighs. "How are they holding up?"

"They're managing as best they can."

What else can I say? Their life is imploding too.

"I wish there was something I could do to help, but I know you'd never accept Konstantin's money."

"Absolutely not. You know I love you, Em, but when it comes to the Marinovs, I want no part."

"I know. I get it. But can you at least come over for dinner and get to know him? I'm sure you'll like him once you do."

I bite back the truth. That'll never happen. The only way I'd sit down to dinner with that family is if someone forced me.

As in tied me to a chair and gagged me.

"I'll think about it. But how are you?" I deflect. "How's life as a… Mob wife?"

That's so hard to say out loud.

My best friend, the Mob wife. What the fuck…

"Oh, you know. Between all the sex and the money, I'm actually exhausted."

"Tragic, really. I'll light a candle for you." An easy laugh falls out of me.

"No, but for real, it's been good. I've been helping Konstantin with his company, which has really helped distract me from…you know…"

My heart squeezes. Emilia's been through hell since she married Konstantin. Betrayal, danger, trauma. But she's the strongest person I know.

"I'm sorry," I tell her. "I wish it hadn't all gone down the way it did."

"Me too." Her words break a little, and all I want to do is hug her.

A woman's muffled words interrupt on her end.

"Ugh, sorry. I've gotta go. Apparently running an empire means I never get to finish a goddamn conversation."

"Go, boss lady," I tease, forcing lightness I don't feel.

"I'll talk to you later, okay? I really miss you." Emilia's voice catches just a little at the end. Barely noticeable, unless you know her like I do. "Let's get lunch soon, okay?"

I press the phone tighter to my ear. "Yeah, let's do that."

"Okay. We'll plan something later."

"Alright. Bye."

She hangs up, and I'm left staring at nothing.

The silence that follows isn't peaceful. It's dense, heavy, creeping around the edges and settling over me like a fog I can't push through.

I should be thinking about the letters. The masked man. The possibility that he's still out there. But my mind doesn't go there. It goes somewhere worse.

It goes to *him.*

The monster. The ghost. The devil incarnate. The man who's found a way to slither under my skin, leaving pieces of himself there like splinters I can't dig out.

And buried under all that, a dark, treacherous part of me wants to know exactly what he'll do when he finally decides to take what he wants…and how long he'll make me beg for it.

SIX

FIONA

The hum of dryers and the faint chemical scent of hair dye wrap around me. My stylist, Marlene, waves me over to her station with that same warm smile she's worn since I first sat in her chair.

Dropping into the seat, I set my purse on my lap, the latest anonymous note still clutched in my hand. I meant to tuck it away before coming inside, but my mind's been running in circles, turning over the same questions, unable to shake the thought that there could be someone else watching me.

Marlene glances down at my hand, tilting her head, her bright red hair flipping over her shoulder. "What's that?"

I slide the note into my purse, and shrug. "Just a note from someone."

A dark brow lifts with a playful glint in her eyes. "Ooh. Secret admirer?"

A short laugh slips out before I can help it. "More like a psychopath."

She chuckles like it's a joke, twisting a lock of my hair between her fingers. "They're all psychopaths, honey."

She's not wrong about that.

Her eyes meet mine in the mirror. "How are your parents doing?"

The question sinks my mood even more.

"Still the same."

She shakes her head. "My God. They're such good people. I hate that this is happening to them." Picking up a large comb, she runs it through my strands. "You think they're going to sell the place?"

As I shake my head, my emotions overwhelm me. "I really hope not. It would break their hearts. They've built that vineyard from nothing. That place *is* them. I just…" My throat tightens. "I wish I could do something to help. But I don't have that kind of money."

If they don't pay the mortgage soon, it's over.

She pins half of my hair up, working with efficient hands as she sprays a bit of water over the other sections, then grabs a pair of scissors. "Are they trying to find some investors? Maybe someone with fresh ideas would be good."

"Yeah, they're actively looking now." I glance at my reflection, forcing a smile.

"That's good. I'm sure it will work out. Tell your mom I said hi, will ya? Haven't seen her stop by in a while."

"She's cutting back on expenses."

Marlene nods, sympathy swelling in her irises.

The rest of the appointment passes in easy small talk, but the note in my purse is like a ticking clock against my thigh.

By the time I reach the vineyard, the late afternoon sun spills gold across the rows of vines. Normally, this view feels like home: rolling hills, neat trellises, the earthy sweetness drifting on the breeze. But this year, the leaves curl at the edges, clusters of grapes hanging smaller, sparser. Even the land looks exhausted.

Inside the main building, Mom greets me with her usual warm smile and a kiss on the cheek. But up close, I catch the fine lines of worry etched around her eyes. Dad's right behind her, pulling me into a bear hug, his hair somehow grayer than it was a few months ago.

"How you doing, kid?"

"I'm good, Papa. How are you guys? Need any help around here?"

"Nah, we're okay." He grins, but it's the kind of smile meant to distract me from the hell they're going through.

I can feel the burden behind it. He's beyond stressed. They both are.

"You look pale." Mom's hands cup my cheeks, like she's checking me for a fever. "Are you eating? Sleeping? Going on any dates?"

"Oh, no. Here we go." A groan slips out as I duck past her toward the sofa in their office. "Ma, please, not today."

She trails after me, completely undeterred. "Not today? What does that even mean?" Her eyes widen in outrage. "You're twenty-eight. If you ever want to get married and have children, the time is now. You may not have a deadline, but your ovaries do."

Oh God, please give me a bullet. Where is Aleksei Marinov when you need him?

"I'm sure there's been a handsome defense attorney or two lately," she presses.

The look I shoot her is both wild and exaggerated. "Are you kidding? I'd never *date* anyone from the other side, let alone marry him."

She scoffs. "Defense attorneys make money, sweetheart."

"Life isn't all about money."

"Oh, really?" She crosses her arms over her chest. "Tell that to our vineyard. Right, Tony?"

Dad's chuckle drifts from the coffee pot in the far right corner. "Do I look like an idiot? I'm not getting involved. I'm Switzerland."

"Coward," she mutters, shaking her head. "You want your daughter to be alone when we're dead? Because that's where she's heading."

"Oh, come on. She's still young. She's got time."

"See?" I gesture toward Dad like he's my star witness. "I've got time."

"Per l'amor di Dio, finirai zitella e con dieci gatti." *For the love of God, you'll end up a spinster with ten cats.*

Oh, no. When Mom starts talking in Italian, we know we're screwed.

"Don't worry, Ma. The right man will come." *Or not.* "I'm just currently surrounded by psychos."

Her gaze sharpens. "How psycho are we talking?"

My jaw drops. "Wow. Nice one, Ma. Whose side are you on?"

She smirks. "What? Sometimes the crazy ones are better in bed."

"Angelica! Come on." Dad groans. "My poor ears."

"What?" She tosses her hands in the air, completely unfazed. "We're all adults here."

Dad scratches his head, shaking it with exasperation. But he loves my mother more than anything. I don't think I've ever seen a love stronger than what they have.

"Alright, enough," I cut in. "No more talk about my love life. Or anything else that'll haunt me forever."

Mom scoffs. "Fine, I'll stop. For now. But I'm serious about the defense attorneys."

"You've made that quite clear." My eyes flick to the desk. "Now, how about we talk about what really matters? Have you found any investors yet?"

The stack of unopened mail in the corner draws my attention: thick envelopes, some stamped with red lettering that screams overdue.

A glance passes between them, and my stomach coils.

"What was that? What aren't you telling me?"

"Nothing." Mom clears her throat, a dead giveaway she's lying.

"We have a few interested parties. We're just…weighing the pros and cons, that's all."

My eyes narrow. "And will they let you keep the majority of the shares?"

She peers at the floor. "We hope so."

I know if they want to keep the doors open, they won't have much choice. But I'll be damned if I allow them to be taken advantage of.

Dad shrugs like it's nothing. "We'll figure it out, sweetheart. We always do."

The words are meant to be reassuring, but they hit like a stone in my chest.

We talk for a while, pretending everything's fine. Mom fussing over whether I'm eating enough again. Dad telling some ridiculous story about a raccoon that broke into the fermentation room last week. For a few minutes, it's almost normal. Almost.

But when Mom's gaze drifts to the window, the shadow returns to her face.

"I wish I could do something to help," I tell them, but my job definitely doesn't come with a huge paycheck.

Dad reaches for my hand, squeezing gently. "You help just by being here."

Mom's smile softens, but there's mischief in her eyes. "Or maybe by finding a handsome man with deep pockets. A defense attorney would do nicely. He can buy the place, and you can run it together."

I laugh, shaking my head. "Not in a million years."

"Never say never," she teases, rising from her chair.

"You're lucky I love you, Ma."

She wraps her arms around me, pressing a kiss to the top of my head. "And I you, tesoro. Everything I do is for you."

"I know."

My parents have no one but me. Mom always said her family never approved of her marrying Dad, mostly because his father wasn't

Italian. That's where our last name comes from. They disowned her after that, and Dad didn't have much family to begin with. His parents died when he was young, and he was an only child.

If there was a way to fix their financial problems, I'd do it in an instant, even if it cost me everything.

SEVEN

ALEKSEI

As she walks out of the main building of the vineyard, she's still wearing that fake smile for her parents' sake as she says goodbye.

It slips the second she's out of their line of sight. By the time she hits the path toward the parking lot, her shoulders are rigid, her steps clipped. That small hand grips the strap of her purse like she's holding herself together with it.

The cameras her parents installed catch everything: the breeze tugging strands of hair across her cheek, the moment she pauses halfway to the car and looks back at the rows of vines like she's saying goodbye. Like she knows this chapter's closing.

And she doesn't even realize who's already writing the next one.

I know all about her parents' troubles, even better than she does. Past-due invoices, the bank calling each week, the money they owe that loan shark who will kill them all if they don't pay. I've made it my business to know everything.

The second she blinks too fast and lifts her chin, something locks up in my chest.

She thinks she's hiding the pain, but she isn't. I see it all. Every fracture, every sharp little edge she pretends isn't there.

Those pieces are already mine, and soon, the rest of her will be too.

Don't worry, detka. I have the perfect solution to all your problems.

A smirk cuts across my lips.

This woman…blyat, the things she drags out of me. Every shred of savagery claws its way to the surface when she's near. If I'm not careful, this thing I feed on, this loathing, could shift into something else. Something harder to kill.

Fiona Clark is my sweetest poison. My greatest challenge. My most dangerous enemy. And when I take her, when I own her, she will beg for an ounce of mercy I will never give.

Toggling to the exit camera, I follow the dust that rises behind her tires. Another keystroke throws her onto a different monitor: the state road, a wide shot from a traffic mast.

I sit back, my office dim except for the multiple screens in front of me. Floorboards creak in the hall, then two soft taps sound at the door, and I know it's my maid, Galya.

"Come in."

She slips inside, her smile warm, though it does nothing but irritate me. "Your brother Kirill is here, sir. Little Lev too."

"Send them in."

They're already at the threshold when she steps aside. Kirill crosses first, wearing that arrogant grin he saves just for me. The one that says he knows exactly where my security feeds are pointed and who I've been watching.

Lev follows close behind, gripping his father's hand tightly, his other hand grasping the strap of his backpack. His eyes flick up to the ceiling, then the floor, then finally land on me. But not for long. He never stares. He takes everything in quietly, like he's recording it all in that brilliant brain of his.

"Hi," he says at last, voice soft and unsure.

I crouch until we're level. "Privet, soldatik." *Hi, soldier.*

Kissing the crown of his head, I move to the bookshelf along the wall and pull out the hardcover book on constellations I ordered last week. His current fixation.

"Eto tebe." *This is for you.*

Reaching out, I hand it to him. His fingers hover, then he takes it carefully, as if it might break if he breathes too hard. He runs his thumb over the cover like he's reading it through touch.

Kirill stands beside him, watchful and protective. A permanent shield. He's been like that ever since his ex walked out when Lev was barely three. She couldn't handle the diagnosis. Couldn't stomach the reality of raising an autistic child. Some mother.

The only reason Kirill didn't put her in the ground for it is because she's the daughter of someone powerful, someone we couldn't afford to provoke. But I would've done it. No matter what.

"Spasebo," he says softly after Kirill bends and whispers the reminder in his ear.

He doesn't look up. Just runs his hand over the book again, like it might vanish if he stops touching it.

But I don't need eye contact, a smile, or some classic version of gratitude. Not from Lev. It's in the silence. In the way he holds the book close to his chest—not like a child with a toy, but like someone who's finally found something meant for him. He doesn't have to say "thank you" because I already know it's there, where it matters most. In his heart.

"Of course." I give him another kiss on his head.

"Go sit and read," Kirill tells him, roughing his dark hair. "Papa will be done soon."

He takes small steps toward his favorite spot: the armchair by the window, overlooking the garden at my estate. He pauses, taps the armrest once, takes two steps back, then sits. One of his small rituals that keeps the world safe for him.

When he's happily reading, Kirill cocks a brow. "Do you do anything other than stare at her all day?"

"I do other things."

Sometimes…

"Like what?" His laugh is low, needling, as he drops into the chair across from my desk.

"Edi na khuy." *Go fuck yourself.*

He tsks, grinning wider. "Not in front of my son."

Kirill glances over at him, then back at me with that same sneer tugging his mouth.

I sink back into my chair, the glow of the monitors around me as I glare at him. "You have to know the enemy inside and out."

As I flip to another feed, there she is again, caught in the grainy lens, waiting for the light to change. Zooming in on her face, I catch the tightness in her jaw.

What's running through that sharp little mind of hers?

Is it me? The ghost of my hands still on her?

The vineyard crumbling under her parents' feet?

Or is it something else? Something I haven't uncovered yet?

Kirill's chuckle yanks me back to reality. "Are you sure that's all she is? Just the enemy?"

"Of course." The words grind out between my teeth.

Of course that's all she is. A venomous woman who should thank me for what I did for her instead of wanting me to rot.

But even if I told her the truth, she would only perfect her hate. That's who Fiona Clark is. She paints the world in black and white, and men like me—men who crawl in the shadows—might as well be the devil himself.

And this devil is going to enjoy proving her right.

Kirill's laugh rumbles deeper until my temper claws to the surface. "You can't even focus on what we're talking about without staring at her. I think you've been infected."

"You're not funny."

"I think I'm hilarious." His grin fades as he leans forward, eyes narrowing, voice dropping low. "But I almost wonder, why not just kill her? It'd be easy. Quick. A needle in her neck…" His glance flicks toward Lev before settling back on me. "Then carve her into pieces small enough for the pigs to feast on."

My smile bends. "Too easy." I tip back in the chair. "There are worse things than death, moy brat. A lot worse."

What I don't say—what I will *never* say—is that the thought of anyone hurting her rips through me like barbed wire. I tell myself it's because I want to be the one to break her. But the truth tastes too much like protection, and I despise myself for even entertaining it.

Kirill folds his arms across his chest, studying me with that sharklike curiosity. "Are you ever going to tell her the truth?"

My gaze drags back to the screen, to her car slipping around the corner of her block. "Maybe. But not yet."

"What are you planning to do with her?"

"You'll see."

My hand curls against the desk as the feed shifts to her car door opening and her body comes into view, every curve crafted to tempt me, whether she knows it or not.

"Moya okhotnitsa thinks she's the hunter." My finger hovers above the screen, tracing the outline of her face. "But she will be the one who gets caught."

Kirill's mouth quirks. "How precious. You already gave her a pet name."

"That's not—"

He lifts a palm with a scoff. "Khvatit vrat." *Stop lying.*

"Edi k chortu." *Go to hell.* My glare cuts harsher than the words. "Why are you even here? To test my patience?"

He shrugs. "Can't a brother visit?"

"You never *visit* unless it's for a reason."

"Never is dramatic. Even for you."

"Khvatit nesti khuynyu." *Stop spouting bullshit.* "Why are you here?"

He leans back like he's settling in, but his eyes turn calculating. That look tells me everything I need to know before the next few words leave his mouth.

"I found something. On Fiona."

The words slam through me. "So, are you going to tell me, or do you need an invitation?"

"Check your email."

"You couldn't just call?"

"And give up seeing the look on your face when you realize you missed this?" He straightens his back. "What kind of brother would I be?"

"A dead one if you keep talking."

He chuckles while my fingers fly across the keys until I find his email with multiple attachments.

The first few are familiar—surveillance stills, faces I recognize.

The Volkovs. Our enemies. The family who's been playing the long game, waiting for us to slip so they can rule instead.

They don't want war. Not yet. They know we would burn them alive.

Konstantin keeps saying it's not time. That patience is strategy. But I have never been patient. I want their blood, want to carve them down to the bone and leave their tiny empire in ruin.

Then I open the next file with photos, and everything inside me locks as I read through what Kirill found.

"What the hell is this?"

"I was just as surprised as you."

How could I have missed this? But it all makes sense now.

"Does Konstantin know?"

"Not yet."

"Slovichy!" My fist pounds on the desk, pens rattling across the mahogany. "Ya ikh vsekh ub'yu!" *Bastards! I'm going to kill them all!*

My jaw grinds as I flip from picture to picture.

This changes everything. They want her. And they think I'd ever allow this? That they have a chance?

Never. They don't know who they're dealing with.

The Volkovs think they're going to be kings. But I was born to be something worse.

It's in my blood, this need to dominate, to crush, to be the best. Our father made sure of it. He didn't raise sons. He forged weapons. Failure wasn't punished; it was erased.

And love? Love was weakness. Love was leverage. Love was a lie.

Power. That was the prize.

And I intend to take it. Starting with her.

EIGHT

FIONA

The moment I turn onto my block after work the following day, that creeping sense claws up my limbs.

He's here.

As I slowly turn down my street, the eerie feeling only continues to grow. The street is quiet, too quiet. Nothing but homes on one side and thick, heavy woods on the other, like they're hiding something just beyond.

My headlights sweep around the final curve of my dead-end street, and for a second, I let myself relax.

He's not here. It was just my mind playing tricks, feeding off my nerves.

But that illusion shatters the moment I reach the end of the block.

There, across from my house, waits a sleek red-and-black sports bike. Leaning against it, leather jacket molded to a body built for intimidation and helmet hanging loosely from one hand, is Aleksei

Marinov in the flesh.

And every nerve in me lights up.

I pull into my driveway on autopilot as I contemplate what the hell to do. Confront him? Walk inside like he's invisible? Like he hasn't been unraveling me with nothing but a look? Like he didn't pin me against my car and flip some switch in me I've been trying to deny ever since?

No. Screw this. I'm not going to just ignore what he's doing.

How dare he keep showing up? How dare he play these games like I'm some prop?

This ends today.

Fuck Aleksei Marinov. Fuck his entire cursed family. I'm Fiona Clark, and I make the rules.

Swinging my door open, I get out, shut it behind me, and march toward him. He just stands there, arms folded across his chest with that insufferably self-righteous look. Like he knew I'd come to him before I even knew it myself.

I keep my gaze pinned to his face, but it's impossible not to take him in. The sharp lines. The leather stretched over his frame like a second skin. He looks like he walked out of a nightmare just to haunt me. Calm, unreadable, and dangerous in ways I haven't even begun to understand.

I hate the way my pulse reacts. Hate the way I feel it everywhere, low and hot and curling. Like my body hasn't gotten the memo that this man is not the hero of my story.

I shouldn't want anything from him. Not his attention. Not his words. And definitely not the way he's gazing at me now, like I'm already his to do with as he pleases.

But some part of me, that small and shameful part, leans into it anyway. Because no matter how many lines I draw, he's always right there standing on the edge, daring me to cross every single one.

Heat flares through my center as the images from what I did last night replay behind my eyes. The sound of water pounding against tile, the ache between my thighs, the way my fingers moved, his growled orders echoing in my skull as I made myself come like he owned that too.

It's sick. Irrational. I despise him for it. For having this much control over my body, for making me lust over him the way I do.

Because that's all this is: pure lust. And that's all it's ever going to be.

My footsteps carry me closer until only a few feet remain between us, and he cocks a brow.

"What the hell are you doing here, Marinov? Planning to make stalking me a sport?"

He chuckles, that sound filled with amusement and menace all at once. "Really? And here I was thinking I hadn't been trying hard enough."

Sick bastard. He's having fun with this.

My fingers twitch with the memory of every shooting lesson Emilia ever gave me. I can almost picture the bullet: dead center, right between those arrogant eyes.

I'm not usually this homicidal, but Aleksei Marinov is a special kind of trigger.

"Trying to provoke me, huh?" I match his stare with one of my own. "Or is this just your lame idea of foreplay?"

His jaw flexes, a dangerous glint in his eyes, and my heart stumbles before I force it steady.

A smirk plays across his lips. "If it is, you are doing an excellent job playing along."

"Don't flatter yourself, Marinov," I snap. "You might have money, power, and a face that makes women forget their morals, but I'm not one of your groupies. You don't rattle me."

His gaze dips to my lips, settling there for far too long. "No? Then why are you trembling?"

His knuckles feather across my jaw, and I attempt to hide the way my body shudders.

I take a step forward instead, toe to toe with the devil. "Maybe I'm just restraining myself. Because if I acted on every impulse I had around you, I'd be burying your body in those woods."

He laughs. "Violent fantasies, detka? Should I be flattered or concerned?"

"Neither." I tilt up my chin. "Just know that if you keep showing up like this, one day I won't stop at words."

His smirk fades just a fraction. "You wouldn't."

"Try me."

There's an unreadable flicker in his eyes before his hand lowers slowly, his fingertip grazing my wrist and dragging upward, mapping the length of my arm. His touch is maddening, and this sensation inside me clenches in protest even as my skin betrays me with a tremble.

"Don't touch me." The words leave my mouth with more bite than I feel, but at least I say them.

That's right, Fiona. Good girl. There's that backbone.

His gaze never wavers, not for a second, as the pad of his finger finds the curve of my collarbone, slinking over it with a patience that makes my breath catch. My body tightens, heat pooling deep in my belly, my pulse thudding where his skin meets mine.

"But look how much you like it when I do."

His fingers find the button at my chest, slipping it open with infuriating ease. Like he's done it a hundred times in his fantasies and is finally indulging in the real thing.

I need to stop him, but I just stand here frozen in place—not from fear, but from a dark curiosity. Because despite everything I've told myself, part of me needs to know what he'll do next.

His breath ghosts against my cheek, warm and laced with venom. "Tell me…how wet does your cunt get when you think about me in the shower?"

Fuck...

My ribs cinch so tight, it's like they might crack.

He knows. Somehow, the sick bastard knows what I did last night. The way I let my fingers slip between my thighs with his name burning through my skull.

"Don't." The word escapes in a breathless tremor, shaken loose from the thunder in my chest.

He leans in, lips grazing the shell of my ear. "Don't what? Don't stop? Because I don't plan to."

Another button slips free, the cream blouse falling open just enough to expose the edge of lace and skin before he presses me back against the bike. The cool metal bites through the thin fabric of my skirt, but it's nothing compared to the heat of his mouth against my throat. Hot, unrelenting, devouring.

His tongue traces the frantic rhythm of my pulse like he set it racing just to savor the wreckage. His teeth graze the skin there—sharp enough to threaten, soft enough to tease—and my knees nearly give beneath the pressure. A needy sound escapes me, and my fingers fist in his hair, tugging hard, desperate to regain control.

But it's already gone. Because when he growls low in his throat, I feel it. Between my thighs, in my chest, twisting up my spine like a warning shot I'm too far gone to heed.

"Still pretending you don't want this?" he whispers against my skin, dragging the words down my neck.

My only answer is my breath catching when his hand slips beneath the hem of my skirt. Rough fingertips graze my thigh, each stroke drifting higher, bolder, crueler in its precision.

I know I should stop him, but I can't do anything except feel. Trapped between disgrace and a hunger so deep, it threatens to swallow me whole.

Because this isn't just lust anymore. It's war.

And I'm losing.

My eyes shut the moment his fingers brush against my core, the thin barrier of my panties doing nothing to blunt the pulse of need spiraling through me.

I arch into the touch, shame flooding my veins as my body obeys him like it belongs to him.

But then it hits me.

The courtroom. That verdict. Him standing there in his suit and superior fucking smirk. The monster behind the mask. The man who ruins lives with a flick of his hand.

The memory cuts clean through the fog of desire, and my spine snaps straight.

What the hell am I doing? How did I let it go this far?

"Let me go. Now."

He doesn't move. Doesn't flinch. His free hand slides up, curling around my throat with unnerving calm.

"I will never let you go, okhotnitsa. And the more you run, the deeper I will bury myself under your skin. Until there is no you without me." His words scorch straight through me, searing themselves into bone.

My knee flies upward before the thought even fully forms, landing hard between his legs. He staggers back, a strangled sound clawing from his throat, eyes wild with disbelief and something far scarier.

Shit. Shit, shit, SHIT!

"You really shouldn't have done that." A muscle tics in his jaw, those hands curling into fists.

But it's the calm that terrifies me more than the anger.

He moves toward me. One step. Another. In that disturbing way predators move when they are deciding whether to maul or play first.

And just like that, I know I'm completely and utterly fucked.

"I…" I don't even know what I'm trying to say.

Sorry?

Screw you?

Please don't kill me?

He takes another step forward.

"You will pay for this." His eyes gleam with murderous intent.

"Wh—what?" I stumble backward, arms covered in goose bumps, the air vibrating with the malice rolling off him.

It's suffocating. All-consuming.

A smirk splits his face, sharp enough to bleed.

"You have three seconds to run, moya okhotnitsa," he growls, a haunting blend of guttural and dangerous. "And you'd better pray I don't catch you."

Then he lunges.

Adrenaline explodes through my body. And I run as fast as I can.

The forest swallows me whole, branches slashing at my skin as I tear through the trees like my life depends on it.

Because it just might.

The ground pitches beneath my feet, soft and slick with leaves and mud, my heels slipping uselessly beneath me. I rip them off, clutching them in one hand as I push harder. Faster. Deeper. The breath burns in my lungs, my heart punching through my ribs.

And somewhere behind me, I swear I hear him laugh. A dark, feral sound that promises one thing: this is far from over.

Twigs slap across my face, thorned vines snagging at my skirt. The hem rips as I charge through the underbrush, the sting of bramble slicing across my feet, but I don't stop.

My heart crashes in my ears, too loud, too fast, drowning out everything except the ragged thrum of panic.

And still, I don't hear him anymore. No footsteps. No rustling leaves. Nothing but silence and the knowledge that he's out there closing in, which somehow makes it worse.

The air thickens around me, saturated with dread. My skin prickles, every nerve on fire. And beneath all that fear, something else winds low in my belly. Something darker. Hungrier.

It's not just fear making me run. It's exhilaration. The high of the chase.

But now's not exactly the time to unpack that particular brand of insanity.

Maybe later. You know…when I'm *not* being chased barefoot through the woods by a trigger-happy psychopath with a hard-on for psychological warfare.

Up ahead, the trees thicken, shadows knotting like tangled rope. If I can just make it there, duck behind one, find cover—

A brutal force yanks me back mid-stride.

An arm loops around my waist like a vise, lifting me clean off the ground. I slam into a tree with a scream, air whooshing from my lungs in a strangled gasp. His body crashes into mine, solid muscle and rage, pinning me in place.

Before I can scream again, one hand clamps around my mouth, the other splaying flat over my stomach to keep me still.

Then his voice scrapes across my skin like a blade. "Did you really think you could run from me, Ms. Prosecutor?"

His nose brushes my throat, breathing me in like I'm the first inhale after a lifetime underwater.

"Do you know how long I've waited for this moment?" His irises blaze as his fingers wrap around my throat. "To have you like this. Gasping. Cornered. Mine. Without metal chained around my wrists."

"What now, huh?" I lift my chin in defiance, ignoring the heat crawling through me like it knows who it belongs to. "You gonna prove what a man you are by choking a woman against a tree?"

His mouth curves, but it's not a smile. It's a threat.

"Net, detka. I am going to do far worse."

Before I can spit back a word, he grabs me, spinning me so fast the world blurs. My front hits the tree, cheek scraping bark, and then his fist is in my hair, yanking my head back until my eyes find his.

Wild. Unhinged.

I let out a small, mocking laugh, knowing what I do to him. What I make him become.

He rips my skirt up without warning, and the slap across my ass that follows lands with bone-deep force, the sound echoing through the trees. I gasp, more from the humiliation than the pain.

And beneath the shame, a raw, hungry need tightens, wanting him to do it again.

"You think it's funny?" he growls against my ear, his breath hot and vicious. "You won't be laughing when I am through with you."

Every molecule in my body lights up as his hand moves between my thighs, rough fingers parting me, stroking through the slick evidence of my arousal.

"Look at that…" He lets out a grunt. "You hate me, and still your cunt is soaked for me."

"That's a lie," I snap, though the crack in my tone tells a different story.

His chuckle vibrates through me, full of wicked triumph, while his fingers play with my clit. Circling. Taunting. Tormenting.

Each stroke makes my muscles weak and my exhales hitch. I clamp my lips shut to stifle the moan building in my throat, but it breaks free anyway, shaky and mortifying.

The metallic clink of his belt echoes through the stillness, and heat floods my chest, spine pulled tight by a raw, animal hunger I have no hope of killing.

One hand holds me pinned, fingers curled tight around the back of my neck, forcing my cheek against the bark once again. My body is strung tight, a live wire sparking under his grip. Every inch of me screams with anticipation, untamed and ready to snap.

Then he drives into me in one savage, unforgiving thrust, and the air tears from my lungs like it's been stolen. A sound rips from my throat—part moan, part cry, choked and desperate as he fills me completely, merciless in his pace.

I'm not ready for this, yet my body opens for him like it's been waiting for him all along.

I crave him. Recklessly. Ravenously.

And that might be the most fucked-up part of all.

Cold metal drags against my walls. I jerk beneath him, eyes rolling back.

Oh God. He's pierced.

"Yes!" I cry as he slams into me like I'm the battlefield and he's hell-bent on burning it all to the ground.

He takes me like it's vengeance. Like every insult, every courtroom blow, every scar I left on his soul demands repayment.

His thrusts are punishing, each one ripping a breathless sound from my throat, grinding me down until there's nothing left but surrender. A beastly growl tears from him as his fingers clamp my hips, bruising me with the kind of grip that swears I'll never forget him.

"You give in to me so easily, Ms. Prosecutor," he rasps. "Even when it kills you."

He pounds deeper, harder. Each thrust is a brutal promise, like he's trying to fuck something out of me. Or maybe out of himself.

His pace turns wild, like breaking me is the only thing that might save him. And God, I want him to. The hard bite of metal rubs against my walls with every drive of his cock, each piercing dragging fire through me, pushing me closer to a place I can't crawl back from.

"Say it." His teeth sink into the curve of my neck, and it only fuels me. "Say you hate me, moya ptichka."

"I hate you," I gasp, the truth dragging out of me on a ragged breath.

"Good girl."

His pace turns ruthless, each drive more feral than the last, like he's making me feel what I just said. One hand fastens around my throat while the other slides lower, rough fingers circling my clit—not to give me pleasure, but to show me what he's capable of.

He pinches. Slaps. Toys with me like my body is his weapon of choice.

"I hate you too. Every defiant inch. The way you make me need this. Make me need you."

His words rip through me, and my body answers anyway, helpless and burning, caught between the heat sparking off us and a desire I can't outrun.

"This is nothing." My nails claw against the bark. "Just sex. You're nothing to me. You never will be."

His fingers knot in my hair and yank, dragging my spine into an arch until every thought burns out. No air or logic. Just the feeling of him. The sheer savagery of his fucking.

"And this is all you're good for," he taunts, fingers clamping around my throat again, pressure tightening as his mouth charts a ruthless path down my neck—biting, sucking, devouring. "A tight hole to fill. A body to break. And mine to take again and again."

Rage tears through me. But with every violent thrust, my body submits to him like it never left.

"Is that supposed to hurt me?" I laugh again. "You want me to cry? Want me to be sad about it? Keep dreaming, asshole. I'm using you just as much."

His hips slam into me in response, cruel and relentless, dragging a moan from my throat that I wish I could bury. My back bends, and I curse him for knowing exactly how to tear me apart.

I melt for him. Yield for him. Break for him.

His touch is callous as he circles and spanks my clit while slamming into me over and over, until I'm crying his name like it's salvation and sin rolled into one.

"Oh fuck, Aleksei! This is too much." His name leaves my mouth like a sob, like a curse, like a plea I never meant to give him.

He pounds into me even harder. "You can take it."

His grip around my throat cinches as I call out his name again. "Aleksei…"

"Yes. That's it." His words are strained and volatile. "Moan for me, detka. Fucking take it all. You're my filthy whore to use any way I want."

The words crash through me like a lightning strike, and it's all I need to let go. My body convulses, clenching and exploding around him in a blinding climax that rips through me with a vicious sob.

I shatter around him, my pleasure crashing through me. Still, he moves inside me, dragging out every aftershock, refusing to stop until I'm limp and quivering against the tree.

His own grunts come in quicker right before he lets out a deep-chested growl as hot spurts coat me, marking me.

Right now, I'm really grateful that I'm on the pill.

When his body finally eases, the tension in his limbs slowly dissolving, he pushes off me as though I'm made of acid, and I can't help the way it stings.

I stay where I am, unable to turn around, to look at him and face what I let him do. My skirt is still rucked up around my hips, my panties twisted halfway down my thighs, but it's the shame slithering higher that makes me sick inside.

My eyes close as I register his belt sliding back into place and the faint click of a zipper, right before his footsteps start away from me.

My God, what was I thinking?

I should be pissed at myself for letting this happen. For letting him in. For enjoying it.

But instead, all I can think about is how empty it feels without him.

Eventually, I peel myself off the tree and tug my panties up before drawing down my skirt with shaky hands, like smoothing the fabric can somehow undo what just happened.

I crouch to wedge my heels back on, but the second the sole hits the ground, pain rips through the back of my foot.

"Fuck—ow!"

A rustle slices through the silence behind me.

"What's wrong?" His voice sends my heart crashing into my ribs.

I whip around, eyes wide. "Jesus!"

He emerges from the shadows, arms folded, that unreadable expression carved into his face.

Something in my chest lurches. I don't know what stuns me more: that he stayed, or that part of me is relieved he did, though I don't understand the reasoning behind it.

"What do you care?" I push past him with a limp I try and fail to hide.

He doesn't let me get far. One second, I'm hobbling forward; the next, I'm airborne, scooped into his arms like I weigh nothing.

"What the hell do you think you're doing?"

"Carrying you." His tone is dry, like it's the most obvious answer in the world. "What does it look like?"

"I can walk just fine."

"Of course you can," he deadpans. "You looked really graceful back there, princessa."

"Maybe don't sneak up on me like some backwoods serial killer next time."

He mutters something in Russian. Definitely a curse. "Are you always this difficult when someone is trying to help you?"

"Only when that someone is the reason I need help in the first place."

"What can I say?" A grin snakes up as he pulls me closer to his chest. "I always clean up my messes."

"God, I hate you."

My attempt at pushing him further away is futile. The man is just too strong.

His lips tug into an even more maddeningly smug curve, infuriating and infatuating all at once. "Wouldn't be fun if you didn't."

He exhales a laugh when I groan, the sound vibrating through his chest, and I hate how stupidly safe he feels.

Instead of pulling away, I let go. Just for a second. Long enough to allow my cheek to rest against the steady rhythm of his heart.

When his arms tighten around me, it's not rough. It's like he's been waiting for me to fall into him all this time.

NINE

ALEKSEI

I kick the door shut with my heel and carry her to the sofa, setting her down like she's fragile when she's far from it. But something about seeing her hurt makes me want to be gentle.

Shto ya zdest delayu? What the hell am I doing here?

Why didn't I leave her in those woods? Why couldn't I just walk away?

Blyat. Ti vapshe idiot. Fuck. You're a real idiot. *She tried to put you in prison, and you're here making sure her little boo-boo is okay? You are not her doctor. And you are definitely not her husband.*

I need to go. This is not my damn job. She shouldn't be a priority, and definitely not someone who deserves my mercy.

But when I heard her cry out, when I saw her limp through the woods like that with pain shadowing her features, something inside me twisted. Something I don't want.

She moves against the cushions and winces. And there's that damn unwelcome feeling again. Her nose scrunches with her pain, and she looks even more irresistible right now than she did in those woods.

"Uh, thanks." She positions herself higher on the sofa. "But you can go now."

Instead of leaving, I head for the stairs.

Ty bol'noy na golovu, I scold myself as she calls out after me. *You're sick in the head.*

"Where the hell are you going?"

A smile winds up my mouth from how pissed she sounds while my footsteps climb higher up her stairs, knowing how much she hates me being in her space. If she only knew how many times I've been in her panty drawer, she would rip my eyes out…and I'd probably enjoy it a little too much.

The first time I visited, it was curiosity. The second, compulsion. By the third, it was full-blown obsession.

I knew the scent of her shampoo before I ever ran my fingers through her hair. I know where she keeps her pills. Her razor. Her vibrator. I know which panties she avoids when she's on her period. Or how she sleeps facing the window—unless it's storming. Then she turns in.

I know too much. And I'm not sorry.

Because while she burns with hate for me, I have already built a cathedral out of her name in my mind. And every time she trembles or cries out my name, it only confirms what I already know.

She doesn't belong to anyone else. Ona moya. *She's mine.*

After grabbing a T-shirt and a pair of her sleep shorts, I head toward her bathroom and pick up the first aid kit too before heading back down. Her eyes lock on to mine the second I enter, and the fire in them singes the air between us. I toss the clothes onto the cushion beside her, and she gives the most dramatic huff I've ever heard, like I have offended her royal sensibilities.

It's maddening. And fucking adorable.

"What the hell? How did you know where those were?" Her eyes narrow. "Have you been inside my house before?"

My lips twitch. "Of course not." I drag the ottoman closer and drop onto it, lifting her foot onto my lap like it belongs there. "Merely a lucky guess."

"Yeah, okay." She crosses her arms. "You're not even trying to lie well anymore."

"I'm losing my touch, it seems." My gaze sinks deeper into hers, my thumb grazing over the bruised curve of her heel. "Must be your effect on me."

"I can't wait until we're done with whatever the hell this is," she mutters, shifting like she's about to yank her foot back, but she doesn't.

"You make it sound like you're not enjoying yourself." I grin. "I'm almost offended."

"That is…*if* you had feelings."

"Oof." I clutch my chest. "The cruelty. Truly. You wound me."

She shoots me a glare hot enough to scorch flesh, and I want to chase the fire.

"Now, if you're done with your dramatics, I need you to change so I can clean your feet before you die of an infection."

"How noble," she drawls, dry as dust. "Isn't that what you want? To watch me die?"

The smile instantly vanishes from my mouth.

No.

The thought hits harder than it should. Her body cold, breathless… It cracks something in my chest.

I don't want her dead. I just want to leave her on the ground gasping for air, knowing I'm the one who took it away.

"I said change, Fiona." My gaze cuts to hers. "Before I strip those clothes myself. Then again…" I tilt my head, eyes trailing down her body. "Considering how you moaned for my cock just minutes ago,

I'm guessing that is exactly what you want."

Her jaw clenches, nostrils flaming. "Look away, asshole."

"Say please."

She launches a pillow at my head, and I catch it midair, grinning like the bastard she knows I am. I turn, though not before imagining all the ways I'll get to know her body all over again before the week is over.

I listen to her movements, each rustle of fabric feeding my sickness. She's taking her sweet time, knowing exactly what she's doing. Letting me stew in it. Letting me remember how she looked. Flushed, panting. How she begged with her body even as her mouth spat venom.

It's not just hate between us. It's combustion. And I'm a fucking arsonist.

"Okay," she says from behind me. "I'm decent."

I glance over my shoulder. "I could've flown to Moscow and back in the time it took you."

She rolls her eyes. "Do us all a favor and make it a one-way ticket."

I pivot fully, stepping into her space. My knuckles brush her cheek, and her lashes flutter.

"Just admit it…you'd miss me."

"Yeah, as much as a cavity."

I chuckle, but it dies fast.

Because she's right. It would be smarter to leave. To forget this madness. To burn every trace of her from my life and pretend she never happened.

But the second I try…something in me snaps.

I can't kill what she makes me feel. The obsession. The rage. The way my blood sings with the urge to destroy anything that touches her, that makes her feel something I didn't give her first.

Only *I* get to break her. Only *I* get to make her come undone.

Nu blyat.

Raking a hand through my hair, I mutter under my breath as I stalk toward her kitchen.

Behind me, she says dryly, "My God, I'm never getting rid of you, am I?"

I don't bother looking back. "Not until you're dead, moya ptichka. And not then either. Because heaven or hell, I'll find you."

Her muttered curse from behind me makes me grin, the sound like music—angry, indignant music, but music all the same.

I grab a clean dishcloth and soak it in warm water, watching it darken in my fist. When I return, she's sitting stiffly, legs stretched out, arms crossed like a shield. Her eyes are sharp, guarded, but something in them flickers when I kneel in front of her. Like she's not sure whether to run or breathe me in.

I take her ankle, resting it over my bent knee. She flinches when my fingers skim up the delicate line of bone.

"Relax, detka." My voice is a whisper meant just for her.

She swallows hard, throat bobbing, but she doesn't pull away. And when our eyes meet, everything slows. The time, my heartbeats, the world around me. It all ceases.

I should hate her. I *do* hate her. But right now, it doesn't feel too much like hate.

It's like possession. Like punishment wrapped in desire. Like my darkness has finally found a home in hers.

She's the enemy. She's everything I swore I would destroy. And still, I want to bury myself so deep inside her that neither of us remembers who is in control.

I press the warm cloth to her foot, gently wiping away blood and dirt. Her skin's scraped raw in places. Nothing deep, but it still carves a hole in my chest. Guilt gnaws at the edges of my control. A feeling I thought was long dead…if I ever had it to begin with.

I've ended lives without a second thought. Buried men without a trace of regret. But with her? All it takes is a scratch.

Her breathing changes, shallow and uneven. Like she doesn't know what to do with gentleness from me. Like it rattles her more than violence ever could. My touch is careful instead of cruel, something that might look like mercy if she was foolish enough to believe me capable of it.

But this isn't mercy. I just don't know what the hell it is.

Her lips part, her chest rising unevenly, and I can't stop staring. Not at her mouth. Not at the way her lashes lower with each stroke of the cloth. Every inch of her is a trigger I want to pull.

And this—this quiet intimacy between us—is more dangerous than fucking her against that tree. There's no adrenaline to hide behind. No fury to use as armor. Just the truth, pressed between us like a fuse waiting to blow.

I drop the cloth to the floor, muscles tight, and grab the antibiotic from the kit. My hands move on instinct, brushing ointment over the wounds like I've done it a thousand times.

But I haven't. Not for anyone.

I go to the other foot, slower this time, dragging it out like a sick bastard just for the excuse to keep touching her. My fingers graze her skin, memorizing the warmth, the fragility she hides so well.

Zachem ty mne nuzhna? Why do I need you?

None of this makes sense. I want to walk out, slam the door, and pretend this didn't happen. But the thought of her here alone, hurting, even with just a cut, makes something vicious twist in my gut.

I want to leave. I need to stay. And the war between those two truths is tearing me apart from the inside out.

When I'm done, I reach for the last scrape and press a Band-Aid over it, letting my thumb trace slow, soothing circles against the soft skin of her ankle.

"Does it hurt?" My voice is quieter now, rough at the edges. "Do you want something for the pain?"

She looks down at me, eyes dark and unreadable.

"No," she breathes. "I'll live."

But I'm not so sure I will. Not if she keeps looking at me like that. Not when every second I spend touching her feels like a confession. Not when I know down to the marrow in my bones that she was meant to ruin me.

I lower her foot gently to the floor, but neither of us moves. The air between us pulls taut. One wrong breath, and it'll snap.

Her hair clings to her temples, damp with sweat, strands wild and curling like they've been gripped by desperation. Her lipstick is smeared, bitten raw from holding back the sounds I'll replay in my mind until they drive me insane.

She looks like a mess. And it is the most beautiful thing I've ever seen.

My fingers twitch against my thigh. The urge to touch her again, just one more time, rips through me. To taste what I've already claimed. To feel her fall apart again just to prove I can make her do it.

But I don't do a thing. Because if I touch her now, I won't stop.

And God help us both if that happens.

Forcing myself to step back, I put distance between us before the hate curdling in my blood shifts into something worse. Something dangerous. Something I do not know how to survive.

Hate, I can handle. Rage, I can harness. But anything more? Anything real? That could break me.

And I do not break. Not for anyone.

I start for the door and grasp the knob, ready to leave her behind.

"Aleksei."

As soon as she calls me, I'm pulled to a halt. I don't look at her as I wait for what she has to say.

"Thank you." Her voice…it's low and sincere, and I've never heard it that way.

But I say nothing. Because there is nothing to say. Instead, I walk out into the night, my footsteps loud in the quiet, every one of them echoing with the same question I refuse to answer.

How the hell did I go from wanting to destroy her to needing to protect her more than anything else in this world?

TEN

FIONA

It's not even ten in the morning, and every step sends fire through the soles of my feet. The torn skin from last night's sprint through the woods still stings with each shift of weight, an aching reminder of everything that happened with Aleksei.

Not just the reckless sex against a tree. The way he bandaged my wounds after. The way he carried me. Like I meant something.

God, no. I shut that thought down immediately.

Who cares if the man cleaned my cuts like the world's most attentive boyfriend? He is still Aleksei fucking Marinov. Cold, criminal, manipulative Aleksei, who dug under my skin like a toxin without an antidote.

There's absolutely no way in hell I can ever allow that to happen again. That was a mistake. An unbelievably pleasurable mistake, if you don't count the pain I'm currently in, but a complete lapse in judgement.

One I don't plan to make again. Ever.

I force the memory down, bury it deep, and refocus on the real reason I'm driving away from the comfort of my home on a morning that should've belonged to peace and quiet.

Mom called earlier, asking if I could come by the vineyard to sit in on a meeting with a potential investor. I said yes before she finished the sentence. The last thing I want is for them to be blindsided by some slick-talking bastard, especially when I have a perfectly honed bullshit radar and a law degree to back it up.

And maybe it's selfish, but I'm glad for the distraction. I need something else to focus on. Something that does not involve replaying the way my body responded for a man I refuse to name, lest I conjure the devil. Or worse, summon that feeling. That unbearable emptiness that followed the second he walked away.

When I pull into the vineyard, I spot a dark sedan already parked out front. The sun is strong, casting long shadows through the rows of vines as I make my way inside.

The man waiting in the office rises when I enter, offering a smile that feels too easy before I give my parents a hug in greeting.

"You must be the famous Fiona. Your parents haven't stopped talking about you." He reaches for my hand with a charming smile. "Pleasure to meet you. I'm Wesley Dawson."

As we shake, I take a moment to study him. Late forties, dark hair, dark blue eyes. Attractive in that polished country club kind of way with his fancy suit and watch, to go along with that easy confidence of a man who's used to closing deals and getting his way.

Which is exactly why my parents need to be careful.

He hands me a business card.

WESLEY DAWSON

CEO, DAWSON EQUITY PARTNERS

Not that I needed the introduction. The moment my mother mentioned his name, I did my homework. No glaring red flags, at least not the kind the internet will tell you about.

Then again, if you searched Aleksei Marinov, nothing would come up about the fact that he once bit a man's neck, tore out a chunk of flesh, and calmly watched him bleed out. Apparently there was a witness. Sadly, I was not invited to that particular performance by the murder machine himself.

"Pleasure's mine." I sink onto the sofa between my parents, keeping my expression neutral as Wesley takes the armchair across from us.

"So…" I lace my fingers together on my knees. "What makes Dawson Equity interested in a modest vineyard in New Jersey?"

His smile deepens. "Vision. Potential." He gestures with an elegant flick of his hand. "And a genuine belief that this place could be something much bigger. I'm not just here to keep your doors open. I want to take this global."

I arch a brow. "And what's the catch?"

He chuckles. "Smart *and* beautiful. I like that."

I meet his gaze with a flat stare. My mother discreetly squeezes my finger. Her silent way of saying *be nice.*

Wesley leans forward and unclips his black leather briefcase, which is probably worth more than my car, then opens a folder and hands it to me.

"I know you're an attorney," he says, all business now. "I'd love for you to read this over today. Tomorrow night, perhaps we can meet to discuss your thoughts."

"Meet where?" I'm already not liking the direction this is going.

"A club. It's where I usually conduct business." The glint in his smile sharpens just enough to set off a quiet alarm in my gut.

Who the hell negotiates contracts at a club?

Oh, right. Rich people. And predators. Sometimes they're the same thing.

"And…" he adds, like he's doing me a favor. "You may want to dress up a bit. I'll pick you up at nine, if that works for you."

Nine? What the fuck? That's late.

Beside me, my father shifts. He hates him. I can sense it radiating off him. But he won't say anything. Not in front of my mother.

I should say no. Tell Wesley we can meet here, or schedule something during daylight hours like normal people. But I'm curious now. I want to see him in a different setting. How he carries himself. Who he talks to.

It's research. A different kind.

"That'll work," I say.

Dad clears his throat, but I ignore it. I give Wesley my number and watch as he saves it and sends me a quick text so that I can give him my address.

"Thank you for your time, Mr. and Mrs. Clark." He rises and shakes both their hands, then turns to me. "And I look forward to seeing you again."

The second the door shuts, the tension snaps like a rubber band.

"I don't like him," my dad mutters, rubbing his stubbled jaw. "And I really don't like the way he was looking at you."

My mother tsks, waving him off. "You're overreacting, Tony. Maybe he's single."

I groan internally. *Here we go.*

"I'm not marrying the investor, Ma."

"You don't even know him."

"He's a schmuck. Una faccia da schiaffi." *Face just begging to be slapped.*

"Tony!"

"What? I'm just saying what we're all thinking."

I sink back into my seat as the two of them start bickering—about who's right, who cares more about saving the vineyard, and who's convinced I'll die alone and be discovered half eaten by my cat.

But I'm not listening. Not really. Because something shifts in the corner of my eye.

Movement. Just beyond the window.

My body goes still, spine straightening as my gaze sharpens. For a second, just one breathless beat, I think I see someone. A shadow. A figure near the edge of the property, barely visible between the slats of morning light and rows of sprawling vines.

Is it him? Would he follow me here?

He's unpredictable enough that it wouldn't surprise me, and obsessive enough that it makes sense.

My pulse stumbles, then kicks into high gear. I lean forward, eyes narrowing, searching. But there's nothing there. Just grape leaves swaying in the breeze.

Still, my skin prickles. I know this feeling. The electric awareness that curls low in my gut when he's near.

Why the hell am I so attuned to him? Is my mind just warning me?

Either way, I don't want to feel anything where Aleksei's concerned. Nothing but complete and utter disdain. I hate the thought of that man following me, watching everything I do.

There's no way he'd come to the vineyard knowing he'd be seen on cameras, right?

Then again, it's not like he'd care. This is a place of business, and he can come here if he chooses.

Then I start to wonder…

Will he follow me tomorrow night?

Would he care? Would seeing me with another man spark something feral in him?

If Wesley so much as lays a finger on me, Aleksei will either tear him apart…or sit back and enjoy the show.

And honestly, I'm not sure which would be worse.

ALEKSEI

The vineyard falls behind me as I pull away. I should be following Dawson, tracking him until I know exactly what he wants.

Instead, I'm already late to the meeting. My grip tightens on the wheel. I hate answering to anyone. Especially my own brother.

Two damn years. That's all it would have taken. Two years earlier, and I would be the one sitting at the head of the table. Giving orders instead of taking them. The one they answer to. But the universe is cruel and Konstantin came first, the Pakhan of the Marinov family, and he wears that title proudly.

I enter his estate, gates yawning wide, the guards letting me in as the cameras track every inch of my Royce.

Emilia swings the door open before I even touch the handle, arms crossed, a slow, knowing smirk tugging at her mouth.

"You're late."

I grunt. "No way. Hadn't noticed."

Her brows arch. "Let me guess: you were too busy stalking my best friend again. You do realize that's not a healthy coping mechanism for loving her, right?"

"I will never love that cursed woman." I brush past her, heading straight for Konstantin's study.

Of course she knows about my extracurricular activities. They all do. Not as though I'm subtle.

"Nice talking to you too, brother-in-law," she calls after me. "You're always so pleasant."

She's already made herself right at home in this family. And while her mouth is a damn menace, I will admit having her around isn't the worst thing in the world. As long as she stays out of my way.

When I enter the study, they're all already there. Anton dead-eyed as usual. Kirill with that smug grin. Konstantin sitting like a king behind his desk, shot of vodka in hand.

"Nice of you to finally join us," he says, tipping his glass to his mouth before lowering it.

I shrug and drop onto the leather sofa between Kirill and Anton. "I'm here, aren't I?"

Konstantin arches a brow, his mouth curving with dry amusement. "And we are all very grateful. Especially considering what we need to discuss."

"And what's that?"

He crosses his arms over his chest. "The Volkovs. And their connection to your lovely Fiona."

My jaw tightens as I bury the chaos churning beneath my ribs whenever someone mentions her name. "She's not mine."

"Not yet," he says with a low chuckle.

I start to snap something back, but he lifts a hand, cutting me off.

"Spare me the dramatics, brother. I have no interest in your love life, or lack thereof. What I want to know is what you plan to do about what Kirill uncovered."

My tone drops. "Nothing."

Konstantin's gaze narrows.

"There's nothing *to* do. I will not let them touch her. That's all there is to it. Anything else?" My teeth grind with irritation that I don't bother masking.

He drags in a long inhale, eyes still trained on me. "And how do you plan to stop them?"

"I'm watching her. I know where she goes, who she sees. I'll know before they move. It will be simple."

"Hmm. Still stalking my wife's best friend, huh? We really do need to find you a new hobby. It's been a while since you have stepped into the ring. Maybe you need to bleed her out."

Kirill laughs under his breath. When I shoot him a glare, he chuckles harder. If he wasn't my brother, I would have killed him by now.

Still, Konstantin has a point. It's been too long since I've fought. Since I stepped into one of our underground rings and let the violence unleash.

Anton follows the conversation with quiet observance, probably wondering why I'd let a woman get under my skin at all.

But of course it doesn't make sense to him. Nothing does. Not since our father shattered a bottle over his head and left him facedown and bleeding on the floor for hours when he was nine. He never called a doctor. No one was even allowed to check on him.

I thought he was dead. I snuck in to see if he had a pulse, but my father caught me and beat me half to death for it.

When Anton finally woke up, the boy we knew was gone. We didn't know it at first. But eventually, we realized he was a shell of who he was. All his emotions were gone. He didn't feel love, anger, or hate. He felt nothing.

And for my father, that was a win.

Anton became his killing machine from a very young age. And ever since, he has been just that. Empty. Efficient. Unbreakable. The one man who's never let emotion cost him anything.

Not like the rest of us.

"One last thing…" Konstantin leans back in his chair, cutting into my thoughts. "Do ensure you don't hurt Fiona. If you do, Emilia will not be happy. And that means I will not be happy." His grin widens. "Do we understand each other?"

My nostrils flare, but I don't say anything. Of course my prosecutor had to be friends with his wife. Because fate is a sadistic bastard with a sense of humor.

But nothing I have planned will hurt her. Not physically, anyway…

Konstantin smooths his tie with a flick of his hand. "We all know war with the Volkovs is inevitable. But for now, let us eat. Emilia prepared lunch. I expect everyone to be on their best behavior."

We file out into the dining room like the civilized criminals we are, settling around the long dining table. I pick at my plate, pretending to care about food. But all I can think about is Fiona.

Where is she now? What is she wearing? Is she still thinking about last night?

I mutter a curse, stabbing at a piece of roast.

I have to stop this. She is the enemy. A threat.

But none of that seems to matter. Because even here, surrounded by blood and power and legacy, all I see is her.

And I do not know how to stop it.

ELEVEN

FIONA

The moment the limo pulls up to the curb, I second-guess everything. The heels, the dress, the decision to get in at all.

When the door swings open and Wesley steps out, that gnawing unease in my gut roars to life. He straightens the front of his suit with an arrogant flourish, as though the whole world's lucky just to see him exist.

"You look stunning." His gaze sweeps down my body like a scanner with too much interest.

I try not to flinch when he takes my hand and brushes a kiss to my knuckles, but every cell in my body recoils. I already hate how close he is. How comfortable he seems touching me.

A chill spiders down the back of my neck. I don't know if it's him or just this eeriness of being watched.

Is Aleksei here? Lurking somewhere? Watching me from some

unseen corner?

My eyes gloss over the street, but there's no sign of him. Still, the buzz beneath my skin refuses to fade.

Wesley gestures toward the open door, and I force myself to move, slipping into the backseat. He slides in after me, and we're too close—his knee brushing mine, his cologne invading the air. I already can't wait to get this damn meeting over with.

The ride is filled with surface-level questions about my family, our vineyard, and his claim at potential. I answer as little as I can, nodding where necessary, letting my gaze drift out the tinted window.

After nearly forty minutes, we pull up to what looks like an industrial warehouse.

My brows furrow. "This doesn't look like a club."

Wesley reaches into a small velvet box, pulling out a black lace mask that he holds out for me. "Put this on."

I don't take it. "Where the hell are we?"

"You'll see," he says with a wink.

My God, the way I hate men who wink.

I should leave. Right now. But curiosity—dangerous, stupid curiosity—settles in my gut, and I slide the mask over my face, instantly knowing I'm going to regret it.

He opens the limo, the cold air biting across my skin as we start toward the door. A few people in masks are already lined up, equally dressed up.

When it's our turn, a man in a red devil's mask steps forward with a black scanner in hand. He doesn't speak or ask who we are, just lifts the device and sweeps it over our masks. A faint beep follows, and without hesitation, he steps aside to let us pass. These clearly must have chips in them.

Inside, the space is nothing like the industrial exterior. Chandeliers hang from exposed steel beams, casting a dim glow over marble floors and leather seating. Maybe this is a club after all…

A masked woman stands by the elevator, pressing a button without speaking. Wesley places a hand on the small of my back and guides me inside like we've done this before.

I really don't like this man touching me.

When the elevator glides open, we step into a large hallway pulsing with distant bass and the hum of decadence. A few steps ahead, two masked men in black suits stand at a pair of double doors. Their eyes flick over us before one of them gives a subtle nod and allows us to whatever waits inside.

As my eyes adjust to the dim red-washed room, the low, sultry throb of music pulses through the air. Bodies move together on the dance floor, hands roaming, clothes slipping, mouths crashing. Some of them are already half naked, tangled in each other like this is foreplay for something more.

I stop cold, my stomach flipping.

"What the hell is this place?" I spin toward Wesley. "You'd better tell me now or I'm out."

He laughs. "Suit yourself. But from what I hear, you and your family need me."

He's right; there aren't any other investors knocking on the door. But we don't need him that much.

I grit my teeth, spine stiffening. "Let's just find somewhere to talk business, and then I'm leaving. And for the record? Dragging me to some seedy club? Not exactly professional."

He scoffs. "You've got a mouth on you, don't you?"

My expression sharpens, pure venom bleeding into every syllable. "Excuse me?"

"Come on, Ms. Clark. Lighten up." He reaches for me like we're old friends, his hand sliding around my waist and pulling me close like he has any right.

I shove him off without hesitation, but he only chuckles, shaking his head like I'm a cute little thing throwing a tantrum.

Every inch of me screams to leave. But I follow him as he walks a few steps ahead, needing to get this over with. I don't want this son of a bitch to think he's intimidating me.

As we make our way down the hallway, I can't help peeking into the open rooms lining the walls. At first, it doesn't register what these rooms are. Then the truth lands like a punch to the throat.

And suddenly the club doesn't feel like a party. It feels like a trap.

Ropes swing from the ceiling. Leather cuffs dangle like ornaments. Sex, skin…so much fucking skin. Bodies grinding in sync, gasps and moans bouncing off the walls.

Bile creeps up my throat.

Oh my God.

"You're disgusting." I step back. "I'm leaving. And if you think there's still a deal, you can shove it up your—"

Wesley's smile morphs into something jagged and feral. Before I can take another step, his hand snaps out and clamps around my wrist, his fingers pinching tight against my skin until I wince.

"Let go of me." I yank against his hold.

But he doesn't. Instead, his face darkens, all charm gone, replaced by something twisted and unhinged.

"Do you have any idea how much I paid to get you here tonight?" He shoves me forward until my back slams into the wall.

I flinch, the air knocked from my lungs.

"Too much," he sneers, his face inches from mine. "More than you're worth. So if you won't give me what I want…" His hand creeps down my chest. "I'll just take it."

Anger crackles beneath my skin, burning through the fear. My pulse hammers, vision narrowing to a single, violent solution.

He has five seconds before I knee him so hard in the balls, he won't be walking straight for a month.

"Get your fucking hands off me!" I lift my knee, ready to end this, but I don't get the chance.

Because in an instant, he's gone.

One second, Wesley's leering in my face, and the next, he's flying backward like a rag doll. Ripped away from me with brutal force.

A man in a plain black mask slams him against the opposite wall so hard, the drywall splits with a thunderous crack.

"Fuck! Get the hell off me!" Wesley thrashes, arms flailing like a fish on land, but it's useless.

The tall stranger's hand wraps around his throat. Tight, unyielding, and utterly calm.

I freeze. Because I know those hands. At least I think I do.

The man doesn't speak, his forearm pressing into Wesley's throat until his sputtering becomes silence, his face turning an alarming shade of blue.

Two more masked men appear. And once the first man releases Wesley with a shove, the others seize him, dragging him off like trash being taken to the curb. He kicks and shouts, sputtering threats about not knowing who they're messing with. But they don't give a shit.

Where are they taking him?

Probably throwing him out. Good riddance. Couldn't have happened to a better bastard.

I force in a breath, brushing a strand of hair off my forehead and trying to steady my hands. My heart's still galloping, but I manage to look up and meet the stranger's eyes.

He's still watching me. Still silent. So still it makes my blood chill.

Those eyes... God, they're familiar. So is the way he moved...

"Um...thank you," I manage, my voice far too calm for someone who almost got assaulted.

He doesn't reply. Just keeps watching me instead, unnerving me.

"I'm not supposed to be here. It was supposed to be a business meeting, but somehow, we—" I stop myself, shaking my head.

Why am I telling this man all this?

"Anyway, I have to go. Have a good night."

As I start to pass him, my shoulder brushing his arm, he doesn't let me get far. He grabs my wrist—not enough to hurt, but firm enough to stop me dead—and pulls me closer.

And the moment I smell that insufferably delicious cologne, I know.

Aleksei.

"I'm almost insulted you didn't recognize me," he murmurs. "I thought we were friends, Ms. Prosecutor." His lips stroke beneath my ear. "*Good* friends."

My body prickles but I ignore it, stepping back.

I can't believe it's him. Does he have no boundaries left?

"Wh-what are you doing here?"

His knuckles brush across my jaw, the hollows beneath his cheeks deepening with the grind of his teeth as he laughs.

"My brothers and I own Rzvrt. Want a tour, moya ptichka?" His eyes drop to my mouth. "Or would you prefer to participate?"

Before I can answer or even think, his arm tightens around my waist, dragging me flush against the hard lines of his body. Heat blooms across my skin, any memory of how I got here dissolving into static. My mind short-circuits, my body completely forgetting who the enemy is.

He slides a hand up my thigh, toying with the hem of my black pencil dress like he has every right to.

I shudder, lashes lowering despite every cell in my body screaming *don't.*

No. This is wrong.

I promised myself I wouldn't let this happen again. That I wouldn't fall under his spell, not after everything. Not when I know who he is.

Yet here I am, melting at the first drag of his fingers like I haven't learned a damn thing.

"Net," he growls, the word slicing through me. "You look at me when I touch you. I want no confusion about who makes you feel this way. Understand?"

My gaze jerks back to his, and I hate how easily I obey. It's like some part of me is wired to respond to him, no matter how hard I fight it.

"Did he hurt you?"

The shift in his tone throws me. There's something beneath it. Anger. Maybe concern. Or something twisted in between.

"No." I shake my head. "I'm fine."

Why the hell do you care?

A muscle in his jaw tics. "Do not worry. He will be handled either way."

"Handled? How?"

Does he mean…

I don't even want to think it.

He leans in, breath hot against my lips, menace flickering beneath the ghost of a smile. "Do not concern yourself with such things. That is my burden, not yours, Fiona Clark."

Before I can respond, his fingers start slowly climbing again, sliding beneath the fabric, rough knuckles dragging fire over sensitive skin.

I gasp on a moan, my body floating on a high. "I-I should go home."

That's the smartest thing you've said today.

It's what I'm supposed to say. What any sane, rational woman would say. After everything that's happened, after everything he's done, I should mean it.

But I don't.

"Mmm." His mouth grazes just beneath my ear, sending a sharp jolt straight to my core. "But you don't want to."

I should tell him to stop. Should remind myself who he is. But instead, my eyes flutter closed. Because it feels too good. *He* feels too good.

And that's the part I can't make peace with. The part that terrifies me. That despite everything, my body still begs for his.

He flicks my panties to the side with one commanding stroke and presses me against the same wall Wesley shoved me into just minutes ago. Only now…I don't hate it.

Now I kind of like this wall. And worse, I like the man pinning me to it.

God, what's wrong with me? I swore he wouldn't get another piece of me. That I wouldn't let him crawl back under my skin.

But he never left. And I don't know whether to scream at him or beg him not to stop.

"Oh fuck," I whimper when he strokes my clit between two fingers, sending heat rocketing through me so fast my knees buckle.

My lips part on a moan I can't hold back, my body already bowing to his command.

People pass behind him. Faces hidden behind masks. But no one slows or watches.

And even if they did, I wouldn't care. Not with what he's doing to me. Not with how easily I'm coming apart for him.

It's filthy, yet perfect, and I crave more.

When two fingers enter me with a deep thrust, I cry out, my eyes closing until his voice rumbles.

"Net. Open your eyes." *Thrust.* "I want you to see who's fucking you."

His gaze immediately locks on mine, like he's drinking in the sight of me losing control. His thumb circles tight over my clit while he pummels harder, deeper, the tension in his jaw betraying just how much he wants this too. His tongue slips out to wet his lower lip, like he's starving for a taste.

The pace quickens. My breaths shorten. Every nerve ending sharpens.

Don't close your eyes. If you do, he'll stop. He'll make you beg.

And I'm already teetering on the edge. One more second and I'll fall apart.

My hands grip his biceps, fingers digging into the thick muscle, and the strength of him makes it all worse. Or better. I can't tell the difference anymore.

His mouth finds my throat, hot and possessive, trailing lower with kisses that turn my skin to fire. Down to the curve of my collarbone. Then lower.

Until he starts to drop to his knees.

Panic lances through the haze.

"Wha-what are you doing?" I whisper, grabbing his arm.

Because I know what he's about to do. And there's no way in hell I'm letting him do that here. Not where someone could see.

Not where I might like it.

But Aleksei just smirks and sinks to his knees, ignoring my hesitation. And the sight of a man like him on his knees for *me* is a kind of power I've never experienced.

He slowly gathers my dress, the fabric whispering up my thighs until it's bunched at my hips. When he throws one of my legs over his shoulder, his gaze burns into mine just as his mouth seals over my core.

"Oh God," I choke out, fingers diving into his hair as his tongue strokes across my clit.

Light and teasing at first, then deeper, more demanding. Every muscle tightens. Every breath stolen.

He devours me like a man starved, groaning into me, tasting me, while I struggle to stay standing, my legs turning weak and useless.

The tempo shifts. Slow. Fast. A wicked rhythm that drags me closer to the edge only to yank me back again. His tongue slides deep, his growl vibrating through every nerve ending as his fingers curl inside me, finding that spot that makes me see stars.

It's too much. It's not enough.

Need barrels through me like a train I can't stop.

"Come on now," he rasps against me, words thick with need. "Let them hear you. Let them see who this body belongs to."

No, no. I don't belong to him. I never will.

Oh God!

His mouth returns, merciless now, driving me straight toward the edge, until I'm shaking, boneless, on the verge of coming apart entirely.

But then he stops.

I blink down at him, chest heaving. "Are…are you kidding me?"

If he leaves me like this, I swear to God, I'll—

But before I can finish the thought, he rises from the floor, towering over me like he owns the air around me. His hand lifts to my cheek, palm warm, steady, grounding me in the chaos he just created.

His eyes are darker now. Ferocious. Ravenous.

Then, before I can breathe, before I can think, his mouth crashes to mine, hard and deep, like he's staking a claim he never intends to relinquish, swallowing every last shred of reason I had left.

And in this moment, I forget.

I forget that this is wrong. I forget why I ever tried to resist him. I forget everything except the feeling of his hands on me, his breath in my mouth, the way my body folds into his like it's been waiting for this forever.

His grip tightens at my hips and he walks me backward down the hallway, never breaking the kiss. Then a door opens, his hand on the handle, mine tangled in his hair, and we stumble inside. The lock clicks behind us, and his mouth still stays on mine.

My fingers are buried in his scalp, pulling him closer, while his work the zipper of my dress. The sound is soft, a whisper under the uneven drag of our breathing. His hands slide down my spine, trailing over the skin I don't like other men to touch.

The skin I'm terrified he'll see.

I try to shove the thoughts down, to focus on the pleasure, on the dizzying rush of it all, but the moment he drags the fabric lower, they creep in and my muscles tense.

He must feel it because he pauses, eyes cutting sharply to mine, gaze suddenly too focused.

"What is wrong?" That flicker of concern returns again, all too real, digging deep into my marrow

Do I lie? Pretend I'm fine? Maybe it's better if he sees for himself and changes his mind.

Maybe I want him to. I *should* want him to. This is bad.

Right?

I swallow hard.

No. Screw it. If this causes him to stop stalking me, touching me, that's actually a good thing. I'm not supposed to be enjoying this. I *should* want him to stop.

"It's just…I-I have vitiligo. My skin…"

He freezes. Takes one step back, gaze narrowing.

And there it is. I knew it.

"Are you sick?" he demands, suddenly right in front of me again, both hands framing my face like he's afraid I might disappear.

His eyes rake over mine, frantic and unblinking, searching for something.

Oh God. Does he think I have a terminal illness? I almost laugh at the sincerity in his tone.

A murderer with a heart. How cliché.

And maybe…kind of sweet? In a twisted, deranged, completely unhinged kind of way.

"No." I laugh. "Regrettably, I'm in one piece. I just… I have this skin condition. It's called vitiligo. I have pale patches on one of my hips that wrap around my back. It's not contagious or anything. But I figured…you should know."

There's a beat of silence. A pause so heavy it makes my stomach clench.

Then his jaw tightens like I've said something offensive. Like he might kill someone just for making me feel like I had to explain that. And it takes me aback.

Why would he even care?

"You thought, what? You would tell me and I'd stop?" His laugh turns low. Lethal. "That I'd want you less?"

In a flash, he yanks the dress down past my breasts, and I gasp, my lungs locking as his gaze floods me. Not just on the exposed skin. On the very depth of me.

And I couldn't do a thing to stop it even if I wanted to.

His laughter is anything but amused. It's more of a warning, a growl.

"You have no idea what you've done to me, Fiona Clark. No. Fucking. Idea." His gaze turns molten, a dark hunger bleeding into every word. "So let me make myself clear."

His thumb grazes the curve of my hip, over the very skin I tried to hide.

"There is nothing you could show me, nothing you could do or say, that would make me stop hunting you. Nothing that would keep me from dragging you down into hell with me."

The words sear through me. Possessive. Vicious. Honest.

"If anything…" His hand tightens around my back, dragging me flush against his chest. "You just made me want to fuck you even harder. Until those foolish little thoughts of yours don't exist anymore."

My nipples tighten under his stare; my knees trembling from the weight of it. From the way his eyes worship and destroy me at the same time.

And God help me, I want that.

I want every last unholy thing he's about to do.

TWELVE

FIONA

He yanks my dress all the way down in one swift motion, the fabric hitting the floor before I even register the loss of it. His mouth crashes into mine as his hands roam, taking in every inch of bare skin. A quick tug at my hips, and the thong is gone too.

I should be stopping this, telling him no. But instead I just stand here, breathing too fast, heart pounding too loud, knowing how wrong this is while wanting it anyway.

His hands grip my hips as he starts to kneel before me, lips dragging over every inch of my skin. Not skipping the patches. Not pretending they're not there.

Instead, he lingers on them. Feathers unhurried kisses over each pale mark like they're sacred. Like *I'm* sacred.

And it undoes me.

Because this, him…none of it is good. It's reckless and twisted and too intense, but I can't pull away. I don't want to. Even when everything in me screams that I should.

It feels too good. Too right.

He flips me around, throwing me up against the wall, and devours me. His mouth clamps around my core, and I cry out from white-hot need tearing through me as he eats me like he's dying for it. Like it's the only thing keeping him alive.

His tongue flicks fast and deep, his growl sending vibrations through me until my knees nearly buckle.

Then I feel it. The press of his finger…slipping into my ass.

Well, this is…new.

And not that terrible.

The harder his mouth works, the less foreign it becomes. My moan splits the air, high and desperate, while I clutch the wall like it'll save me, like anything can save me now.

"Aleksei, oh God!" My release hits hard, crashing over me, stars exploding before my eyes.

"Again," he grunts, pushing his finger deeper into my backside, curling it as his tongue licks and sucks like he's trying to rip another orgasm from my soul.

I don't know how I need to come again, but it's more demanding now.

"Say my fucking name again."

And I do. I chant it. His name is all I know as the sounds of my wetness echo between us. Obscene, filthy, hypnotic.

His thick fingers plunge inside me, stretching, thrusting, owning me. The faster he moves, the more my body breaks apart. I can't stop it. I don't want to.

And when his tongue flicks just right, when the pressure builds so tight I can barely see, I fall.

Hard.

"Yes, yes, yes!" I scream, hands tangled in his hair, body

convulsing around his fingers and mouth as the orgasm hits like a tidal wave, wrecking me completely.

His beastly groan tears through my clit, his mouth wet and possessive against me, dragging every last tremor from my body until I'm nothing but boneless pleasure and rasping breaths.

Then he rises. Slowly. Predatorily. His mouth glistens with me, lips curved in dark satisfaction.

"You're a squirter, Ms. Clark?" His mouth hovers over mine, sending my heart skipping. "Mm…" He grazes his lips across mine, tongue sweeping over the seam like he's savoring me all over again. "That is very dangerous information."

My brain short-circuits.

I'm *what*?

Before I can find words, his hand fists in my hair, wrapping the strands tight around his wrist. He grazes my bottom lip with his teeth just enough to make it sting, then pulls back with that maddening, arrogant look. The one that says he knows exactly how far under my skin he's gotten.

He strides to a leather chair positioned like a throne in the center of the room. Only then do I take in the rest of our surroundings.

A dresser. A long wooden table. Gags. A metal leash and bar. A chair with a mounted collar. Another table, this one leather with cuffs attached, definitely meant for straddling.

Heat floods my chest.

Where the hell are we…and why is my body throbbing at the thought of him using any of this on me?

"You want to try all of that, don't you?" He sinks onto the chair, undoing two buttons and rolling his sleeves past the thick veins of his forearms.

His gaze tracks every inch of me, every spot he touched and tasted, and it's as though I'm being stripped all over again.

"No." *Yes.*

What the hell is wrong with me? Have I seriously forgotten how hard I worked to get this bastard into prison?

He crooks a finger. "Come here."

I take one hesitant step forward.

No. Don't you dare do what he says.

He stops me with a look, then points to the floor.

"Net. You'll crawl to me." His tone drops lower. "Slowly."

I let out a small laugh. "There is absolutely no way in hell I'll ever do that."

My gaze falls to the thick ridge of his cock straining beneath his slacks, and my body pulses, aching with the memory of what he did to me.

He chuckles. "Oh, but you will, Ms. Prosecutor. You even want to. You just don't want to admit it."

He's not wrong. I do want to. I even like him bossing me around. Which is a whole new level of self-loathing I wasn't emotionally prepared to unpack while stark naked in front of a Russian mobster with control issues.

He leans forward, eyes burning into me. "Your shame makes you lie, but your body doesn't. You want to submit. You want me to take everything. To break you open and fill you until you forget your name."

My breath hitches. It's like he knows everything about me. Even things I've never said out loud.

"I can give you that, Fiona. I can give you everything you need, but only if you obey."

My heartbeat thunders. "The last thing I want is pleasure from you."

He chuckles, savage and cold. "Still pretending I don't own your body?" He lounges back, the bulge in his pants impossible to ignore. "Because I just made you come so hard you squirted for me like a desperate little slut. Don't lie to me, detka. I guarantee no man has ever made you come like that."

His triumphant smirk deepens, and I want to cut it off.

"I won't ask again." His voice drops, rougher now. "Or maybe you want me to take it instead. Is that it? You want me to rip the obedience out of you?"

He stands, and with every inch of height, my lungs tighten. Power comes off him in waves, and I'm caught in its gravity. His hand fists my hair, dragging me closer until his mouth hovers over mine.

"Get your damn hands off of me." I make some half-assed attempt at pushing him off, but it's all a game, he and I both know it.

It's what we do. What we both like, this sick little game we seem to be playing.

"You make me do this," he growls, like I'm to blame for the hunger spiraling in him.

He drags me by my hair toward the table, fingers brushing over the metal chain and collar attachment.

My stomach flips. My thighs clench.

I don't know what I expected, but the collar sliding through his hand lights up every nerve ending in my body. He turns to me with fire in his irises, brushes the hair from my neck with an intimacy that burns, and then…

Click.

The cold metal locks into place around my throat.

My pussy aches, toes curling. I don't know what it is about this, but I seem to like it.

His gaze devours me, pupils blown.

Is this happening? Did he really just chain me like a dog?

"Obedient looks good on you. Almost too good."

"Obedient?" I laugh. "I will never heel for you. Ever."

"We'll see." He tugs once, hard enough to make my pulse spike. "Should I make you crawl, or will you be a good girl and do it for me?"

The metal sinks into my skin with a satisfying sensation, and I'm edging again, on the cusp of pleasure, wanting to drown in everything he gives me.

But I still won't do it. I won't give him the satisfaction.

His dark laughter ricochets through the room, echoing off the walls. Then he firmly tugs the leash, giving me no choice but to follow. He sinks back into the chair like a king claiming his throne, one arm draped lazily over the side, while the leash stays wrapped in his possessive grip, a silent command that makes my blood burn and anger spiral through me at the same time.

His fingertips trail down the middle of my chest with maddening slowness, drawing an invisible line straight to the place I need him most. And when he touches me there…God.

My back arches, a moan clawing up my throat as lust floods between my legs.

His hand slides lower. Deeper.

When I squeeze my thighs together, a last-ditch attempt to reclaim control, to pretend I still have any, he smirks.

"That won't help you, Ms. Clark." His voice is a rumble laced with hunger, dark eyes fixed on mine as he drives his fingers deeper, rougher, relentless now. "You can't lie to me. Not when your body already belongs to me…to use however the fuck I please."

Another sharp thrust makes my spine arch, a strangled sound breaking out of me as his other hand slides up, gripping my throat. His thumb circles my clit with devastating precision, the pressure just shy of cruel.

I try to resist. I do. But it's too much. Too good. Too dangerous.

I hate him. Yet I want this.

And somewhere in the blur of pain and pleasure, I surrender to it all. Again.

"Please…please—" The words rip out of me on a broken gasp.

The chain around my neck tightens. His fingers pound harder. A dark, untamed grunt vibrates from his chest as he grabs my hips and lifts me like I weigh nothing, positioning me over his face.

Before I can blink, he's devouring me. Tongue greedy. Mouth unrelenting. Forcing me to ride it, to break apart all over again.

"Oh God!"

I've never felt this much. Never wanted this much. Every nerve is lit. Every inch of my skin flayed open.

My head spins. My heart slams against my ribs. My body shakes with the kind of desperate pleasure I didn't know was possible.

His grip on my hips tightens, grounding me while he sucks me and fucks me with that sinful mouth, consuming me like I'm the only thing keeping him alive. He yanks the chain, pulling at my throat as his tongue fills my hole, stealing every moan, every scream, every wreck of my soul. It's his now.

When the release hits, it's violent. Shattering. My whole body trembles as I break open, pleasure crashing down in waves so intense, I nearly black out.

I'm dripping over his mouth, shaking uncontrollably, and he keeps going. Sucking my clit harder, lapping up everything I give him like he's starving for it. For me.

My thighs twitch, hips jerking against him, and still he holds me there tight in his grip, fixed to the wicked, greedy heat of his mouth.

By the time the quakes in my body finally begin to ease, I can barely pull in a full breath. He lowers me just enough to tear the mask from my face, then his own, and the second our eyes meet, something inside me detonates. His gaze is molten, trained on me with an intensity that steals whatever air I have left.

He drags me down slowly, like he wants me to feel every inch of the descent, and then his mouth closes over mine, urgent and insatiable. A kiss that swallows the last of my strength and makes me cling to him like he's the only solid thing left in the world.

His fingers sink into my hair, keeping me pressed to him, to whatever this is that neither of us can stop. He kisses me like a man who's just found heaven and intends to claim every inch of it. The taste of my own arousal on his lips lights up a fierce, hungry need inside me, strong enough that I drag him closer.

This is the dirtiest thing I've ever done, and somehow…it's the hottest.

Because it's with him. Aleksei Marinov. My sworn enemy. The man who fills my every dark fantasy.

And now he's here, pressed against me. Hard. Massive. His thick erection grinds against me, stoking my desire that doesn't burn out, only builds.

I need to come again. Need to feel him. Not just inside me. I need him in my mouth, his taste sliding down my throat. I want the power, the control.

What would he sound like? Act like?

As if he hears the thoughts, he pivots back, one hand locking around my jaw, the other going to his belt.

"On your knees, Ms. Prosecutor," he growls. "You know how to use that mouth in court. Let's see how it does wrapped around my cock instead."

The words hit like lightning—sharp, electric, wild.

No. Don't do it. This is wrong. He's *wrong.*

Remember everything you stand for. Your principles. Your morals. Your fucking job.

But before I can think better of it…I drop. Knees to the floor. Submission like a drug in my veins. He smirks, slow and lethal.

And somehow, that arrogance doesn't enrage me like it should.

It thrills me.

THIRTEEN

ALEKSEI

She pops the button of my pants and drags the zipper down, and all I can think about is that mouth. I want her on me, lips wrapped around my cock, giving me the kind of pleasure that wipes out every thought in my head.

She's becoming an addiction.

No, worse. A disease I don't want cured.

It's almost sadistic, how much I want her. Like fate dropped her in front of me just to see how far I'd go before I snapped.

But the way she's beginning to obey, beginning to understand the way this is going to work, it's too perfect.

She's mine to command. To mold. To bend until her mind breaks and the only thing she begs for is *me*.

When I kick free of my pants and shoes and my cock springs loose, she wraps her small fist around it, her fingers unable to circle me completely. The crown pulses hard under her touch, a raw throb of need, and when her thumb skims the king's crown piercing, a curse breaks from my chest. Her tongue flicks out, tracing the metal, circling the swollen head in slow, wet drags that make my vision go black at the edges.

"Blyat…" The word snarls out of me as my hand clamps on the back of her head. "Take it all."

I need that tightness. Need to feel her throat stretch around me until she forgets how to breathe.

She parts her lips and slides down over me, eyes glued to mine, and my body answers with a violent shudder I can't stop. I don't even try.

Clutching her hair, I push her deeper, driving her down until her gag vibrates around me. The sound is perfect, and I hold her there, my cock pressed to the back of her throat, watching her struggle to take it.

"That's it, detka," I growl. "Swallow every inch. Choke on it."

Her eyes water, mascara running in dark streaks down her cheeks, and the sight only fuels the hunger tearing through me. She keeps going, taking me deeper, bobbing her head, tongue flicking over the metal at the tip while her other hand toys with the pubic piercing.

The thought of her doing this for another man makes my vision go white.

Jealousy is not something I've ever felt before, not over any woman. Yet with her, it hits like a knife under the ribs.

Why her? This is the last thing I need. I want to rip her out of my goddamn subconscious.

The harder she takes me, the tighter her lips seal, her muffled moans vibrating around my cock until I'm fighting not to spill down her throat. Her gaze hooks mine, tongue sliding out to circle the skin around the head.

"Nu blyat…tvoy rot…" *Fuck…that mouth…*

The fire in her eyes flares hotter at the words, her grip tightening, sucking me harder like she knows exactly what she's doing to me.

Too good at it. Too proud of it.

Another curse rips out of me as I tug on her hair and drag her off, my cock sliding from her lips, slick and throbbing.

My jaw locks, every muscle straining to hold back because I refuse to finish anywhere but inside her. Where she will feel it, remember it, know who filled her.

I drag her up by the leash and rise to my feet, walking her toward the bondage table like the filthy little prize she is. I flip her over, chest pressed to the leather, her elbows bent beneath her, ass in the air.

"How many men have had that mouth?" I give the leash a sharp tug.

She laughs—that same taunting, reckless laugh she's given me before. "Too many."

Rage floods me like venom. I grab the cuffs and shackle her wrists, locking them down, then her ankles, securing her wide to the table.

"You think that is funny?" My hand knots in her hair and yanks her head back, making her gasp. "We'll see who's laughing soon."

"What does that mean?" she pants, teeth sinking into her bottom lip, that maddening mix of anticipation and defiance twisting through her features.

A low, feral chuckle escapes me as I walk to the table across the room, grabbing a crop. But not just any crop. This one's fitted with an electromagnetic charge I have been meaning to try.

What a perfect little canvas to test on.

I stalk back toward her, dragging the crop up the curve of her ass and watching her shiver. "If you don't like it, tell me and I stop. Understand?"

She nods for only a second before I strike. A clean, snapping blow across one cheek. She flinches, but doesn't make a sound.

That won't last.

I hit her again. And again. Her skin begins to pinken, the marks blooming under my control.

Then I flip the switch. This time, when the crop lands, she jolts, a gasp slipping from her lips, followed by a desperate moan, a sound that makes my cock twitch.

I don't stop. Each shock sharpens her cries, each blow coaxes more. I drink in the sight of her trembling beneath me, her fists clenching against the cuffs, her body straining toward something she will never ask for.

Until I lower the crop between her thighs.

Her clit is already swollen and flushed. I flick it, and she bucks.

Then I strike it, just once, and her moan turns into something jagged and needy, like pain and pleasure tangled into one desperate scream.

I do it again. And again. Each cry breaking louder. Each jolt dragging her closer to the edge. Until *I* decide when she goes over it.

And not a second before.

My cock throbs to feel her wrapped around me, but that'll wait. I'm not done with her yet.

I leave her trembling against the table and move to the dresser. My fingers work the combination on a bound leather case, anticipation crawling under my skin. When I take what I want from inside, her eyes go wide.

The sight of her fear and curiosity sends a dark satisfaction flooding through me.

"You have no idea what I've got planned for that tight cunt of yours."

She squirms against the cuffs, hips shifting, glistening and spread for me like a feast. I click the vibrator on and press it to her clit, teasing circles until the tip slides inside. Her moans dissolve into panting whimpers as I push it deeper, feeding her more with each pass, watching her unravel.

She throws a glance back at me over her shoulder, hair sticking to her damp skin, breath stuttering.

I grab a fistful of it, dragging her head back, my mouth trailing across her ear. "You're a perfect little toy, moya ptichka."

"I'm not your toy." Her eyes flash, denial dripping from every word, a last spark of insolence I want to taste.

"You're whatever I decide you are."

Before she can answer, I slam the vibrator deep until it's seated in her. Her knees buckle, nails digging into the leather.

And then, slowly, I push my cock in beside it.

Her strangled gasp breaks into a moan. "Oh my God, what are you—oh f-f-fuck!"

"Such a filthy whore," I growl, sinking deeper. "Taking everything I give you."

My palm cracks across her ass, and she whimpers. I start to thrust, slow at first, then harder, keeping the toy where it is until she's screaming her yeses into the leather, her body collapsing under the weight of it.

I don't let up. I keep pounding into her while the vibrator thrums inside, pushing it deeper with my other hand, keeping her pinned open and helpless until she's clawing at the table, trembling on the edge.

Her walls clench, taking me in deeper. Her cries sharpen, turning needier, more desperate.

"Oh God, yes, don't stop."

"Mm…" My voice drops to a low command against her neck. "Beg for it, ptichka. Tell me how badly you need my cock to finish you. Tell me how desperate you are."

Her groan claws up her throat, and I sink in harder, grinding through the need.

"Beg," I snap, my fingers curling in her hair. "Or I'll leave you like this—tied up, aching, dripping—until you ask me properly."

She gasps, hips jerking, but I hold her in place, still buried deep, with the toy pulsing alongside me.

"You want to come?" I roll my hips once, nice and slow, pushing into her. "Then let me hear it." I give her another ruthless thrust. "Beg like a good girl."

She whimpers. "Please…please, I—I need to come."

My eyes close on the sound of her voice quivering, cracking under the weight of her own desire. That surrender in her tone, the way she falls apart just to get a taste of release, it feeds something unholy in me.

Everything she owns is already mine. And soon, she will be too.

With a low snarl, I shove her face into the leather and slam into her again, losing myself as rage, desire, and months of bottled-up obsession pour through every hard thrust.

She made me like this. She twisted something inside me. And now I'll break her with it.

When she finally comes, it's with my name torn from her throat like a curse, her body convulsing as she comes so hard she soaks the floor beneath her.

And I keep going. Driving into her again and again until she's shaking, sobbing, drained of everything but the memory of me, the feeling of my cock, the bruises I left, and the truth she can't escape.

She'll hate herself for how much she wanted it. And I'll make sure she never forgets who made her this way.

FIONA

The air hangs heavy with the stench of sex and my own shame. It clings to my skin like a second layer, wrapping around me tighter than the cuffs he's just now unlocking.

I can feel it in every breath I take. The filth. The humiliation I try to swallow down.

My legs barely hold me as the restraints fall away, muscles

twitching in ways I don't want to examine too closely.

Used. Open. Branded by his touch.

And I let it happen. Again.

I can't look at him. I can't even look at myself. Not like this: flushed and sticky and ruined in a way that's as emotional as it is physical.

What the hell is wrong with me?

My fingers rub at the red welts on my wrists, trying to remember the version of myself who didn't melt when he touched me or crawl into the fire just to feel something.

Behind me, Aleksei moves without a word, reaching for his pants and getting dressed like this is just another day for him. Like none of it meant a damn thing.

And maybe it didn't. Not to him.

But it meant something to me. Because I don't just sleep around, especially not with men I attempt to put in prison.

I'm really winning at life lately.

I turn away, not wanting to look at him anymore, reaching for my dress instead and fumbling with the fabric. My stupid, traitorous hands shake as I sweep it over my body. I don't like being rattled this way.

Why the hell do I keep coming back for more?

Because he gives you the best orgasms.

Am I seriously that easy?

His footsteps approach before I feel him behind me, the heat of his body brushing my spine.

"Need help?" He tugs the zipper up slowly.

His voice is low, smooth, and impossible to ignore. It still lights me up from the inside out. My nipples tighten. My jaw locks. I despise the way my body still answers to him like it's his fucking possession.

He continues zipping the dress, his hand brushing the nape of my neck before trailing down to my thigh, and I flinch.

But he doesn't stop. His fingers catch the hem of my dress, tugging it down with infuriating care like I'm some delicate artifact instead of the mess he made me.

When he's done, he doesn't move. His palms remain against my hips. Familiar. Possessive. Unwelcome.

Or at least that's what I try to tell myself.

Because my eyes flutter shut the moment he touches me. My body doesn't care how wrong this is. It only knows his hands, what he makes me feel.

"Aleksei…" I breathe, trying to step forward, to break the spell.

But his arm snakes around me, dragging me back into him like I'm his to hold.

"This was a mistake. All of it."

He hums, low and unbothered, his mouth skimming along the side of my neck. "Is that what you tell yourself after every time you scream my name?"

His words cut deeper than I want to admit. Because he's not wrong.

"You beg for it, then pretend it didn't happen." His exhale fans down my throat, and I feel it everywhere. "You act like fighting me makes it less real. Like losing to me doesn't make you wet."

My cheeks burn. My stomach twists. Disgrace twines inside me, but not for the reasons it should.

Because he made me feel wanted. Desired. Worshipped and defiled in the same breath. And I loved it. I loved it all.

Even now, I want to lean into him. Let him fuck me again. But I won't.

"I don't want you," I whisper. "I'm using you."

He laughs under his breath, then flips me around so fast I stumble. That large, masculine hand wraps around my throat, caging me, making me ache all over again.

"Either way…" he says, rough and possessive. "You belong to me, detka." His lips slowly drop to mine, teasing them slowly. "You can hate it. You can fight it. But I'll always be in control. You will never be rid of me."

My pulse slams against his palm.

"You haven't won," I grit out. "You haven't won a goddamn thing, Marinov. Trust me."

His smile is crooked. Poisonous. Like he knows something I don't. And the chill that slips down my spine tells me he might.

"Hope you got your fill. Because I'm done. With this. With you. With all of it. And I mean it this time."

My words don't waver, gaze sharp.

He drops his hand away and simply watches me. That same maddening smile. Like he's already rewritten the ending I've yet to read.

"Oh, Ms. Clark…" His eyes gleam. "You have no idea how wrong you are."

The words hang in the air long after I rush out, impossible to shake. And for the first time, I'm not sure if I've just ended something…

Or if I've walked straight into a trap I'll never dig out of.

FOURTEEN

ALEKSEI

The door closes behind her, but I don't move. Not right away.

Not when my blood is still thrumming with the taste of her. Her scent rooted in the air. Her sounds echoing in this room like a memory I'll take to the grave.

I see it all. Feel it again like it's happening now. Every twitch. Every tremble. Every war she waged and lost.

She will pretend it meant nothing. She will lie because she has to. It's the only way she survives this.

But I know the truth. I felt it. She's powerless against me. Just the way I like it.

It's in the way her body opened for mine. The way her breath caught when I kissed the skin she tried to hide. The way she whimpered when I wrapped that collar around her throat, and the way she loved every second of it.

My perfect, self-righteous prosecutor.

I gave her the fantasies she won't ever admit she has. And now she's running. Again.

I drag a hand through my hair, jaw tight as I button my shirt.

Let her run. Let her cling to whatever illusion of choice she thinks she has left. It won't matter.

Because I own her now. Body. Mind. Soul.

And anyone who tries to get in the way of that? Will bleed for it.

Speaking of bleeding…

I have unfinished business, by the name of Wesley Dawson. Exiting the room, I head down the hall, opening the door to a secure stairwell. Our men greet me with a nod, knowing exactly where I'm headed.

To the room no one ever comes out of.

My boots echo down the metal steps, each one a countdown to a reckoning that should've happened the second that svolich laid eyes on Fiona.

I should've ended him at the vineyard. Should've dragged him behind the barrels and slit his goddamn throat the moment he smiled at her.

But I waited. Watched. Wanted to know who he was before I killed him.

Because I would never have allowed him to invest in the vineyard. That was not an option he had.

Then he did something worse. He hurt her. And now he's going to bleed for it.

I didn't know he was a member of Rzvrt. We have too many to keep track of.

But I followed her on the cameras the second he picked her up. And to my surprise, they were coming right to me.

I waited to see if she would let him touch her and how much I'd be able to watch before I killed him just for breathing the same air as her.

And now? He's stripped to the waist, wrists chained above his head, swaying like carcass meat in the middle of the basement. My men got started without me.

Good. Saves me time.

Wesley's eyes widen the second I step inside. That flicker of fear brings me satisfaction. His ribs are already mottled with bruises, a cut splits his lip, and a thin stream of blood snakes down his thigh where somebody got creative.

"Having too much fun without me?" My laugh bounces off the concrete as I head for the weapons my men laid out for me on the small table in the corner of the room, picking up the brass knuckles I enjoy using.

"Da." My cousin Dimitri smirks as he wipes his hands on a towel. "On khotel dat' kazhdomu iz nas po millionu, chtoby my ego otpustili." *He wanted to give each of us a million to let him go.*

The rest of the men chuckle, stepping aside to make space for me.

"Is that true, Wesley?" I slap him forcefully, just to see his head snap back. "Were you going to bribe my men to betray me?"

He lifts his head and groans, blood bubbling at the corner of his mouth when he tries to speak.

I don't give him the chance. The knuckles drive into his gut once, twice, hard enough to make his whole body jerk like a puppet on a string, his groans loud and beautiful.

"Tell me who sent you."

But I already know. I'm just waiting to see how long it takes him to crack.

I hit him again and again. He whimpers, his knees buckling. Heading back to the tools, I drop the knuckles and pick up a golf club this time. Swinging it lazily from hand to hand, I watch him start to shake.

"P-p-please," he stammers, chest heaving. "I-I'll tell you whatever you want."

"Who sent you? Why did you go see the Clarks?"

"They…they paid me, okay? They said all I had to do was make them think I wanted to invest and then sign the vineyard to—"

I step closer, the smell of his fear rising with each shallow inhale.

"To who?" My voice drops to a growl. "Speak."

"F-f-fuck!" His whole face tightens, terror carved into every line.

"Believe me." I lean in until my shadow swallows him. "I'm much scarier than whoever paid you. Open your mouth and give me a name before I grow tired of it and decide to rip your tongue out."

"Alright! Alright!" he sobs. "His name is Daniil Volkov. Very scary guy. He wants the vineyard. I don't know why, I swear. I only know what they paid me to do."

I pat his blood-slicked face, the way you might a dog that finally obeyed. "That was very helpful."

He gasps like oxygen will save him. It won't.

"And Fiona?" I ask, taking a slow step forward, tone turning razor-sharp. "Did they tell you to touch her? Were you told to lay your filthy fucking hands on her?"

"No! No, I swear. That was a mistake. I didn't know she was yours. I was just—"

"You do now." I swing the club hard until it connects with his face with a crunch, ripping into his cheek.

His scream tears free, short-lived, before I swing again. And again. And again.

Bone cracks. Blood sprays. Skin gives way to meat. I don't stop until there's nothing left but pulp, until even his mother wouldn't recognize what used to be her son.

The club clatters to the floor when I'm done. Rinsing my hands in the sink, I splash water on my face, meeting my own gaze in the mirror.

She made me kill for her when I should've killed her instead. A long time ago.

What a fucking twist of events.

I turn to my men. "Burn the body. Dispose of the ID."

They nod without question.

The Volkovs will pay for this. They all will. I'll rip out every vein one by one until there's nothing left to kill.

And Fiona? She might hate me, but she'll never have to worry about another man touching her again.

Not while I'm still breathing.

FIFTEEN

FIONA

My cell buzzes on the bathroom sink the next morning, an incoming text from Emilia saying she's leaving in five to meet for our lunch date.

I try to add extra concealer to the bags under my eyes, but it's no use. I slept maybe three hours. Just enough to relive every second of last night in stuttering flashes.

His hands on my skin. His mouth dragging confessions from places I didn't know existed. My own voice, begging.

I don't want to think about it. But I can't stop either.

Lunch with Emilia couldn't have come at a better time. I need normal. I have to remember who I am and why staying away from Aleksei is goal number one. Indefinitely.

Heading out of the house, I glance around for signs of him, but there are none. No black SUV idling by the curb. No shadow hovering near the edge of the trees. Still, my shoulders stay tight, my instincts humming with that low, persistent warning I haven't been able to shake.

On my way to the car, I detour toward the mailbox, purse slung over one shoulder, keys already dangling from my fingers.

I'm not expecting anything. Just the usual junk mail, maybe another credit card application I'll shred without reading. It's too soon for another letter. They never come this close together.

But then I see it. Tucked between bills and advertisements. Unmarked. White. Same as all the others.

My heart pumps louder.

I tell myself to wait. To open it after lunch so it doesn't ruin my mood.

Sliding into the driver's seat, I slam the door and rip the envelope open like it's burning through my fingers.

> How much would you pay to know what your family did?

The words hit like a blow to the chest, sending shock waves through me.

This has to be a joke. Someone is trying to mess with me, make me doubt everything I know. But I won't let them. I shove the letter into the glove compartment and slam it shut, like that's enough to seal it away.

They won't win. Not this time. This ends now.

I'm done with the letters. Done with Aleksei. Done with all of it.

By the time I pull into the lot, Emilia's already walking into the café, flanked on both sides by Konstantin's cousins, Maksim and Dimitri, who look like the musclebound mafia version of Secret Service. They follow her wherever she goes. It's their job now. Konstantin takes her protection very seriously, and I'm relieved about that.

When I head inside, Emilia spots me immediately and waves me over.

"Hey!" she says, standing to wrap me in a warm hug.

I smile and rest a hand on her belly. "How's our future lawyer doing?"

"He's kicking like he's got something to prove," she laughs, glowing. "I swear, he thinks my bladder's a trampoline."

"His dad must be proud already."

"You have no idea," she mutters with a smirk.

Maksim flashes a grin. "Miss Fiona. Lovely to see you."

"Hi… Thanks." I offer a polite smile, caught slightly off guard. I know who they are, but we've never exactly chatted over croissants.

"Aleksei still bothering you?"

I roll my eyes. "Unfortunately."

Maksim shrugs like it's out of his hands. "You could give him a chance. He might grow on you."

"Like mold?"

"Exactly," Dimitri deadpans. "Persistent. Impossible to kill. You'd never be lonely."

"No, thanks, boys." I raise a brow. "I like things just the way they are."

Without the oversized Russian who knows how to use his hands…

I clear my throat before that thought finishes.

Maksim leans in with a whisper. "You know, he calls out your name in his sleep."

I nearly choke. "Oh, does he now?"

"It's sweet," Maksim adds, perfectly serious. "Almost…romantic."

"Kinda pathetic too," Dimitri says with a shrug. "But hey, who am I to judge? I have never been in love."

"Believe me, that man does not love me."

"In my family, this is exactly how we show love."

Emilia's cackling beside me, barely holding in her water.

"Oh really?" I tilt my head, needing this topic to end ASAP. "Good to know. Now tell me, do you guys take turns tucking him in at night too?"

"We have a schedule," Maksim says.

"I'm sure he appreciates it." I laugh despite myself.

Dimitri grins. "You never know. We might end up family."

I still, smile tightening.

"Yeah," I mutter, shaking my head. "That's never gonna happen."

"If you say so." Dimitri flips a hand.

The two of them saunter off to a table in the corner, still chuckling like devils, while Emilia's grin lingers across the table.

The second they're out of earshot, she leans in. "Don't listen to them. I'm sure he's not calling out your name. He's most likely using your face for target practice."

"Ha. Ha." I shoot her a playful look while she giggles into her ice water.

I try to hold on to the laugh, but it slips, tension settling over me when I think about the letter, Aleksei, my parents' vineyard, everything…

It's too much, pressing in on all sides.

Emilia's expression shifts. "Hey, is everything okay?"

I try to deflect, fingers twisting the edge of my napkin, but the pressure's been building too long. She's my best friend. She'd never tell Konstantin anything, not unless I asked her to.

"Remember that investor I was supposed to meet yesterday?"

"Yeah. Wesley, right?"

I grimace. "That's the one. We met. He…took me somewhere."

Emilia's brows draw. "Where?"

I wince. "Rzvrt. Some club the Marinovs apparently own. Do you know it?"

Her jaw drops. "Shit. Yeah, I do."

"I couldn't believe it. The sleazeball took me there without telling me what kind of place it was. And when I tried to leave…he grabbed me."

Her whole body stiffens. "I'm gonna kill him."

"Pretty sure Aleksei already did. Or came close."

Her head snaps toward me. "Wait, what?"

I glance down at my hands. "He showed up. Ripped Wesley off me like it was nothing. Then his men dragged him off somewhere."

"Go Aleksei." Emilia smiles. "Maybe I've been too hard on him."

"Nope. We still hate him."

Her grin widens. "Right. Of course. Carry on."

I shift, hesitating. "I didn't see Wesley again, but...somehow, Aleksei and I..."

Emilia leans forward. "Yeah?"

Her smirk is pure mischief now.

"We..."

"Use your words, counselor." She's really having too much fun with this.

Groaning, I cover my face, peeking at her between two fingers. "We slept together."

"Oh, what was that?" She cups a hand to her ear.

"You heard me."

"I did. I just wanted to hear it again."

I toss a napkin at her. "Shut up."

She swats it away, eyes gleaming. "So...how was it?"

"Better than last time," I mutter. "At least it wasn't up against a tree."

Her eyes grow.

"I'm sorry, WHAT?! You've been holding out on me?" She folds her arms across her chest.

I sigh. "It's a long story."

"Oh, we're not leaving until I hear every detail. Start talking."

"I didn't mean not to tell you. I just...didn't want to talk about it. It was awful. Not the...you know... That was..." I wave a hand. "But the fact that I let it happen. Twice. What the hell is wrong with me?"

Her expression softens. "I'm not judging. Obviously."

She holds up her left hand, flashing the diamond that could blind a man.

"This is it, though," I say, trying to convince both of us. "I scratched the itch. It's done."

"Totally." She nods like she believes me. "Whatever you say."

"I mean it."

"I believe you." She pauses. "I just think it'd be fun if we were sisters-in-law."

I groan. "You're insane. I would never, *ever* marry that man."

"Sure." She sips her water, unbothered. "But if you want kids, you're going to have to actually start dating again."

I narrow my eyes. "Have you been talking to my mother?"

"No," she says with a suspicious amount of innocence. "But maybe I should."

"God, please don't."

We burst into laughter, and for the first time in days, it's like I can breathe again.

Emilia grounds me. She always has. She reminds me I'm still the girl who dreamed of being a lawyer. Of doing good, putting away the bad guys. The girl who didn't fall for mobsters with dark eyes and hands that make you weak.

But the truth creeps in anyway. The way Aleksei looked at me last night, like I was something he treasured. The way he traced every inch of me like a map he already knew.

And I wonder, just for a second, how crazy it would really be if I was his wife.

No. No, no, no.

I shake the thought loose, but Emilia's gaze sharpens like she sees too much.

"You gonna be okay?"

"Yeah." I force a smile. "I think your crazy might be contagious. I need to quarantine. Immediately."

She smirks. "You'll get used to it."
"Let's not get ahead of ourselves."

SIXTEEN

FIONA

There's a weight in my chest before I even leave the house. A pressure that has nothing to do with Aleksei, yet everything to do with him. Because even when I haven't seen him, I feel him, like smoke clinging to my skin long after the fire's gone out.

It's been a week. A full seven days since I let him touch me again. Since I dropped to my knees for him and hated how much I liked it.

I haven't heard from him. Haven't even seen him. But I know he's still watching.

I check the mailbox out of habit before getting into my car, my hand remaining on the cool metal just a moment too long before I lift the lid. No letter today. No envelope with mocking, cryptic threats.

Maybe whoever's sending them finally got bored. Or maybe this is just more of their game.

I exhale a slow breath as I slide behind the wheel and try to clear my head. I need to if I want to make a good impression on the new investor Mom was going on about yesterday. She didn't give me much info when I asked, which I did find weird, but I think after Wesley, she's being extra cautious.

All she knows is that Wesley backed out after meeting me. That's what his text said the next day, though I'm not convinced he even sent it. If I had to guess, it was Aleksei who made him write it.

Maybe he's already dead. I haven't looked into it. I don't want to know.

Either way, Mom's been pissed. She didn't see it coming, and I get it. She thought Wesley was a sure thing. She even asked what I did to scare him off.

I told her the truth. That he was a creep. That he put his hands on me. That we didn't need someone like that anywhere near our family business. She agreed. And Dad swore he'd kill him, which is laughable, because the man couldn't hurt a fly.

When I pull into the lot beside the main building, a few cars are scattered around, but one stands out: a sleek black Bentley that definitely doesn't belong to anyone here. Must be the investor.

Straightening my spine, I grab my bag and head inside, knocking once on the office door.

"Come in," my mom calls out.

I step inside and immediately notice the tension. They're sitting on the sofa, whispering until the door opens. My mother throws on a smile that's way too bright, and my father...won't even meet my eyes.

The hell is going on?

I remain standing, arms crossed. "So, where is he?"

Dad scratches the back of his neck, avoiding the question, while Mom rises slowly.

"He's out walking the property. Said he wanted to get a sense of the place before we all sit down to talk."

Something twists in my gut. Unease settling like a stone. This already feels wrong, and I don't know why.

Then she reaches for my hands and grips them tight. Too tight.

"Fiona," she says gently. "I need you to go into this with an open mind, okay?"

My stomach knots. "Why? What's going on, Ma?"

Her eyes gloss, blinking too much, like she's holding something back. "This investor…he's serious. And this might be our only chance."

I glance at my dad, but he's not looking at me. He's just staring into his lap, his hands clenched so tight that the skin over his knuckles has gone pale.

"What aren't you telling me?" The tension continues to grow. "Dad?"

He lifts his head, breath hitching like he's about to confess to a crime. "Fiona, I—"

But then I hear it: the voice that lives in my nightmares.

"Good morning, Ms. Prosecutor."

No. No, no, NO!

All the blood rushes out of my body.

"It's good to see you again." Every syllable is soaked in smug satisfaction.

I don't want to turn. I already know what I'll find. But I do anyway.

Leaning against the doorway—coffee cup in hand, hair coiffed back, black shirt tucked into tailored slate-gray pants that hug the rippled muscles of his thighs—stands Aleksei Marinov.

All the air leaves my lungs.

This isn't happening. It can't be happening. My parents know what he is. Who he is. They know what his family is capable of. They would never do this.

Would they?

I squeeze my eyes shut, praying he'll disappear. That he's a mere hallucination. But when I open them, he's still there. Still watching me. Still looking at me like this has already been decided.

Over my dead body.

"No," I snap as I whip toward my parents. "Absolutely not."

"Just…hear him out," Mom pleads, words thin with desperation. "Please, Fiona."

"We are not dealing with that family, Ma! Are you kidding me right now?"

"Wow, Ms. Clark. You think so highly of us. I'm honored."

"Go fuck yourself, Aleksei. No one's talking to you."

"Fiona!" Mom scolds like I'm a child.

"Oh, come on, Ma," I scoff. "I've said way worse to him."

"She has," Aleksei murmurs, that irritating grin curling across his face…and God, my stomach flips for all the wrong reasons.

This is all wrong. Every part of it.

"All I'm asking is that you hear him out." Mom runs a hand down her face, every inch of her tight with exhaustion. "If you don't like what he says, then… Then that's that."

But we both know what she means.

If I say no, we lose everything. The vineyard. Their legacy. The only life they've ever known.

How the hell am I supposed to let that happen? But how am I supposed to accept help from Aleksei Marinov?

My eyes drag back to his, which are full of some unreadable intensity that makes my skin prickle. I turn, unable to handle the way he's looking at me like he's already won. Instead, I focus on the two people who raised me. Who gave me everything. Who are now drowning, and he knows it.

He came here because they're desperate and he knew I'd want to help.

Is that why he took Wesley?

Not because of what Wesley did to me…but because he wanted to hurt me through my parents? Is this all just another game?

"I'm not here to cause trouble," Aleksei says calmly, eyes fixed on me.

That's because you are *trouble.*

"I'm only asking for a moment of your time. A simple conversation. We can walk the grounds if you'd prefer some privacy. Then you're free to say no."

God, I want to scream. But talking in private *is* a good idea. I don't want my parents to be here when I tell him to fuck right off if he thinks I'll allow him to hurt them.

"Fine." My gaze flicks to my parents. "I'll be back."

"Okay, honey." Mom tries for a smile, but it wavers. "We'll be here."

And my father…still won't look at me. Now I know why.

Aleksei moves ahead to open the door, his arm sweeping wide like it's some kind of courtesy. I step through, and he falls in beside me, close enough for the air between us to tighten. His cologne drifts over, woodsy and clean, and to my disgust, it stirs something in me. A dangerous kind of comfort.

The sun has climbed higher, but the warmth doesn't reach me. Not with him beside me. I swear, I can't escape this man no matter what I do.

His arm slides around my waist and drags me against him as we round the corner past the tasting patio, while his voice dips low, a slow rasp that curls along my skin. "It's been too long since I've had you this close. Have you missed me the way I've missed you?"

"I actually forgot you existed."

He laughs under his breath, turning me to face him with a smooth twist.

"Liar." His fingers catch my chin, tilting it up until his mouth lowers, hovering a breath from mine. "I know exactly how wet you get when you're fighting me. And I like it a little too much."

So do I.

No. Stop that!

"My parents could be watching." I try to shove him off, but he doesn't budge.

"Let them." His lips graze my ear, setting my nerves alight. "They should get used to seeing me right where I belong."

I close my eyes, forcing a breath into my lungs before I push at his chest. "Cut the act, Marinov. Why are you here? Is this another one of your games? Because I swear to God, if you so much as think about hurting my parents—"

His laugh is dry, almost cruel, and he finally lets me go. He strolls toward one of the patio chairs, moving with a calmness that makes my stomach knot. The patio's empty; it's too early for guests. Thankfully.

He pulls a chair out for me as if we're at a polite lunch, not a hostage negotiation. Against my better judgment, I sit.

He studies me for a beat as he lowers himself opposite me, his gaze unblinking. "Whether they're hurt depends entirely on you."

A chill slides through me. "What the hell is that supposed to mean?"

He smooths a hand down his shirt like he's already bored of the conversation. "We had a nice talk before you arrived, and now it's all up to you. Their entire future is in your hands, Ms. Clark."

My pulse drums hard against my ribs. "Then stop circling and get to the point."

His grin spreads. "I offered them a deal. One that saves the vineyard, secures their future, and wipes away their debts."

"What kind of deal?"

"Marinov Holdings takes control. We invest, expand, make it profitable, while keeping fifty-one percent of the shares. But…" He pauses, letting it hang between us, and then leans forward, elbows braced on the table, his eyes catching mine. "There's one more condition."

I force my face neutral even as dread crawls up my spine. "And what's that?"

His gaze skirts up my body. "You marry me."

My jaw drops and a strangled laugh escapes. "You're joking."

But his expression doesn't shift. His features harden instead.

"Oh my God… You're actually serious."

"I don't joke about business, Ms. Clark." His voice is calm, too calm. "You want to save your parents? Become my wife. Bind yourself to a man who will never love you."

Every word is filled with contempt, and I feel it in every inch of my body. Has this been his plan all along?

My spine stiffens. This is a death sentence.

"Why? Why would you even want that? This is your life too. Why the hell would you want to be tied to someone you despise?"

"Because…" His hand glides over my throat, light and deceptively gentle at first, until his fingers curl around my neck and squeeze. Hard enough to try to make me feel powerless. "When you swore to destroy me, I made a promise too." His grip tightens. "That one day, I'd take everything from you."

A cold rush floods my veins.

"And now…" His thumb traces the line of my jaw. "I've found the perfect way to do it."

He crowds into my space, his stare burning like a fuse.

"You wanted to see me rot behind bars. But instead, you'll have the distinct honor of wearing my ring. Bearing my name. And every day you share my bed, share your body…" His fingers constrict, forcing a breathless gasp from my throat. "I'll remind you that you failed. That your entire life exploded in your pretty little face and *I* lit the match."

"You're sick." My teeth clench so tight my jaw trembles.

"Perhaps. But you're mine now, moya okhotnitsa, for better or worse."

I try to jerk back from his grasp, but he won't let me go.

"I won't do it."

"Fine." He releases me with a shrug, stepping back like none of this matters to him. "I'll let your parents know the deal is off. That their daughter chose pride over their survival. But know this: if you don't accept, I will take *everything* from them. Every penny will burn to the ground until they have nothing but the clothes on their backs, and even those, I will take from them."

Fear tears through my chest like a scream that won't come out. I stare at him, at the cold certainty in his eyes, and I know…

He's not bluffing.

He turns, strutting away without a backward glance like he didn't just detonate my entire world. My breath comes fast, my heart hammering like it's trying to claw out of my chest.

I can't do this. I can't marry him. He's going to make my life a living hell.

And if he wants kids? God, I can't have children with him.

The farther he gets, the deeper the terror drags into my bones.

I open my mouth. "Wait!"

He pauses, slowly turning, his gaze drifting over his shoulder like he already knows what I'm about to say. "Yes?"

My lips part. My mind splinters. I can't think. But I can see my parents in that office: the fear in their eyes, the weight of their future pressing down on them.

They've done so much for me. College. Law school. Even helped buy my home. How do I turn my back on them?

But how do I marry this man?

Yet what choice is there, really? It may seem like he's presenting me with one, but it's not much of a choice. It's all smoke and mirrors.

Still…this doesn't have to be permanent. Emilia might be able to help. If Konstantin steps in and talks to his brother, this whole thing could end. Maybe Aleksei won't want to go through with the marriage. Maybe he'd divorce me if he does. There has to be a way out of this for me, but my parents don't have that option.

Bitterness rises in my throat as the words claw their way out.

"I'll do it," I whisper. "I'll marry you."

His smile cuts across his face, polished and poisonous. "Of course you will."

God, I want to wipe that haughty look off with my fist.

"I have conditions, though," I bite out as he draws closer.

He dips his head slightly, one brow arched. "Naturally. Shall we discuss them over champagne?"

"I'd rather swallow broken glass."

"That can be arranged." His fingers barely skim up my hand, but my body screams for more. "You do understand that there's no getting out of this marriage, don't you?" His hand climbs higher until it wraps around my throat. "You will be my wife until your very last breath."

He drops his arm and starts to leave, but not before he adds, "How does it feel, Ms. Prosecutor? To have no control?"

My hand balls into a fist.

"Welcome to your new life, Mrs. Marinova. I trust you will find it quite agreeable. Maybe." He chuckles.

I can't believe I agreed to this. I sold my soul to the devil and singlehandedly just made the worst mistake of my life.

And I'm not sure there's any way back.

SEVENTEEN

ALEKSEI

She was always going to say yes. If she hadn't, I would've made her.

There was never going to be a world where Fiona Clark walked away from me. She was always going to be mine.

She came for my freedom, so now I have hers. That's how this works.

I'm going to enjoy watching her walk down the aisle, knowing how much it's killing her to give in. To give herself to me.

She thinks this is a loss for me? That marrying her was some kind of defeat for me too?

No. This was the win. She's the prize.

I didn't lose anything. I claimed her. Branded her. Bought her. And now I get to do whatever I want to the one woman who wanted me caged more than anyone.

She doesn't realize it yet, but I'm going to enjoy this marriage more than she can possibly fathom. If I ever divorce her, it will be because I've grown tired of the fire in her eyes. But something tells me I never will.

Because giving her freedom again? Letting her have the life she thought she would build for herself? That future is dead. She's bound to me now. Tight as a knot that can't be undone. Fused through blood, betrayal, and the sweet taste of revenge.

That's who we are. What we will always be.

"When will this sham of a marriage be official?" The words scrape up her throat like they physically hurt.

I grin, and the flare of fury in her eyes only makes it sweeter. "A week. At my home. Invite whoever you want. The more the merrier, wife."

A muscle pops in her chin at the word.

She'll get used to it. In time.

"So, this won't be some big wedding or anything, right? Just your family, I assume?"

I tilt my head, catching the flicker of panic in her eyes. No, I hadn't planned on anything grand. I was going to keep it simple.

But now? Now I want the whole world to watch.

"Of course it will be big," I say smoothly, savoring the sharp breath she pulls in. "Everyone I know will be there. When a Marinov gets married, it's a big occasion."

She stiffens like she's bracing for impact. "One week isn't enough time to plan something like that."

I lean in, lowering my voice just enough to make her nerves prickle. "Then you don't know my family. It will be done."

My hand lifts, fingers curling under her chin, thumb dragging over the softness of her bottom lip. My cock throbs at the contact. At the faint tremor in her breath.

That mouth. I've tasted it. Claimed it. But I want more. So much more.

Now it's mine. To own. To ruin. To savor.

It's a sickness, this obsession. But I've stopped trying to cure it.

I force myself to step back before I lose control. She has that effect, making my blood run hot.

"I'm not wearing a wedding dress." She plants a hand on her hip like she's still in charge of something.

A dry laugh escapes me. "I would much prefer if you wore nothing at all, but since I cannot have everything I want, you'll be a good little wife and put on a gown. In fact…" I check my watch. "The gown I chose for our special day should be arriving at your place in about two hours."

Her mouth drops open. "What?!"

My knuckles drift down her cheek, my gaze taking in every inch of her. Every defiant, filthy, beautiful inch.

"*No* was never an option for you, I'm afraid."

She flinches, though desire flickers through her like a traitor.

"I took the liberty of choosing ivory. I remember how good it looked on you."

Her eyes narrow. "How the hell do you even know my size?"

I smirk.

She groans, shoving my arm. "You are actually insane. It's a tragedy I never managed to put you behind bars."

"Ah, but then we wouldn't have our happy little union. And that, detka, would've been the real crime." I cup her cheek again.

Her body tightens beneath my palm before she slaps it away, and I can't decide what I enjoy more: her resistance or how easily I can break it.

"We need to set some ground rules."

I chuckle. "And what would those be?"

"I'm not quitting my job."

"Fine. We could use a lawyer in the family." I lean closer, lowering my tone. "But what will you do with me? Pretend I don't exist? Lock me in a closet like your shameful little secret?"

"Yes, exactly." Her glare narrows. "I'm glad you're understanding how this is going to go now. In my world, aside from Emilia, you're nothing but a man I once tried to send to prison."

I grin, brushing my lips along the edge of her temple. "That's the most romantic thing you've ever said to me, moya ptichka."

"You bring it out in me."

"What else? Go on. Tell me what you want. I'm in a giving mood."

"Separate bedrooms. Non-negotiable."

A loud, humorless laugh tears from my throat. "That's cute. But no."

Her brows slam together. "That's not up for debate—"

I cut her off, grabbing her waist and dragging her flush against me. She sucks in a gasp, chest pressing to mine.

"You don't seem to get it yet." My gaze snaps to those furious, perfect eyes. "Every night, you'll be in my bed. Right where you belong."

Her hands push at my chest, but I don't move. I won't.

"I'll do whatever I want to this body, whenever I want. Because I own you, Fiona." My mouth brushes her ear. "Every inch is mine to defile. And I intend to."

Her lashes dip as my lips hover a hair's breadth from hers. I can feel her tremor, the tiny fissures spiderwebbing through her walls. One more push and she'll crack, whispering my name the way I want it.

"It'll never mean anything," she breathes.

My lips graze the corner of hers. "That's exactly how I like it."

Then I crush my mouth to hers, my tongue forcing its way inside. She fights me at first, palms braced against my chest, but resistance with us never lasts.

Her fingers tug at my shirt, and she hauls me closer. She moans for me, low and wrecked, and it hits me like a shot of adrenaline. My hand slides into her hair, fisting tight as I deepen the kiss, her body melting into me, hips shifting on instinct she won't admit.

Blyat. She's perfect. Too perfect. And I hate her for what she drags out of me, while at the same time craving more of it. It's a cruel addiction, and I want to punish her for it.

I pull back just enough to see her face: flushed, lips swollen, eyes dark with the same need burning through me.

"This is going to be fun," I whisper against her jaw, still tasting her on my tongue. "I can't wait to spend the rest of our lives together, Mrs. Marinova."

She swallows hard. "Do you promise not to hurt my parents or their business? Because if you do anything to them…" Her gaze hardens. "I will kill you in your sleep."

A low sound vibrates in my chest while my teeth drag across my bottom lip. "Do you purposely say things like that just to excite me?"

She groans, smacking my chest. "I need to hear you say it, Marinov."

I catch her wrist, bringing it to my mouth. My eyes stay locked on hers as I press a slow kiss against her pulse point.

"I keep my word. Your parents will be safe, as long as you behave." I lean closer, my grip tightening just enough to make her body twitch. "But if you don't…" My tone dips. "I'll burn it all to the ground and give you a front-row seat. We understand each other?"

There's something feral in the way her face twists, rage burning so bright it turns almost beautiful.

"You think forcing me into this marriage is some kind of win?" She shakes her head with a laugh sharp enough to cut. "You're a pathetic man who has to hurt someone else to prove a point. Hate me all you want, Aleksei, but you're still a criminal. And I'm still a prosecutor." She tilts her chin up, eyes blazing so hot it knocks the breath from my lungs. "I did my job. And I'd do it again."

The fire in her makes my cock harden like stone. I grab her throat, my lips hovering over hers as my fingers squeeze just enough so she learns to mind her manners.

"If you wanted foreplay, detka…" My mouth traces hers. "All you had to do was ask."

My hand drifts down, trailing up the inside of her thigh. She trembles and her lips part, a gasp caught between fury and something far more dangerous.

"Look at you…" My thumb brushes her bottom lip. "Look how easily you bend for me. You are mine now, Fiona. In every sense of the word."

Her eyes flash, filled with the kind of fury that would make most men back away.

Not me, though. It only makes this sweeter.

"I will never be yours, Aleksei Marinov. No matter how hard you try. No matter what you wish or dream, it will never happen."

My smirk hooks at one corner of my mouth. "We'll see about that."

She tears herself out of my grip, cheeks flaming as she backs away. I let her go. For now.

"One last thing." I straighten my jacket, already turning to leave. "You'll be moving in with me. Your things will be collected the day before the wedding. Be packed by then, or I will take the liberty of doing it for you."

"You're pure poison, Aleksei!"

I glance back over my shoulder, the edge of a smile tugging at my lips. "I have a feeling you enjoy a little poison running through your veins."

Her chest heaves. "You're fucking crazy."

I step toward the door, watching her from the corner of my eye. "Welcome to hell, my love."

I blow her a kiss, and she flips me off.

God, I fucking love her fire.

FIONA

There's a moment, as I'm standing in my kitchen with the kettle whining behind me, when I genuinely wonder if this is some kind of psychological break. If I've officially snapped completely and gone full padded room.

Because there's no way this is real. No way that just two hours ago, a man I despise told me we're getting married. That my wedding dress is arriving soon.

I didn't even ask what kind of dress. I was too busy trying not to scream.

The kettle clicks off with a sharp pop, and I pour water over a tea bag I don't remember choosing. I clutch the mug tightly, breathing in steam and chamomile like that's going to fix any of this.

I'm marrying Aleksei Marinov.

I haven't even told Emilia. What do I say?

But it's different for her. Even after everything, she chose to stay. And Konstantin never hated her the way Aleksei despises me. He's going to make sure I suffer.

A knock hits the door before I can spiral any further. Setting the mug down on the counter, I move reluctantly, knowing it must be the dress. When I open the door, I don't expect it to be two women who look like they've stepped out of a *Vogue* shoot.

"Mrs. Marinova?" The taller one beams, knowing full well that's not my damn name. Not yet, anyway.

Ugh. The thought makes me want to vomit.

"I'm Claire, and this is Kelly. Mr. Marinov said you knew to expect us."

I catch the black Ralph Lauren garment bags and the red Cartier and Chanel bags.

Well, if I have to marry the devil, I might as well look pretty doing it.

"Right. Yeah." I open the door wider, stepping aside so they can glide in with the dresses and whatever else they've got.

They remove their shoes by the foyer, and I lead them to the bedroom, where they lay everything on the bed.

"Mr. Marinov was very specific. Lace, thin straps, sweetheart neckline, mermaid silhouette, flared tulle, and small beaded diamonds along the floral appliqué near the hem," Claire says, unzipping the first bag.

"He said all that?"

"He had notes," Kelly adds cheerfully. "He really cared about getting your dream wedding dress right. As a surprise, he said."

Color me fucking shocked.

When they unzip it, my eyes grow. The dress is stunning. Too stunning. The kind of gown you picture in fairy tales…if the fairy tale was written by someone who enjoys psychological manipulation and brutal dominance. And if I'm being honest, if I was ever going to get married for real, it would be in something just like this.

I've never imagined my own wedding. I was never the type of girl who stared at dresses and rings and wondered what her future husband would look like or be like.

And I definitely never pictured myself getting married to a Russian mobster.

My eyes catch on the delicate straps and the shimmer of the beadwork near the train. The way the lace flutters at the bottom. It's the most beautiful thing I've ever seen, and it makes me want to hurl my mug through the nearest window.

"Would you like to try it on?" Kelly asks.

No. Yes. Can I keep the dress, but not the fiancé?

I nod stiffly, not trusting my own mouth.

"The designer wanted to make sure Mr. Marinov was satisfied, so the gown was created in two sizes." She clears her throat.

"And your satisfaction is important too, of course," Claire adds quickly, realizing how that sounded.

Right. Of course. This is all *about me.*

"We'll step out to give you some privacy," Claire goes on. "When you're ready, just let us know."

"Okay."

As soon as they leave and close the door, I take the first gown and place it on the carpet, stepping into it.

When I pull it up, it's surreal, like I'm putting on someone else's life. Someone who doesn't know what it feels like to be backed into a corner by a man with eyes like weapons and threats laced in every smile.

I call them in, and they start squeezing me into the corset. Once they're done, they stare at me like I'm a doll on display.

"You look so beautiful!" Kelly gushes, while I want to roll my eyes until they fall out.

"Here, let's get you into the shoes he chose." She grabs a pair of silver heeled sandals that look like they cost more than my monthly salary. "He included your sizes for everything, so these should fit. You must be so excited!"

"Yeah," I mutter. "Ecstatic."

They laugh like I'm joking.

Claire fastens the earrings next. Diamond studs so bright, I swear I see into the future.

She grins as she takes a step back. "Perfect."

"Let's get you to a mirror." Kelly guides me toward the long one in my room.

And when I see myself, I stop short. Because I look…beautiful.

"How much is this dress?" My palms glide down the soft fabric, knowing it must be thousands, easily.

They exchange a look.

"That's not important, now, is it?" Kelly says.

"It is to me." I hit them with a glare through the mirror. "How much?"

"Uh…" Claire clears her throat. "It's, um, one point five."

"One point five?" My gaze narrows. "Thousand?"

She laughs. "Of course not. Million."

I choke. "Wh—what?"

"It was custom. Specially made for you."

I whirl around. "What do you mean, custom?" My heart pounds; my head spins. "When did he order this dress?"

Another look between them. More hesitation.

"You might want to ask Mr. Marinov—"

"No," I snap, the edge in my voice sharp enough to cut through her. "I'm asking *you*."

Claire swallows. "It's been over two months. I don't know the exact date."

My heart drops into my stomach.

He's been planning this. The marriage. The vineyard deal. All of it.

I can't breathe.

"Undo this dress, then get out."

"But—"

"Now."

They nod quickly, clearly sensing that I'm about to lose it. Kelly undoes the lace string of the corset while Claire helps undo the straps of my dress. As soon as they take the other garment bag, they scatter out of the room, leaving me alone with the future I never asked for.

I sink onto the bed, the weight of a million-dollar dress still clinging to my skin. If it wasn't for my parents, I'd rip this dress to shreds and send him a care package with its remains.

But I can't do that. I have to play the long game, even if it costs me everything.

EIGHTEEN

FIONA

Every time I closed my eyes, I saw him again.

Cold. Cruel. So damn sure of himself. That smug little curl of his mouth the second I let those unforgivable words slip out.

I'll marry you.

Now it's the next day, and I've been running on autopilot since I walked into the office while that stupidly expensive dress hangs in my closet, reminding me of what's coming next. My stomach heaves at the thought, and I can barely concentrate on my work.

The case files blur, and I swear I've typed the same line in a report three times and still can't remember what it says. Hours have passed with me staring at my monitor while the edges of my world quietly unravel.

Even Dana noticed.

Mid-afternoon, she leaned over my desk, her brows knitting in that soft mother-hen way of hers. "You okay?"

Of course I lied. Said I was tired. Headache. Not enough coffee.

What was I supposed to say?

Hey, remember that mobster I tried to put behind bars? I'm marrying him next week. No big deal.

She didn't push, but I could see it in her eyes: she didn't believe me.

Maybe that's why she invited me out after work. Drinks with some of the other ADAs. A little unwinding, a little gossip. Normally, I'd have smiled, made some excuse, and gone home to Netflix and wine.

But today? Why the hell not? My life already feels like it's over. Might as well toast to my own funeral.

Because what's my other option? Go home and stare at the walls? Count down the hours until I'm Mrs. Marinova, serving a sentence in a cage I walked into myself?

I glance at the clock. Almost time to go.

My stomach flips. Not because I'm afraid of walking into a bar with a few coworkers. But because I don't know if *he'll* be there. If he'll follow. If I'll look up from my drink and find him watching from some dark corner like he always does. Like a curse I summoned and can't outrun.

God, when did my life turn into a twisted reality show?

I'm just out of the Uber, heels clicking against the cracked pavement outside the bar, when my phone buzzes and Emilia's name lights up the screen.

"Hey." I tuck the phone between my ear and shoulder as I adjust my purse strap.

"Hey yourself. You there already?"

"Yeah. Just got to the bar. Dana and a few of the others beat me here. I had to finish a brief before heading out."

"Well, have fun. And sorry I couldn't make it. Being pregnant at a bar sounds about as appealing as a root canal."

A faint smile tugs at my lips. "I get it. I just...wanted you here." I fight the disappointment. "But I don't blame you."

There's a beat of silence.

"Okay," she says gently. "What's going on? You sound...off."

I stop just shy of the door, staring at the wash of neon light across the sidewalk.

"You're going to find out sooner or later anyway." My throat tightens as I force the words out. "Aleksei threatened to ruin my parents if I didn't marry him. The wedding's supposed to be next week."

There's a sharp inhale before she says, "I'm gonna kill him."

"No." My answer is quick, almost panicked. "Don't. I can't risk him doing something to them."

She exhales, slow and furious.

"My parents need a win right now," I say, quieter. "I don't care what happens to me, but I won't let him drag them down with me."

"I'll help. I'll talk to Konstantin. We'll figure something out. He's not going to get away with this."

My eyes flutter to a close. I didn't even need to ask.

"Thank you. Seriously."

"You never have to thank me. We'll talk later, okay? Love you."

"Yeah. Love you too."

Ending the call, I shove my phone deep into my purse and square my shoulders. Then I push through the door into the hum of music, low lights, and the kind of bar noise that makes your thoughts scatter. Dana's already waving me over, with two of the other women from the office crowded around a high-top table.

"There she is!" Dana grins. "We already ordered a round. Hope you're ready."

She hands me a pink shot, and I don't even bother asking what it is.

"Cheers!" She clinks her glass against mine, the others following suit.

"Cheers," I mutter, lifting my shot like I'm toasting to my own execution.

The liquor burns going down, and I already want another. I flag down the bartender, and as I ask for a refill, Dana arches a brow, amused.

"Okay, girlfriend, let's go!"

Thank God tomorrow's Saturday. I can sleep off the poor choices and pretend, for a few blissful hours, that my life isn't in flames.

The next shot dulls everything. The rage, the dread, the way Aleksei makes me feel like I'm flying only to rip the ground out from under me. By the third, my limbs start to loosen and I feel a strange buzz under my skin.

"Damn, girl," Dana laughs. "What's gotten into you tonight?"

"Nothing," I say too quickly, waving her off. "Just felt like cutting loose."

We move to the dance floor, and I let them pull me into the center, the bass thrumming through my chest like a second heartbeat. The lights blur, bodies swaying in a tangle of limbs and laughter. For a moment, I let myself get lost in it, not thinking about my future husband at all.

Until I feel hands at my waist, and I stiffen, half expecting a tall, broody Russian with a five o'clock shadow and sexy hand tats. But alas, all I find is a cheap replacement.

"Hey," a man says, grinning down at me. "You wanna dance?"

"No." I shake my head and force a polite smile. "I'm getting another drink."

I weave through the crowd, ignoring the way he trails after me like static cling. Back at the bar, I slide onto a stool and take a breath.

He pulls up beside me. I open my mouth to order, but he beats me to it.

"It's on me."

Every part of me knows I should say no. But my head is still buzzing and, well, maybe I just want one last man buying me a drink before the new one kills them all.

"Sure. Why not? Thanks. A dirty martini, please."

He nods at the bartender, and as he orders, my phone vibrates in my bag. I fish it out and see her name.

MOM

Tesoro, can we talk? Are you okay? What happened with Aleksei?

She's been calling all day, but I haven't had the energy to talk to her.

What's there to say? I'm hurt she'd even want this for me. It's one thing for me to do it for them, but it's another when your own parents think you should.

I shove the phone back into my bag and turn to face the stranger again. He's decent-looking. Dark eyes, sharp jaw. Almost handsome.

Just not Aleksei handsome.

Don't. Don't even go there. You definitely need more alcohol if you're comparing random bar guys to Russian criminals.

"Here you go." He hands me the glass.

"Thanks." I take a sip, the liquor biting sharp enough to make my eyes sting.

He starts talking—something about work, I think—and I lie easily. Say I'm in marketing. Something vague enough not to invite questions.

Then it's travel. Something about a trip to Spain, or maybe Portugal? I nod. Smile. Laugh when he does.

But I'm not really here. My gaze keeps flicking to the corners, waiting for him to appear like he always does, but I can't seem to focus. Everything in front of me is starting to blur. Dana and the girls are still dancing, but now there's two of them. Or maybe four?

My head thumps.

"Shit," I whisper, pinching my temples.

The room warps. The guy on my right seems to glitch, his figure stretching, then snapping back in front of me.

"I…I need to go." I push to my feet too fast.

The ground lurches. My drink sloshes. My stomach flips.

"Whoa." His hand catches my elbow. "Hey, you okay?"

I try to speak, but my tongue's thick. "I…I think I should g-go home. Can you…can you call a car?"

"Yeah, of course."

I blink rapidly, trying to find Dana through the crowd. She was here. I swear she was just here. Where is she?

Oh God. I'm going to be sick.

I stumble. His grip tightens.

"I need air."

"Okay, come on. We'll wait outside. The car will be here in two minutes."

I nod, but it feels like my head's made of lead. Everything feels wrong. And all I can think is, why does it feel like the floor's falling out from under me and why the hell did I drink this much?

I'm going to regret this tomorrow.

His arm slips around my waist, and my mind goes straight to Aleksei. How furious he'd be if he saw someone else touching me like this.

If I'm supposed to be his wife, I'm guessing sleeping around isn't part of the arrangement.

But…does that mean he *can?*

The thought crashes through my haze like a sledgehammer.

I can't ask him. That would make it seem like I care.

But what if it's not about caring? What if it's about setting boundaries? About demanding respect? That doesn't mean he matters to me. Everyone deserves respect.

Am I even making any sense right now?

Cool air hits my face, and I realize I'm outside. The man is still holding me. Still steering me. My God, this is humiliating. I never get like this.

"I-i-is the-the cab here?" I slur.

"Shit, I think we missed him."

Oh no. I can't wait all night.

"I can just take you home. Another cab will take too long."

"Nooo, that's…okay." My words stumble over themselves.

No way am I getting in a car with a stranger.

He chuckles. "Honey, relax. I'm not trying to hurt you. You look like hell. I'm just trying to be a gentleman."

His arm tightens. Too tight. My pulse spikes. I try to pull back, but my limbs are sluggish, my vision smearing like wet paint.

He opens a door. Black? Blue? I can't make out the color.

Oh my God.

"Get off of me." I push, but it's weak.

"Shut up and get in before you cause a scene, stupid lush whore."

Fear clamps down on me, cold and suffocating.

He tries to shove me inside. I fight, weak and uncoordinated. When I open my mouth to scream, his hand slams over it.

Pure terror slices through me.

This is it. This is how I die.

Then, out of nowhere, he's gone, ripped away from me like a toy snatched from a child. I stumble, gasping.

Shapes move in the dark. Three? Four? But my vision won't focus.

Strong arms wrap around me, holding me upright.

"No…" I groan, trying to shove him away. "Leave me alone."

"Shh, detka. You are safe now."

That deep, familiar voice cuts through the haze, and relief slams into me so hard my knees nearly give. But beneath it, something else pulses. A note I've never heard from him before.

Pain.

He cradles me against the strength of his body, and my lashes flicker, head lolling against his solid chest that smells just like the cologne he always wears.

"Aleksei?"

"It's me, detka. You're okay. I have you." I can feel the agony drip from every syllable.

My fingers curl into his jacket, and the fight goes out of me.

Because no matter how twisted this is, no matter how much I hate him, a part of me knows I'm safe now.

ALEKSEI

She's quiet, hardly breathing, her limbs limp and tangled in my sheets with my comforter tucked around her. I almost like the sight of her here in my bed, amongst my things. Like she's always been here.

I sit at the edge, elbows braced on my thighs, watching her chest rise and fall like I've forgotten how to do the same.

I should have gotten there sooner. Should've skipped the fucking boardroom, canceled every meeting, torn apart the city if I had to. Instead, I let her slip through the cracks and straight into the hands of a predator.

Now she's pale and curled in on herself like a wounded animal.

It will never happen again.

I clench my fists so hard they shake.

From this moment on, she won't take a single breath without protection. If she doesn't like it? Too damn bad. She will learn.

My hand trembles as I reach for her face, brushing a strand of hair from her cheek. She doesn't stir, but I do. Inside, I'm an inferno.

Thoughts of what that padonok could've done to her tear through my mind like shrapnel. He drugged her, and that alone will cost him his life.

For now, he rots in the cellar, chained like the animal he is. Until I decide it's time to play. And when I do, he will beg for death long before I grant him the mercy.

I don't know how long I sit here—minutes? hours?—before she stirs. A low groan breaks from her lips as her fingers curl around the edge of the sheet like she's trying to hold on to something solid.

"Aleksei? Where am I?" she whispers, eyes barely open.

"Shh. It's early. Go back to sleep." I can't help cupping her cheek. "You're safe."

The words sound strange coming from me. Too gentle. Too soft.

She flinches slightly, like she's caught between sleep and some lingering nightmare. Her lips part, but she doesn't say anything. My thumb grazes the sharp line of her cheekbone. Her skin is warm, sweat slicking her hair to her temples.

Her eyes glisten with unshed tears, and the sight of it does something unspeakable to me. To see her like this, so still, so stripped bare by fear and whatever hell she lived through tonight…it carves into me with a blade I didn't see coming.

I could lie to myself. Pretend I'm unaffected. Tell myself I'm here because she belongs to me now. That I was only protecting my property, and anyone who lays a finger on her answers to me.

But that wouldn't explain why I haven't left her side. Why I have stayed awake since the moment I brought her here. Why I'm *still* here.

I try to convince myself it's duty. That I'm doing what any man in my position would.

She's going to be my wife. Her safety is my burden now. Her pain, my problem to handle. Any harm that comes to her is an insult to me.

That's the truth I cling to, the story I feed myself. But it feels hollow.

Because as I dip the cloth into the bowl of cool water beside the bed and press it gently to her forehead, something cracks wide open inside me.

Deep down, I know this is more than obligation. And I hate it.

She groans, her eyes still filled with exhaustion as she shuts them, and I drop the cloth back into another bowl. Easing down beside her, I let my weight sink into the mattress as carefully as I can. For a second, I think about staying upright, keeping a distance. But then she makes this sound—a tiny, broken whimper—and I can't stay away.

So I do what I swore I never would. I slip beneath the covers and pull her against my chest.

She melts into me like her body knows mine. Like some primitive part of her accepts me. Her cheek finds its place above my heart, her breath hot and damp through my shirt. It's strange, this feeling of holding her, of giving comfort, of her giving comfort to me. I wrap one arm around her waist and bury my face in her hair, breathing her in.

Lavender. Sweat. Intoxication. Fiona.

My grip tightens as she falls back asleep.

"I will kill him," I whisper, almost to myself. "And I'll make it slow."

My lips press to the top of her head, my eyes shutting.

This is wrong. I shouldn't be here. Should've handed her off to someone else the second I made sure she was safe. But I couldn't. And I don't know what the hell that says about me.

She shifts again and mumbles something into my chest. My name, I think. Or maybe just a sound. But it's enough.

"I've got you, moya ptichka," I breathe. "I'll always have you."

NINETEEN

FIONA

The first thing I notice is the smell.

Clean linen. Faint cologne.

I'm not in my bed. Everything feels off.

My eyes crack open against the splitting pain behind them, and the second thing I register is the sunlight, blinding me until I want to hide behind sleep again.

But fragments start surfacing.

His voice whispering beside me. Arms wrapped tight around my body. The steady weight of him pressed against me, like he wasn't going to let go.

I remember the parking lot. The way he pulled me into his chest. The way I let him. And…I think he held me last night.

No. That can't be right. He wouldn't.

Would he?

Sitting up, I look around the room. The space feels just like him.

Dark wood with modern touches. Expensive. Masculine.

My head pounds harder. Did he really find me? Did I really get that drunk and almost get myself into real shit?

I pinch the bridge of my nose and push the blanket off, and that's when I freeze.

My clothes are gone. In their place is an oversized white T-shirt I don't recognize. I stare at it, nausea spiking.

I'm wearing his shirt.

Panic crawls up my spine. I bolt upright, and the world tilts, the sudden motion sending a wave of dizziness crashing through me. My stomach churns, and I press a shaking hand to my forehead, trying not to throw up.

When did he take my clothes off?

Did I let him? Did I even know? Would he really have done that to me while I was in such a state? That would be a new low, even for him.

My mind claws for answers, but I don't remember anything more.

I stagger for the edge of the bed and spot my phone on the nightstand. My fingers shake as I grab it and hit the screen.

Eight missed calls. Twelve texts.

DANA

> Fiona? Please tell me you're okay.

> I swear to God, if you don't text me back, I'm calling the cops.

> I'm going to lose my damn mind. Are you DEAD?

That one makes me laugh.

FIONA

> I'm okay. I'm safe. I'm so sorry I didn't respond sooner. I think I was drugged.

She replies instantly.

DANA

WHAT?! Where are you now?

I pause. How do I answer that? Because I have no idea where I am. I can guess I'm in Aleksei's home, but there's no confirmation. No details except the scent of his cologne.

Before I can reply, the door opens. And he's there.

The air shifts the moment our eyes meet, some unseen current crackling between us and lighting something in my chest.

He steps in, gray sweatpants slung indecently low with no shirt on. My eyes catch on the tattoo stretched over his chest: a lion ripping apart a wolf, flames curling in every direction.

It's brutal. Violent. Unapologetic. Just like him.

He's carved from danger, every inch of him a warning. The kind of man who doesn't just break rules, but builds his power from the ruins.

And yet, despite everything, I can't imagine him crossing that line and taking advantage of me. Not even if he despises me.

"You're awake."

I close my messages and toss my phone on the bed.

"I—" My voice cracks. I try again. "Where am I?"

His brow furrows. "You're at my house."

Just as I assumed.

"Why am I in your shirt? What happened to my clothes? Did you…"

"No," he says sharply, cutting me off. He strides to the edge of the bed and hands me a bottle of water and two white pills. "You threw up in my car. Your clothes were ruined. I took them off. In the dark. I didn't look. I'm not that kind of man."

Relief washes over me.

I take the pills with a shaky sip, hoping he's telling the truth. He lowers himself onto the bed beside me with a kind of care that unsettles me. It's like I'm something fragile he's not sure how to hold without breaking. And I hate it.

Or maybe I don't.

Because I don't know what to do with this version of him. This quieter, almost nurturing presence. I'm used to the crazy, impossibly domineering Aleksei.

But this? This tender version? It throws me off-balance. And as much as I want to reject it, question it, pretend it's not what I need, I can't lie to myself.

I *do* like it. Maybe too much.

His hand finds mine, fingers wrapping around it before he lifts it to his mouth and presses a kiss to my knuckles.

"How do you feel?" he asks, low and gentle.

"I…like I got hit by a truck," I whisper. "I don't really remember much. Just…the parking lot. I think. And you?"

Something sharp flickers in his expression. "You were drugged."

I suck in a breath.

Oh God…

"But don't worry," he adds, a mischievous glint in his irises. "He won't ever touch anyone again."

My stomach drops. "What does that mean?"

"It means…" His mouth curves. "Exactly what you think it means."

I can't be listening to this. It might as well be an admission of a crime.

My heart thuds. "You weren't with me…last night, were you? I could've sworn you—"

He shakes his head too hard, like he's trying to rid himself of the thought. "No. You were alone."

How can that be? I swear I heard him. Felt his arms. Was it a dream?

A part of me aches at the confirmation. Not because I wanted him here, but because…well, maybe I did.

God, what's wrong with me?

"If you want to shower…" He rises to his feet. "Your things are in the bathroom. Same products you use at home."

I jerk back. "You went to my house?"

"No." He scoffs. "I was preparing for the inevitable."

My body goes rigid. Does he mean he bought them in advance and kept them for when I was here? For when I married him? He really was planning this…

"If you're hungry, my chef has made lunch. I can have it brought up to you."

"Lunch?" I glance at the clock on the nightstand. "What time is it?"

"Noon. You've been out for a while." He looks me over slowly. "You look better. I was worried."

That last sentence is so quiet, I almost miss it.

Almost.

He turns to go.

"Aleksei," I call out, surprising both of us.

He pauses.

I swallow past the knot building there. "Thank you. For…whatever you did. For not leaving me."

He doesn't smirk or throw one of his sharp, condescending replies. He just nods, but there's something raw in his face that takes me aback.

Then he's gone, the door clicking shut behind him. While I sit here, tangled in his sheets, drowning in his scent, wondering how the man who threatened to ruin my life could be the same one who made sure I lived through the night.

TWENTY

FIONA

T he warm water has washed away the grime, but not the dread curling inside me as I relive what I remember. What that piece of shit could've done to me.

I swear, I'm never drinking again.

My headache is little more than a dull whisper now, nothing like the hammering from earlier, and the soup his staff sent up after he left was exactly what I needed. I'd never tried borscht before, the rich red broth with potatoes and beets, but it settled in my stomach with a warmth that felt almost comforting.

Back in the bed, I press my fingers to my temples while replying to more of Dana's frantic messages, telling her I'm okay and with a friend. That seems to make her feel a bit better.

As comfortable as this bed is, I'm going to have to go home sometime soon. I can't stay here anymore and pretend Aleksei and I are best friends now.

What a weird thought.

A hard knock comes, and I know it's him before he walks in—with a shirt on this time. Unfortunately. He should look softer like this. Less dangerous, more human. Except he doesn't. Not even a little.

Glancing down at his hands, I find my clothes neatly folded.

"You look better," he says, stepping inside. "The color has come back to your face."

"I'm starting to feel like myself."

"That's good. Here." He hands me the clothing. "They've been washed and pressed."

"Thanks." They're warm, smell clean and floral. "I think I'll go home."

His body instantly tenses. "No, you will not." He moves closer, grabbing my chin, his thumb leisurely grazing my bottom lip. "You'll stay until tomorrow. That way I can be sure you're okay."

His tone leaves no room for arguments, and quite honestly, I wouldn't mind sleeping in this bed another night.

Especially if he held you…

No. Absolutely not.

But even though my mind wants to fight it, my body warms at the thought.

"How was the food?"

I'm immediately glad for the interruption his question offers.

"It was really good. Please thank your chef for me."

"You're welcome." His smirk stretches.

I'm confused at first, my brows furrowing.

"I made it."

My mouth pops open. "Really?"

"You sound surprised. Do I not seem like the kind of man who can cook a meal?"

A small laugh escapes me. "Not really, especially not one that doesn't actually kill me."

"See, it's why I didn't tell you it was me." He laughs, dropping his hand away. "You wouldn't have eaten it."

"You're probably right," I admit with a reluctant laugh.

"Are you up to taking a walk?"

"Why?"

When I narrow my gaze, he continues. "I want to show you something."

There should be hesitation. Maybe logic and distance and all the things I swore I'd uphold. But my fingers slide into his without resistance, and the moment our palms meet, heat blooms up my arm and settles in my chest.

We walk down a sweeping staircase, his hand in mine. Marble lies underfoot, iron banisters curling like black vines.

He doesn't speak, and neither do I. But the silence crawls beneath my skin, winding tighter with every step.

Outside, the sun is too bright, the sky too blue. Like the world's trying too hard to look normal. Something about it feels wrong, like it's off-kilter, and I can't explain why. But I feel it.

We pass through a glass door, and the backyard unfolds like something out of a painting.

But it isn't a backyard. It's an estate. Endless green stretching like it forgot the world beyond the fences. A stone fountain shaped like a lion glimmers in the distance, water pouring from its snarling mouth.

I narrow my eyes as figures appear in the distance. Some of Aleksei's men, I think, standing in a circle.

"Where are we going?" I ask. "What are those men doing?"

He doesn't answer me, just holds my hand tighter like he's daring me to run. Once we get closer, the men turn to us, parting enough for me to see what was hiding behind them.

No, not what, but who.

A man. On the ground. Hand and feet zip-tied in front of him.

Bloodied. Bruised. Barely conscious.

My pulse spikes. "What is this, Aleksei?"

"This," he says, mouth twisting into something cruel, "is the man who drugged you."

I take a step back, sucking in a sharp inhale. "No. No, Aleksei, I can't…I can't be here. I can't be seeing this. Do you understand me?"

His fingers wrap around my jaw, his mouth nearing mine, his breath warm and calm. Too calm.

"You *will* see it. Because I want you to understand what happens when someone dares to hurt what's mine. And you *are* mine, Fiona. Whatever twisted form this takes, you are a Marinova now. I will *never* let anyone hurt you again."

He lowers me onto a stone bench, and I don't even notice it until the cold bite hits my thighs. His hand cups my cheek as his gaze sucks me in. There's something terrifying in it, but something protective too.

Then he makes it worse and kisses the top of my head with a gentleness that feels like it belongs to someone else. The tenderness clashes so violently with everything I know him to be, it leaves me breathless. It's like being touched by two men at once—the monster and the guardian—and I don't know which one to fear more.

"Please," I whisper. "Let the court handle him. I'm begging you."

He leans in, gaze unreadable. "You're in my courtroom now, Ms. Prosecutor."

As he steps toward the man, my clasp tightens on the edge of the bench, fingers digging into the cold surface.

He seizes the man by his hair, jerking his bloodied face upward into the fading light. The man can barely lift his head on his own. One eye is swollen shut, the other wide with terror. A deep gash splits his cheek open, bleeding freely down his jaw. His cries are broken, soaked in the kind of fear that only comes when death feels close enough to taste.

"I'm sorry," he sobs. "Please. P-p-p-please don't kill me."

Aleksei keeps hold of the man's hair, his voice almost gentle, but threaded with a fury so sharp it slices straight through me. "When I'm done with you, ublyudok, you will beg to die."

His hand moves to his waistband, drawing out something that flashes silver before I register what it is.

A blade. Long. Curved. Gleaming like something unholy in his hand.

I go still. No part of me wants to see what comes next. But when I start to turn away, his voice lashes the air like a whip.

"No."

My breath catches.

"You will watch, moya ptichka. You will remember. This is your husband. This is what he does for you."

For a moment, our eyes collide, and I'm hit with the terrifying truth.

This is his promise. This is the real Aleksei. The murderer, the torturer, the bloodthirsty villain in every one of the fairy tales I read as a child.

When he slashes across the man's forehead, it happens so fast, I almost miss it…until blood starts to spill like tears that will never dry. The man shrieks, the sound twisting into something inhuman.

I jolt, my fingernails scraping against the rough stone of the seat beneath me. I want to close my eyes and vanish. But I can't. He won't let me.

And some twisted part of me doesn't want to.

The second cut is slower. It carves down the man's arm, skin peeling back like paper too thin to hold shape. Crimson floods down his side, soaking his shirt. He howls, his legs jerk, body writhing like a wounded animal caught in a trap.

One of Aleksei's men steps forward and hands him something. At first, I can't tell what it is. But when Aleksei seizes the man's trembling hand and the metal catches the light, I see it. Garden shears.

My stomach turns. I shake my head, begging him silently, praying he won't.

He smiles, vicious and cold. And when the man tries to fight, Aleksei slams an elbow into his face. Cartilage cracks. More blood spills. Then, without pause, he clamps the pruners down and snaps.

A finger drops. A scream tears through the air.

I slap a hand over my mouth, gagging. I want to look away, but I won't appear weak.

I've seen horrors in my line of work. Bodies torn apart by violence. The aftermath of human cruelty. But never like this. Not this close, not when I can taste the blood at the back of my throat.

He can't kill this man in front of me. I'd be a witness.

Unless…

Unless that's the point. Once we're married, I can't be forced to testify.

This performance isn't just retribution. It's strategy. A message. A warning. A vow.

And he's making sure I don't miss a second of it.

Aleksei doesn't stop. He takes another finger. Then another.

The man's screams crumble fast, turning into torn gasps and wet, stuttering sobs. The words he tries to choke out twist into nothing, falling away until only a rough whimper remains.

He's losing too much blood. He won't survive much longer.

"Are you still with me?" Aleksei slaps the man's cheek, and his head lolls like a puppet cut from its strings. "Let's wake you up."

He chuckles. And that calm, amused sound turns my stomach more than the violence ever could.

One of his men steps forward, holding…a blowtorch.

Oh God…

My world tilts, nausea rises too fast to fight, and I barely make it to the grass before everything comes up.

"You don't touch her!" Aleksei's command tears through the air, thunderous and absolute.

Suddenly he's beside me, his hand on my back. He crouches low, wiping my mouth with a cloth when I'm done, then tilts my face up to meet his.

"I will take you back. I think I proved my point." His thumb glides over my cheek, a whisper of warmth that lingers longer than it should.

When his lips touch my forehead, I can't bring myself to pull away, helpless to the strange comfort of it all.

He rises, and I force myself to look. Just in time to see the glint of his gun.

A single shot cracks through the air. Right into the man's chest. The red in the grass spreads like ink on water.

But Aleksei doesn't look down. He simply stands there, gaze fixed on me. And right now, I don't know how to truly feel.

Because beneath the nausea, beneath the scream clawing at the inside of my throat…there is something else. Something worse.

Satisfaction? Some twisted form of relief?

He did this for me. He killed someone who hurt me.

And the craziest part? It doesn't scare me.

Not him. Not the gun. Not the blood soaking the grass.

What scares me is the part of me that feels avenged. The part that whispers he was right to do it. Because if this doesn't repulse me, if this feels like justice, then maybe the monster isn't just standing in front of me.

Maybe she's already inside.

ALEKSEI

She hasn't quite grasped the depth of my depravity. Not until now.

She looks at me like I'm something out of a nightmare. And she's not wrong. I am.

Only she still doesn't see the full picture. She doesn't understand that when I destroy a man for touching her, it's not just brutality. It is sending a message the world won't forget.

Cross this line, and you don't crawl back.

And today, she learned that lesson firsthand.

Aleksei Marinov doesn't forgive. Doesn't forget. Never lets anything go.

I saw the horror in her eyes as I carved screams out of him. I saw the way her throat worked like she couldn't swallow, the way her fingers trembled as she tried not to break in front of me.

But under all that fear, there was something else. It flickered in her pupils, in the way she couldn't look away, in the breath that hitched not just with disgust, but with a raw, ugly want she'll never admit out loud.

She liked it.

That alone should make me stop and push her away. But all it does is feed the psychosis she's injected me with.

I run a hand down her back as she lowers herself back to the bench, no longer appearing sick. When I saw her that way, I almost regretted the whole thing. I should have let her rest longer before I ended him. She's still carrying the residue of what that bastard pumped into her veins.

And yet I almost wish he was still alive. Just so I could take my time and really make him understand what happens when someone touches what's mine.

One of my men steps forward, offering a damp washcloth, and I drag it across my hands. The blood smears before it fades, then I toss the ruined cloth on the grass.

She looks up at me, and the vulnerability there, the way her hands knot together on her lap, nails digging into her palms… She doesn't know whether to run or thank me, and I can taste the war inside her.

I crouch in front of her, letting my knuckles brush along her jaw, soft enough to be mistaken for tenderness. "Are you feeling better?"

She nods, her chest swelling up and down, and my eyes can't help but track the movement. I can't stop the way my body reacts to being this close to hers.

"Come." I take her hand, easing her to her feet.

She's barely upright before my arm slips under her legs and I lift her against me. Her brows arch, lips parting like she wants to argue and tell me to put her down, but no words come out. Instead, she lays her head against my chest like she belongs there.

And that's the problem. Because the second she rests against me, that vicious instinct flares. To hold her tighter. Shield her from the world I just blew up.

It makes no sense to have this urge to soothe her when I've spent so long creating chaos in her life. But when I saw the way she reacted to what I was about to do to him, I couldn't do it. It was like something cracked in me.

I tell myself it's not kindness or concern. It's about being the one who can help her. That power.

But the lie sits heavy. Because the truth is uglier.

I just wanted to help her. It always seems to come back to that.

My father would be ashamed. He raised us to be strong, ruthless, untouched by weak emotions. And Fiona is the one thing that shatters every lesson he ever drilled into me, the kind of temptation that makes me forget the man I was meant to be.

But none of that matters. This marriage is nothing more than payback. A reminder that I hold her future in my fist and I always will. And I'll make damn sure she never forgets it.

I carry her through the house and up the stairs, straight into my bedroom. Into my bed. I should've taken her to a guest room. But the thought of her lying anywhere else made something twist in my chest.

"If you want to sleep some more, I will get you one of my shirts again."

She nods, and I help her sit on the edge of the bed before moving to the drawer. I hand her a clean T-shirt, and she accepts it quietly before I turn away, giving her privacy. If I don't, I'll end up forgetting my manners, and the last thing she needs right now is me inside her.

I should've brought her clothes here. Something soft and comfortable instead of those pants and silk blouses she wears. The ones I fantasize about tearing off her every time she looks at me like I'm the enemy.

Even now, while I wait facing the wall, all I can think about is chasing her through the woods, pinning her to that tree, and taking every inch of her.

But what follows isn't lust. It's the memory of her whispering my name after I tended to her wounds. The way she thanked me when I didn't deserve it. The way it felt to take care of her, for no other reason than wanting to.

"Okay. You can turn around now."

Her voice is small. Worn down to the bone. And all I can think about is how much I miss the woman who gives me hell. The one who fights me with every breath. The one I can hate.

Because this quiet version of her? This girl in my shirt, in my bed? She scares me more than anyone ever has.

I help her settle against the pillows, adjusting them until her body sinks into the mattress just right. She doesn't speak, just watches me with those guarded eyes that used to burn with defiance.

Now they search mine like they're trying to figure out if I'm the monster she should fear or the one who just saved her.

I pull the comforter up, tucking it snug around her like she might slip through my fingers if I don't. My hand stalls at her shoulder, then drifts higher, brushing a strand of hair from her face. Her chest rises with a shallow breath, like she's afraid I'll pull away if she moves.

If only it was that easy to resist her. My life would be so much simpler.

"I'll see you later." The words are dry on my tongue.

I turn and close the door behind me before she can answer, the latch clicking into place. But I can't seem to move, back against the door, like some magnetic force is keeping me here.

Seconds tick by, and I'm left thinking about her on the other side, in that bed alone, pretending she's fine.

"Blyat…" I mutter as violent inhales rival through me, my hand snapping to the knob.

I shove off the door, taking a step away, then stop, my fists clenching. And without stopping myself, I twist the handle and push the door open just in time to catch her wiping a tear from her cheek.

She freezes.

"Were you crying?" My voice cuts sharper than I mean it to, but it's too late to soften the edge.

"What? No. I…" She clears her throat, the lie landing thick between us.

But I see it. The tears still clinging to her lashes. The flush in her cheeks.

I move on autopilot, lifting the comforter and sliding in beside her.

She startles, peering at me with a twist of confusion. "Wha–what are you doing?"

I don't answer because I don't know what the hell I'm doing at all. I just know I need to be here, need to hold her.

My arm finds its way under her, pulling her in tight. Her body goes still for half a breath before she settles, pressing into me with a soft groan.

When her arm curls around me, I stop thinking and let myself feel. The weight of her in my arms. The way her breath syncs to mine. The quiet, unbearable peace.

And for the first time in longer than I care to admit, sleep doesn't

feel like something I have to fight for. It just takes me.
Because when she's here, the war quiets.
And I hate how much I need that.

TWENTY-ONE

ALEKSEI–AGE 12
SOLNTSEVO DISTRICT, RUSSIA

The hood over my head itches like hell, and my wrists burn where the zip ties cut into my skin. The van shakes beneath us, every bump in the road making Anton jolt beside me. I slip my hand into his and squeeze, feeling him stiffen and tremble. He's terrified, and I can't do shit to help him.

We were with the bodyguards when the SUV was taken over by thugs in masks. My other brothers stayed after school for some meeting, so it was just me and Anton. The men came out of nowhere, guns pointing at all of us.

They fought our bodyguards and shot them, then dragged us into a van while we kicked and hit them as best we could. But there were at least five of them, and we didn't stand a chance. Then the hoods were shoved over our heads and everything went black.

The van jerks to a stop, and I immediately tense. There are footsteps before a door slides open, and then hands are yanking us out.

Something hard and cold jams into my back, and I know right away that it's a gun. The guy at my back shoves me and I stumble forward, my heartbeat slamming in my ears.

"Bystreye," he grumbles. *Faster*.

We're forced inside somewhere. I can't see much, but the air changes. It's not cool anymore, replaced by a nasty smell of some kind. Like mildew or something gross like that.

Someone pushes me down onto a hard floor. "Syad i ne dvigaysya." *Sit and don't move.*

I obey. Can't give them a reason to kill my brother.

I don't recognize their voices. It's probably just another set of enemies my father has made. He has plenty, and he trained us for this very thing.

But nothing prepares you for it. Not the fear or panic. It's different when it actually happens.

Though I worry for Anton more than myself. He's only eight.

Pain means you're alive. Use it to your advantage. Do not let them break you, my father would tell us when he would pit us against one another in a fight.

The loser would be locked up in a cellar for days as punishment, scraps for food, just a little water to get by until the next time. We knew we didn't want to be locked up again, and that survival instinct would kick in and we'd fight harder for it not to happen again.

Except with Anton, I would lose just so he didn't have to face it. But my father was smarter than that. He'd see right through it and would punish Anton anyway.

Plastic bites tighter into my wrists, and I hear Anton grunt.

"Ne trogay yego!" I yell. *Don't touch him!*

A voice laughs in front of me before someone pulls off my hood.

The light stings my eyes. I blink hard as my gaze adjusts. The room looks like a basement. Cement walls. No windows. One hanging bulb overhead. Five men. All of them with guns.

One of them steps forward. A scar runs down his face, teeth crooked when he sneers.

"You want to take your brother home?" the man asks, his Russian accent thick.

Him speaking English doesn't help me figure out who they are. We speak both too. Father made sure of it. *It's important for business,* he'd say.

I nod, but I know there's a catch. There's always a catch. That's why we're here.

He crouches in front of me. "Then tell me where your father keeps the jewel."

My stomach turns. We're going to die here.

I know exactly what jewel he means. Our father's most prized possession, stolen from some European museum years ago. People have killed for it. Died for it. And when it comes to us versus the jewel, we're nothing.

Loyalty and honor above all.

That is what he drilled into us.

Don't break. Don't talk. Don't beg.

So when the bastard punches me in the face, I just smirk through the blood. He wants me scared. I won't give him that.

"Oh, you think it is funny?" he growls. "We will see how funny you think I am."

He turns, and grabs Anton, ripping the hood from his head.

My whole body lunges forward. I can't let them hurt him. He's just a kid. Yeah, we have all seen a lot of shit, been dealt a lot of it too, but this will be too much for him. He will break.

"Maybe your little brother knows." He pulls Anton's hair, forcing his head back.

Anton grins, a defiant, shaky kind of grin. "I don't know anything."

He's trying so hard to be brave, but I can see the tremor in his leg, the way his shoulders shake.

He doesn't know anything. But I do.

The man leans closer to him. "Last chance."

And Anton—my stupid, fearless brother—spits, "Fuck you."

The man slowly drops his hand, like he's enjoying this. He crosses the room, and for one second, Anton looks at me, chin trembling and eyes shining.

"Vso budit khorosho," I whisper. *Everything will be okay.*

But that's a lie.

When the man comes back, he's holding something long and black in his hand. A whip.

My stomach twists so hard, I think I will be sick.

"Maybe now you will talk," he says.

The first crack splits the air like lightning, and Anton screams. It hits his thigh, loud and sharp. The sound echoes in my chest until it hurts to breathe.

He hurts him again and again. Anton's cries fill the room, and every one of them feels like it's aimed at me.

"Tell me where the jewel is!" the man shouts, glaring at me while he hits Anton, this time on the other leg, bright blood breaking through his skin.

I can't. I can't tell them. If I do, my father will kill us both. And worse, he will be proud doing it.

"Pain means you are alive," I say fast, locking eyes with Anton. "You are a lion. You fight to the death."

His body rocks with his sobs, but he nods as another strike comes.

"Don't hurt him! Do whatever you want to me."

The man chuckles, but it causes him to stop and move toward me. "If you want me to stop, you know what you have to do. Tell me where the jewel is!"

My body rocks with harsh breaths, but I don't say anything. It's not an option.

He crouches down until I can smell his disgusting breath. "I will break you, boy."

Then he flips open a knife and slices my shirt right down the middle. Cold metal presses hard into my chest, leaving a thin line of blood.

I grit my teeth, ignoring the pain like Papa taught me, and stare him dead in the eye.

Another man hands him a lit cigarette. I don't get it. Until I do.

He presses it into the cut.

The burn is instant and unbearable. I groan, jerking against the zip ties, the smell of my own singed flesh turning my stomach. He does it over and over until it covers my entire chest, until the pain makes me want to die.

"Where is it? Tell me and you can go."

"Kill me." I laugh. "I won't talk."

"Please stop!" Anton snivels. "We don't know. Our dad doesn't tell us that stuff!"

I remain quiet. Because even through the pain, even through Anton's sobs, I hear my father's voice.

Don't betray the family. Don't break.

Anton sobs beside me as one of the men presses a gun to his temple.

The man with the cigarette grins. "Last chance. Tell me where the jewel is, or he dies."

My chest heaves. "No, don't! Please! Don't hurt him! He is just a kid!"

"We were all kids once."

I cry for the first time since I was six. Hot, angry tears spill down my cheeks. I can't lose my brother.

The man cocks the gun. Anton looks at me. His lips tremble, but he doesn't speak.

"Three...two..."

No, no!

Loyalty over love. Family is the oath you swear to.

"One."

The gun goes off.

"Anton!" I scream his name, the sound tearing through me.

He flinches, his small body jerking. But…there's no blood? No hole.

He's alive?

"What the—"

The men start laughing. All of them. Like this is a joke.

I stare at Anton, shaking so hard my teeth clack. He's crying. I'm bleeding. And none of it makes sense.

They didn't kill him. Why?

Then…footsteps.

When I look up, I choke on the air.

My father stands in front of us, hands behind his back, disappointment written all over his face.

"I thought today might be the day you made me proud." He circles us like a wolf, his voice calm. Too calm. "But I see now I have to push harder to make you into men. Because this…" He gestures to us. "This crying. This begging. It's pathetic."

He stops in front of me and crouches, grabbing my jaw in his hand. His fingers dig into my cheek until it hurts.

"You failed," he says softly. "You are always such a disappointment."

I grit my teeth, forcing myself to stare straight at him. The pressure on my throat tightens when his thumb brushes under my chin. I want to look away, but I don't. Because weakness is what he wants to see.

And I will die before I give him that.

But his words hurt deeper than the whip. Deeper than the burns on my chest.

He turns to Anton.

"And you." He scoffs. "Have I taught you nothing?"

Anton freezes, but he doesn't speak.

"You have to stay strong. You look death in the face and smile. Do you understand?"

Anton nods fast, tears streaking down his face. Father straightens, adjusting his cuffs like we're beneath him.

"Take them home," he orders one of the men. "I can't stand to look at either one of them."

Then he's gone. Just like that.

The room is silent except for my brother's uneven breathing and the sound of someone cutting through the zip ties.

They drag us back to the van, and I can't feel my legs. My skin still burns, but it's nothing compared to the deep, rotting pain in my chest.

I sit beside Anton, staring at the window, but seeing nothing except the way my father looked at me.

After a minute, Anton's hand snakes to mine, but I pull away.

Love is weakness. It hurts you. Destroys you.

And when you find it, you tear it apart with your teeth before it tears you apart first.

TWENTY-TWO

FIONA

It's been a couple of hours since he dropped me at home. The drive was utterly silent, like he regretted coming into the room and holding me.

Being in his arms felt strange. Wrong. Like some twisted form of comfort after everything I'd just witnessed.

It wasn't the blood that haunted me. It was his face. The way he looked while hurting that man. Like he enjoyed it. And the way he stopped the moment I got sick, like he actually cared. That was… unexpected.

I've always known who Aleksei Marinov is. His name alone sends ripples of fear. I've built a career chasing men like him, spent years believing I was immune to that kind of darkness.

But there was something different in the way he looked at me tonight. Something possessive. Final. He didn't just punish that man for what he did to me. He claimed me with every blow.

And part of me—some sick, buried part—actually felt…protected.

None of this is right. Not how I sat there and watched. Not how I understood it.

But what scares me the most is the question I can't shake.

Would I ever go that far? If someone I loved was in danger, could I kill for them?

God, I hope I never have to find out.

Pinching the bridge of my nose, I breathe in slow, fighting the dull ache building behind my eyes. The tea on the table's gone cold while I've been sitting in the kitchen for over an hour staring at nothing, trying to convince myself that none of this is real.

But it is. The dress fitting happened. The way those women said *Mrs. Marinova* like it was already written into law. The diamond earrings that sit in my nightstand, mocking me with how beautiful they are. How permanent it all feels.

And there's nothing I can do. That's the most suffocating feeling: being helpless. My parents are the most important people in my life. No matter how many times I've thought about telling Aleksei I've changed my mind, I can't do it. I can't hurt them.

The vibration of my phone on the table startles me, and when Mom's name flashes on the screen, my stomach flips. I hesitate, thumb hovering over the answer button.

Maybe I should let it ring. Pretend I'm asleep. Busy. Dead.

But then guilt gnaws at me until I sigh and answer.

"Hey, Ma."

"There you are." Her tone's soft, but already cracking at the edges. "I've been calling and calling. You didn't answer. We were worried. How are you holding up?"

A sharp and bitter laugh slips out before I can stop it. "Let's see. I'm about to marry the man I tried to put in prison, so I'm doing real great here, Ma. Thanks for asking."

"Oh, tesoro…" She exhales, the sound caught somewhere between a sigh and a sob. "I'm sorry this is happening. I wish it didn't have to be this way."

I shouldn't have said all that. It's not their fault. They didn't ask for any of it.

"It's okay, Ma. It'll be fine." I lean forward, elbows braced on the table. "Don't worry about me." The lie tastes sour, but I keep going anyway. "He's actually…not so bad."

Are those words seriously coming out of my mouth? These are scary times.

There's a beat of silence on the other end. Then a snort, and suddenly, my dad's voice joins the line.

"Not so bad? He's the devil," he mutters. "Tu stai sposando il diavolo." *You're marrying the devil.*

A short laugh breaks out of me, tired but real.

Tell me something I don't know.

"The wedding's in a week," I say, almost to myself. Maybe trying to make it seem real, even though it's the last thing I want.

Dad clears his throat, and I can picture him pacing in the kitchen, rubbing the back of his neck the way he always does when he's trying not to yell.

"This is not how I imagined walking you down the aisle, stellina. You were supposed to be smiling. In love. Not…" He trails off, like saying it aloud might break him. "Not this."

"It is what it is, Papa."

"You don't have to do it," he says suddenly. "If you say the word, I'll find a way. We'll lose the vineyard, the house, everything. It doesn't matter. You don't need to do this for us."

But I do. Aleksei holds their future over my head, and I'm not willing to let him ruin their lives when I can stop it.

"Papa," I whisper, swallowing the tightness in my throat. "I *want* to help. You and Ma have done everything for me my entire life. It's my turn."

"It shouldn't be this way. You shouldn't have to sell your happiness to save ours."

"Sometimes life doesn't give you a choice." I try to smile, even though they can't see it. "Sometimes you just…take what's left."

There's a pause, then Mom sighs. "You always were the strong one. We are very proud of you."

I huff out something between a laugh and a scoff. "Yeah. Strong. That's one word for it."

"We'll make this right," she says. "Somehow. I don't know how yet, but we will."

I don't answer. Because *making it right* feels like something out of a fairy tale. Something that doesn't belong in the world I'm about to marry into.

"I love you both. Please don't worry. I'll be fine." I force a weak laugh, trying to make myself believe it. "I mean, he hasn't killed me yet, so that's progress."

"That's not funny, Fiona," Dad mutters, hard as stone.

"It's a little funny," Mom throws in.

Despite everything, the corner of my mouth lifts. She and I laugh while he groans something about women being impossible. A long pause stretches between us before I speak again.

"I tried on a wedding dress he got for me." The words come out hollow, like this is someone else's wedding.

There's a beat of hesitation on the other end.

"How was it?" Mom asks.

"Pretty. Expensive. Too expensive."

"You'll be the most beautiful bride," Dad says, gentler now. "Even if the groom is a figlio di puttana." *Son of a bitch.*

"Tony!" my mother snaps.

"What? It's the truth! What you want from me, huh?"

She sighs dramatically. "Ignore your father. You'll be stunning. And if your marriage is not good, I'll kill the bastard myself, okay?"

I snort, the sound breaking through the lump in my throat. "Okay, Ma."

They continue to talk, and the conversation stretches long enough that I close my eyes, letting it linger around me like a blanket.

For just a moment, I let myself forget what's coming.

I don't tell them I'm scared. I don't tell them I sit there wondering what it will be like to be his wife. What it will cost me.

Or that lately, when he looks at me…I don't feel scared at all.

When the call ends, the silence returns, thicker this time, like it's pressing down on my chest. I stare at the wall for a while, then let my gaze drift toward the closet door where the wedding dress hangs. The symbol of everything I've already lost. And everything I'm about to lose.

I press my palm to my sternum, trying to steady the panic rising in my throat.

It doesn't go away. I think of his hands on my face, the way his thumb brushed my jaw as he told me I was his.

He meant it. Every word. And a small, shameful part of me wants to know what it would feel like to belong to a man like him. Not out of fear, not because of the threat over my family, but because there is a twisted, hungry part of me I don't know how to face.

"God," I whisper to the empty room. "What's wrong with me?"

I have about a week left. One week to make peace with the fact that Fiona Clark is gone.

And in her place, Fiona Marinova will be born. Whether I'm ready for her or not.

TWENTY-THREE

ALEKSEI

I've stared death in the face. Watched men beg and break. Felt the crunch of bone beneath my fists, the warmth of blood on my hands.

But standing at this altar? This feels far more dangerous.

Because she might not come. Because a part of me isn't sure she should.

On the outside, no one can tell what is going through my mind. But inside, a sliver of something sharp turns low in my chest.

She's late. Not by much. But enough that I start to wonder…will she run? Would she dare?

Kirill lets out a quiet laugh beside me, posture lazy, hands folded behind his back like we're not surrounded by enough firepower to overthrow a small government.

"Think she drove off yet?"

"She could try." I flick a speck of lint from my sleeve. "But there's nowhere she can go that I won't find her."

He grins. "Romantic."

Konstantin steps closer, palm clamping around my shoulder. "Are you sure this is a good idea? Especially with everything we know about her. This could bring us a lot of problems."

"This is the only way, and you know it."

"Perhaps. But she's also a prosecutor. Marrying her could burn everything we've built."

"Says the man who married a fed."

He laughs under his breath. "Ex-fed." Then his voice drops. "But know this, brother. Fiona may be your wife, but Emilia is mine. And Emilia loves her. If you hurt someone who matters to her…I'll take it personally."

My face nears his, and I meet his stare head-on, my blood pumping louder in my temples. "Love has made you soft."

He closes the distance, expression sharper. "And obsession has made you blind. You keep pretending this is just about business. About revenge. But I've seen the way you look at her."

I say nothing.

"You claim you don't care, but you watch her like a starving man watches bread. You have stalked her, chased her, protected her. Not because you had to, but because you couldn't help yourself. You keep saying she means nothing, but you have built a cage just to keep her close."

I adjust the cufflink on my wrist, eyes narrowing as he fixes his jacket and backs away.

"You're addicted to the idea of her," he continues, and the temptation to pull out my gun and use it is too strong. "And every time she gets too close, you push her away. Then you try to sew the hole up afterward like it didn't tear through you. But love can get to anyone, even you."

My jaw flexes. "You finished?"

"Almost," he adds just as the first notes of the violin begin to play. "Try to be a decent husband. It is the only way this doesn't end with both of you miserable."

I ignore him, keeping my eyes trained on the entryway where she's meant to appear. "She makes me miserable."

"No," he says simply. "She doesn't. And that is the part you hate the most."

I despise it when he's right.

She drives me mad. Cuts beneath my skin. But I crave her like oxygen.

The crowd rises.

Then she appears, flanked by her parents, the only ones she invited.

And the second I see her, my heart beats faster, even when I beg it not to.

She's veiled and radiant, the gown hugging her body in a way that steals the air from my lungs. Worth every dollar I spent.

Her eyes slam to mine, her head high, back straight. She looks like she's ready for the next battle, and I grow hard just thinking about our next fight.

Every step she takes toward me only tightens the pull—this sick, hungry need I keep trying to fight. To crush.

But Konstantin was wrong. Love has nothing to do with this. This is nothing more than need. Possession. Obsession that's been festering ever since the day she first sat in that courtroom, lips cunning, promising to take everything from me.

Her parents say something to her, then her father presses a kiss to her temple before turning his attention to me.

"You hurt my daughter…" he fires as he shifts her hand into mine. "And I'll find a way to make you regret it."

I nod once, not offended in the slightest. I would do far worse if she was my daughter.

He holds my gaze a second longer, then steps back, guiding his wife to the front pew as Father Pasha begins the ceremony.

But I'm not looking at anyone else. I bring Fiona's hand to my lips and kiss her knuckles. Her fingers twitch in my hold.

"You look beautiful, moya ptichka."

She doesn't smile. Instead, she leans in, her tone razor-sharp beneath the veil. "You're making a huge mistake. And you may think you're only hurting me with this sham of a marriage, but you're hurting yourself too, Marinov. Because I will never love you, and everyone needs that."

I laugh under my breath, the sound vibrating in my chest as I kiss her hand again. "Your love is the last thing I want. Believe me."

I don't let go, tightening my grip instead. She glares at me, heat flaring behind her eyes, and all I feel is fire. The kind that burns. The kind that brands.

The priest starts speaking, but his voice fades behind the roar in my head. All I hear is her breath. The shift of her gown. The crack in her voice as she repeats the words she's forced to say.

Then Konstantin leans in, speaking low behind me. "Don't waste this chance to have more than he ever let us have."

I say nothing.

Because I'm not wasting it. I'm claiming it. I'm claiming her.

But love? Love makes men weak. Makes them forget who they are. What matters.

Just because he forgot that doesn't mean I will. I won't falter, and I won't fall.

Not for her. Not for anyone.

TWENTY-FOUR

FIONA

The ceremony is over.

The fake vows, the diamond rings on my finger, the man gripping my hand… I survived all of it. Somehow.

Now I'm standing in the middle of his estate under a silk-draped tent strung with crystals, surrounded by more criminals than a Manhattan courthouse on indictment day.

Roses. Peonies. Velvet chairs. White centerpieces that probably cost more than my car.

It's all stunning. And suffocating.

My wedding reception looks like a war council disguised as a black-tie gala. There must be a hundred people here, probably more. Everywhere I look, someone is watching me, their eyes taking in every detail.

The room is packed with designer suits and dresses, like everyone showed up to audition for a *Vogue* spread.

And me? I didn't invite anyone. Not a single friend. Not a single coworker. Because how do you invite people to witness your legally binding fall into hell?

Come celebrate as Fiona Clark marries Aleksei Marinov, the man she once tried to put away for life! Open bar. Armed guests. Please RSVP.

I'd laugh if it didn't feel like I might scream.

People keep walking up to us, congratulating us like we're some happy couple and I'm a blushing bride who wasn't emotionally blackmailed into marrying a man who may or may not bury someone alive before dessert.

I really wouldn't put it past him.

Aleksei plays the role well: smiling tightly, nodding politely, his hand resting low on my back like he owns me. Which, to be fair, he kind of does.

I'm trying to remember all the names and faces of those I don't know, but they start to blur the moment the Quinn family arrives, also known as Irish Mob.

"Congratulations," Eriu, the youngest sibling, says warmly, her brown hair pulled back into some elegant braid I could never pull off.

She kisses my cheek like we're old friends, and she has this light about her that shouldn't belong in this world, but somehow does. Her husband, Devlin, gives a polite nod and a firm handshake. There's a pause when he turns to Aleksei. A subtle shift in the air before they shake hands. Like there's history there neither of them wants to revisit in public.

Tynan Quinn, the head of the family, follows, his expression stoic as he greets us. I swear he could pass for a Marinov with that stare. But his wife is softer, more open.

"I'm Elara," she says, offering a gentle hug. "It's very nice to meet you. You look beautiful."

"Thank you." I fight the instinct to excuse myself and hide in the bathroom.

God, I just want this day to end. None of this is normal for me—to interact with these people, to break bread with them.

Tynan's brother Fionn and his wife, Amara, come next. It's obvious by his easy grin that he's the more laid-back member of the family. Well, as laid-back as the Mob can be.

Then another Quinn arrives—Cillian this time, with two women beside him, both stunning and dark eyed. Though the older one carries a smile that could melt steel.

"Hey, I'm Dinara," she says, extending a hand. "Aleksei's cousin. And this is my sister, Tatiana." She gestures toward the younger one. "My condolences, by the way."

Her lips quirk as her gaze flicks to Aleksei.

He raises a brow. "Careful."

"What?" She laughs, flipping her hand in the air. "It wouldn't kill you to smile. It's your wedding, after all."

"You're not funny," he mutters flatly.

"I think she's hilarious." Cillian slides an arm around her, kissing her cheek like there's nowhere else he'd rather be.

And for a moment, something in me twists. Because I want that. Not just the kiss. Or a man. But the ease of it. The quiet intimacy of being with someone who makes it feel simple.

I glance across at Aleksei, and the muscle in his jaw tics. When his gaze drops to my mouth, I wonder if he knows exactly what I'm thinking.

I clear my throat. "So, is every Quinn in attendance? Because I'm trying to remember everyone's name and feel like I'm failing."

Except that's a lie. I know the names of each one.

Eriu glances around. "Well, my sister should be—"

"Saving the best for last," comes a voice behind her, and Eriu instantly grins.

A woman steps forward, tall and striking, flipping her bright red hair past her slender shoulders. As she approaches, she does nothing to hide the holster around her thigh, clearly visible through the slit in her black gown like it's part of the outfit.

"I'm Iseult Quinn, and this is my husband, Gio Marino."

A tall man with dark eyes nods. "Nice to meet you."

I know exactly who the Marinos are. They're Italian Mafia, the ones who run the Messina crime family, one of the five families in New York.

And just behind them, the boss himself arrives: Michael Marino. Dark features, expensive suit, and the long scar on his right cheek only makes him that much more terrifying.

He gives me a firm handshake while his wife, Elsie, beams at me like this is a Hallmark movie.

"I'm sorry my brothers could not attend," Michael says. "They sent a gift."

"It was last-minute." Aleksei throws a hand in the air. "We understand."

Dinara leans into me while Aleksei talks to Michael. "You're going to need a family tree when this is over."

She's not wrong.

"How many crime families are actually here?"

She lets out a laugh, like I've asked if the sky is blue. "All of them. It'd be an insult if even one didn't show. Usually they send a representative, or the head of the family comes."

"Right." I nod slowly. "Totally normal."

Silly me. How did I not know that?

"You'll get used to it."

I scoff under my breath. "Highly doubt that."

"Nervous?"

"Only mildly terrified."

She smirks. "Good. That's the appropriate response to marrying a Marinov."

I spend the next stretch of the reception nodding politely, smiling when expected, and repeating *thank you* until it loses all meaning. My cheeks ache. My feet hurt. And the whole time, it feels like I've been dropped into the center of a den of wolves.

Except I'm the only one here without a weapon.

By the time Adriano Scutari of the Grazia family approaches, I'm exhausted and need a nap.

He walks with the kind of ease that comes from power, a calm and confident stride that carries a quiet threat rather than comfort. He's maybe around Aleksei's age, even a little older.

The Grazias might be respected in legitimate business circles, but everyone here knows they're just as cutthroat as the rest.

Adriano reaches for my hand, bending slightly to kiss it.

He never gets the chance. Aleksei is there in a second, a shoulder angled between us, hand on my waist.

"You don't touch what doesn't belong to you," he says, each word a warning.

Adriano raises both palms, grin still firmly in place. "Of course. My apologies. We're here as friends. My family and I hope to leave any…recent tensions in the past." His eyes flick to mine for a beat too long.

What the hell was that about? My gaze darts to Aleksei, who hasn't moved, every muscle in his body strung tight.

Do these two families not get along? I haven't known of any problems between them. Not anything known amongst the legal world, anyway.

Adriano moves on to say hello to the Quinns, and when he approaches young Tatiana, her lashes dip, her body shifting. She clearly has a thing for him. When he picks up her hand and kisses the top of it, she just about melts.

I lean into Aleksei. "I think your cousin likes him."

"Too bad," he mutters. "She's not marrying into that family."

"Why not?"

His features tighten. "Not your concern."

I arch a brow. "Aren't I your wife now? Shouldn't I be aware of such things?"

That gets his attention. "Oh?"

His arm slides around my waist, heat pouring off him as he pulls me closer. His eyes flicker with something possessive and altogether dangerous.

"You're my wife now, huh? I thought this was just pretend… or how did you call it? A sham?" His fingers claim my chin, mouth inches from mine, breath hot against my lips.

"That's right. Still is." My voice wavers, but I don't back down. "I just said I should know, seeing as how I'll now have to tolerate you."

"Mm." He leans in, his mouth grazing mine. "Then show me, katyonak. Show me how well you can tolerate me."

His words strike low, curling right through my core.

"How should I do that?" I whisper.

His grip tightens at my waist, dragging me flush against him. "Kiss me. Show me what a good wife you can be."

My breath hitches, every nerve ending pulsating as I lean in and give him a small peck.

"Is that what you call a kiss?" His tone is low, lethal, his fingers snaking into my hair as he tips my head down. "Kiss me like you mean it. Like you're begging me not to destroy your family. Like you're begging for your life."

For a heartbeat, reason claws to the surface, then drowns in the heat of him. The part of me that knows better flickers out, and the part that wants him, craves him, takes over completely.

I surge forward, crashing my mouth to his. My fists twist into the lapels of his jacket as I pour everything into the kiss. Every edge of fury, every pulse of desire, every breath I shouldn't give him, but do anyway.

It's not soft or sweet. It's a collision. A surrender. A war we both lose.

He meets me with equal hunger, kissing me like he wants to punish me for wanting him, like he wants to ruin me for anyone else.

But this isn't just a kiss. It's possession. He consumes me, and I let him.

Worse, I welcome it.

Because in this moment, I want the fall. I want him. I want the plunge and the wreckage that follows.

Soon enough, I forget everything but the man kissing me like he's waited a lifetime to do it.

And I hate how much I never want it to end.

ALEKSEI

The moment her mouth finds mine, feverish and angry all at once, I lose my fucking mind. One hand tangles in her hair, the other fastened on her hip, dragging her closer like I can mold her into me.

She tastes like defiance laced with surrender, and I kiss her harder, just to see which one breaks first.

She whimpers into my mouth, and I want more.

I want the dress off. Want her bare beneath me, flushed and cursing and clinging to me with the same vicious fury I can't shake. I want to drag her inside, peel the fabric off inch by inch and watch it pool on the floor before I take her against my walls, in my bed, anywhere I want her, until she remembers nothing but my name.

But not yet. That's for later, when there's no one here but her and me and the heat that never seems to die between us.

When we finally break apart, she's breathless, lips swollen, chest rising and falling like she's run a mile. Like every man in this room just watched her come in my arms.

I see them. Some look at her like they wish she was theirs. Others stare at me like I've lost my mind.

A prosecutor, they're thinking. *You married a goddamn prosecutor.*

There's no hiding who she is. Her face is public record. The case made headlines. Everyone knew I'd been caught—and worse, they knew it was her. The woman who tried to bring me down. I can almost see the headlines even now.

Prosecutor takes aim at the Marinov empire. Will she be the one to bring them down?

She gave it her all. I have to give her that. But failure was inevitable. I was never going to go to prison, no matter how hard she tried.

She smooths the front of her dress and starts toward her seat, but I catch her hand before she gets far.

"Dance with me, Mrs. Marinova."

Her brows arch. "You dance?"

"You sound surprised."

"I am." Her finger trails slowly down the center of my chest, featherlight and dangerous. "You're always so…stiff. I didn't think you had it in you."

"Mm. Is that so?" I lean in, close enough to feel her breath catch. My mouth grazes the shell of her ear. "You should know by now, detka, I don't back down from a challenge."

"Let's see what you've got, then." She laughs, an unguarded, rich sound that punches straight through my chest like a damn knife.

She's never laughed like that for me before, and it tears through every raw nerve I have.

I clench my jaw, shoving that feeling down. This is nothing. It's just a dance. A distraction. Nothing more.

I lead her toward the dance floor just as the music shifts and slows and pull her in, one hand resting at her waist, the other cradling her hand in mine while her arm slides around my neck.

And just like that, we fall into step. Like we've been doing this forever. She tilts her face up to mine, eyes flicking over every inch like she's trying to read me. There's wariness in her gaze. Curiosity too.

And I can't look away.

Konstantin's words echo like a curse in the back of my mind, a truth I don't want to hear but somehow need. Because this moment, with her here in my arms, feels like more than a dance. And I don't know if I want to push her away or pull her closer and never let go.

She's not even trying to seduce me, and still, no one else comes close. That dress clings to her like a damn invitation. Her mouth, still swollen from our kiss, tempts me right back in. And her eyes…

Her eyes hold the storm I've spent a lifetime trying to outrun. And for one breathless second, I can't imagine losing her.

She has no idea what's circling around us or the danger she's in, and I'm the only thing keeping the wolves at bay.

She can't know the extent of it. If she finds out, she won't survive it.

If anyone comes for her—*when* they come for her—I'll be ready. I'll spill blood so fast, the rivers will run red. I'll bury their families, torch their homes, carve my warning into every wall they hide behind.

Because she's mine now. And God help the man who forgets it.

But if she ever learns the truth, if she uncovers even a fraction of what I haven't told her, she'll never forgive me.

That used to mean nothing. Now…it somehow matters, and I don't know how to reconcile that.

I tighten my grip on her waist, her body curving into mine, warm and trusting, and I despise myself for not telling her the truth. Her fingers trail along the back of my neck, nails grazing skin, and I lean in to press a kiss to her forehead.

She tilts her head back just enough to meet my eyes. "Are you okay?"

I almost laugh. "I don't think you've ever asked me that before."

"Don't get used to it." Her mouth tugs into a half-smirk, but her thumb brushes my jaw like she doesn't mean a damn word.

Leaning down, I kiss her again. Slower this time. Softer.

Like I'm trying to memorize the shape of her before it all burns to the ground.

TWENTY-FIVE

FIONA

The wedding ends, but the night isn't over.

The bedroom door shuts behind us with a soft click, and just like that, we're alone. In his house. In his room. *Our* room.

And the very thought is suffocating.

My things have already been unpacked, tucked into drawers and hung in closets by his maids like I belong here. Like I've always belonged here.

A princess in a castle built on blood and power. And he's the warlord who claimed it all.

Aleksei shrugs out of his jacket, watching me the entire time, his gaze heavy enough to feel like a touch. He begins to unbutton his shirt, and I can't look away even when I want to. Each flick of his fingers pulls at something inside me, something hot and wanton and almost cruel.

The fabric parts, and I see the tattoo inked across his chest. That lion, feral and victorious.

It's violent. Beautiful. Terrifying. A perfect reflection of the man himself.

It stares at me with bared teeth and wild eyes, tearing into the wolf's flesh the same way he's torn into every fabric of my life.

But as I look closer at the artwork, I see something I never saw before. Beneath the ink, beneath the sharp lines and vivid colors, are scars—round and raised ridges clawing across his skin like some monster tried to tear its way out and failed.

My stomach twists. I shouldn't care. I shouldn't feel this strange tug in my chest. Not pity, but something deeper. I shouldn't be wondering if he got the tattoo to hide the scars, or what hurt him enough to leave it there. Yet I do.

There's a part of me—some stubborn, idiotic part—that wants to reach out. To let my fingers skim over the marks and ask how they happened. Who made him bleed. Or maybe who he bled for.

But I don't. Because no matter how human those scars make him seem, he's still who he is. And I'm still the woman trapped in his empire, pretending I don't feel the walls closing in.

He stands across from me like the king of all things dark, and for the first time, I understand why people follow him, fear him. He doesn't have to command power. He just *is*.

And that might be the most dangerous thing about him.

He catches where my attention falls, his jaw gritting tight, and I instantly look away. Flicking my hair over my shoulder, I sink onto the edge of the chaise, tugging at the straps of my heels.

"Jesus," I mutter as one finally slides off. "Whoever designed these should be tried in international court."

He pauses halfway through unbuttoning his shirt, that razor-sharp gaze cutting straight through the dim light. "Do your feet hurt?"

I nod, already starting to rub them, but the relief is barely there.

He doesn't wait for permission. His shirt hits the floor in an instant, leaving only the dark slacks riding low on his hips and the kind of temptation that makes it hard to think. When he starts toward me, something tightens in my gut, hot and wild and a little afraid. Not of him, but of how badly I want him to keep walking.

To reach me. To touch me. To ruin everything just by looking at me like that.

He lifts my foot into those rough, calloused hands that have broken men, pressing into the arch. My head tips back, a shameless sound of pleasure slipping out of me.

"Better?" his deep voice whispers.

I can't even find words. Just a breathy moan that barely qualifies as a yes. Because it's not just relief flooding me. It's desire. Twisting. Thrumming. Alive.

My eyes fall to a close as he moves to the other foot, his touch firmer now, like he knows exactly what he's doing to me. What I like. When my lashes flutter open, his stare is there waiting—dark and seared on mine.

And I know what he's thinking.

I'm not supposed to want this. I promised myself the last time was it. But how am I supposed to hate the way he makes my body feel when he touches me this way?

I want his hands slipping under my dress. I want to feel free and alive, the way only he can make me feel.

And as soon as the thought comes, I curse myself.

What the hell is wrong with you? You're here because he threatened your parents and forced this on you. Not because of the way he touches you or how good it feels.

Except good doesn't even cover it. It's addictive. Dangerous. Life-altering.

Reckless. You forgot reckless.

I squeeze my eyes shut and groan internally, from frustration this time. Because I already know I'm losing this fight.

"Get up," he says as he stops the massage, and my gaze lifts on instinct.

I don't even ask why. I simply obey as though something in his tone tugs at me like a thread being pulled tight.

He doesn't move at first, just watches me standing there in my dress like I'm on display. Like he's carving this moment into memory, as though he wants to own it too. His hands land on my shoulders, turning me around slowly as he steps behind me.

And suddenly he's everywhere—his chest brushing my back, his breath grazing the shell of my ear, warm and unsteady like he's holding on to the last bit of restraint. Rough hands trail down my arms. A firm drag of his palms over skin, like he's reminding me I'm his now.

"Let me take off this dress." His fingers work the ties of the corset back. "I'm sure you want to slip into something more comfortable."

Yes. You.

Bad Fiona. Very bad. You are to stay far away from your husband, especially in bed. As far as you're concerned, he has crabs.

And yet…

My skin grows taut beneath his fingers, every glide of his hands setting off sparks I swore I was done reacting to. Each pull of the corset loosens more than the dress. It's pulling apart my resolve, seam by seam.

I shouldn't want this. But the second his fingertips trace down my spine, my body forgets every reason it's supposed to resist. A shiver dances through me just as the final tie slips free…and so does my grip on sanity.

The bodice slackens. The dress surrenders, sliding down my curves until it gathers around my feet. I stand there in nothing but a lacy thong and bare skin, rooted in place by the weight of it all.

"Turn around," he says, his tone humming with arousal as I step out of the dress. "Let me look at you."

I obey before I can think better of it, facing him fully. My hands tremble slightly at my sides, but I don't try to cover myself because there'd be no point.

He'd just take it. Like he took everything else.

ALEKSEI

She can't deny it.

Whatever this is between us burns hotter with each moment, and now that she's here in my home, in my space, she can't avoid it.

She trembles when I touch her. Follows every command like it's law. Like I've already rewired her from the inside out. And blyat, maybe I have. Maybe somewhere between hating me and giving in to me, she started craving the control. *My* control.

My gaze drags over the swell of her breasts, nipples tight and aching for attention. Her lashes flick down when my fingers glide along her hips, ghosting over the skin she once tried to hide. When my hand lingers on the paler patch at her side, she stiffens, like she's bracing for rejection or for me to pretend I don't see it.

Instead, I drop to one knee. My mouth grazes the spot, and she groans, fingers tangling in my hair, our eyes locked as I press a second kiss to the opposite side. Then another. And another.

By the time I stand, my cock aches to be inside her. To have all of her. But I pull her against me, my mouth just close enough to take everything I want.

I brush a strand of hair from her shoulder, letting my fingers trace the line of her collarbone before gliding down the center of her chest. She doesn't pull away, watching me instead—eyes wide, lips parted, as though she's daring me to go further.

My God, she's so beautiful, it makes me violent. Brings out a need to mark her with something more than just my name.

My palms find her hips, guiding her backward until the backs of her knees meet the edge of the bed. One light press and she sinks down, her gaze never leaving mine.

"What are you doing?" She catches my wrist, staring up at me with breathless exhales as my fingers hook into the strap of her thong, needing it off too.

"Don't play shy now, Ms. Prosecutor. I've seen and tasted every inch of you already."

Her chest rises, her teeth pulling her bottom lip as I work her panties down, exposing her pink cunt. It glistens, slick with signs of her arousal, with the need she tries to bury. But it's there, staring right at me, and all I want is a taste.

Her cheeks flush as my finger slowly drags through her slit, grazing her clit as she gives me a little moan. I tease her with it, opening her up and sinking inside her to my first knuckle until she's writhing, her toes curling.

My mouth lowers to her bikini line, breathing her in before I drag my lips over her core. The tip of my tongue flicks her clit and her hands fist in the sheets, eyes squeezed shut like she's trying to pretend it isn't me making her feel this good.

"No. Open your eyes." *Thrust.* "I want you to see who's fucking you."

Two fingers ease inside her just as she obeys.

"Keep them that way. From now on…" I sink deeper as she cries out. "You do not close them when I touch you."

My thumb grazes her center and her body tenses, winding in pleasure.

The urge to take her, fully and without mercy, rips through me, consuming all reason. I want to bury myself inside her until there's no part of her left. But I want her desperate first, begging for it like she did at the club.

The second my fingers leave her, her thighs clamp shut, denying me the view. It twists something vicious in my chest, the way she still pretends she can set the rules when the truth is every move she makes happens because I let it.

Heading to the dresser, I pick one of my T-shirts and hand it to her. She slips it on fast, tugging the hem down the middle of her thighs like I haven't already memorized the terrain of her bare skin, mapping every inch of it with my hands, my mouth.

"Why are you giving me your shirt?" she asks, voice tighter.

"This is what you sleep in now. Unless you'd rather sleep in nothing. Trust me, I wouldn't object."

She swallows hard, slipping beneath the covers like they'll shield her, as if hiding from me is still an option.

Sladkiya moya. *My sweet girl.* She hasn't learned. Nothing in this house hides from me. Especially not her.

I start undoing my belt, the metal catch releasing with a soft clink that makes her tense. Pants slide off, and I leave the boxers on…for now. Just to show her I'm quite capable of being a gentleman.

She turns away just as I switch off the bedside lamp, and darkness swallows the room whole.

The mattress dips beneath my weight as I climb in beside her. She's so close, I can feel the heat of her. The soft rustle when she shifts, like she's searching for comfort she doesn't want to ask for.

I should leave it at that, let the silence stretch.

I got what I wanted. She's here. Mine. Wearing my shirt. Sleeping in my bed. Miserable.

But that damn pull—the one I've tried to ignore—rises again, curling low and hot, dragging against the sharp edge of my pride.

It's not just the wanting to take her. It's the way I want to pull her into me. Wrap an arm around her waist. Let my fingers splay across her stomach and breathe her in. It's the sick, maddening way I crave the quiet weight of her body against mine because I liked the way it felt. Like something inside me settled when I held her last.

That should repulse me, make me shove off this bed and sleep somewhere else just to put distance between myself and whatever the hell this is.

But I don't move. Instead, I stare at the ceiling, listening to her breathe like she's trying to slow it down and fight the same demons that claw at me.

She moves again. A faint exhale escapes her lips, tinged with frustration and want. She rolls her shoulders, then goes still, keeping her back to me.

That's when I can't stop my hand from moving. Just one touch. One press of my palm to the curve of her hip. My fingers slide over the soft cotton, and she freezes.

Neither of us says a word, but I swear in this quiet, I feel her press the smallest bit closer, just enough for her body to meet mine.

Nu blyat, that one silent answer undoes something in me.

In a single move, I pin her against me, chest to spine, my nose in the scent of her shampoo, a concoction of something coconut and vanilla.

"I ache for you, Fiona," I say against her throat, the words slipping out before I can stop them. "Do you ache for me?"

She hesitates. Just for a second.

"No."

My lips curve into a slow smirk as she trembles beneath my hands, her chest heaving like she's been holding her breath since I touched her.

"You try to lie..." My fingers drag lower, slipping between her thighs until I find her soaked for me. "But your body already confessed."

She gasps as I slide into her wet slit. "Oh God..."

I groan at the way she reacts, slick and desperate around my fingers.

"Spread your legs," I growl. "Let me feel how much you hate me."

"In your dreams, Marinov."

Wrong answer.

"That was not a request." I let out a low laugh, groaning from her sultry tone. "You want to play stubborn?"

She squirms, trying to twist away, but I grip her thigh, forcing her leg up until she's pinned open against me. I give her pussy a quick slap, my palm following with a rough stroke that makes her jerk against me. Before she can catch her breath, I flip her onto her back, pinning her beneath me, my arm locked beside her head.

Her gaze finds mine, wild and defiant, but beneath that fury, I see it. The fear of how much she wants this. Of how much she wants *me.*

"My pretty girl…" My lips ghost over hers. "You were throbbing for me before I even touched you. Don't insult us both by pretending otherwise."

It's adorable. Futile. This resistance of hers. But nothing good will come from it.

I drag her shirt up her body, letting it bunch around her ribs. My cock slips through my boxers, grinding against her soaked center, piercings dragging over her clit with each slow, punishing roll of my hips. She writhes beneath me, fingers digging for control she'll never get.

Lifting her leg, I drape it over my shoulder, watching the head of my erection stroke against her, coated in her slickness. It takes every ounce of discipline not to take her right now.

"Ask me." My hips arch into her. "Beg me, and I'll give it to you."

"I'd never even beg you for water if I was on fire."

In one fluid motion, I flip her onto her stomach, shove her thighs apart, and pin her down with the weight of my arm. My hand comes down hard on her ass, the crack echoing through the room, and before she can even gasp, my fingers are inside her.

Her cry rips through the dark as I give it to her hard. "Oh God, yes!"

My mouth finds her ear, voice a graveled strain. "I'm your God now, moya ptichka. Pray to me."

I drive into her harder, rougher, until my fingers are soaked, her cries turning ragged as my cock throbs. I crave to be inside her, but there's something I want more. Something she's going to give me, whether she wants to or not.

I flip her without warning, my back hitting the mattress and her landing on top of me, hair wild, lips parted.

Her thighs straddle my waist, hips moving, unhurried at first, then faster, rubbing her soaked cunt across my chest like she's trying to brand me with it. Reaching over, I turn on the bedside lamp. Warm light spills over her skin, and I grind my teeth at the sight: face flushed, hunger permeating through those eyes. Before she can argue, I drag the shirt over her head, tossing it to the floor. My cock kicks up against her, desperate, but I hold back.

"Grab the headboard," I growl. "And ride my face until I can't fucking breathe."

She hesitates, teeth tugging into her bottom lip like she's deciding whether to obey or fight.

"No, thank you," she whispers.

A dark laugh rumbles out of me as I shake my head slowly. "Takaya neposlushnaya malishka." *Such a disobedient girl.*

Her gasp hits the air like a gunshot, hands scrambling for balance as I yank her up and onto my mouth.

Then I bury my face between her thighs. My tongue rolls through her cunt, sucking and biting like I've been starving for her. And maybe I have. Because nothing tastes like this. Feels like this. And I'm not stopping until she's praying my name like a goddamn hymn.

Her hips buck, trying to escape the pressure, but I grip her ass and hold her down, pinning her to my mouth. She's not running from this.

My tongue plunges into her, then circles back up to flick her clit, over and over, until her thighs shudder and her breath shatters in stuttering gasps.

"Don't…" Her hands thread into my hair, yanking me closer. "Aleksei, oh God, don't stop."

I groan against her, tongue flattening and dragging slow and hard, sucking her in like I'm dying of thirst and she's the only thing that'll save me.

Her taste wrecks me. Her scent burns through my bloodstream. And every time she pulses on my tongue, I swear it's a prayer being answered.

She arches as her muscles clench, thighs locking around my head as she cries out. Then she breaks, falling apart on my tongue, her orgasm crashing over her like a wave strong enough to drown us both.

I hold her through it, licking every last tremor from her body until she slumps forward.

But I'm nowhere near done. I flip her onto her back, her chest heaving like she just ran a mile. I strip off my boxers and wrap my fist around my cock.

"I want you slow this time." I stroke the head of my cock through her soaked pussy. "I want your eyes open. Watching me feed you every inch."

Her nails score down my chest, and she doesn't look away. Not even as I press inside her, inch by inch, filling her until her back bows.

Her eyes roll back, her legs lock around my waist, and I thrust again, deeper this time. She wraps around me like gravity—inescapable, inevitable—and all I can do is hold on and lose myself in it.

"Feel that?" I whisper into her ear, grinding deeper. "That's how well we fit."

She moans, her walls clinging around me like a vise. I slam into her, chasing the way her body grips mine, and she meets me thrust for thrust, sweat slick between us, need building to a breaking point.

Her fingers dig into my back as my lips find her neck, and when she whispers my name…blyat, it undoes me.

I snake a hand between us and find her clit, rubbing tight circles until she shatters all over again, body convulsing as she screams into my shoulder.

And I follow. With a growl, I bury myself deep and come with a force that leaves my vision tunneling, my body locking, my heart threatening to beat out of my chest as I empty every last drop into her, her name falling from my lips like a confession I can't take back.

I stay there—inside her, against her, tethered by something I don't dare name—until her breathing slows and her fingers curl softly against my chest.

And for a second, I don't feel like a monster.

I feel like I'm hers.

TWENTY-SIX

FIONA

I stretch slowly, limbs tangled in expensive sheets, the remnants of sleep still clinging to my skin. My arm drifts across the mattress in search of warmth, only to meet cool linen and empty space.

He's gone.

Something sharp and unnamable flickers through me. Not disappointment, because that would imply I expected him to stay. I didn't. I don't. The less I see of Aleksei Marinov, the better. Space is safer. Distance keeps this...whatever this is...in the box it belongs in.

A dull ache throbs between my thighs as I push myself to a seated position, ignoring all thoughts of him. I shouldn't think about the way he touched me, the way his hands held me like I was something breakable while his mouth whispered things that made my heart trip over itself.

Look how good we fit.

I want you slow this time.

Lies dressed up as something sweeter. Temporary fantasies woven between sheets that were never meant to hold meaning.

My fingers find the edge of the comforter, gripping it tight for a moment before I throw it off.

The air is cool against my bare legs, but not enough to clear the thoughts I don't want to acknowledge, thoughts that cling even when I tell myself it was just sex.

That's all it's ever been. No matter how gentle he was. No matter how good it felt. No matter how much of me he seemed to see.

My focus lands on the rings. The diamond glints in the morning light, paired with the band he slid onto my finger…and the problem is, I don't hate how they look.

Shaking those thoughts loose, I climb out of bed, ignoring the slight sting in my muscles as I move. I'm beyond exhausted, but I have work and there's too much to do for me to be late.

Slipping the rings off, I place them in the nightstand drawer. There's no chance in hell I'm wearing them to work. When I told him no one can find out about us, I was dead serious.

Dressing quickly, I slip into a cream blouse and black slacks, step into low heels, and dab concealer beneath my eyes, praying it hides the kind of exhaustion that sleep never touches.

Halfway down the hall, the scent of coffee and something savory drifts to meet me. My stomach grumbles before I can stop it. I really hope he has green tea.

At the base of the staircase, a man in all black waits. Broad shoulders, a holstered gun at his side, face carved from stone.

"Good morning, Mrs. Marinova." He tips his head to the left. "I will show you to the kitchen."

Mrs. Marinova.

God.

I give a tight nod and follow him past a series of ornate doors until we reach a gleaming white kitchen that feels too alive for a man like Aleksei. Sunlight pours through oversized windows. The counters shine. Everything smells like comfort.

At the stove, a woman moves with purpose, her back to us, stirring something in a heavy-bottomed pot. Her gray hair is twisted into a bun, her floral apron snug across a no-nonsense frame. She radiates the kind of presence that says she'll feed you with one hand and smack you with the other if you mouth off.

She turns, expression warm.

"Hello. I am Galya," she says in a thick Russian accent. "Come sit, Mrs. Marinova. I am sure you are very hungry after wedding night."

My ears grow hot instantly as I freeze halfway to the table. Whether she means the ceremony or what happened after, I don't want to know.

Before I can die of mortification, Galya turns back to the stove, plating dish after dish across the counter. Eggs, pancakes, fruit, and something golden and fried that smells buttery and amazing.

She sets a plate down in front of me, followed by a mug of…green tea? How the hell did she know?

He must've told her, but how did *he* know? I've never even drunk it in front of him.

"This is blini." She points to the round, thin pancakes. "And this is draniki." She gestures toward a circular-looking fried thing. "Is like potato pancake. You eat."

"Thank you. It all looks delicious." I'm not used to eating a big breakfast, but I can make an exception.

"I am glad." She wipes her hands on the apron. "I am happy too because Mr. Aleksei needed woman's touch in this house."

My laugh almost slips free. I want to tell her this isn't that kind of arrangement. That this marriage is just a contract, a solution to a problem. Temporary. Conditional. One breath away from collapse. For me, anyway.

But I don't. Instead, I offer a polite nod, pick up my fork, and try not to think about how Galya's words make something tighten in my chest.

Poe strolls in, meowing as he rubs his tail around my foot before heading for his bowls in the corner. He's definitely made himself at home already. I'm not even sure he'd come with me if I left.

I'm still eating when two men walk in, all in black like every other one of the men around this damn place. They just stand there watching me. I have no idea if I'm supposed to address them, dismiss them, or ask if they're waiting for a seat at the table. The silence stretches, growing louder by the second.

"Uh…" I glance toward Galya, who seems completely unfazed by the silent giants. "Would you guys like something to eat?" I tilt my head toward the counter.

Both shake their heads in unison.

"Net, spasebo," one of them answers in a heavy Russian accent.

"Alright, then…" My voice trails off as I glance between them, then back to Galya, who ignores us, cleaning up some dishes instead.

Finally, the man on the right takes a step forward. "I am Viktor." Then he motions toward the one beside him. "This is Leonid."

I offer a slow, cautious grin. "Nice to meet you?"

"We are assigned to you," Viktor says plainly. "Mr. Aleksei sent us."

My stomach twists. "For what?"

"To follow you," Leonid adds. "We are your bodyguards now."

Oh, hell…

"You're joking."

They don't so much as crack a smile.

"Okay, yeah, no." I rise from the table, napkin hitting the plate with a soft slap. "Absolutely not."

They continue to silently stand there like my words mean nothing. We'll see about that.

"Give me a second." I leave my plate behind, grab my cell, and step into the adjacent dining room to call Aleksei immediately.

He answers on the second ring. "Hello, wife. How may I help you?"

His low rumble curls through me in a way I hate. "I need you to call off your watchdogs."

A dark chuckle greets me. "No."

"They can't follow me to work. People will see. I'll lose my job."

"You are my wife now. My danger is your danger," he throws in causally. "Unless you would like to end up face-down in a ditch somewhere, you will do exactly what I say. Or so help me…" His tone sharpens.

The fury builds so fast I swear I can feel it in my teeth. "You're such a bastard."

"Every time, moya ptichka," he replies smoothly. "Now, unless you need me to pick out your outfit too, I have things to do."

"Fine," I grit out. "But they better stay back, far enough that no one notices. No one at work can know about this. Do you hear me?"

He pauses, just long enough to let me feel the silence.

"Losing your job wouldn't be the worst thing," he finally says.

"It would be for me. You have no idea what I sacrificed to earn my place. You won't take that from me too."

Another pause before he adds, "Horosho. I'll tell them to keep their distance. But that's all you get. Goodbye."

The line cuts off before I can say another word. When I return to the kitchen, Leonid is glancing down at his phone.

"Did he call you?" I ask him.

He lifts his chin. "Texted."

"Good. Let's go before I'm late."

"You don't want to eat some more?" Galya's words are gentle, but the disappointment in her expression hits harder than I expect.

"I'm sorry," I say softly. "I just lost my appetite."

Grabbing my bag, I adjust my blouse and walk out the front door with both men shadowing me.

I don't know if I'll survive this new world I'm in.

The office is quiet, save for the hum of the overhead lights and the occasional clack of someone's keyboard down the hall.

My screen glares back at me, a wall of text I've already read five times without absorbing a single word. I swear I've typed the same paragraph twice, maybe three times, and none of it is sticking or sounding right.

With a groan, I delete the entire passage and start again, but all the while, I can't stop thinking about Aleksei.

His mouth. The way he looked at me. Not in that arrogant way he usually does. It was different this time, almost tender. Like he was searching for something in me he didn't want to admit he needed.

God. No. Stop.

I drag my hands down my face.

Focus. This is just sex. It's always been just sex.

I repeat it silently, like a mantra. Because the man is dangerous. A criminal. And the second I forget that, I lose.

A soft knock on the door pulls me out of my spiral just before Dana breezes in, a coffee in one hand, her oversized tote slung over the other arm.

"Hey," she says, pausing halfway across the room. "You good? You look...off."

I blink up at her, forcing my features into something close to neutral. "Just tired."

She sits down across from me, not buying it for a second. "Did you ever report that guy?"

I don't have to ask which guy she means.

"No," I answer too quickly. "Honestly, I don't want to think about it anymore. It happened. It's over. He didn't try anything, thankfully. I just want to forget."

Her brow lifts. "How do you know? That he didn't try anything?"

Shit.

"Because…someone I know showed up right before he could. He took me home instead."

Dana leans back, eyes narrowing just slightly. She doesn't trust that answer, but she also knows when to push and when to let it go.

"Do I know him?"

Clearly, she's not in the let-it-go stage right now. Awesome…

"Nope." I fold my arms over my chest. "I'm fine, I promise. I'd rather focus on work because we need to finish the Soto brief, in case you forgot."

You know, the one I can't seem to focus on.

Her brows lift like she knows exactly what I'm doing, but she plays along anyway. "Nice pivot. And yes, I'm almost done with my part. You?"

"Almost done too."

Dana tilts her head. "You sure you're okay? Because honestly, you look…I don't know. Nervous. Glowy. A mix of both."

"I'm using a new highlighter."

She snorts. "That's not it. Did you get laid last night?"

"What?" My voice catches, too loud in the quiet room. "No! Of course not."

She leans back in her chair, arms folded. "Geez, you'd think I'd accused you of murder. A little sex wouldn't kill you."

I try to laugh it off. "I barely go out. You know that."

"Well, whoever this *friend* is, he looks good on you." Her salacious grin brings unnecessary heat to my face.

Before she can dig her teeth in any deeper, there's a knock at the door and the secretary walks in, arms full of envelopes.

"Morning, Ms. Clark. Your mail."

"Thanks," I say, maybe a little too eagerly, as I grab the stack and place it beside my laptop. "Appreciate it."

Dana watches me for a beat longer, then glances at the stack of mail before flicking her attention back to me.

"Well…" She sighs, stretching as she stands. "That's my cue to go be productive. Or pretend I'm being productive. I'll come annoy you later."

"Looking forward to it."

She smirks. "But just so you know, I *will* find out about your new friend. I'm very resourceful."

"I'm terrified." I roll my eyes.

"You should be."

"Yeah, yeah. Bye, psycho."

She chuckles, shutting the door behind her,

Shaking my head, I grab the unopened mail, knowing I won't be able to focus on anything else until I've sorted through it all and tossed the junk. I sift through the stack of mail without much thought: legal briefs, case updates, nothing too exciting.

Until it is.

My fingers stall on a plain white envelope—no postage, no return address—and I know instantly what it is.

I inhale sharply, not wanting to open it.

Somehow, I'd forgotten about the letters and the threats. But here it is again, staring back like it never left.

Thumb brushing along the seam, I glance at the door, unable to shake the feeling that someone's on the other side. Watching. Waiting.

I roll my chair closer to the window and glance down at the parking lot, but there's no one except a bunch of cars and the two men Aleksei assigned to stalk me. Turning back to the envelope, I open it slowly, anxiety winding its way up my spine with every inch of the tearing seal.

Inside is a single sheet of paper with words typed up.

> You really think he can save you, Mrs. Marinova?
> You have no idea what I am capable of.

A chill slides beneath my skin. The paper rustles as I drop it, and my hands haven't stopped shaking.

I read it again, slower this time, letting each word settle deep in my chest. My gaze drifts toward the window once again, scanning the sidewalk, the parked cars.

Nothing moves. No one stares back.

But someone was close enough to deliver this without being seen.

I fold the letter and tuck it back into the envelope, pushing it to the bottom of my drawer beneath a pile of legal pads. Out of sight, but not out of mind.

The back of my neck prickles. Whoever sent this knows I moved out. That I'm married. They have been watching me, and for the first time, I'm positive this isn't Aleksei.

It's someone worse.

TWENTY-SEVEN

ALEKSEI

Once the meeting ends, I have no intention of going home. The thought of walking through that door and pretending I can exist in the same space as her…it's unbearable.

I could go to one of our bars, drink until the world blurs, and sleep it off in the back office. But even that doesn't tempt me.

What I need isn't a drink. It's destruction. My hands crave the violence of it, the release, the pain that comes after.

Tonight, I'll disappear into the gym at home where she won't find me and tear this unrest out of me with every hit I land. This chaos. This hunger. This obsession. I'll beat it out, muscle by muscle, until there's nothing left of her inside me.

Kirill is one of the last ones still here, rising from his chair and buttoning his jacket as he moves toward the exit.

"Are you leaving, or do you plan to sleep here?" His mouth jerks.

My jaw tenses; I'm not sure what the hell to say. "Yeah, I'm going.

What about you?"

He shoots me a dumbfounded look. "Diner with Lev. It's Monday."

Nu blyat, I forgot. Lev has his routines, and this is one. Every Monday, they go to the same diner not far from where they live.

Kirill starts toward the door, and I follow.

"Can I come?"

He stops just before the elevator, eyes narrowing. "Why? Shouldn't you be off entertaining your blushing bride?"

I grit my teeth. "Zamalchi." *Shut up.*

The corner of his mouth twitches. He's enjoying this far too much.

Kirill presses the button for the elevator, then glances over. "Already having problems? That has to be a record."

"This marriage means nothing," I bite out. "*She* means nothing."

"Of course." Sarcasm threads through his calm tone like a knife.

I don't care what he thinks. This has never been about me. This marriage is all about her and how much she despises it.

But the thought of her unhappy doesn't bring me much satisfaction. Not like I thought it would.

Doesn't matter. This is for the best. The less time I spend near her, the better. The less she talks, the easier it is to pretend I don't care what she thinks of me. That her moods don't sink their teeth into mine. That I didn't spend the entire goddamn day thinking about her. How her morning went. Whether she actually ate the breakfast Galya made. If she smiled. If she felt safe.

I even called Viktor, pretending it was about logistics, just to hear him confirm she got to work without trouble. Then I texted him again hours later to check on her.

I don't know what the hell is happening to me, but somewhere between the hate and obsession, she's carved herself into every part of me.

The elevator ride stretches in silence while his words echo in my head, gaining weight with every floor we descend until they settle like lead in my chest.

Once I'm in my car and he's in his, I grip the wheel harder than I should, that familiar dull pressure blooming behind my ribs again. A throb I can't ignore. A burn that's got her name written all over it.

This was supposed to be simple. A transaction. A way to break her down slowly, on my terms.

Instead, she's breaking me.

By the time I pull up to Kirill's, he's already outside, strapping Lev into the backseat. I kill the engine and head toward his car, planning to ride with them.

He eyes me with a smirk. "What, your car broken?"

"Don't feel like driving."

"Horosho," he says, opening the door. "Let's go."

Twenty minutes later, we roll into the lot. Kirill settles the car in the last row, hidden in the far corner. In the backseat, Lev's flipping through the pages of his book, headphones on, oblivious that we've arrived.

I reach for the door handle, but Kirill stops me with a low grunt. "Podajdi." *Wait.*

I still, following his line of sight with a raised brow.

Two rows down, a young woman, maybe mid-twenties, steps out of a rusted Volkswagen. She stretches like her body's been folded too long, knuckles pressed into the small of her back, then drags a hand through her light brown hair.

Her eyes scan the lot as if she's making sure no one is watching.

Then she opens the car door, pulls out a toothbrush and a half-empty bottle of water, and slips behind the edge of the lot. She rinses, spits, then wipes her mouth with the back of her hand.

When I glance at Kirill, his entire expression changes, tightening and sharpening as if something set him off. He's probably thinking what I'm thinking: either she's weirdly committed to oral hygiene or she has been sleeping in that car.

That makes me more interested.

"She yours?" A smirk carves itself out as I tilt my head toward her.

His glare cuts.

"No," he growls. "I haven't touched her. But do not think for a second that I won't kill you if you do."

I've never once heard him this intense over any woman, not even Lev's mother.

This girl matters. Maybe more than he wants to admit.

"Ya ponil." I nod once, clapping his shoulder. "Bezdomnaya devushka tvaya." *Got it. Homeless girl is yours.*

"She's not homeless," he snaps. "Or she wasn't supposed to be."

"What does that mean?"

But he ignores me.

The girl disappears into the diner, and Kirill finally shuts off the engine.

"Come on," he mutters. "Let's eat."

He helps Lev out of the car, and we head inside. The second we step through the door, a hostess approaches with a bright, overly rehearsed smile.

"How many?"

"Three." Kirill's voice is flat, almost cold.

Her smile flickers. "Right this way."

She grabs three menus and turns toward the nearest open booth, but Kirill doesn't budge.

"That section." He tilts his chin toward the far end of the diner.

"Of course."

And the moment we round the corner, I understand why he made this request. The girl from the parking lot is working this side.

"So…" I lean across the table once we're all seated. "Homeless girl works at the diner. Does she know you own it?"

"Net," Kirill bites out.

That reaction? It tells me everything. There's something going on here, and I intend to find out what.

I glance over at Lev seated beside him, flicking through a menu like he's memorizing it for a test, headphones resting over his ears.

The girl starts toward us, and Kirill immediately sits up straighter. Interesting.

When she reaches us, she grins brightly, her cheeks heating up when she looks at my brother. "Hey, guys. Good to see you."

I catch her name, Sloane, on the tag pinned to her apron as her gaze sweeps the table.

"Can I get you started with some drinks? The usual for you, buddy?" she asks Lev.

Lev slides off his headphones, eyes still on the menu, but the subtle nod he gives tells me he's listening.

"And for you, sir?"

Her voice is soft, but not timid. And after all my time observing people, I can tell there's something careful about the way she carries herself. Like she's used to holding things together even when they're falling apart.

"Aleksei." I let my name curl off my tongue with a smirk.

"Aleksei," she repeats, her smile widening.

I don't miss the way Kirill's jaw tenses as she says my name.

"We will put in our food order too," he adds.

Sloane nods. "Of course." Then she looks over at Lev with a conspiratorial smile. "I'll make sure the chef gives you extra curly fries today. Pinky promise."

Lev looks up and stares. Not just a flash of a glance, but full-on eye contact.

"Th-th-thank you," he says, just above a whisper.

Across the booth, Kirill freezes, like something in him just broke wide open. He's staring at his son like he's not sure if he's dreaming. Like one wrong move might shatter it.

And I get it. Because I know what this means. Lev doesn't speak often. When he does, it's usually with effort or if Kirill prompts him. To see him look at her and say thank you on his own…it hits Kirill hard. It hits me too.

She turns to us, not realizing how monumental this was. "What can I get you guys?"

We both order, and she jots everything down before heading toward the kitchen. As soon as she's gone, Lev slips his headphones back on like nothing happened.

I lean in closer toward the table. "Are you going to tell me who Sloane is, or do I need to start digging?"

He shoots me a warning glare.

"All I'm saying is, the boy needs a mother. And he obviously likes her."

"No."

"Why not?"

He doesn't answer right away. "Too young."

"That's not the reason."

"She's just a girl who works here. That's all."

I let him have the lie. For now.

Fifteen minutes later, she's back with our food. Chicken nuggets and fries for Lev, burgers for us. Lev looks down at his nuggets like they are something sacred. Then, without a word, he unzips his backpack and pulls out a chocolate bar, still wrapped, and holds it out to her.

The shift is instant. Her face crumples, tears filling her eyes that she can't blink away fast enough.

"Oh, wow," she breathes, her voice cracking. "Thank you, Lev. But I can't take that. It's yours."

"Take it," Kirill says firmly.

She peers over at him, her lips parting like she wants to argue, but she stops herself and just nods. "Okay. Thank you, Lev. You're always so sweet to me."

She turns and struts off, still clutching the chocolate to her chest like it means more than she knows how to say. Right before she disappears into the back, she peers at Kirill, and I grin.

I might need to start tagging along to the diner more often. This is entertaining.

When dessert comes, Lev gets a chocolate chip cookie, but she brings two and sets the second one down in front of him like it's a secret between them.

"This one's on me," she says with a wink. "For the chocolate."

Kirill watches her. When she catches his stare, her cheeks flush.

"I'm sorry," she says quickly. "I should've asked first. I just thought—"

He lifts a hand, stopping her mid-ramble. "It's fine."

And for the first time since he stepped inside, the corner of his mouth twitches. Barely a smile, but it's there.

She lets out a quiet laugh, relief softening her features. "Alright, then. Just let me know if you need anything else."

Then she slips away, darting into the kitchen.

"She likes you," I tell him.

"She doesn't know me, and she doesn't want to."

"Doesn't matter. She still likes you."

Kirill says nothing.

When we're done and getting ready to leave, he stalks toward the counter, stops beside her, and pulls a folded stack of cash from his wallet.

"This is for you." He grabs her hand and presses the bills into her palm.

She looks down at it, eyes widening. "Wait, this is too much…"

But he's already walking away.

FIONA

By the time I walk through the front doors after work, all I want is a hot cup of tea and maybe a quiet hour with a book by the fireplace in his den.

I kick off my shoes and leave them by the bench in the foyer, then hang my bag on the hook in the hallway, phone still in hand. The staff moves around me in practiced silence, wiping down surfaces that already gleam. The guards posted throughout the house do little to hide their presence, and the weight of their stares makes the place feel less like a home and more like a beautifully furnished prison.

"Aleksei here?" I ask, turning toward the nearest guard.

He meets my eyes while standing with his arms crossed, expression unreadable as he answers in a clipped tone. "Boss is at work."

The disappointment creeps in so fast, I barely catch it. It settles somewhere low and uninvited, curling in my stomach before I have a chance to reason it away.

His absence should come as a relief. A break from his madness, from the intensity that slithers around him like he's one with me. I should be grateful for the space.

But…I'm not.

Some stupid part of me imagined walking in and finding him waiting. Maybe not smiling or warm, but present. A nod. A look. A question about my day. Anything.

But why? Why do I care? Why do I want that? Am I that desperate to find someone who gives a shit? Who wants to burn the earth down just to have me?

Or have I somehow stepped into the dark side without realizing I was there to begin with?

My God, this is a nightmare.

Keep your shit together, Clark.

I shove the thoughts away and start toward the den, not bothering to change yet.

"Boss said your clothes coming soon," the same guard adds, as if that's supposed to mean something.

I pause and glance over my shoulder. "What clothes?"

"Don't know."

Well, that's great, because neither do I.

"Thanks," I mutter, already pulling my phone from my bag, my thumbs moving quickly.

FIONA

Did you buy me clothes? Because I have my own.

The reply comes faster than it should, like he'd already been waiting for it.

ALEKSEI

You are my wife now. That means you represent me, so you will dress the part.

I snicker.

FIONA

I'm not showing up to work looking like a walking luxury brand ad.

ALEKSEI

Wear what you want to court. But when you're with me, you will wear what I give you.

Frustration flares in my gut, but I don't bother replying. What's the point? There's nothing left to say. But one thing's for damn sure: he's not going to tell me what to wear. Not ever.

I type the message, then hesitate, my thumb frozen over the screen.

FIONA

Are you going to be home for dinner?

Is this normal? Too much? It's just a question. One anyone would ask. Right?

It feels strange. Too domestic. But not entirely unreasonable.

And just like that, I start imagining it. Him as some powerful CEO, me doing what I love. Both of us coming home, collapsing on the couch, and laughing at something stupid before I crawl into his lap, look into his eyes, and whisper how much I missed him. How much I love him.

A sigh slips out before I can stop it.

That life doesn't belong to us. It never will.

When I peer down at the phone, dots appear before they disappear, then blink back to life again. My pulse ticks up.

Just say it already. What the hell are you doing?

Finally, his reply lands.

ALEKSEI

No. Eat without me. I have business.

The words land with more weight than I want to admit. They shouldn't matter. He doesn't owe me anything—not his time, not his attention, not even a damn dinner. This marriage was never about love or a partnership, and it sure as hell wasn't built on mutual respect. So if he wants to stay gone and let work take priority over me, that's fine. I can't be upset about something that was never real to begin with.

I press my lips together, pulse tight in my throat, and close my hand around the phone until my knuckles ache. Then I toss it onto the couch with a bit too much enthusiasm.

Seconds later, one of the maids appears. "Would you like some tea?"

Just what I need.

"Green tea, if it's not too much trouble."

"Of course."

I drift into the den and curl onto the far corner of the sectional, tucking a throw blanket over my lap. The floors gleam, the artwork is museum-worthy, and every surface whispers wealth.

The home is beautiful and immaculate. But it doesn't feel like mine.

When the tea arrives, I cradle the mug between my palms, letting the warmth soak into my skin while my thoughts circle the one man I shouldn't want, but do anyway. And there's not a damn thing I can do about it.

What I could use right now is something as simple as a friend. Someone to talk to, to tell about my day, about the notes I've been getting, about how exhausting it is wanting something real with someone who lives in a world so completely opposite of mine.

I finish the rest in slow sips, the tea lukewarm now but still decent. Heavy footsteps approach, and I glance up to find another guard.

"They're here," he says. "The clothes. They are in your room."

"Thanks."

I set the mug on the end table and head upstairs to my bedroom, where clothes hang from portable stands and more wait in bags on the floor. I let my fingers glide over silk and satin, tailored seams and sculpted waistlines, wondering what Aleksei will see when he looks at me in these. A possession? A prize? A placeholder?

The clothes fit beautifully. Too beautifully. Pencil dresses, evening gowns, tops, skirts, blouses and high-waisted slacks, blazers that sharpen my shape.

I look in the mirror and barely recognize myself. Like I'm playing dress-up in a world that isn't mine.

Once I'm done, I peel the clothes off like I'm shedding a costume.

Like if I move quickly enough, I can shake off whatever version of myself was starting to believe I belonged in them.

I hang the pieces I'm keeping and leave the rest on the rack, telling the guard to return them or have whoever brought them come collect them.

When dinner rolls around, I hesitate. The thought of sitting alone at the far end of that ridiculously long dining table makes my stomach turn.

I've eaten alone more times than I can count. I've spent years by myself, when the silence didn't bother me, when solitude was a choice, not a consequence. But tonight, it feels different.

Tonight, it feels like punishment.

Maybe it's the size of this house. The way the quiet stretches too far and echoes too loud.

Or maybe it's him. The way Aleksei has wormed his way into places I didn't think anyone could reach, his absence somehow heavier than his presence ever was.

I shouldn't crave the company of a man who married me out of vengeance, out of some twisted game of power. But I do.

And no matter how hard I try to fight it, I'm not even sure I want to be free of him anymore.

ALEKSEI

It's after midnight when I step through the door, removing my boots and leaving them by the door. I tell myself I'm heading for one of the guest rooms. That's the plan. Sleep alone. Keep my distance.

But my feet don't turn right. They carry me left and down the hall, toward the master suite.

Toward her.

I should make some attempt to stop, but it's the last thing I want. The last thing I need. I want to feel the way she breathes beside me, her warm skin on mine. All the things I never imagined myself wanting, especially from her.

The door's already cracked open, the faintest sliver of light spilling across the hallway floor. She must've forgotten to close it all the way. Or maybe she did it on purpose, hoping I'd join her.

The room is dark except for the moonlight painting pale shadows across the bed. And there she is.

Fiona.

I can see her hair, the way it spills across the pillow. Her body snuggled beneath the blanket. And I envy that thing because I want her wrapped around me like that.

Everything in me says to turn around, go back downstairs, and pour a drink. Pass out on the leather couch in my office if I have to. Anything to keep these unwanted feelings from growing.

Instead, my hand presses against the door, easing it open without a sound, and I step inside.

I tell myself one last time to walk away and be smart. To protect what little control I have left, because this feels like stepping into a war I've already lost. The odds are stacked. The cost is too high.

But I would trade every weapon in my arsenal just to feel her body next to mine.

Slowly, I move toward her, each step a surrender I swore I would never make. And then I'm standing over her, watching the only woman who has ever gotten under my skin, who challenges me in ways no one else ever has. Her stubbornness, her fire, the mouth that never holds back. I crave every last piece of her.

I reach out before I even know what I'm doing. My knuckles barely graze the curve of her cheek. Warm. Smooth. Too goddamn soft for a world like mine.

And then…she whispers my name. So quiet I almost don't hear it.

"Aleksei…"

My hand freezes.

Say it again, detka.

And she does, like she heard me. For a second, I almost believe she's awake. That she knows I'm here, standing over her like some pathetic fool who can't sleep without looking at the woman who's wrecked him.

But she's not. She's out cold, saying my name in a nightmare—or worse, a dream.

I don't belong there. I'm not the man you dream about. I'm the one you survive.

I step back, every muscle pulled tight. My father's voice slams into me, echoing through the hollow spaces he carved out long ago.

Caring is weakness.

Women are distractions at best, poison at worst.

Your only job is to protect this family.

Affection is nothing more than a liability.

You don't want what you can't control.

Every lesson he taught me replays on a loop as I keep staring at her, knowing he was right. I watch her for a few more seconds, like maybe standing here long enough will make the urge pass.

But it doesn't. It just grows and presses harder. Right now, the only thing I want, the only pull I can't seem to resist, is to get into this bed, wrap my arms around her, and pretend for one fucking night that nothing else matters.

Instead, I force myself to turn around and close the door behind me.

But even as I walk away, that throbbing in my chest is there, reminding me that in all the noise and blood, the only quiet I crave lives in that room.

And I hate how much I need it. How much I need *her*.

TWENTY-EIGHT

FIONA

Morning light spills through the tall windows, casting long streaks across the marble as I make my way downstairs. I'm already dressed for work, just hoping to grab a quick bite before heading out. I sigh as I turn toward the kitchen, already knowing he won't be there.

Last night, I could've sworn I felt him near me. Or maybe that was just a dream. A hazy impression I can't quite remember, but can't fully shake either.

Then I walk into the kitchen and stop cold.

He's seated at the counter, looking like something out of a magazine. Navy trousers hug his powerful thighs, and his pale blue shirt stretches just enough across his shoulders to make me stare longer than I should. The sleeves are rolled to his forearms, veins on display, a diamond-studded watch catching the sunlight.

He looks like power. Effortless, commanding power. And way too good-looking for my sanity.

Jesus. Why does my husband have to be so hot?

Not a thought I ever imagined having, but here we are.

"Good morning." His mouth lifts by a fraction. A hint of a smile, nothing more.

"Morning," I manage, keeping my voice casual.

He doesn't get to hear whatever cracks underneath, or how some part of me might have…missed him. If that's what this is.

Before I can sit, he rises and moves toward the stove.

"Tea?" he asks.

I nod, not sure what to think as he grabs a green tea bag and wraps it around a spoon before pouring steaming water into a mug. He crosses the room and holds the cup out to me just as I lower myself onto the seat beside his.

His fingers faintly brush against mine when I take it. It's nothing. Just a touch. Barely there. Yet it moves through me like a current, seeping into every corner of my body and lighting up places I've tried to keep dark.

His eyes flick, catching mine. Searching, maybe seeing too much.

I drop my gaze and busy myself with straightening my napkin like it suddenly matters.

He doesn't move. Just stands there a beat too long, close enough that I can feel the weight of his stare on my skin. Then he steps back, returning to his seat, his chair scraping against the floor cutting through the silence.

But before he sits, his eyes drop to my left hand. "You're not wearing your ring."

The rough way he says it makes my body prickle, tone dripping with that quiet kind of dominance that always gets under my skin.

I shrug, flat and unapologetic. "Nope."

His gaze doesn't leave my hand. "Where is it?"

"In the nightstand. Where it belongs."

He doesn't move at first. Just peers at me in that calculating way, like he's debating whether to punish me now or later.

He suddenly pushes his chair back in a way that makes me tense. "I'll go get it for you."

"Don't." I lift my hand up. "I'm not wearing it to work. And that's final."

His jaw flexes. "Then you'll wear it at home. And everywhere else."

"That wasn't part of the deal."

"It is now." He pulls himself in, grabbing his coffee mug, calm as ever. "Next time I see that finger bare, I'll glue it on myself. Do you understand me, Ms. Prosecutor?"

My mouth parts, ready to argue, to remind him that he doesn't own me. But the words never make it out. Not when his voice sounds like that. Possessive in a way that slides down my spine and twines deep. Like every line I've drawn is just waiting to be erased. And a big part of me doesn't even want to stop it.

We eat in silence, the clink of silverware the only sound between us. I try to focus on my breakfast, pretending I don't feel his eyes on me every few minutes.

"I won't be home for dinner tonight," he finally says.

I don't know what I expected. Something meaningful, maybe. Something real. But it's not that. Just more distance and disappointment. More of this hollow ache I hate admitting he causes.

My fork stalls halfway to my mouth. "Oh, really? Working late again?"

Or fucking someone else?

"Yes." His response is clipped, not even an ounce of warmth. "Is that a problem?"

No. Of course not. I don't care what you do, or who you do it with.

But the thought of him with another woman, touching her the way he touches me, sends a hot, bitter rage tearing through me.

I shake my head, gripping the fork painfully tight. "No problem at all. The less I see of you, the better."

I mean to sound indifferent, but it doesn't come out that way. It feels like something splinters in my chest as the words leave my mouth. Something I won't be able to glue back together.

He doesn't answer right away, just looks at me. Long enough that it punctures something raw inside me.

"I'm glad." His lips wind a fraction. "I'm here to make you happy, lyubov moya."

What the hell does that mean?

I really need to start learning Russian.

He reaches into his jacket pocket and pulls out a black credit card, placing it on the table between us. "This is for you. Use it for whatever you need. Go shopping. Take a spa day. Buy a new car if you want to. It has no limit."

I stare at the card like it's some kind of insult. "I don't want your money."

He leans back, something close to amusement tugging at his lips.

Without hesitation, I shove the card back toward him. His gaze darkens as he rises and closes the space between us. That familiar scent of his cologne clings to him as he stops in front of me, tipping my chin up between his fingers and forcing my eyes to meet his.

"Like it or not, you are a Marinova now. You represent me. So act like it."

I force out a humorless laugh. "And what exactly does that mean? What do I represent? A violent man who terrifies everyone who crosses his path? A man who traps a woman in a marriage she never wanted?"

His eyes narrow, the warning in them unmistakable, but I don't care. I'm too tired of holding my tongue.

"You'd rather see me miserable than let me go," I press, my voice trembling with something too jagged to name. "And for what?

Because I did my job? Because I put people like you in prison?"

I stand slowly, lifting my chin, and those deep, dark eyes never leave mine. The air between us thickens, charged with something volatile. One wrong word, and this entire moment could ignite.

His nostrils flare, but he doesn't say a word. He just stands there, all silent and still, watching me with that unreadable expression like he's already dissected everything I just said. My ribs tighten around each breath, the heaviness of his silence more unnerving than any threat.

I shake my head, turning to walk past him. "I'm done here."

"But I'm not," he growls.

Before I can take another step, his hand wraps around my wrist and I'm yanked forward and spun into him so fast my breath catches. My chest collides with the solid wall of his body as he pins me there, one arm banded tight around my back, the other gliding up, fingers tipping my chin until his mouth hovers near my ear.

"You really don't know what you do to me when you talk like that." His warm breath tickles against my skin. "So bold. So defiant."

I swallow hard, every nerve ending on fire.

"But watch how you speak to me, moya ptichka. Because there are consequences."

"And what are those?" My pulse thuds in my throat.

His gaze flicks to my mouth. "I'll punish you for it."

Heat slams through me.

"And you will love every second," he adds, grip tightening at my waist like he knows, like he feels it too. That pull. That need.

Something reckless twists through me.

"Maybe you should kill me." I brush my lips over his before nipping his lower one, just hard enough to draw a groan. "It's the only way I'll get out of this marriage anyway."

His laugh is low, rough, as he grabs a handful of my ass and pulls me against him.

"That would be too easy." His mouth ghosts over mine. "This…" His gaze dips to where our bodies meet. "…is a lot more fun."

Yes. That's right. That's all we are. This passion, this intensity, is nothing more than skin and flesh.

My throat tightens from the tornado of emotions crashing against one another—rage, fear, desire, and confusion, all twisted into one impossible knot.

His thumb drags over my lower lip. Testing. Teasing. And neither of us moves or wants to run. Not from this. My back is against the wall before I can convince myself to stop, and my body—that traitorous, aching thing—is responding to him in ways my mind can't control.

"Say it again." He wraps his fingers around my throat.

"Say what?" I breathe, my nipples pebbling beneath my bra.

"That I should kill you."

My chin lifts, a half-smile pulling at my lips. "Kill me and get it over with."

His growl is low and full of something feral. "I don't want to do that."

Then his lips find mine, fierce and desperate, like he's trying to erase the space between hate and want. And I kiss him back like it's the only thing keeping me alive.

His fingers thread into my hair, tugging just enough to tilt my head, to deepen the claim. The kiss tears through every wall I've built, and I melt into it, gasping when he grinds against me, his arousal thick and unmistakable through his slacks. His other hand fumbles at the buttons of my blouse, roughly popping them open until the cool air hits my skin, my bra exposed under his gaze.

"I hate you," I whisper against his lips.

Hate the way you undo me. Hate how much I want you.

"Good." His growl vibrates against my skin as he drags his mouth down to my throat and bites. "Hate me harder."

He yanks the zipper of my skirt, tugging it down before his belt clatters to the floor. I don't remember how we got here, but it's the only thing I want. He lifts my legs around his waist, shifts my panties aside, and drives into me in one hard, greedy thrust.

I gasp, clutching at his shoulders, the stretch of him dizzying, overwhelming, perfect.

"Blyat, I've missed you," he mutters against my neck, and I have to choke back the stupid rush of pleasure that comes with hearing it.

Maybe he only means the sex, but the rough scrape of the words cuts deep, curling around something inside me that refuses to believe he didn't mean more than that. A raw and needy moan slips from my throat, my nails raking up his back when he circles his hips. His muscles tense beneath my fingers, the only warning before he drives into me harder, deeper, his rhythm brutal and unrelenting.

"Oh God," I cry out, clinging to him like he's the only solid thing in a world gone sideways. "Don't stop."

And he doesn't. He only picks up the pace, pulling back to peer into my eyes. Forcing me to see him. To feel all of it. I drown in the storm of him, every thrust unraveling me until I can't think, can't breathe, can't be anything but his.

The walls shake with the force of his body, with the sound of us. Anyone in this house knows exactly what's happening, and I don't care.

His hand finds the space between us, fingers circling my clit, and I detonate. A strangled cry tears from my throat as I come undone, biting down on his shoulder just to keep from screaming. He follows with a guttural curse, ramming deep like he's trying to brand this moment into both of us.

Then it's over.

When he lowers me, the silence, the distance…it all returns with a vengeance. Without a word, he steps back, refastens his clothes, and hands me my skirt with barely a glance, raking a hand through his hair like I'm nothing.

I'm still leaning against the wall, blouse open, body trembling, lungs clawing for air, but he doesn't even look at me. Just turns and leaves. The silence he leaves in his wake wraps around me like a chokehold.

Because I don't know what I hate more: that he walked away like I mean nothing, or that some part of me wanted him to stay.

ALEKSEI

It's only supposed to be sex. A release. A means to an end.

That's what I tell myself as the door clicks shut behind me and I slide into the car, her taste still on my tongue.

But it isn't. And that's the goddamn problem.

I drop my head back against the seat, knowing I should've stayed away. It's the only option left to make it through this marriage without losing control.

She's my wife on paper. My enemy by design. But every time she looks at me—unflinching, furious, daring me to strike first—something in me cracks. Everything I was taught, everything I've lived by like a code of honor, starts to slip.

Because she doesn't just make me forget the rules. She makes me want to break every damn one.

I drag a hand over my jaw, still hard and strung tight with the memory of her pressed against me, her body soft, but her eyes fighting every second of it. She never fully submits. Not even when she's trembling, gasping my name, and shaking apart around me.

That's what makes her dangerous. Not her job. Not the way she tried to destroy me in court. The way she feels: too real in my arms.

This was supposed to be revenge. Now I'm not sure who's paying the price.

TWENTY-NINE

FIONA

It's been a week since that breakfast. A week since I last saw him.

And every day, it gets harder to pretend that I'm okay with that.

Some nights, I wake to the faint trace of his cologne clinging to my pillow. Other times, I swear I feel the dip in the mattress beside me, like a ghost of his body was there and vanished before dawn. But then morning comes and he's still nowhere to be found. His side of the bed remains pristine, like he was never there at all.

I don't know if I'm imagining it. If my mind is playing tricks on me, weaving him into the empty spaces simply because I don't know how to fill them anymore. He's become a quiet, yet insistent ache in the background. The only part of him I have is his ever-present bodyguards, one car length behind me wherever I go, reminding me that even when he's gone, he still owns every corner of my freedom.

But every night, I lie awake wondering where he is. Who he's with. Whether his hands are on someone else. Whether his mouth is whispering to another woman in Russian, telling her all the things he's never said to me.

Is he falling for her? Will he give her everything I told myself I never wanted?

I can't seem to get the images of him with other women out of my head. It's like a damn life sentence—seeing that, feeling the anger, sadness, and jealousy all wrapped into one insufferable emotion.

When did I start caring this much? Was it gradual? Slow enough to slip past my defenses without setting off alarms? Or did something inside me break the day I met him, and I've been bleeding out ever since?

I don't know who I am anymore. I used to be sure. I used to believe in right and wrong. In justice. In the thrill of hearing "guilty" read aloud in court.

Now, all I feel is chaos.

You seriously need to get it together. Remember who he is.

Men like Aleksei don't fall in love. They conquer. They consume. They leave behind nothing but wreckage, and I swore I'd never let myself become another broken piece in a long line of casualties.

But knowing something doesn't make it easier to live with. A sharp pang stretches in my chest as I grip the steering wheel, eyes fixed on the endless stretch of road as I veer off the main highway, pulling into the gravel lot near the tasting room of the vineyard.

The second I park, I register the sound of music floating through the air. The quiet hum of staff outside setting up chairs beneath the pergola and arranging lanterns for what looks like an event.

For the first time in a long time, there's life here. Real life. Not desperate hope or barely hanging-on optimism.

My throat tightens as I step out of the car and spot my parents standing near the patio, talking to two vineyard employees. My mom's laughing at something, her hand resting lightly on my dad's arm while he says something back, and she swats his shoulder with a grin.

They look happy, and it was all I wanted for them.

When they notice me, Dad grins and Mom's eyes light up.

"Tesoro!" she calls with a wave of her hand.

I cross the gravel, letting them pull me into hugs, the smell of grapes and soil and old oak barrels wrapping around us.

"You look tired." My mother brushes my hair off my face. "You work too much."

"Or maybe it's not the work," my father mutters, glancing over at her with a grunt. "Maybe it's il diavolo vestito bene." *The well-dressed devil.*

I give him an exhausted smile. "It's just been a long day, Papa. That's all."

He narrows his eyes. "You're lying."

I open my mouth, but he cuts me off.

"You're not happy." He looks at my mother again, voice rising. "Look at her. You're going to let this happen?"

She says nothing, just lowers her gaze and squeezes my hand gently.

"I'm fine," I say, more forceful this time. "I promise."

"No, figlia mia, you're surviving. This is not right."

I don't have the strength to argue. Instead, I change the subject.

"The vineyard looks beautiful." I turn toward the rows of green stretching down the hill. "There are so many people here. Are all the staff back?"

My mother nods. "Yes. We can pay everyone now. The deliveries, the vendors. Even the restaurant is opening for full hours this week."

"And the outstanding bills?"

"All paid," she says quietly. "He did what he promised."

Well, at least he's good for something other than mind-blowing orgasms.

But my parents don't have to know about my complicated marriage. I'm just glad to give them this. I'll let them believe I'm okay for long enough to secure their future. Then I can figure out how to walk away.

Even when I don't know what I want anymore.

ALEKSEI

The punching bag doesn't hit back. That's the problem.

I slam my fist into the center again, the leather groaning from the force. Sweat drips down my back, the heat of the basement gym at Kirill's pressing in, but I could be in a prison cell for all I care.

Every strike I throw is a curse. A prayer. A plea for silence in a mind that won't shut the fuck up. Her face flashes behind my eyes, and I hit harder.

The soft groan she made when she said my name in her sleep.

A kick slams into the bag, rocking it on its chain.

Her scent in my nostrils, even though I never stay long enough to sleep beside her.

Another hit. My knuckles throb, but I don't care.

Every goddamn night, like clockwork, I come home late enough to know she's asleep and slip into bed beside her, just long enough to breathe her in, to feel her warmth against my chest. And before the sun rises, I'm gone again. Because if I stay longer, I won't be able to leave.

I told myself it would be enough. That just being near her would quiet the monster inside me. But it hasn't. It's only made me want her more.

I don't think she knows. Or maybe she does and pretends not to. I wouldn't blame her. She should hate me. If anyone deserves it, it's me.

"You're going to kill that bag, brother," Kirill drawls from the bench, where he's slipping into his own pair of gloves. "Should we be worried?"

I grunt and land another jab. "You talk too much, like nasha babushka." *Like our grandma.*

He chuckles and gets to his feet. "And you are running from your wife too much. We all have our problems."

My eyes glare hard. "She's nothing."

The taste of that one word burns.

"Do you actually believe your own lies?"

"Maybe I should divorce her," I mutter.

But the thought hits like violence every time I consider it.

"Then why don't you?"

Because the thought of her not being mine—of her being with some other svolich, laughing with him, touching him—would split me open like a goddamn grenade.

"You don't want her gone," Kirill says, reading me too easily. "You wanted her in chains. To own her, control her. And you thought you wouldn't feel anything. But it didn't work out that way, did it?"

My teeth grind. "You tell me. How's it going for you and the homeless girl?"

His expression twists, that flicker of rage flashing in his eyes.

"Ah," I sneer. "You think you can push and I won't push back."

"That's different," he spits out. "She's not my wife."

"Maybe not yet. But it's only a matter of time, right?"

"Wrong."

Yeah, that's what I once said about Fiona. Now here we are.

I throw another punch, harder this time. Anton steps in to hold the bag, while Kirill stalks to the other end of the gym and starts taking his frustration out on a different target.

We all bleed. Some of us just hide it better.

"I don't get it," Anton says, his voice distant. "What is it about these women that makes you all give a shit?" He stares like he's studying a language he will never speak. "I want to understand."

My mouth dries. Because how could he understand?

I've wondered what it's like to be him. Incapable of guilt, rage, remorse. It must be freeing. Maybe confusing too.

"It is weakness," I say. "You're not missing anything."

"Then kill her." He shrugs.

I can't. Because a week without touching her is already too fucking long. Because I watch her every day through security feeds at her office, stalking her with cameras, knowing it's the only way I can see her all day.

And what kills me is that I want her to want me, even though I swore I'd never need that from anyone.

"Want me to do it?" he asks casually.

Something in me snaps. I grab his collar and yank him close, our faces inches apart.

"You even think about touching my wife, and I'll carve you open. Ponatna?" *Understand?*

Anton nods slowly, absorbing it. "You are right. It is weakness."

My hand drops. He doesn't understand what she does to me. No one does.

And maybe it is weakness, but it's also the only thing that feels real. The only thing that makes me feel alive.

"Fight me," he says. "Maybe I can beat it out of you."

Kirill chuckles from the ring. "My God, Anton. You're such a romantic."

Anton ignores him, eyes fixed on me in challenge.

"Fine." I strip my gloves off. "Let's go."

When he hits me square in the jaw five minutes in, I welcome the snap of pain. Because it's better than thinking about her. Better than knowing I'll go home tonight, crawl into bed beside her for twenty silent minutes, and leave before the sun comes up.

Even better than admitting I need her more than air, and that I'm too fucked up to deserve any of it.

THIRTY

FIONA

Another day. Another hour in this mausoleum of a house where every echo reminds me I'm alone.

I kick off my shoes by the door, missing my own home more with each passing minute. The creaky floorboards. The scent of my favorite candle drifting from the kitchen. The tiny chipped mug that didn't match anything else in the cabinet.

I miss the warmth of a cozy home. Of knowing every corner and crevice. Knowing who I was when I lived there.

Poe's meow cuts through the quiet as I sink onto the massive sectional. He leaps up gracefully, tail flicking once before he curls it around my side as he rubs against my waist.

"No, Poe." My fingers brush through his soft fur. "Of course I don't miss him. What gave you such an awful idea?"

He meows again, this time sharper, and I glare halfheartedly at him.

"So what if he's ignoring me?" My eyes narrow. "I should be happy. I mean, I *am* happy."

He gives another meow, and I huff.

"Oh, shut up. What do you know?"

He flicks his tail and jumps to the floor, leaving me alone.

I let out a sigh. What else is new? I'm always alone.

I press my fingers against my temples.

No. No, we're not doing this tonight.

Grabbing my phone off the sofa, I scroll to Emilia's name, thumb hovering. Distraction. That's what I need. Something to pull me out of this spiral.

FIONA

Are you home?

She replies instantly.

EMILIA

Yep. Wanna come over? I'll show you the baby's room. We just finished setting it up.

My heart tugs. This is exactly what I need.

FIONA

I'd love that.

EMILIA

Finally. Get your ass over here before I change my mind.

The smallest smile bends my mouth. I close the texts and head to the closet to retrieve my shoes, then walk back out to my car.

The drive doesn't take more than fifteen minutes before I arrive on their private road. The Marinov estate sits at the end of a winding road flanked by trees in a deep forest. Men in dark clothing allow me through the gate as I ease my car forward.

After sliding into a spot beside the driveway, I climb the cobblestone steps, angelic white columns greeting me as I ring the bell.

Inside, the foyer gleams with polished white marble and a chandelier so massive it looks like it could crush a person if it ever decided to fall. Emilia meets me halfway across the floor, her arms open and her grin wide.

"So glad you came," she says, pulling me into a hug. Her small belly presses against mine.

I can't believe she's going to be a mom.

"You look beautiful." I step back to take her in. "How are you feeling?"

"Pretty good. Just tired all the time. And you?" She links her arm through mine and pulls me into the den. "Tell me everything."

I let out a sigh as she leads me to the den, where we lower ourselves onto the white leather sofa. A lit fireplace crackles in the corner, a tray of tea and cookies resting on the coffee table.

"I'm fine. Everything's good."

I'm not sure why I'm lying. Maybe because the truth is harder to digest.

"You're fine, my ass. I know that face. You've got something bottled up so tight, it's practically vibrating through your skin. So talk."

My lips twitch despite myself.

She softens, reaching out to brush my hand. "Come on, Fi. You know you can talk to me."

I stare into the fire, muscles drawn tight, and then it all comes out.

"I don't know what the hell is going on with me," I whisper. "I never wanted to feel this way." I pinch the bridge of my nose. "But it's like I can't stop it, you know?"

"Feel what?" She scoots in closer to me.

"Aleksei. He's never home, and I'm supposed to be relieved, you know? But I'm not." I let out a dry laugh. "It's like he went from total psycho to kind of sweet to completely distant just like that. Every day, I wake up in that house and he's not there. Every night, I go to sleep wondering where he is. Who he's with. And I shouldn't care. God, I shouldn't care." I grip my hair in a tight fist. "But I do, Emilia. And I hate that I do."

Emilia says nothing, just lets me talk.

"I hate how empty that house feels. I hate that I'm starting to notice the way my chest tightens when he's not around. I hate that I look for signs that he was home while I was asleep, like some idiot sniffing pillows." I shake my head at myself.

What happened to me?

Is this what she felt when she first got involved with Konstantin? Because she tried to resist him. She didn't want him. But now they're married and she's happy.

Can I have that? Could I even let myself have it with someone like Aleksei?

Emilia squeezes my hand, mouth pinching sympathetically.

"I'm scared." The words tumble out before I can stop them. "Because if I let myself want this, want him, then what does that say about me?"

Silence stretches between us for a few agonizing seconds.

"That you're human, Fiona. Nothing in life is ever black and white. You know that. Somewhere deep inside, you do."

She's right, but still, this is different.

"That would mean accepting what he does for a living. Accepting crime and murder—and worse, making excuses for it because he's mine. I just…I don't know how to do that." I slant my head. "I hope I'm not offending you, and I'm sorry if it comes across the way it sounds, but I just have no one to talk to about it and—"

She throws a palm into the air. "Don't do that. Come on, Fi. We've been through so much together, and you think I'd be offended at that? Please? You don't think I sometimes sit here and think about how objectively insane all this is?"

"Tell me how to fix it," I beg. "Because I'm not you, and he's not Konstantin. He doesn't care about me or want me that way. He wants to use me. And it's a cold day in hell if I'll ever allow him to do that."

Even though I've allowed it plenty, but like she said, I'm only human.

"You're right. He isn't Konstantin. But maybe underneath all that assery, there's actually a human being in there somewhere."

"Assery? That's not even a word." I let out a laugh, my body feeling lighter the more we talk.

"It's not? Because it should be."

I blow out a breath. "I don't think this can ever work between us."

"I hope it can, because he has no plans to divorce you. I had Konstantin talk to him, and he won't budge."

Great...

"Maybe you should talk to him. Tell him it's bothering you that's he's never home."

My laugh falls out of me, dry and hollow. "And make myself sound like a pathetic, lovesick idiot? No, thank you. But even if I wanted to, I can't on account of, you know, him never being around."

"Right." She nods. "God..." She leans back. "I never thought we'd end up with two Russian mobsters. They should write a book about us."

My face twists. "Mm, yeah, no. I prefer if they didn't."

Heavy footsteps grow closer, and Konstantin appears.

"Fiona." His smile stretches. "How nice it is to finally see you in our home, sistra."

He comes closer, and I very reluctantly get up and greet him with a quick hug. Though if I had a gun to my head, I'd admit I actually kinda like him now.

I shudder at the thought.

He walks over to Emilia, pressing a soft kiss to her lips. One hand cradles her cheek, the other resting protectively on her belly, and the back of my nose stings. Blinking back my emotions, I push a few strands of hair behind my ear.

When they finally pull apart, their eyes stay pinned, their love so palpable it feels like something I could reach out and touch. God, I envy that.

"So…" Konstantin settles on the other side of her. "I didn't mean to eavesdrop, but I couldn't help overhearing something about my brother never being around, and that it's bothering you." He tsks softly. "Well, we can't have that. How can I help?"

"Other than forcing him to sign the divorce papers?" I mutter. "I don't know, maybe start by telling me where he is and who he's with."

He flips a hand in the air. "How about I take you to him?"

My eyes widen, and when I glance at Emilia, her expression mirrors mine.

"Wait…you know where he is?"

"Of course I do. I know everything that goes on." The sly grin that follows makes it clear: *of course* he does. "So, do you want me to take you?"

A chill runs down my body, like it's telling me something. "Uh… am I going to hate this?"

"Probably." The corner of his mouth tips up. "Is that alright, moya lyubimoya? I will just drop her off and return."

"Sure." She shrugs. "But make sure she's not alone. I don't trust your brother."

He snickers. "She won't be alone. Kirill and Anton will be there."

Emilia pops a single brow. "That's not saying much."

He can't help but smirk.

"I'll go, but not until you show me the baby's room," I tell her.

"It's settled, then," Konstantin says. "You girls have fun. I'll be here answering my emails, and when you are ready, we will go."

"I love you," Emilia says as she rises, going over to kiss him.

And when she does, his entire face softens, his hand clasping the back of her head as he pins his forehead to hers. It's intimate in a way that feels sacred, and I have to look away and give them their moment, clinging to the foolish hope that maybe someday I'll have something that real.

"Ya teba bolshi lyublu."

I don't know what any of that means, but if I had to guess, he just told her he loves her too.

I sit stiffly in the front seat, the leather cold beneath me as trees whip past in the dark, nothing but shadows and sky out the window. The headlights catch on the road in sharp bursts, slicing through the silence like warnings I can't decipher.

I don't know where we're going. Konstantin still hasn't told me. And the longer he stays quiet, the more the unease builds.

Finally, just when I'm about to ask, he speaks.

"My brother," he says, voice even but distant, "was shaped by our father. Molded, really. Like steel in fire. All of us were."

I glance at him from the corner of my eye. He doesn't look back. His gaze stays fixed on the road, one hand loose on the wheel, the other resting on his thigh.

"Our father was…cruel," he continues. "In ways I won't bore you with. Unlike me, Aleksei wanted his approval. A kind word, for him to say he was proud. But it never came. All he received was more cruelty until whatever part of him craved love died too. You see, not everyone gets over that sort of thing. It's in you, and sometimes it is loud."

A lump forms in my throat while my fingers twitch in my lap, a strange ache building beneath my ribs.

For the first time, I feel bad for my husband. For what he must've lived through. For the scars on his chest.

Did his father give him those?

"But Aleksei…" Konstantin goes on, almost contemplative. "He wants more. Even if he doesn't know how to get it. And I think you might be the one person who could show him."

I exhale slowly, his words sitting heavy inside me.

"My brother cares about you." He glances over. "And just as it is for you, I'm sure this is all confusing for him. The things he feels for you. But if there's even a chance you want a life with him, don't give up on him. We would welcome you into this family with open arms."

"Th-thank you." I look out the window again, blinking away my emotions, heart ticking faster than I want to admit.

A life with Aleksei. What would that even look like?

Would it ever feel safe, or would it always feel like I'm standing on the edge of a blade, waiting for him to cut me just to see how much I'll bleed?

"He's stubborn," Konstantin says with a faint smile. "Since we were kids, he always was, so you may have to give him a little extra time to come around, but he will."

A quiet breath slips out of me, something between a laugh and a sigh. Maybe it's amusement. Maybe it's exhaustion. At this point, I can't even tell the difference.

"I don't know what I want," I admit. "I don't know if he'll ever get over our past. Or my job. And I don't know if I'll ever get over who he is. And shit, he threatened my parents, for fuck's sake."

Konstantin shrugs like it's no big deal. "In our world, threats are leverage. A way to make people do what we want. And for my brother…that's the only currency he thinks he has with you."

That definitely doesn't make me feel better. It makes me feel like a pawn. Like every moment we've shared is tangled in strings he pulls tight around my throat.

But I don't say any of that. I just press my lips together and let the silence swallow it whole, wondering what it would even look like to be loved by a man like Aleksei Marinov, and whether love from someone like him could ever come without a price.

THIRTY-ONE

FIONA

The car slows as we pull onto a narrow side street, the low thum of traffic fading behind us. I glance out the window, expecting…I don't know. Some dimly lit restaurant, or maybe a hotel where I'll walk in and find Aleksei nursing a drink, probably with some other woman laughing at his side.

The thought makes my stomach turn, and I brace myself for whatever Konstantin dragged me here to see.

But when we stop and he steps out, I realize we're in front of an old bar. The paint is chipped from the brick, and the windows are tinted so dark I can't see anything inside. The sign above the door flickers red and white, casting ghostly light across the sidewalk. Not exactly Aleksei's usual style.

I follow Konstantin to the entrance, my heels clicking against the concrete. A massive man in black stands outside, arms crossed, tattooed neck flexing as he turns to greet us.

"Boss." He steps aside.

Konstantin doesn't reply with words, just a sharp nod and a slight tilt of his head toward the door before guiding me inside. The bar is loud and warm, packed with people shoulder-to-shoulder, and the sharp scent of alcohol immediately burns my nostrils.

But we don't stop there. He takes a sharp left and heads toward a heavy red curtain draped across the back wall. My heart starts to race.

"Where are we going?" I try to keep my voice even.

He laughs softly. "Don't worry. I promise I am not trying to kill you."

"If you say so."

He pushes through the curtain and leads me down a narrow flight of metal stairs. Every step echoes. The deeper we go, the louder the noise gets. Shouting. Cheers. The clink of glasses. It doesn't sound like any bar I've ever been to.

Another set of double doors waits at the bottom. A second bouncer opens them for us, and the moment we step through, I freeze.

The space opens wide in front of us. There are no windows, just concrete walls and low-hanging lights casting everything in a smoky, yellow glow. Music thumps from somewhere overhead, almost drowned out by the roar of the crowd. In the center of the room, surrounded by a cage and rope, two men are fighting. No gloves to be seen. Blood streaks one man's chest, and the other's knuckles are raw and red.

Waitresses in black minidresses weave between low tables scattered around the perimeter, trays of shots and beer balanced expertly in their hands. Rows of chairs form a half circle facing the pit in the center, like a makeshift arena. Some people stand along the back, shouting over each other, while others lean forward in their seats, eyes locked on the fight. There's a man near the edge collecting cash—probably for bets, though I can't be sure.

My entire body tenses. "Why are we here?"

Konstantin turns and looks directly at me. "Because it's where he is. Come."

Everything inside me screams to turn around, but I follow him past tables, through the haze of smoke and sweat, until we reach the front row. Then I see them.

Kirill lounges causally in his chair, his attention on the fight. But it's Anton beside him who makes my pulse hitch. He's dressed in all black, watching me approach with no warmth in his eyes. No expression at all. Just a quiet, terrifying stillness. When he lifts his chin in a silent greeting, it feels like a threat. And still, it takes everything in me to look away.

"Privet, sistra," Kirill says when he notices me. "Didn't expect to see you here." His gaze slides to Konstantin. "Our brother won't like this."

"She needed to be here," Konstantin replies calmly. "It's good for him."

Kirill shrugs like it's no big deal. "If you say so." Then he gestures to the empty seat beside him. "Come. Sit."

I sink into the chair, scanning the ring, nerves coiling tight in my stomach.

Konstantin leans in. "I should get back to Emilia. Make sure she gets home."

"We'll take care of her," Kirill says without looking.

Then Konstantin's gone.

"So…where is Aleksei?"

Kirill smirks, lifting a glass from the cup holder. "You'll see."

His answer does nothing to ease the tightening in my chest. My hands twist in my lap as the crowd grows louder.

The match ends. One man collapses to the ground, and the other lifts his blood-soaked fists in victory. My stomach turns.

When the second match is announced, I register the first name, something Russian, and it doesn't mean anything to me. But as soon as the second name is called, my heart slams into my ribs.

"Aleksei Marinov."

"Oh my God. He fights?" I ask Kirill, jerking forward in my seat.

My eyes dart to the entrance of the ring, and there he is.

"He used to. A lot," Kirill says. "But he hasn't in a while, not until you."

"What do you mean? Why?"

Kirill laughs. "Never mind. Just watch. He never loses."

Aleksei emerges from the shadows like a nightmare I haven't stopped dreaming. Shirtless. Blood streaked across his shoulder, maybe from an earlier fight. His face is a mask of violence. Jaw clenched. Eyes sharp and deadly.

He hasn't seen me yet. But I can't stop staring, like I've forgotten how to breathe.

Then the fight begins.

Every movement he makes is calculated destruction, his fists landing with precision, his body a weapon. He doesn't flinch or pause. He hits like he's exorcising something, like every strike is meant to silence the war inside him.

Blood splatters from his opponent. Still, he doesn't stop. He goes harder.

Watching him like this feels wrong, like I've stumbled into a moment I was never meant to see. But beneath the brutality, I see it: the way he takes a punch to his torso without blocking, like he wants the pain. Like he needs it.

My lungs forget how to work.

Because I want him to win. I want him whole. I want him safe.

The crowd roars with every hit, but it's background noise. All I can focus on is him. The sharp flex of his muscles, the way he dodges each swing without even breaking rhythm. And when the other man starts to falter, Aleksei just keeps going, methodical and merciless, until the man hits the ground with a sound that silences the room for half a breath.

Aleksei doesn't stop. He circles once, making sure it's over, then stands tall under the harsh lights. His chest rises and falls steadily, not a single trace of blood on his face. He looks like he could go another ten rounds and walk away untouched.

Then…he turns.

Our eyes meet.

The noise fades, every shout dissolving into a dull hum. The air between us tightens, and it's like the whole world pulls taut around that one look. His expression doesn't change, but something flickers there. Disbelief, maybe. A quiet jolt that mirrors the one tearing through me.

My heart kicks painfully against my ribs, and I can't seem to tear my gaze away. Neither can he.

He doesn't move toward me. Doesn't say a word. He just stares, frozen in place, like the fight, the crowd, all of it ceases to matter.

And that's when it happens. The punch comes hard and fast.

"Aleksei!" I shout.

But it's already too late.

ALEKSEI

Every strike I throw is supposed to do one thing: take me further away from her. Empty the chamber in my head where her face lives, where the memory of her hands and the way she looked at me the last time we spoke slinks beneath me and won't leave.

I came here to punish my body so I would stop thinking of her. Each punch, each kick, is a promise to myself that I will not be undone. Not by her. Not by anyone.

My opponent is solid, bred to fight and take the kind of pain I give.

But unfortunately for him, he won't be getting out of this cage alive.

Still, with each connection—the crack of knuckles on bone, the thud as elbow meets ribs—I keep seeing her. The way she called my name in the dark. The way she spits words at me like a challenge. The tilt of her chin when she refuses to be afraid. Her face sits like a flare behind my eyes, and the more I try to extinguish it, the brighter it burns.

A right hook crosses the man's jaw, and he crumples. The cage hops with a roar, and I step back, ready to finish. When I raise my arms in victory, the crowd cheers louder, and I stare around the room, knowing why they came. They want to see me finish him…and I always give the people what they want.

The second my eyes sweep the room, my pulse spikes.

For a moment, I think I'm seeing things because I have been starving for her. So badly it's started to feel like a sickness.

My attention fastens on her, and for one split second, everything shifts. The cage, the crowd, the fight…it all fades.

It's just her. She's the only thing I see.

Which is why I don't notice the punch coming. Until it slams into the side of my face like a hammer, snapping my head sideways and ripping me back to reality.

And that is what happens when you let a woman distract you. It's what my father always said.

He would be embarrassed if he saw me now: staggering, wobbling on my knees, my hearing cutting in and out as the world distorts around me.

The copper tang of blood hits my tongue, sharp and bitter. I swipe it from my mouth and glare at the man who landed the hit, but the real fury spirals inward. I deserve worse.

Because I know better. I've been trained better.

And still, one look at her—just one—and I let my guard drop.

"Yebanyy amateur," I mutter under my breath, spitting blood on the mat. *Fucking amateur.*

Before I can recover, he's on me, knees pinning me down, fists raining with precision. Pain bursts sharp, then dulls into a heavy rhythm that rattles through my skull. The crowd blurs into noise, the cage lights blinking overhead like distant stars.

"Aleksei!" Her desperate voice cuts straight through the chaos. "Aleksei! Get up!"

It slices through everything. The roar, the pain, the noise. Until it's the only thing I hear.

She shouts my name again, and the pitch in it, fear and something like command…that sound reaches the last shred of the animal inside me.

My fingers find the bastard's eye, and I dig in hard. When he screams and rolls off me, that's all I need. I snap back.

Then I make him pay. I hammer him with fists like winter hail in Moscow. Cold, unforgiving, relentless. I don't just fight; I destroy. I give him everything I have and then some, blow after blow, until he's nothing but bone and blood and twitching weakness beneath me.

I don't stop. Not when he gasps. Not when the ref yells. Not until the blood on the mat spreads wide and his face is something unrecognizable.

When they finally drag me off him, the crowd explodes, but it's all distant. Muffled. My chest heaves. My fists drip. My face is a river of blood, but most of it isn't mine. And still…

I'm only looking for her.

The second my arm is raised, she's already moving, pushing past the ropes, ducking into the ring like she can't stand another second of distance between us. Her eyes are wide and filled with concern, her steps urgent, focused only on me. And the sight rips something open inside me I didn't know was still there.

"Your face." She cups her mouth. "You need to see a doctor."

"I'm fine." The referee walks away and returns with two rags, handing one to her and the other to me.

I clean my hands and chest while she presses the other to my cheek, and all I can do is look at her, forgetting why I ever hated her in the first place. Her fingers are clumsy and perfect, and I let her touch me because she is the only thing that has kept me human.

And I want to be human…for her.

"You're bleeding like a fountain." She grimaces. "I'm not sure if this will help. We have to get you to a doctor."

"No. I'm fine."

She shakes her head. "You're absolutely not fine. Please just promise me if it doesn't stop in the next few minutes, you'll go."

Her tone cracks at the end, and it does something cruel to me. I've taken bullets and blades without flinching, but her voice breaking like that feels like the deadliest blow I've ever taken.

What the hell is she trying to do? Kill me?

"What are you doing here?" I ask, trying hard not to split in two, to be the man my father taught me to be.

But with every second, this woman, my wife…she makes it harder to live without her.

"Konstantin brought me."

"Ya yevo ubyu," I mutter. *I will kill him.*

She frowns. "What?"

"Nothing." I clamp down, needing to get away from her before I kiss her and get blood all over that perfect mouth. "We're going home."

As soon as I grab her hand, her warmth shoots through me like a drug. I help her out of the cage and slip into my sneakers and sweatshirt before heading for the exit.

She tries to twist away with the familiar knife-edge of sarcasm. "Oh, you're actually coming home this time? How nice of you."

"I did not think you noticed." I let out a dry laugh.

The way she stares at me, it's filled with a sliver of vulnerability.

Has she missed me the way I've missed her?

She hands me the cloth. "Hold that before you bleed all over the damn floor."

I take it because it matters to her. *I* matter to her.

And I want to matter.

I don't say goodbye to my brothers as we step outside, my car waiting for me at the curb. Our fingers brush when I help her inside, and instinctively, my arm curls around her, dragging her body flush against mine.

"Spasebo," I whisper, my mouth so close to hers I can feel every exhale warm against my lips.

"For what?" she breathes, her voice barely a sound.

"For taking care of me."

She doesn't answer, just nods, her eyes too full of emotion. Of questions. Of things neither of us can say.

I want to kiss her. I want to forget everything else exists and pull her under with me.

Reluctantly, I let her go, closing the door behind her with more force than necessary. As I round the car, my hand curls into a fist to keep from reaching for her again.

When the engine roars to life, I watch her through the corner of my eye while she stares out the window. And I know with bone-deep certainty, I've never wanted anything like I want her.

No matter how much I try to fight it, I know that whatever this is between us will not bend to rules or reason.

It will take what it wants, no matter the cost.

THIRTY-TWO

ALEKSEI

She walks in ahead of me as we step into the house, dropping her keys in the dish by the door. When she faces me, her eyes are sharp as they scan me, landing on the dark stain spreading beneath my sweatshirt.

"Kitchen. Now."

I lift a brow, mouth curving. "Are you giving me orders?"

"You're bleeding and won't see a doctor. I think it's in my job description to at least try to stop you from dying."

My gaze drops to her mouth, to the way her lips move when she takes charge. That authority in her voice does things to me I can barely contain. It takes everything in me not to spin her around and show her exactly what that tone does to me, right here against this wall.

"Stop looking at me like you're two seconds from tearing my clothes off and get your ass in the kitchen so I can patch you up."

My knuckles graze her jaw, lingering just long enough to feel the heat of her skin. "I like it when you get bossy, detka."

She draws in a shaky breath, and my heart squeezes too damn hard from how much I need her.

"This is not happening," she murmurs, peeling my hand off her. "Now be a good boy and listen to your wife for once."

My God, what she does to me.

I follow her into the kitchen, watching the way her hips sway, already picturing how she'll look with her hands pressed to the countertop and my name like a song from her lips. I ease into the kitchen chair as she moves across the room, disappearing into the hallway closet and coming back with the first aid kit, already snapping on gloves.

"You're my nurse now?"

She doesn't even look at me as she sets the kit on the table. "Someone has to be. It's obvious you can't be trusted to take care of yourself."

A low laugh rumbles out of me. "Is that right?"

She steps between my legs, standing so close I can smell the faint trace of her perfume.

I dip my head, brushing my mouth near her ear. "Tell me what else I can't be trusted with, moya ptichka."

She freezes. Just for a second. But it's enough to know she felt it too.

She dabs hydrogen peroxide on the cut and winces. "You need stitches."

"Much to your disappointment, I will live. Just clean it."

Something passes in her eyes, like maybe the idea of me dying doesn't please her as much as I thought. Wordlessly, she grabs antiseptic, cotton pads, and gauze, then gets to work. Her hands are careful and firm as she presses against the wound, and all I can think is that I would take a hundred more hits just to feel her touch me like this again.

"This will leave a nasty scar."

"Add it to the rest."

She pauses, eyes on mine, like there is something she wants to say, but she can't figure out how.

Is she wondering about the scars on my chest? Does she want to know how I got them?

Would I tell her?

Maybe I would, because a part of me does not want to hide myself from her anymore.

Once she finishes with the bandage, she steps back, arms crossing over her chest. "Hopefully you're still alive by the morning."

"I'm deeply moved that you seem to care so much."

She rolls her eyes. "Don't get too excited. I'm just not a cruel person."

"I'd say you're cruel." My hand rounds the small of her back and I grab her hips, pulling her up onto my lap until she's straddling me.

"How's that?" she whispers, throwing her arms over my shoulders.

"The mere sight of you, the feeling of you…" My lips brush hers, and a groan escapes me. "It feels like a punishment. The worst kind, Fiona."

"Aleksei…" My name on her lips feels like she's begging me for something I don't know if I'm ready for.

"You should go to sleep. You have work in the morning," I tell her.

But I can't seem to pull away, my fingers sliding into her hair. I want so badly to kiss her.

"Yeah, right… Work." She sucks in a shallow breath, slowly slipping her arms from my shoulders.

It hurts to let her go, but I do it anyway.

She slides off me and stands there for a moment, her eyes on mine, and something flickers across her face. "Good night, I guess."

She wants me to stop her. To join her. But I don't.

"Sleep well."

I curse myself for not getting up and following her as she scurries out of sight. Once she's gone, I sit there like an idiot.

It shouldn't feel like this. Like wanting her is a wound I keep digging into.

Why can't it be easy? How does Konstantin do it and remain true to who he is? I don't know if I have that in me. If I do, it's buried so deep under everything I've done, everything I am, that I'll never find it.

Something inside me locks up when she's near. It pushes back, makes me say things I don't mean, makes me cold when all I want is to hold her.

She thinks I've been avoiding her because I'm indifferent, but she's never been more wrong.

If anything, Fiona should be relieved. Because I don't know how to love someone without destroying it.

And she deserves better than that. She deserves better than me.

FIONA

I don't expect him to follow me upstairs, but some stupid, naïve part waits for the sound of his footsteps anyway.

They never come, though.

It's better this way. That's what I tell myself as I strip out of my clothes and pull on one of the silk camisoles he bought me.

The silence stretches around me as I sit at the edge of the bed and stare at the wall, the corner of my vision catching on the faint outline of the open door. I hate how much I care. That I noticed the way he didn't wince when I pressed down on his wound, the way he didn't even flinch when I cleaned it. Like he's used to the pain. Like it's a friend he grew up with.

God, what kind of childhood leaves someone like that?

I pull my knees to my chest, wrapping my arms around them as I rest my chin on top. His words replay in my head.

It feels like a punishment.

Is that what I am to him? Or was that his twisted way of saying I matter?

I should be angry. I *am* angry. He's been cold, distant, shutting me out in every way that matters. Then he says things like that?

Kirill's words echo again.

He used to. A lot. But he hasn't in a while, not until you.

Why? Why did he start fighting? What do I have to do with that? Did he start fighting to numb whatever feelings he's hiding behind?

I turn onto my side and pull the covers up, trying to force myself to sleep. But my mind won't shut off. I can't stop thinking about the way Konstantin looks at Emilia, how he touches her like she's everything to him.

I want that. So badly.

I don't know when I fall asleep, but I do. Eventually.

And the next thing I feel is the shift of the mattress beneath me, the faintest pull of weight as the bed dips behind me. I stir, disoriented, heart kicking up once before I hear it: his voice, low and rough and barely more than a whisper.

"Sleep. I'm here."

Aleksei.

Quiet surrender washes over me as a smile winds up my mouth and I sink into him, too afraid to open my eyes to see if I'm dreaming. The heat of him sinks into my back, hesitation in his breath before his arm curls around my waist, and I know this is real. It has to be.

He exhales against the back of my neck, his nose brushing the curve of my shoulder like he needs to remind himself I'm real. That I haven't disappeared. When his palm pulls me tighter, my throat thickens as I wonder if he came here because he couldn't stay away or because he knew I was hoping he would.

And whether it even makes a difference.

I wake up reaching for him.

It's automatic now, this foolish little twitch of hope that he stayed. That maybe, just maybe, last night meant something.

But the sheets are empty. Of course he isn't there. Why would anything change with Aleksei?

I lie there for a few more seconds staring at the ceiling, trying to shake the tight knot building in my chest.

It's stupid. This is stupid. Clearly there's never going to be anything real between us.

I seriously need to go back to the days when I wanted to stab him in the eye with a fork. Those were much simpler times.

I drag myself out of bed and into the shower, the water hot and satisfying against my skin, trying to wash away the memory of his touch. But it clings. Like everything else about him.

When I arrive at work, the day moves in slow motion. I can't focus at the meeting. Can't focus in court. Even when Dana starts gushing about the new guy she's seeing over lunch, I'm only half there, nodding in the right places and pretending to listen while my mind replays the same damn reel on repeat.

Him. Last night. The way I felt when he touched me.

Why am I like this? Why do I keep hoping he'll give me an ounce of something real? Every time I think I see it, he tears it away like it was never there.

By the time I'm heading back to the office, I'm ready to scream into a pillow or maybe set something on fire. Preferably him.

My phone buzzes on my desk, and when I find his name there, my heart gives a little kick.

Great...

> **ALEKSEI**
>
> Dinner. You and me. Tonight at 7.

That's it?

No hello. No apology for disappearing. Just a command. Like I'm a possession he left on the nightstand and expects to be waiting, smiling and compliant.

I roll my eyes so hard, I'm surprised they stay in my skull.

> **FIONA**
>
> I'm not hungry.

The response comes fast, like he's been waiting for my reply.

> **ALEKSEI**
>
> You will be, Mrs. Marinova. Trust me.

I snort.

> **FIONA**
>
> That so? What are you going to do, force me to the table? Because the only way I'd ever sit at the same table as you is if you tied me up and gagged me.

I hit send before I can second-guess it, and just as I'm grinning at my own audacity, his reply pops up.

> **ALEKSEI**
>
> This dinner is sounding more and more appealing by the second.

I scoff. Of course he turns it into something dirty. That's the only damn thing he responds to.

> **FIONA**
>
> There will be no dinner.

> You'll be eating alone, as usual. Feel free to choke on your overpriced steak.

There's a pause. Three dots blink on the screen like he's typing. Then they vanish.

Good. Let him stew in it the same way I've stewed in his absence every night since he started this stupid game of avoidance.

I toss the phone onto my desk and spin my chair to face the window. I tell myself again that I'm not going. No matter what he says or does.

He wanted distance? Well, here it is, baby.

But a part of me, some irrational part, wants him to drag me to that stupid table and tie me up just to prove he can.

THIRTY-THREE

ALEKSEI

I skipped the last meeting of the day. Investors flew in, so the board expected me to stay, but I left anyway.

Because tonight matters more. *She* matters more.

Fiona doesn't know it yet, but we *are* having dinner together. No isn't on the table. She will be there.

The second I step into the house, I kick off my shoes and shrug off my coat, my hands already itching to find her. I scan the kitchen and den, but she's nowhere to be found, even though I know she's home.

"Gde ona?" I ask one of my men. *Where is she?*

"Naverkhu." *Upstairs.*

I take the stairs two at a time, and when I open our bedroom door, she's stretched out on the bed, a book in hand, wearing tiny athletic shorts and a thin white tank top that leaves nothing to the imagination.

She was wearing those clothes with my men around? She's going to pay for that.

When she notices me come in, her lips quirk, but her eyes don't go to mine.

God, she maddens me. And when she's close, everything rattles inside me. It's like I want to say a thousand things, but I do not have the language for any of it.

"Is that how we are playing this, detka?"

She does not glance up immediately. When she finally does, there is a small, careful lift at the corner of her mouth that isn't quite a smile.

"I'm not playing anything. I'm simply declining your offer."

She picks her book back up, eyes moving across the page like she's actually reading it. But I know better. I move closer, closing the space between us until I'm right beside her.

"Come eat with me," I say, letting the words slip into the quiet like a dare. "I won't ask again."

"No, thank you." Her grin widens as she flips her page. "I'm good right here. Thanks for asking, though."

She pats my arm, a clear dismissal, but my skin is too busy burning from her touch to care.

I drag a finger up her bare thigh. "You want to make this difficult, don't you?"

"Of course not." Her lips twitch, that almost-smile turning into a dare of its own, like she's testing just how far she can push me.

It's adorable. Infuriating. Addictive.

"Lucky for you, I happen to like difficult."

She barely looks up before I hook an arm around her waist and flip her over my shoulder. She yelps, a burst of startled laughter escaping her. The sound cracks something wide open inside me, pure and bright and unguarded.

"What are you doing?" She half laughs, half gasps, pounding a playful fist against my back.

"Taking you to dinner." I adjust my grip as I stride down the hall.

"Konstantin said I needed to be a proper husband."

"This is definitely *not* what he had in mind! Put me down!"

"Net. You said the only way you'd sit with me was if I tied you up. I'm a man who takes requests seriously."

Her laughter cuts off in a disbelieving sound. "That was not a request."

"I think it was." I give her ass a firm slap, satisfied by the way she jolts. "I think you wanted this."

Once we reach the dining room, I set her down on the chair. The table glows under the soft halo of candlelight, crystal glasses catching the amber flicker of flame. A full meal is laid out—steak, potatoes, roasted vegetables—and for a moment, she just blinks, the fight in her eyes softening to confusion.

"You arranged all this?" she asks, breathless.

And seeing her happy, it makes me want to do this for her over and over again.

"I told you we would have dinner." I loosen my tie, rolling it slowly between my fingers.

Her eyes follow the movement, and just like that, the energy between us shifts. Disbelief melts into hunger, the sharp edge of her defiance dulled by something far more dangerous.

"I wasn't aware this was what you meant." She straightens her tank top, trying to regain her footing. "It feels like a date."

"What if it was?" I approach her slowly, tie in my grasp. "Would you say yes?"

I tip her chin up, her mouth so close I can sense her breath on mine.

"Answer me." My lips stroke hers, and she groans.

Blyat. I was a fool for ever thinking I could resist such a tempting creature.

Bringing her hands to her lap, I wrap the tie around them. The silk glides over her skin as I knot it tight enough for her to feel it.

I lower my head until my mouth grazes the curve of her neck. "You still haven't answered my question."

"That's because you haven't earned my answer."

All the blood rushes to my cock. My hand finds her throat, her pulse ricocheting against my palm.

"I will earn it."

She shrugs one shoulder, mouth curving into something wicked. "We'll see."

My thumbs drags across her bottom lip. "You're here. That's a start."

"You didn't give me a choice."

"That's because you haven't given me one either."

"What does that mean?" she whispers.

My knuckles drag down the soft slope of her cheek, my muscles twisted tight. I want to say things to her that I have never said to anyone. They're there, heavy on the tip of my tongue, begging to be spoken. But I don't know if she wants to hear them. If she feels the same way.

We are so different. For this to work, she has to accept who I am, what I do, and I don't know if she will ever be ready for that.

"It means you make it impossible to think about anything but you."

Her chest rises and falls. "Is that why you've been ignoring me?"

"Yes."

Something stirs in her eyes.

I fill a plate with food, the scent of garlic and seared steak rising between us. She watches as I cut a piece and set it carefully on her plate, then lift the fork toward her lips. The candlelight casts her skin in gold and shadow, and for a moment, I just stare, remembering the first time I saw her. The steel in her spine, the fire in her eyes.

She stunned me then. She still does.

She leans forward slowly, brushing her mouth to the edge of the fork as she takes the bite. Her lips part, tongue flicking briefly against the prongs, and blyat, it lights me up from the inside.

"I'll be a good girl," she murmurs after swallowing, glancing down at her restrained wrists. "You can let me go."

I smirk, leaning in. "We'll see how good you can be after I'm through with you."

"What does that even mean?"

The corner of my mouth kicks up.

She lets out a breathy laugh. "You're insane, you know that?"

Her cheeks flush, desire sparking in her gaze.

"Da." I grind my jaw as I stare at her full lips. "But only about you."

"Mm, I don't think that's true. I would say you're objectively insane."

A rough, genuine laugh escapes me. "And what does that say about you, Ms. Prosecutor?" I cut into the steak. "Getting turned on by an insane man such as myself."

She lets out a small huff. "I'm not."

I lift another piece to her mouth, my eyes trained on hers as I press it between her lips. "Don't deny it."

The back of my hand drags up her knee, her thighs clamped shut before I part them harshly.

"I'm not. You just don't like hearing the truth."

I chuckle, brushing a fingertip through her center and feeling the warmth through her shorts. "You're not wearing any panties…"

She gives a small shake of her head. My fingers strain, pinching her clit just enough to make her shudder with a broken moan, and the sound goes straight to my cock.

I tsk softly, letting my gaze trail over every inch of her. "And you thought dressing like this, practically naked while my men are stationed all over the house, wouldn't earn you a heavy punishment?"

My palm massages her through the fabric, slow circles that make her hips jerk and her eyes roll back, her body already giving me what

I want.

"I…I didn't think you'd care."

"I care, Fiona." My hand slides into her shorts, discovering her soaked. "Mm, look what I just found…"

"Oh fuck…" She gyrates on the chair as I toy with her, sliding inside her before rubbing her clit with her own wetness.

When she closes her eyes, I stop. "You know the rules, detka. Close your eyes and you don't come. Keep them open and Daddy will reward you."

"Aleksei, please…"

I laugh. "I didn't mean you'd get your reward now." I squeeze her clit, and she groans. "Silly girl."

"You're gonna drag this out, aren't you?"

"Of course I am." My grin widens as I slip out of her and bring my fingers to my mouth, tasting her with a low, satisfied grunt.

Her cheeks flush, her nipples hard and visible through her tank top. But it still isn't enough for me. I pick up an unused steak knife and drag it toward her chest, and she watches every inch of the blade as I slice through her shirt, leaving only enough fabric to hang across her stomach. Her breasts spill free, and a growl breaks out of me, my erection growing stiffer as I take in all of her.

"Ti moya." *You're mine.*

She gasps when I catch one hardened tip between my fingers, rolling it until a cry slips out of her, and then I give the other the same attention. The knife lowers to her shorts, and I pull at them, making a hole with the tip before I slowly start to cut at the center.

She holds her breath, her eyes widening.

"Better stay still. I wouldn't want to wreck such a perfect cunt."

Her breathing turns uneven, a mix of fear and desire trembling through her as I let the blade cut just enough to give me access. I grab the torn fabric with both hands and rip it wider, exposing her completely, her pussy slick and open to my greedy stare.

"Now, how about you finish eating?"

"I don't want to eat. Please, Aleksei. It hurts."

"Mm…" My finger flicks her center. "A little pain never killed anyone." I slice into another piece of steak. "Now open up and swallow."

She obeys, her eyes holding mine as she chews and swallows, all the while the fingers of my free hand sink deep inside her, curling exactly where she needs it.

She cries out, the words breaking from her in a desperate rush. "Oh my God… I need this, please."

"I know you do." My lips brush hers, my teeth catching on her lower one in a slow bite. "But you don't deserve it yet."

Picking up a piece of potato, I feed it to her, keeping her mouth busy while my other hand toys with her, teasing her, dragging her right to the edge only to rip it away again. Her body is ragged with need, every breath uneven, her cunt aching for relief. When I finally push three fingers inside her, I drive deeper and harder, watching her brows knit and her mouth fall open on sounds she can't even control.

She's the most incredible thing I've ever tasted, and she's all mine.

Sliding out of her, I bring my fingertips to her lips. "Taste what I do to you. Feel how drenched you get for me. Every drop is mine."

She whimpers as she sucks my fingers clean, her irises locked on me the entire time. My hand slides into her hair, gripping tight as I kiss her, tongues tangling in a hungry, messy clash. Then I pull back and push my chair away from the table.

"Get on your knees and suck every inch of my cock."

Her eyes widen for a heartbeat, that flash of shock making me throb before she rises and slowly sinks to her knees in front of me while I shove her chair out of the way. She waits there as I undo my belt, the clanking of the buckle only making her shudder before I unzip my pants and release myself.

Fisting the crown, I squeeze tight, using my other hand to tug on her hair, dragging her closer. "I want to feel the back of your throat, moya ptichka. Only then will you get your reward."

Pushing her down my length, I control the pace. When she groans against me, taking me deeper, my head falls back, a rush of pleasure stealing the edges of my thoughts until the whole world blurs.

This is heaven. Or hell. I can't tell the difference anymore. All I know is when I'm with her, nothing else matters.

My hand tightens around her hair. "Ty menya unichtozhila." *You've destroyed me.*

She goes harder as soon as I say those words, like she somehow understood them, how deeply I meant them. She takes all of me, inch by inch, right down to my soul, like she's pulling it out of my body and keeping it for herself.

There's no me without her. Not anymore.

When she swirls her tongue over the piercing at my tip, I'm lost. With a grunt, I shoot down her throat, grabbing the back of her head and pinning her there as I finish. And watching her gag and her eyes water makes me want to come all over again.

Roughly, I pull her up and bend her over the table, my fingers thrusting inside her, my grip firm on her throat as I lean in close, my mouth at her ear.

"Ot menya nichego ne ostalos. I ya voz'mu ot tebya vsyu." *There's nothing left of me. And I will take everything from you.*

My fingers curl and ram so deep she cries out, spilling all over my hand before I slide out and thrust my cock so roughly the table rattles. I clasp her hair and increase the pace, her body quivering beneath me, her cries echoing.

This feeling, this woman… She's everything. And I never want it to end.

"Oh God, Aleksei! I'm coming again."

Her head turns to me, her eyes taking me in while she sucks me dry as I give her all of me. Everything I have belongs to her, and I would kill my own father for this if he were alive. Because no one, and I mean *no one*, will take her away from me.

With a sharp snap of my hips, I empty inside her, my arm rounding her stomach to keep myself buried. To make sure she doesn't leak out a drop.

And right here and now, I hope I get her pregnant. Because I want that. Blyat, in some twisted way, I want that with her.

When her body finally stills, her exhales jagged, I press a slow kiss to her shoulder blade.

"I think the whole house heard me," she says with a breathless laugh.

"Good. Then there will be no question about who you belong to."

"I don't—"

"Try it. Try to deny you're mine and I will fuck you all over again just to prove how wrong you are." I graze my teeth against her shoulder, and she lets out a soft, helpless sound, pressing her ass into me like she can't help it.

My palm slaps her hard, and she jolts.

"Give me a minute and I'll be hard again."

She pops a brow, her laughter the sweetest medicine. "I wasn't asking for more."

My fingers slide into her hair, and I pull her mouth to mine. "Like hell you weren't."

I kiss her slowly, letting it all consume me and take me to a place I never thought I would go. When she pulls back, her gaze sinks into mine, undoing me all over again.

"How am I supposed to make it upstairs looking like a lion tore off my clothes?"

I chuckle as I flip her around and tear off her shirt, pulling her shorts down and letting both pieces of clothing fall to the floor. Confusion settles in her gaze, but not an ounce of her grows shy.

I like that. A lot.

"How is this helping matters?" Her mouth lifts at the corner.

"You'll see, my impatient wife."

My fingers reach for the buttons of my shirt, slowly undoing each one. She watches every movement, her eyes heavy-lidded, and the longer she looks at me like that, the hungrier I become. When the shirt is free, I guide her arms through the sleeves and button it just enough to cover her before I zip myself and lift her into my arms.

Together, we make our way up the stairs, climbing until we reach the bedroom. When I lay her down, she gives me a look that says she's afraid I'm about to walk out, but I know I'm not going anywhere tonight.

I strip off my pants, keeping my boxers on, and grab two T-shirts from the drawer. I pull mine over my head, then help her out of my dress shirt before slipping the soft cotton over her. I regret it the second it's on. It's like a crime to hide that much beauty.

"You're staying?" she asks quietly.

I nod and slide in beside her. "I am."

Her eyes warm, and something in my chest warms with them. She lets out a sigh and sinks against me, her head resting over my heart.

I hold her close, wishing I could find a way to prove my father wrong. Wishing I could figure out how to stay the man I am and still keep her.

THIRTY-FOUR

FIONA

My body aches in the best way. I should hate it: the bruised hips, the faint burn in my thighs, the way my lips still feel swollen from his mouth.

But I don't. I like it. I like all of it.

I reach for him without thinking, my arm sliding across the sheets like he's mine to hold.

But he isn't there. And the warmth he left behind feels cold at the same time.

Sitting up, I glance at the clock. Seven. On a Saturday. There's no meeting this early, is there? So where the hell did he go?

I tug on leggings and a hoodie and make my way to the bathroom, not bothering to look in the mirror. I already know what I'll see. The flush on my neck. The guilt in my eyes.

We keep doing this dance. His hands on me, his voice in my ear, the way he looks at me like I'm some kind of prize he can't decide if he wants to cherish or ruin. Then he disappears, acting like none of it meant a thing.

By the time I make it downstairs, Galya is already setting out breakfast, the warm smell of eggs and buttery pastries filling the kitchen.

"Good morning, moya dorogaya," she says warmly.

"Morning. I'm going to take my tea and a danish out back. I just want some air."

She doesn't ask questions, just hands me a to-go cup and folds napkins around the danish like she's packing me off for school. One of Aleksei's men appears and sets my sneakers beside me without being asked. Having these people do everything for me is strange, but I can't say it's entirely awful.

"Thanks. Do you know where Aleksei went?"

He shrugs. "He left early. Didn't say."

Of course he didn't.

I pretend it doesn't bother me, that my stomach didn't just cave in a little. Instead, I head around the back of the house, moving past the tall hedges toward the garden that stretches beyond the pool. I follow the path slowly, chewing my danish while the tea burns a warm line down my throat with every swallow.

What the hell are we even doing? This thing between us, it's not built to last. I'm a prosecutor. He's…Aleksei. And even if I wanted to pretend that we exist outside that, the world wouldn't let us. Sooner or later, someone will find out.

Then what? What would I even say? That I married a man who made my knees shake and my morals blur?

I toss the empty cup and napkin into the trash can by the bench and turn to head back. But when I do, he's standing right in front of me, like I somehow wished him here.

For a second, I'm sure I'm imagining it: him shirtless, sweatpants slung low on his hips, hair damp and clinging to his forehead as if he ran miles just to get to me.

But when he takes a step forward, I know he's real.

"Can we talk?" I ask, releasing an exhausted sigh.

He nods. "Sure."

I start heading along the edge of the pool, and he falls into step beside me. Glancing at him, I attempt to find the right words while he watches silently.

"Look, I've had some time to think, and…"

"Yes?"

Just say it. He probably feels the exact same way, or he wouldn't be ignoring you the way he has been.

"Whatever this is between us…it's not going to work."

He stops, forcing me to face him.

"Is that so?" His mouth quirks like this is some challenge.

"That's right. I know you know it too. We're two completely different people. And I know for you, this whole thing started as some twisted way to screw with me, and maybe it backfired. Or maybe it didn't. I don't know." I laugh, drained from it all. "But I can't do this anymore, Aleksei. If you want to punish my parents, go ahead. They'll survive. I'll survive. But I won't stay married to someone who can't decide if he wants me or not."

His features don't so much as twitch, but something flares behind his eyes.

"I'm serious." I take a step toward him, my hand closing around his forearm.

He's warm. Solid. Real in a way that makes me feel alive. And it makes the next words hurt even more.

"If all of this was just about power, then fine. You win. But just let me go. Divorce me."

He doesn't answer.

"Please, Aleksei. I'm not built for this."

He tilts his head, that maddening smirk playing at the edges of his mouth. "I like it when you beg."

God. That smugness. I want to slap it off his face. Or kiss him, which is worse.

"I'm not joking," I snap. "You know this isn't working. Don't you want to be with someone who actually makes you happy? Someone you want to wake up next to?"

He doesn't say anything, and that silence tears something open in me.

I swallow past the sharp ache rising in my throat. "Because that's not going to be me."

It nearly kills me to say that out loud. But it's the truth. It has to be.

I try to soften it. "Maybe we can be friends."

"Friends?" he repeats, as if I've just told him I want to become a nun.

"Why not?" I let out a weak, humorless laugh. "We're practically family anyway. Emilia's like a sister to me. Konstantin is your brother. This could work. We don't have to hate each other. We just don't have what it takes to make whatever this is work."

He tilts his head. "Marriage."

"What?"

"This thing between us," he says. "It is a marriage."

"It's really not."

"Oh, I disagree."

I fold my arms across my chest. "Most people—normal people— they meet, date for a while, fall in love. Then one of them gets down on one knee and asks the other to spend forever with them. You know what I got? A threat. A contract. A goddamn ultimatum. So no, this is anything but a marriage."

His hand comes up to my cheek, and the moment his palm touches my skin, it throws me completely off-balance. Because the look in his eyes is so raw and unguarded, it breaks right through me.

"Ya ne mogu zhit bez tebya," he says, the words slipping out in a low, rough murmur that carries too much meaning for me to pretend I didn't hear it.

"What?" My heart hammers.

His gaze grows heavy, almost aching, as his fingers slide into my hair, guiding me closer with a tenderness that makes it hard to ignore. "You're a pain in my ass."

But the softness in his face doesn't match the words, and I'm almost sure that isn't what he said. I try to say the words to myself over and over so I can look them up later, but I know I'll forget.

"I'm not joking," I whisper, even though every part of me leans toward him instead of away.

"Neither am I." His voice deepens with something so honest and painfully real that it settles in my chest and leaves me struggling to remember why I ever thought pulling away was possible.

No. Do not get sucked back into this. It's what happens every time.

"I'm done. Okay? I said what I said, and that's it. I'm not letting you turn this into something else. I'm going inside. Have a good day."

I step back, but the edge of my sneaker clips the stone, my foot twisting out from under me before I even understand what's happening. I gasp, arms shooting out for balance.

Then I hit the water. The warmth crashes over my head and steals the breath from my lungs. The moment I break the surface, I register a loud splash behind me.

"Fiona!"

I push the hair out of my face, gasping just as Aleksei surfaces beside me.

"Are you okay?"

I nod, still gathering air, and his grip tightens as the water moves around us in gentle waves.

"If you wanted to escape me that badly, you just had to say so. Jumping in is a bit too extreme, Ms. Prosecutor."

"What can I say? When it comes to you, I'm prone to making bad decisions."

"I like being your bad decision."

Before I can react, he pins me against the side of the pool, his body pressing into mine, arms planted on either side of me, caging me in. The water ripples around us, but everything inside me is still and electric all at once, like the entire world has narrowed to the heat of him, the closeness, the way he fits against me as if he was always meant to be here.

His eyes darken as they search mine, and even though we're dripping wet, it's as though I'm burning from the inside out.

"You can't say things like that to me." My fingers brush the edge of his jaw.

Droplets cling to his skin and slide down the strong lines of his face, and watching them makes something twist deep inside me.

"Why not?" His thumb traces over my bottom lip with a slow, careful sweep that sets every nerve in my body on edge.

"Because…" I swallow hard. "Because I'll start to think you actually care about me."

His expression shifts in an instant, something sharp flickering through his eyes. A mix of pain, disbelief, and a quiet anger that seems aimed entirely at himself.

"You think I don't care?" The question comes out strained, as if it drags something painful with it.

I nod, but it's small, hesitant, barely a movement at all. He exhales, and the sound that breaks from him feels torn from somewhere deep inside, too vulnerable for a man like him to disguise. Then he lets out a laugh, but it's hollow, the kind that carries nothing but exhaustion and defeat.

"You're all I think about," he says quietly. "All goddamn day and night."

His hands rise to cradle my face, his thumbs pressing gently to my cheeks as if trying to ground himself in the feeling of me.

"You've become the center of my world, Fiona."

What?

My heartbeats stumble in my chest.

He leans in until his forehead rests against mine, like he needs the connection just to stay upright. And when his eyes open to meet mine again, the truth in them is so clear, it sends a shiver through me.

"I don't know what to do with that," he admits on a sigh, the words almost trembling. "You don't understand. I've never felt anything like this before. I wasn't allowed to."

The words crack something inside me. He's never looked more human than he does right now.

"But you…" he continues. "You're different. I did not want you to be. I fought it. I tried to control it, control you, but I couldn't. I can't. And I accept it now."

His lips touch the corner of my mouth, a soft, aching brush that loosens something deep inside me even as I try to hold myself together.

"I want you," he says, the words coming out rough, almost breaking. "I want you with everything I am. I don't want to lose you."

He stays close, his breath warm against my lips, and my eyes sting under the weight of what he's giving me so openly. Then he pulls back just enough to see my face, as if he needs to watch every glimmer of my reaction.

"So please, tell me you want this too." His next words are barely a whisper. "I don't know how to do this, Fiona. I wasn't raised to love. I wasn't built for it. But I will do whatever you need, however you need it. Just…don't walk away. Teach me."

I can't breathe. I can't think. I can't reconcile this man with the one who once threatened everything I cared about. My gaze drops, completely overwhelmed, and he lifts my chin with gentle fingers, guiding my eyes back to his.

"Look at me, Fiona. I'm yours. I always have been."

Something inside me slices wide open, and before I can stop

myself, I'm already reaching for him, closing the space in a rush of need I can't contain. I crash my mouth to his with a desperation that feels like stepping off a cliff and somehow surviving the fall.

My hands tangle in his hair, my legs wrapping around his waist while water sloshes around us as he lifts me against him. I don't want space. I don't want distance. I want to feel him, all of him, pressed against me like he's part of my body. Like maybe if I hold on tight enough, he won't disappear when the sun comes up.

His hands grip my hips, and we kiss like it's the only language either of us understands. There's nothing careful about it. It's fire meeting gasoline. Violent, needy, real.

I've spent so long running from this man, hating him, fearing him. But right now, all I want is him holding me like I'm his lifeline.

And maybe, just maybe, he's mine too.

ALEKSEI

Her laughter bounces off the stone path as I hoist her over my shoulder like she weighs nothing. She squeals, telling me to put her down.

"Net." My voice rumbles low as I grip the backs of her thighs to keep her steady. "This will teach you to walk away from me."

I smack her ass hard enough to make her yelp, then she laughs louder. That sound—her laughter, wild and unguarded—has become my favorite thing in this world.

I carry her through the back doors and down the hallway, past a startled Galya who makes a sound of disapproval and mutters something about soaking wet floors. I ignore her. My entire focus is on the woman in my arms as I bring her into a guest bathroom.

She's still laughing when I kick the door closed behind us and set her down carefully, fingers curling around her waist to keep her close. Her hair is dripping, her hoodie clinging to her in a way that does things to me. She tilts her head up, eyes wide and uncertain, lips parted like she's trying to understand whatever is happening between us.

I'm not sure either. I have never said anything like that to any other woman. But with her, all I do is *feel*.

"Davay," I say, tugging the soaked hoodie over her head. *Come on.* "Let's warm you up."

Her arms lift, letting me strip her bare. I peel away every piece of fabric. Her breathing stutters, and I can't tell if it's the cold or me that has her shaking. She bites her lip, eyes never leaving me as I step out of my sweats and leave them on the tile.

When I turn on the shower, steam begins to fill the space, spiraling upward in soft clouds. She steps under the water without a word, and I follow, the heat closing around us. The water runs over her in steady, warm streams, sliding through her hair and down the curve of her neck. She tilts her head back, eyes drifting shut, and I'm not sure she realizes what that simple movement does to me, how it pulls something deep inside my chest.

Reaching for the shampoo, I pour a small amount into my palm and guide her to turn away from me. My fingers slip into her hair, spreading the lather slowly, working it through each strand with a kind of patience I have never given anyone in my life.

The warmth of her, the quiet of the water around us, makes me want this moment to last for as long as she will allow it. She releases the softest sound when my fingertips glide across her scalp, and the sound shoots through me. She relaxes back, her head resting against me.

"That feels nice." Her words drift in a hazy, content sigh.

"I want to make you feel good."

A faint smile curves her lips. "I bet you say that to all the girls."

"Nikogda."

Her eyes open, lifting to meet mine. "What does that mean?"

"It means never," I tell her, cupping her cheek.

"Oh…" The word comes out shallow, almost shaky.

She looks at me like she wants to say something more, something she is not sure she should.

But I told her the truth. Every woman before her was nothing. A forgettable night or a power play. Maybe it started out that way with her too, but it's more now.

I rinse the shampoo out before adding conditioner to her ends, working it through her long hair, and she leans against me again. Water rushes down her back as I rinse her strands, my palms trailing down her shoulders, her arms. She's soft and wet and perfect, and it terrifies me how much I want to protect that softness. How much I need it.

My knuckles trail slowly down her spine, and she shivers at the touch. "I can't remember what life felt like before you."

She goes still for a moment, then turns to face me, water gliding down her skin. "Was it better or worse?"

Reaching for the soap, I take my time working it between my hands, wanting to trace every inch of her with the care I've never shown anyone. "Would it make me weak to admit I prefer my life with you in it?"

A soft smile lifts her lips, her lashes lowering as I smooth the lather over her. Her fingertips slide up my back, and the simple touch quiets the dark restlessness inside me.

"Not as much as it makes me to admit I've fallen for a man I had no business falling for."

I let out a growl, backing her up against the wall. "We are two very complicated people, aren't we, Ms. Prosecutor?"

My cock grows thicker at the sight of her brows knitting, the way her beaded tips beg for my tongue.

"We are…" She lifts to me, nipping my lower lip, and I curse under my breath. "But maybe a little complication makes life worth living."

In an instant, my mouth is on hers, the kiss hard and demanding. She tastes like everything I have never deserved and everything I wish I was worthy of.

When we finally break, her fingertips brush along the rough stubble of my jaw, and my eyes fall shut as I take in the warmth of her touch, the way it sinks straight through my skin. Every time my hands move over her, I feel it: the subtle tremble in her muscles, the small catch in her breath. Her body responds to me in ways she does not seem fully aware of, and it pulls something fierce out of me. It makes me want to test the limits of that quiet trust she keeps giving me, to see just how far it might reach.

I kneel slightly, picking up the soap and gliding it along the backs of her legs, behind her knees, between her thighs. Her gaze is on me, strong and unwavering, like every part of her always is.

When I'm done, she takes the soap from me as she starts working it over my chest, dragging the bar down the center, then using her palms to spread the suds. My muscles tighten as she traces along the edges of the scars on my chest, cracking open something buried deep.

"Where'd you get these?" Her voice is quiet. Careful. Like she's afraid of the answer.

I watch her hand. Not because I don't know what to say, but because I'm not sure I've ever said it out loud.

"My father," I finally answer, and the words taste like rust. "He liked to play games."

She lifts her eyes to mine, and I see it there: pity.

"Games? What kind of games?"

I let out a dry laugh. "Loyalty. Strength. Obedience. Whatever he decided we needed to prove that day."

She doesn't interrupt, just listens, her hands still moving like they can erase the past.

"I was maybe six the first time he made me hold a knife to my brother's palm. Said if I didn't do it, he would hurt him worse. Said it was love. That proving you would sacrifice anything for your family was the highest honor."

"Jesus, Aleksei."

"I could not do it." My head shakes from the memory. "So Konstantin took the punishment for me. I was always a failure in our father's eyes."

"No." Her emotions twist in her features as she curls her body closer to mine, arms wrapping around me like she's trying to shield me from something she never could. "You're not a failure. He was." Her hand holds my cheek, and I ache for it. "He wasn't a father to you. That's not love."

I lean into her touch, like I'm surrendering into something bigger. "I swore if I ever had children, I would never be like him. Never raise my hand, never make love something they had to earn by bleeding for it."

I pause, pressing my forehead to hers, breathing her in like she's the only thing tethering me to the present.

"You're the only person I've ever told that to."

"Why me?" she asks, barely above a whisper.

"Because I think…you're the only person I've ever trusted to hold it."

Tears fill her eyes as she rises on her feet and presses a kiss to my mouth. "I'm so sorry."

My palm slides into the back of her neck, gripping tight. "There's nothing to be sorry for." I kiss her temple. "This is the life I had, and I accepted it a long time ago. But what I can't accept…is you continuing to think I don't care."

A small inhale shudders through her.

"I did push you away, yes, but only out of necessity. More for my own survival. Or for the survival of the man I thought I had to be."

"And now?"

I pull back just enough to see her face, my fingers sliding through her hair. "Now, I don't know what our future looks like. I don't know if we even get one. But I want to try. I want you to tell me you want that too, moya ptichka."

A smile appears through her tears. "This whole thing is crazy, and I don't know how the hell we can make it work, but I want to. I want you, Aleksei."

My chest tightens in a way I can't explain.

I'm used to violence. Power. Revenge. But not this. Not the hope that I have a future.

She stares at me like she's seeing past the darkness, and my lips meet hers softly, carefully. Like she's breakable and I'm learning how not to destroy everything I touch.

"What does moya ptichka mean?" she asks as she pulls away.

I brush a damp strand of hair from her face. "It means my little bird."

She tilts her head. "Why that?"

"Because you're the only thing I've ever wanted to cage and set free at the same time."

Her eyes glisten. "That's beautiful. And a little terrifying."

"I'm not a good man, Fiona." My knuckles slope down her cheek. "But you make me want to be."

She lays her head against my chest, right over the scars, and I hold her there, wondering if this is what it feels like to be forgiven for sins you haven't stopped committing.

I want to tell her I'm falling in love with her. But the words don't come. Not yet. The ghosts in my head still whisper too loud.

But maybe…she's the one who will silence them.

THIRTY-FIVE

FIONA

Aleksei kneels in front of me, towel in hand. The cotton is soft against my skin, but it's the way he touches me that steals the air from my lungs. Slow, purposeful, like every part of me matters.

Neither of us speaks. We don't need to. There's a silence between us that hums with understanding, like something unspoken has shifted and we both felt it. I watch the movement of his hands as he dries the water from my thighs, my stomach, my arms, taking his time like he's savoring this.

He helps me slip into a robe and ties it gently, then reaches for a towel and wraps it around his waist. I wonder if he feels the same pull in his chest that I do. If it aches the way mine does when he looks at me.

Tugging on the belt, he drags me up against him, his mouth falling to mine, and it's not possessive like before. It's quiet and beautiful, the kind of kiss that rewrites everything you thought you knew. He lifts me into his arms, and I don't hesitate, curling into him like he's my home.

We move up the stairs, each step carrying us further into something neither of us can undo.

Once we reach the bedroom, he sets me gently on my feet, his hands sliding to my waist and drawing me in until there is no space left between us. I reach for his towel at the same moment his fingers find the knot of my robe.

The towel slips from his hips first, the fabric falling away with a quiet hush, and he stands there completely bare…but not just his body. He's letting me see him. All of him. And I don't want to look away.

As his chest rises, my eyes trace over skin I've already memorized: scars, muscle, tension barely leashed beneath the surface. There's a crackle in his gaze when it meets mine, but he doesn't rush. He just brushes his fingers against the tie at my waist.

The robe loosens and slips away, pooling softly around my ankles, and his hands settle at my hips while his gaze moves slowly over me, as if he's cataloging everything he thought he'd never be allowed to keep.

But for the first time, I'm letting him keep it. All of it. Every part I used to hide.

He steps in, closing the gap between us, and when our skin meets, the heat of it sweeps through me in a way that's almost overwhelming. It's not rushed or frantic, but something deeper. Something like certainty settling into my bones.

My arms lift around his shoulders, pulling him even closer until there is no distance left between us. Nothing but the thrum of two hearts beating far too hard.

When he kisses me, it's quiet at first, gathering strength, building into something deeper and far more powerful. I meet him willingly, because I want to. Because I trust him. His hand cradles the back of my neck as he takes me backward, his mouth still on mine. When the backs of my knees hit the bed, he stops, his ragged exhales fanning across my face.

"You feel like home, moya ptichka," he says against my lips, laying me on the bed without waiting for me to say something back.

I don't even have the words except that I feel the same, though a part of me is still afraid to say it out loud.

He climbs over me, every line of his body fitting perfectly against mine. He kisses down my jaw and across my collarbone, his hands roaming like he's staking a claim. His mouth finds the curve of my breast, and I gasp as his tongue circles before his lips close around my nipple.

Pleasure sparks, but beneath it, something warmer catches fire. Something like need, yet reaching far deeper than anything physical. It scares me a little, but in a way that feels right, like falling toward something I don't want to escape. He kisses his way back up, resting his forehead against mine.

"Ti moya," he murmurs, voice hoarse.

I cup his face. "Yes. I'm yours."

The look he gives me in this moment, like I've just given him the whole world, burns itself into my chest.

When he pushes inside me, all I feel is him. He lets out a low, rough groan as he braces himself above me, and my legs instinctively curl around his waist, pulling him nearer. We move together in a slow rhythm, neither of us wanting this to end.

There's nothing between us. Nothing to hide behind anymore. No lies, no walls, no pretending. Only the press of our bodies and the truth neither of us can run from.

His fingers slide between us, circling my clit with just enough pressure until I come apart, his name spilling from my lips. My release hits hard, crashing through me, and he watches every second of it like the sight alone unravels him more than anything else ever could.

A rough growl rumbles out of him as he follows, his face buried in my neck, his hand tangled in my hair like the idea of letting go would split him in half. His warmth shoots through me, filling me, branding me inside and out.

He stays there, still inside me, his body wrapped around mine like he's afraid letting go will make us come apart. I press a soft kiss to his shoulder and give him the one truth I've never dared say aloud.

"I don't want to go back to a life without you either."

ALEKSEI

I wake up with a smile on my face. That alone is foreign.

It takes a moment to realize why my chest feels so light, why the air in my lungs feels full. Then she shifts beside me, soft skin brushing mine, and everything inside me settles.

Her hair is a tangle against the pillow, her breathing steady, her lips parted just enough for me to catch the faintest sound of it. I do not remember the last time I felt like this, like I could stay in one place and the world would still keep turning.

Happiness.

That's what this is, I think.

True, unshakable happiness. And it is unsettling.

Because it just as easily can be taken away.

I brush a strand of hair from her face, and she stirs, blinking her eyes open. Her lips curve when she sees me, and for a moment, everything inside me goes still.

"Good morning." She yawns.

I trace the line of her jaw with my thumb. "It is quite the good morning."

She stretches lazily, her body sliding against mine, and I groan. It takes every ounce of discipline not to pull her back under me.

She props herself on one elbow. "I'm gonna take my mom to get her hair done today. She hasn't done it in a while, not since the vineyard started falling apart, and she'd never let me pay. But she can afford it now."

"That is a good idea. But I won't let her pay. Get whatever you want to."

"Thank you." Her knuckles roll down my cheek while I brush my fingers through her hair.

"We should also have them over for dinner this week. What do you think about that?"

Her whole face brightens, and I know I said the right thing. "I would love that."

She leans in and presses a small, quick kiss to my mouth, like she is about to get out of this bed, away from me. My palm finds the back of her head, holding her there for a second longer because I cannot help it.

She laughs. "You're not letting me go, are you?"

"Not yet." I seal my mouth over hers. "Never, if I can help it."

She lays her head back on my chest, fingers tracing idle patterns on my skin. The quiet stretches between us, comfortable and peaceful.

When the hell have I ever felt peace like this?

After a while, I say, "I have to go out for business for a little while, but I will be home for dinner."

"Good." She nuzzles closer. "But you don't have to leave yet, right?"

"No." I pull her tighter. "I am right here, lyubov moya."

She grabs my hand and holds it right over her heart. I do not move. I could stay like this forever.

For a man who has spent his entire life surrounded by death, this is like…rebirth.

After a few quiet minutes, I tilt her chin up. "I have a surprise for you."

Her brows rise. "Oh, yeah? What kind of surprise?"

A small smile tugs at the corner of my mouth. "I will tell you over dinner."

She narrows a suspicious gaze. "You know I have zero ability to be patient, right?"

"I know." I smirk. "That is what makes it fun."

She groans, a mix of annoyance and playful surrender, before dropping her head back onto my chest. "Fine. I'll be good."

"Or don't…" I grab a fistful of her ass, and she bites the corner of her mouth.

She hums softly, the sound muffled against me. "You're in quite the good mood this morning."

"I have a reason to be."

Her gaze lifts to mine again, searching, curious. "And what's that?"

I drop a kiss on her forehead. "You are in my bed and you don't hate me."

Her eyes fill with emotion, and I hope she believes me. The surprise I have planned for tonight will show her that I am serious. That I am willing to try for her. *With* her.

But as I hold her tighter, kissing her hair, a darker thought creeps in. One that reminds me what I had to do to make her mine.

And if she ever finds out, she will never forgive me.

THIRTY-SIX

FIONA

"You have no idea how happy I am to see you back in this chair." Marlene beams, scissors in hand, as she fluffs the ends of my mom's freshly trimmed hair.

My mother lifts her chin, a rare light softening her cheeks, one I haven't seen in far too long. "I'm happy too, believe me."

"Well, you're glowing, honey. Whoever this new investor is, I hope they know what a gem they've got in your family." Marlene clips the last section of her hair.

I squeeze my mother's hand, and she turns her palm to thread her fingers through mine.

"It's all thanks to my Fiona," she says, her voice thickening around the words. Then, with a tender look, she adds, "La mia luce nelle tenebre." *My light in the darkness.*

The phrase hits me square in the chest. I stare at her through the mirror, catching the familiar crinkle by her eyes.

"It was all worth it in the end."

And I mean it. Even if my job's hanging by a thread. Even if nothing about this arrangement is normal. Seeing her like this, alive again, is worth everything.

"Well…" Marlene declares as she dusts off the cape and steps back with satisfaction. "I, for one, am relieved. I was really worried about you and Tony."

My mom laughs, her fingers running through her newly styled hair. "We may be getting old, but we are tough."

"That's right, you are."

I rise from my seat, slipping my coat back on before pulling my wallet from my bag to grab Aleksei's credit card. "What do I owe you?"

Marlene holds up a hand like I've just insulted her. "Absolutely nothing."

"Wait, what? No, Marlene, come on. Let me—"

"This one's on me." She waves off my protest with a flick of her wrist. "As a congrats for things looking up."

I glance at my mom, who's already tearing up.

"Thank you," she murmurs.

The small gesture overwhelms me too.

"Don't mention it." Marlene pulls my mother in for a hug. "You look gorgeous, by the way. And I'd better see you again soon, you hear?"

She nods as they pull back. "You will."

We say our goodbyes and head outside together, my mother's arm looped through mine as we make our way to the car. She slides into the passenger seat, and I close the door before circling around to the driver's side.

Once we're on the road, the quiet settles between us for a moment before she finally peeks over.

"So…" she says, like she's been waiting for the right moment.

"How are things with Aleksei?"

I keep my eyes on the road, fingers tightening around the wheel.

"They're…actually okay," I admit, the words sounding strange even to me.

"Okay," she repeats slowly, as if turning it over in her own head. "So there *is* something between you two?"

I shrug, not wanting to make a thing of it. Not yet, anyway. Things are still uncertain between us, and I don't want to run before I walk.

"That's good." She looks out at the road, eyes distant, like she's miles away in her thoughts. "Se c'è anche solo un po' di amore, vale la pena tenerlo stretto." *If there's even a little bit of love, it's worth holding on to.*

My chest constricts.

"I want you to be happy, Fiona," she continues. "I know this isn't what you imagined. And it's not what I imagined either. But sometimes happiness doesn't come the way we think it will."

"You're right. I just didn't think that happiness would come in the form of the Russian Mob."

She lets out a chuckle. "You'd be surprised where true happiness sometimes comes from. You take it where you can get it."

I glance over at her, the wind gently tugging strands of her hair loose as she stares out the window like she's remembering something far away, and I wonder what that could be.

The tires crunch over the gravel as I pull into the driveway of my childhood home, and something inside me softens. The house is small and older than I am, but it's warm and lived-in. Paint chipping on the baby-blue shutters, a cracked front step that no one's ever fixed.

My mom squeezes my hand before opening the door, and I follow her inside. We remove our shoes and head to the kitchen, and Dad looks up from the table, half a crossword filled in, glasses low on his nose.

He immediately smiles, his eyes crinkling. "Ciao, stellina. Come stai? Dimi, come ti trata il diavolo?" *Hello little star. How are you? Tell me, how's the devil treating you?*

I laugh, shaking my head. "The devil may have a bit of an angel he's hiding."

He scoffs. "Lo crederò quando lo vedrò." *I'll believe it when I see it.*

"He actually wants to have you and Mom over for dinner," I say, unzipping my coat. "Maybe tomorrow night?"

Dad raises a brow like he's waiting for a punchline, then peers over at Mom. "I don't know if that's a good idea."

She waves him off. "I think it's a great idea. Tomorrow night is fine. Your father will come around."

"Yeah, yeah," Dad mutters to himself as he heads for the coffee pot and reaches for the canister. "Coffee?"

"Sure." I slide onto a chair.

We settle around the kitchen table, mugs steaming in our hands. The warmth seeps into my fingers as I listen to Mom tell a story about the neighbor's dog escaping again and chasing after the mailman. And for a few precious minutes, it's like old times, and I didn't realize how much I've missed that.

But the moment doesn't last.

A sound drifts in from the back of the house, faint at first, as if carried on the tail end of a distant echo. A single dull thump, barely enough to register as anything out of the ordinary.

Mom pauses mid-sentence.

Then it comes again, louder this time. A heavier knock that seems to vibrate through the floor.

What the hell?

I glance at my parents, and the shift in their expressions is instant. The ease drains away, replaced by a wary stillness that knots in my stomach.

"Stay here," Dad whispers as he moves toward the kitchen drawer and slides it open, pulling out the old Glock I know he hasn't touched in years.

My pulse spikes. I grab my phone and text both of my bodyguards, asking them to check the back of the house. But a response doesn't come.

A cold wave crashes over me as I stuff my phone into my jeans. Something is very, very wrong.

"Let's go upstairs," I tell them, rushing toward the front of the house.

As Mom starts to get up, the back door slams open, the sound exploding through the house like a gunshot.

Fuck!

"Mom, go," I whisper sharply.

But the words barely leave my mouth before two masked men burst into view, dressed head to toe in black, guns raised and pointed straight at us.

"Don't move!" one of them barks, attention rooted on me and Dad, unaware that Mom is still partway up the stairs.

She goes rigid, trembling, trapped between running and freezing. Dad steps in front of me without hesitation, lifting the gun with both hands. I witness the tremor in his fingers, the fear he's fighting to swallow down.

"You want to play, old man?" the guy on the left jeers. "I'll put a bullet in the girl before you even get a shot off."

A muscle in my father's jaw trembles.

"Dad," I whisper. "Please lower it. They'll kill us."

He doesn't look at me, but something in his shoulders flinches.

"What the hell do you want?" he demands, his grip still white-knuckled on the gun.

"We just want the girl." The man gestures at me with a lazy flick of his weapon. "She comes with us and everyone lives. Even her. It's that easy."

My father's voice drops to a growl. "You'll have to kill me first."

The man snickers, like he finds my father pathetic. "That can be arranged."

My mother lets out a soft, broken whimper, while I can barely breathe. Every instinct in me screams to run, to get them both out of here, but there's nowhere to go and no time to think.

"What do you want with me?" I step up beside my father, lifting my chin, refusing to give them the satisfaction of fear. "Who sent you?"

"You don't get to ask questions." His eyes flash behind the mask. "You do what I say, or every person in this room dies."

"No." I shake my head slowly, retreating a step. "I'm not going anywhere with you."

He raises his gun higher and begins to advance, each step purposeful, the room shrinking with every inch he closes in. "Then I start pulling my trigger."

He reaches me in two strides, his hand clamping around my arm. The other man keeps his gun trained on us, unmoving, waiting for the moment things go violent.

"Don't touch her!" The sound that leaves my father isn't fear—it's fury.

He lunges forward, trying to shield me. But the bastard swings the butt of his gun and cracks it against Dad's skull. Mom screams as he brings the weapon down again. Blood spills across Dad's forehead, running down his temple, and something hot and vicious ignites in my chest.

"Stay down," the man snarls. "Or I kill you and your wife right now."

Dad collapses to the floor, the gun slipping from his hand. For one horrifying second, I think he's gone. The room tilts, panic clawing up my throat as the men drag me toward the back of the house.

But when I look over, I see it: one of Dad's eyes cracking open, a faint flicker of movement as his fingers inch toward his fallen gun.

He's alive.

Relief washes over me. If he can get a shot off at the one not holding me, fast enough to make the other turn for even a split second, I might have a chance to grab his weapon and fight back.

It's all I've got. A desperate, razor-thin hope. And Dad has no idea what I'm trying to do.

A sharp pop shatters the room.

The gunshot echoes through the house, and the second man drops with a cry, clutching his leg. The one gripping me jerks in shock, his gaze flicking between his partner and my father, who is still on the ground, the weapon steady in his palm.

That moment of hesitation is all I need.

I drive my knee into my captor's groin, hard. He doubles over with a choked curse, and I seize the gun in his hand, yanking it free as he tries to recover.

"You bitch!" he roars, still hunched and reaching for me.

Before he can lunge again, I fire.

Once.

Twice.

A third time.

I don't think; I just pull the trigger, the recoil jolting through my arms as the bullets slam into his stomach, groin, wherever I can get them. He stumbles backward, eyes blown wide behind the mask, then crumples over the wooden floor.

When I look at the other man, he's still alive, bleeding heavily from his leg and scrambling backward in a panic as I kick his weapon out of reach.

"Don't. Fucking. Move." I lift the gun and aim it at him.

My hands are shaky, but still, he gets the message.

Mom breaks into sobs, her hands covering her mouth while Dad groans and slumps against the wall, blood wet against his temple. My fingers tremble so hard the pistol almost slips from my grip.

"Dad, are you okay?" My voice cracks as I call over to him.

He nods, though it's barely more than a dip of his chin. "Are you?"

"I-I-I'm fine. I need to call Aleksei."

Still holding the gun trained on the man, I fumble my free hand into my pocket and yank out my phone. My thumb shakes as I tap his name. It rings once before he answers.

"Privet, lyubov mo—"

A strangled sob rips out of me. "Aleksei, please. You have to come to my parents' house."

"Tell me what happened." His tone snaps from warm to lethal in a heartbeat.

"Two men in masks broke in." My breath hitches. "One's dead. He's here in the kitchen. The other one is bleeding on the floor from his leg, and I can't reach the guards. I don't know if they're…if they're alive…"

I register immediate shuffling and voices.

"Are you hurt? Are your parents?"

"My dad's bleeding from his head."

"I'm fine," Dad calls weakly.

Mom is already moving, grabbing a rag from the kitchen and pressing it firmly against the wound when she returns.

"Put me on speaker," Aleksei says.

"Okay…" I don't even have the energy to ask why.

His words fill the room, dark and razor-sharp. "Make sure that piece of shit is listening, okay, detka?"

"He's looking right at me."

"Don't you fucking look at my wife, svolich." The way he says it turns my whole body tense. "And listen closely. When I get there, you'd better still be on that floor. If you are not, I will take whatever DNA is left and find every living relative you have. I will skin every single one of them alive. Your mother. Your third cousin twice removed. All of them. Do you understand? Tell him to nod."

The tiniest curl pulls at my mouth when the bastard flinches and nods like a terrified child.

"He is."

"Good. Now take off your mask, or my wife will shoot your other leg."

I will?

Panic ripples through me. I haven't even processed the fact that I killed someone. The adrenaline is gone, leaving only the sick twist in my stomach. I don't know if I could pull the trigger again, even if I had to.

The man tightens a fist, breathing heavy, losing blood by the second. But he pulls the mask off anyway.

When he reveals his face, there's nothing special about him. Dark eyes and hair. Mid-thirties, probably. The kind of man you would pass on the street without looking twice.

"Take a picture of him just in case."

"Okay." I snap a shot and send it to Aleksei.

"Good girl. Now leave him there and go upstairs and lock the door, then move the dresser in front. Don't open for anyone until I am there. Do you understand?"

"Yes."

"Go now, but do not hang up."

I hurry to my parents. Dad tries to stand, but nearly buckles, still clutching the gun, so I slip my phone into my pocket, then lock an arm around him and support his weight. We move up the stairs as fast as possible, Mom leading the way.

Aleksei is still on the line as he shouts to the others in Russian. Car doors slam. Engines roar to life. Every sound tells me he's coming and nothing will stop him.

We reach my parents' bedroom, and I lock the door behind us. My mind races, spinning through every possibility.

Were these men hired by whoever has been sending me notes, or by someone else entirely? Is this because of Aleksei or because of me? I can't piece any of it together.

"We're going to move the dresser now," I tell him, placing the phone and gun on the bed as my parents help me shove the heavy furniture across the floor until it sits firmly against the door.

"I'll be there soon," he says, then goes quiet. "I'm sorry."

The words are heavy with a regret so thick it sinks straight into me.

"It's not your fault."

"It is, but I will take care of it. Keep your gun with you. If anyone tries to open that door before I arrive, shoot first."

"Okay."

He releases a hard breath. "With everything in me, Fiona, I swear I will hunt down every person involved in this and I will tear them apart. No one touches you and lives. Do you hear me? *No one.*"

I do hear him. Every word hits straight in my bones.

My heart knocks against my ribs as I stare at the barricaded door, waiting for the sound of engines outside. Waiting for the man I once swore I could never love to come save the family I would die for.

ALEKSEI

Ya ikh unichtozhu. I will destroy them.

That is all I think about as the engine roars while I speed through the street. Konstantin is silent beside me, Kirill and Anton in the back, a convoy of SUVs full of our men swallowing the road behind us.

Fiona is still on speaker, her breathing faint but shaky. I can just imagine how afraid she was. What they could have done to her.

I slam my foot down harder, weaving through traffic like the laws of this city do not apply to me, blowing past lights and signs without registering a single one. The only thought in my head is her name. The only picture behind my eyes is what they could have done to her.

She fought for her life tonight. And I was not there.

Blyat!

My grip tightens around the wheel until the leather bites into my palms. Fury boils through me, climbing up my spine in a way that is almost uncontrollable, but beneath it sits something far more dangerous for a man like me.

Fear. Not for myself, but for her.

The realization slams into me with the force of a crash.

I could have lost her today. Lost the one person who slipped through every crack in my armor without even trying. And if she had died, there would be nothing left of me worth saving.

Konstantin taps two fingers against the console, pointing to the phone. A silent order to mute her.

"I am putting you on mute for a second, but I'm still here," I tell her.

"Okay." She sounds strong, and I'm glad for it, though that bastard's death won't be any better for it.

I press the button, silencing her line.

"What?" I ask my brother.

"Viktor and Leonid are still not answering. They have either been captured or they are dead."

"They would never let themselves be captured."

He nods as the truth settles between us. If they aren't answering, we already know the outcome.

We are all used to death. We've seen it with family, friends. It shouldn't be as easy as it is, but we don't have much choice other than to move on.

Konstantin glances at me again. "Emilia does not hear about what happened to Fiona. I do not want her upset."

"She won't."

"And Fiona?" Konstantin asks.

"She won't say a word," I grit out. "She would never stress her out when she is pregnant."

My fingers curl tighter around the wheel. Fiona's voice is still in my ears, trembling when she told me what happened. Konstantin watches me for half a second longer, then nods, and I immediately unmute her.

"Fiona? I'm here."

"Everything okay?"

"Yes. Konstantin was worried about Emilia finding out."

"Well, none of you better tell her anything."

Konstantin smirks, and I shoot him a look that says *told you so*. He tosses his hands up in surrender, but we both know he's only trying to protect his wife in the same way I'm trying to protect mine.

"Stay with me. Keep talking if you need to. I'm getting closer."

The SUV surges forward, engine growling beneath my hands as the speedometer climbs, matching the ferocity in my chest. Homes and buildings smear into colorless blurs. Every turn, every stretch of road, is nothing but space between me and her.

When I reach that house, I will tear the truth out of the bastard who touched her. And then I will make damn sure she is never out of my sight again.

THIRTY-SEVEN

FIONA

The bedroom is too quiet. The kind of quiet that makes every creak in the floorboard sound like a gunshot. Every gust of wind outside is like breath on the back of my neck. I told Aleksei to call when he's here, because having him on the phone was making me more anxious.

My parents sit on the edge of the bed, my mother gripping my father's free hand so tightly her knuckles are white. She whispers prayers in Italian under her breath, the same few lines on repeat like she's trying to build a wall of protection around us. My father's leg bounces uncontrollably, the gun still clenched in his other hand.

I lower to the floor with my back against the nightstand, one hand clamped around the revolver. More of those men could come for us, and the thought makes every hair on my body stand up.

I can't sit still. My mind won't stop replaying everything that happened tonight. The gunshots, the blood, the way that man looked at me in the last seconds before he died. The thought alone forces me up, and I drift toward the window, careful not to let the curtain shift even an inch too far.

Outside, Viktor's and Leonid's SUVs are still parked at the curb, but there's no sign of them. Nothing but the sickening crawl of dread tightening in my chest.

My mother cuts through the fog. "Fiona, come back. Don't let them see you, just in case."

I step away, pulse hammering like a war drum. "Aleksei will be here soon. We're going to be okay."

My father lets out a harsh breath, the blood caked around his forehead now. "I should have killed them both when I had the chance."

Mom shakes her head. "And they would have killed Fiona if you had. We are alive. That's what matters, Tony."

She squeezes his hand until he exhales.

"You're right. That's what matters."

Sudden footsteps downstairs have my heart dropping to my stomach. My father stands beside me while my mother gasps, her hand flying to her mouth.

"Wait here," I whisper, already moving before either of them can stop me.

The doorknob turns. My phone rings.

I lift the gun with both hands, finger tight on the trigger, and I don't hesitate. I already know I will pull it if I have to. I will kill again if it means protecting the people I love.

"Fiona," Aleksei's voice booms from the other side.

Relief crashes into me so hard, my knees nearly give.

We shove the dresser aside, and the second I wrench the door open, he's there—eyes wild, chest rising and falling hard, hair a chaotic mess like he's been raking his hands through it nonstop. He stares at me for a long moment, drinking in every inch of me, looking for wounds, for blood, for anything that might mean he arrived too late.

Then his hands are on my face, warm and frantic. "Are you hurt?"

I shake my head. "No. I'm okay."

"Slava Bogu." His forehead drops to mine and he kisses me slow and deep, his arms crushing me to him like he needs the proof that I'm real.

When he finally leans back, he doesn't let me go. His face stays buried in my neck, breathing me in, as if he's grounding himself in the scent of my skin.

"I was worried."

The rawness in the words hits me in the chest, and I wrap my arms around him just as tightly, holding on like I'm afraid the world might rip us apart again.

Behind him, his brothers and several of their men file into the room, weapons drawn, eyes sweeping every corner.

Aleksei turns to Kirill. "Take her parents to the SUV and have the men stay with them."

My parents both hug me before they head out.

When they're out of earshot, I ask, "Did you find Viktor and Leonid?"

By some miracle, I hope they're alive, but I'm not banking on it.

He nods. "They're dead."

I cover my mouth with my hand, tears swimming in my eyes. "I'm so sorry."

"It is not your fault." His hands grip mine, brows furrowing. "You did nothing wrong."

I know it isn't, but somehow, it feels as though it is.

"You did good, moya okhotnitsa." He smirks. "Your shots were perfect."

He lifts my hand and presses a slow kiss to my knuckles and doesn't let go. Not when we walk out of the house. Not when we reach the car. Not even when the door shuts behind us. His fingers stay wrapped around mine the whole way home, and somehow, that tether is the only thing keeping me together.

ALEKSEI

My hand is still locked in hers when we walk inside, unwilling to let go. My men fan out through the entryway and hall, every one of them on alert.

Konstantin gives a few orders, sending half the crew to guard the perimeter and half to stay with Fiona and her parents. He knows I would burn the world down if I found one gap in our protection.

The air smells faintly of coffee and lemon polish. One of the maids appears, a tray in her hands filled with tea, coffee, and pastries. She sets it carefully on the table in the den and bows her head, her eyes flicking toward Fiona before she vanishes again.

Fiona stands by the window, arms wrapped around herself. She hasn't said a word since the car, and I don't know what the hell is going on in her head or how I can fix it. Her parents huddle close together on the sofa, her mother whispering something to her father.

I step toward her. "You should eat."

She shakes her head. "I'm not hungry."

She killed a man tonight. The first one is always the hardest.

I still remember mine. I was ten, and it was on my father's orders. The man begged on his knees, pleading for me not to do it, that he had a wife and kids waiting for him. But still, I pointed the gun at his chest and pulled the trigger.

For weeks, I had nightmares. I saw his face everywhere I went. I couldn't escape it. But eventually, it went away, until killing became no different than eating or sleeping.

But Fiona is not me and she never will be. She will need time, and I will give her every second of it.

"You did what you had to do," I tell her. "You should be proud."

She lets out a brittle laugh, one that doesn't reach her eyes. "I don't feel proud. I just feel relieved it wasn't us, but I can't stop seeing it."

"I understand." I pull her into my chest, holding her there. "You're strong. You'll be okay."

Her shoulders sag, like she doesn't quite believe me.

I press a kiss to the top of her head before easing back. "I have to go for a bit."

She looks up fast. "Where?"

But in her gaze, I can tell she already knows. I have unfinished business.

"The one who's still alive. He won't be for long."

"Oh." Her expression tightens, the reality settling heavy between us. "Right."

"Anyone who touches what's mine doesn't get to live, detka. You know that."

"I do." She swallows. "That doesn't make it easier."

"I know." My hand curves around the back of her neck and I lean in, giving her a soft kiss.

"I don't want you to go," she says quietly.

I draw her in again, her face pressed to my chest. "I don't want to go either. But every minute that man breathes is a minute I can't. Every second he's alive, I see you standing there again—shaking, terrified, holding a gun. I need him gone."

Her eyes soften as she peers up. "Aleksei…"

"I will not be gone long." My thumb traces the curve of her lower lip. "You stay here. The men will not leave this house, do you understand? You are safe here."

She nods slowly, her hand coming up to rest over my heart. For a moment, I almost stay. I almost give in to the pull she has over me. But that's not who I am.

This is my fight. My vengeance. My blood to spill.

"I'll be fine," she whispers. "Just come back to me."

Those words shouldn't feel like a vow, but they do. They settle in my chest like an oath I'll bleed to keep.

I kiss her again, longer this time. Deeper. The kind that bruises. The kind that tells her exactly how much of me she owns.

"I'll come back," I promise against her lips.

When I turn to leave, she grabs my forearm.

"Don't be reckless. Don't get yourself killed."

I stare back at her. "I will not be the one dying. I swear."

Her lips part, but no sound comes out, and I leave before I can change my mind.

The moment I slide into the SUV, my men climb in behind me. I take the wheel, ignition roaring to life beneath my hand, and we tear down the long road toward Konstantin's estate, where the surviving man is being held.

The house shrinks in the rearview mirror, but Fiona's touch stays trapped against my skin.

As I press the gas, I make a promise to myself, to Fiona, to the ghosts that made me what I am: the man who touched what's mine will beg for mercy. And I will remind him there's no mercy left in me.

The pigs shift restlessly in their pen, snorting and stomping as the scent of blood thickens the air, heavy enough to make the whole place feel alive. The only sound I care about is the ragged, uneven breathing of the man tied to the chair in front of me.

His leg wound has been wrapped just enough to keep him conscious. His face is so battered that he's almost unrecognizable: one eye swollen shut, lip split, cheek already a deep purple. He whimpers when I step into his line of sight dragging the electric bone saw across the grass, making whatever is left of his soul recoil.

Konstantin stands beside me, arms folded, the faintest trace of amusement in his voice. "It is in your best interest to tell my brother everything. He is a little bit cranky today, and if he has to drag it out of you, you will wish these pigs would get to you sooner."

He pats the man on the head like he's a misbehaving child, then steps back. My other brothers say nothing, watching with a cold stillness.

"You have one chance," I tell him. "You waste it, and we do this the very painful way."

Except, of course, no matter what he tells me, I will torture him to death.

"I told you." He gasps. "We were hired."

"By…"

He hesitates, and I tsk disapprovingly. I crouch beside him, my fingers brushing the grass, then reach for the aluminum bat I left resting against the feed bin, leaving the saw beside him.

"Still don't know who gave the order?" I drag the bat up his leg, and he pisses himself.

I should beat him dead just for that.

He opens his mouth, but before the words can form, I swing. The bat connects against the side of his thigh, a sickening crunch splitting the air. With his scream, birds scatter from the trees.

I bring the bat down again, this time against his shoulder. Then his other leg. Then his ribs. He howls, a wet gurgle in the back of his throat.

"Tell me who sent you." The bat connects to his kneecap, shattering in its wake.

"I don't—don't know their names." He shrinks into himself. "They didn't give us names. Just—just told us to bring the girl. Someone wants her."

I go still. "Who?"

"I don't know!"

I swing again. "Think harder."

"Fuuuck!" His exhales grow shallow, teeth rattling.

"I don't know his name. No one does. We got paid by a middleman."

"Tell me who."

He shoots off a name and a number. American. I'm sure it was the Volkovs who paid him.

The bat falls from my hand, and I grab the saw again. It hums to life as I put it on. Loud. Piercing. A mechanical shriek that has dread growing in his irises.

"Wait, no!" His body quivers. "Please…please, man, don't!"

"You came for my wife." I crouch down. "You pointed a gun at her. You made her kill. You made her cry. And that is unforgivable."

"I-I-I'm sorry. I'll help you, okay? Anything you want. I'll be your man."

"I do not need your help. I have my family for that."

His scream rips from his lungs as the blade makes contact with this shoulder, his arm severing as blood sprays across my face. And it fuels the flames already consuming me.

But I do not stop. I saw through flesh and tendon, through bone and muscle, until the arm drops to the floor with a sickening, wet thud.

The pigs shriek behind me, scenting the fresh meat.

Konstantin nods toward the pen. "Toss it in. They've been starving."

I pick up the severed limb and throw it over the gate. The pigs fight over it instantly, squealing in delight.

"Do not worry, I will have more soon."

The man yells again as I take his other arm. He's thrashing, half delirious now, his legs kicking weakly.

Anton steps forward, pulling his face up by his hair. "Let's make him watch."

He turns him toward the pigs. They are louder now. Wet, savage chewing. One of them grunts as it fights another for the bone.

When I take his leg, he barely has any strength to scream. I let the saw fall this time.

"You hear that?" I whisper in his ear as I watch the pigs. "That's your death calling."

"Please," he whimpers. "Kill me."

"No. They will."

"Noooo…please…"

I keep him conscious as long as possible, letting him feel it. Feel the blood leaving his body, the terror rise as his strength fades.

And when he's just barely holding on, I lean in one last time.

"Tell the devil who sent you."

Then I slit his throat and lift him over my shoulder before throwing him into the pen.

The pigs do not wait. They're just as starved as I am.

For blood. For revenge.

And I won't rest until I find every single man who thought they could touch her and live to tell about it.

THIRTY-EIGHT

FIONA

The guest bedroom door clicks shut behind my parents, the quiet snap of the latch too loud in the silence. I tell them I need a shower, an excuse more than anything, but the water might do me some good.

I make it back to Aleksei's bedroom—*our* bedroom—and close the door behind me, heading for the en suite. The moment the shower roars to life, whatever fragile strength I've been holding on to begins to fracture. I undress slowly, almost mechanically, my fingers clumsy as I strip each piece away.

When I step beneath the spray, I brace both palms against the tile, letting the water beat across the back of my head in hard, steady bursts. I shut my eyes, but nothing inside me quiets. The man's face is still there.

His eyes when I pulled the trigger. His body hitting the floor. My father bleeding. My own hands shaking so violently I could barely hold the gun.

And none of it washes off.

The tears roll down my cheeks, and I can't suppress them anymore.

We almost died.

I killed someone.

A small sob breaks free, like my body is finally able to feel it all.

The door creaks open behind me, and I catch Aleksei walking up to me through the glass.

"Fiona? Are you crying?" He pulls open the door.

I shake my head, wiping at my cheeks even though it's pointless. He already heard.

"No. I'm fine."

The muscle in his jaw flexes, and without another word, he yanks off his hoodie, shoves his sweats down, and steps out of them like nothing else in the world matters except getting to me.

He doesn't ask permission. He simply steps inside and closes the door behind him, the steam curling around us as he pulls me into his arms.

The moment I feel him, I break. My body sags into his, my sobs muffled against his chest. His hands trace down my back in calm, reassuring strokes, easing the frantic tremor beneath my skin.

"I'm here." He drops a kiss to my temple. "It's over now. You're safe, moya ptichka."

My vision blurs as I look up at him.

"I don't want to see it anymore," I whisper. "His body…after I killed him. I need it to stop."

"It is hard the first time." His hand comes up to frame my cheek. "But remember this. Your father and mother would be dead if you hadn't done it. You would be…" He trails off, like he can't bring himself to imagine the very idea of me gone.

I tilt my head, searching his eyes through the mist. "When did it stop for you?"

I don't even know if he ever felt what I'm feeling now, but I need him to tell me that eventually, it won't be like this.

His thumb brushes under my eyes, sliding away the water and tears that mix there. "The first time I killed someone, it haunted me for weeks. I would wake soaked in sweat, heart pounding like I was still there."

Something inside me stills. "How old were you?"

He hesitates, just for a moment. "Ten."

The word lands like a stone dropping straight through me. My mind struggles to make sense of it. Of the boy he was and the man he was forced to become.

He clasps the back of my neck and leans his forehead to mine. "I will be here for you through all of it. Whatever you need, however long it takes. And as long as I am alive, no one will ever touch you or your parents again. That is not a promise. It is the truth."

I wrap my arms around him and rest my head against his chest, listening to the steady beat of his heart and wondering how someone born into that kind of violence could become this.

Gentle. Safe. Mine.

Turning off the water, he reaches for a towel, wrapping me in it before drying himself with another. Then he lifts me like I weigh nothing and carries me to the bed, setting me down carefully. He grabs one of his shirts and slips it over my head, then pulls on his own clothes and climbs in beside me.

Settling onto his back, he winds an arm around my waist and draws me over him until I'm stretched across his chest, held firmly in the warm, hard strength of his body.

"Is he dead?" I don't know why I'm asking when I already know the answer.

"Yes." His fingers trace soft, lazy patterns on my back.

I close my eyes. Not in horror or relief, but in resignation.

This is who my husband is. I'm a prosecutor married to a mobster.

I don't think I'll ever get over it.

"Do you want to ask me anything else?"

I lift my head and look down at him. "Do you know who sent them?"

He goes quiet, and something twists in my gut. "Not yet."

Did he just lie?

"I know you're scared, but I won't let them get near you. Not again. I will find them all and hunt them down because this is who I am, Fiona. This is who your husband is."

There's something brutal in his stare, something wild and untamed like the lion he proudly bears on his chest. But I see something else: his fear that this is where I pull away. That I won't want him anymore.

Instead, I lean in and press a kiss to the scar just beneath where the lion tears apart the wolf. "Then I guess it's a good thing I'm your wife. Because I'm not going anywhere."

His breath stutters. Then his arm squeezes around me and he tilts my jaw closer, kissing me slow, the passion and affection seeping through his pores.

I get lost in his kiss. In the way his hands roam my body. In the way he flips me under him and slides inside, rocking slowly as he stares deep into my eyes, making me forget everything but the way it feels when we're together.

THIRTY-NINE

FIONA

"Come on. What are you afraid of?"

Aleksei's words drift across the warm breeze, laced with that familiar teasing edge as he taps the seat of the sleek black-and-red sports bike between his thighs. The same one he leaned against the day he chased me through the woods.

That feels like a lifetime ago. Everything has changed, yet somehow nothing has.

Like the impossible question lingering in the back of my mind: how do I stay with him and still keep my job?

"Well, for starters, the fact that you could kill me." I'm only half teasing, but the idea of riding with him sends a spark through me.

He's been asking for days and I keep saying no, yet some part of me craves the thrill of it. The freedom, the wind in my hair, the long stretch beneath us as he flies down the road.

He holds out a helmet, resting it on his knee, one hand wrapped around the handlebar. I cross my arms and arch a playful brow, but I don't step toward him.

It's been a week since the night I pulled the trigger, and even though time has blurred the edges of the memory, I still can't forget it. The man's face. The fear. The blood.

Aleksei has been there in every way he knows how, even trying to convince me to take time off work. But I couldn't. My job matters to me. I can't just disappear, not with so many cases depending on me.

His smile softens. "I would never kill you, lyubov moya. I'd die before I let that happen."

Those words seep through my chest, and I make my way toward him, throwing my arms around his neck.

"You're such a romantic."

"I take after my brother."

I actually laugh, an honest sensation I haven't felt in days. "Wait until I tell Konstantin you said that."

He groans. "No, please, anything but that." His hand goes to his chest like he's been wounded. "I have a reputation to uphold."

I shake my head, letting the ease of the moment cloak around me and make me forget the ugliness for a while.

Fuck it.

I slide onto the seat behind him.

"Good girl." He kisses the tip of my nose and secures the helmet around my head.

When I lean forward, my arms find their place around his waist, and it's stupid how right it feels. Like I've done it a thousand times before. Like this is where I was always meant to be.

"Are you ready?" He glances back at me over his shoulder, mouth threaded with that smirk he always wears.

My heart gives a little thump. "As ready as I'll ever be."

Please don't kill me…

"I promise to take it easy on you." He revs up the engine. "I'll go slow."

"You? Go slow? That'll be the day."

He chuckles right before we move, gliding down the long driveway of the estate, past the stone walls and security gates and the parked cars. The wind rushes around us, and I squeeze my eyes shut for a second, letting the sensation crash over me. There's something about being on the back of this bike, arms locked around a man like Aleksei, that makes the world fall away. It's reckless. Exciting. Dangerous in a way I've never craved before.

"Go faster," I tell him, and he answers with a laugh before the bike surges forward, wind tearing past us.

For the first time in days, everything falls away. The death. The cryptic notes buried under a stack of files in my office. The fear that someone is coming after me. That my parents could be next.

They're still in the guest suite down the hall. Aleksei insisted they stay until the threat is gone. He even assigned men to guard the vineyard while they're at work, and for that, I'm grateful.

He takes a smooth, effortless turn, and we coast along a back road lined with trees, the sun melting low on the horizon. Reaching back briefly, he places his hand on my thigh, squeezing gently. Like a reminder.

I'm here. I've got you.

I squeeze him tighter, burying my face in his back, letting the warmth of his body and the hum of the engine quiet the noise in my head.

Later, we'll go back, and it'll all drown me again. But right now, I can pretend for just a little while longer that this ride is the only thing that matters.

That maybe, in the eye of the storm, we've found something that feels like peace…and even something deeper than that.

"I seriously cannot believe you guys kept this from me." Emilia's eyes narrow as she glares between Konstantin and me, her disbelief so exaggerated, I half expect her to throw her hands in the air. "Do you all think I'm some fragile little thing who needs handholding? That I can't handle hearing my best friend almost got her face blown off? Because I can."

She's not wrong. She could probably out-shoot half the men Konstantin employs, and she's had her fair share of close calls. But still, Konstantin insisted it was better not to tell her. Said it would stress her out. And now that she overheard Kirill talking about it earlier, here we are.

"Katyonak." Konstantin reaches across the table and takes her hand, bringing it to his lips. "I love you. I love our baby. I didn't want to stress you out or put your health at risk."

She huffs, but her lips twitch like she's trying not to smile. "You just have to be all sweet and protective, huh?"

"Of course." He shrugs with a calm grin. "Why else would you keep me around?"

"For the orgasms. Obviously." She says it so casually, I nearly snort tea through my nose.

"Well, I'm glad you don't want to kill him anymore."

"Give me an hour. I'm sure I'll be pissed again." Flashing him a deathly look, she turns back to me, her face softening. "As for you, are you okay? Who do I need to kill?"

"I think Aleksei has that part covered." When I smile, there's a heaviness I can't seem to shake, no matter how hard I try. "But seriously, I wish I knew who's doing this. And why."

"We will take care of it," Konstantin says, and the tone of his voice leaves no room for argument. "We will not rest until every last one of them is dealt with."

"But who are they?" I ask, needing something, anything, that can help me piece together what's going on.

A name. A reason. A connection.

He holds my gaze, his expression unreadable. "Enemies. That's all you need to know."

Not the answer I wanted.

Konstantin eventually leaves us, something about a meeting, but not before he kisses her again like the world is ending. And for them, it almost did once. I think that's why they're so fearless now. Because they've already walked through fire and survived.

Emilia and I move to the patio with fresh mugs of tea and settle into the cushioned chairs under their gazebo. The late afternoon sun is warm against my skin, the garden alive with the chirp of crickets and the rustle of distant trees.

It should feel peaceful, but it doesn't.

She watches me in silence for a few moments, long enough that I finally look up and catch her expression filled with concern.

"You're not okay," she says. "You don't have to pretend with me."

My throat dries. "I'm trying. I really am. But I can't stop seeing him. That man. The one I shot."

Her expression doesn't change. She just nods.

"Yeah. That doesn't go away overnight."

"I keep thinking about all the ways it could've gone wrong. What if I'd frozen? What if I hadn't even been able to get the gun? We would've been..." I trail off, swallowing down the sudden burn behind my eyes.

"But you're all fine. Because you did everything right."

"I killed someone."

"He was gonna kill you. *You* saved your family."

Silence stretches again before I say, "I know I had to do it. I don't regret it. But I just can't believe I did that, you know?"

Emilia leans back in her chair and exhales. "I killed people when I was with the Bureau. A few, actually. And the first time...God. I threw up. I couldn't sleep for days. I kept thinking, what if I could've found another way? What if I made the wrong call?"

"And now?"

"Now I know that sometimes the only way to survive is to end the threat. It doesn't make you a monster. It makes you human."

I nod slowly, letting her words sink in. "I guess I just wish I could go back to not knowing what it feels like. To just being a prosecutor who believed in justice and rules."

"You still are." She shrugs.

I exhale slowly and nod. "Thanks, Em."

"I'm always here for you, anytime."

We sit in silence after that, sipping our drinks and letting the sun melt into the horizon. And I let her words settle into me, reminding myself that it was either him or us.

FORTY

FIONA

The next five days bleed into one another, and Aleksei and I find ourselves growing closer, finding a sliver of normalcy amidst the chaos that is our life. Each morning, I walk into work as if nothing in my world has changed, as if I'm not married to one of the most dangerous men in the country.

The ring stays on a chain beneath my blouse, hidden but close to my heart. The only way I can keep him with me without inviting questions I can't answer.

I don't ask what Aleksei does while I'm gone. I don't want to know. Not because I don't care, but because I care too much. If I let myself dwell on the details—on the blood, the brutality, the darkness—I might break. So I compartmentalize. I focus on my case files, the mountainous to-do list I have each day. And when I come home to him, I let myself breathe again. Let myself sink into his arms, where I feel more myself than I ever have.

It also helps that our families blend together so smoothly. We see Emilia and Konstantin when we can, and my parents are beginning to soften to the idea of him. My father even shared a glass of wine with him last night.

Then there's Aleksei. He's there for me in every way that matters, and he seems to know just what I need before I even do. With each passing day, I find myself falling more for him until it turns dangerously close to love, though neither of us has said it.

I melt against his side, the low hum of the movie fading into nothing as his arm settles around me. My eyes drift shut, breathing syncing with his without even trying. These quiet moments are the ones I crave. The ones where the chaos outside doesn't exist.

When the movie ends, Aleksei turns toward me, brushing a stray curl away from my cheek.

"I have a surprise for you. It's something I wanted to show you before everything happened." That usual wicked glint in his eyes is softened by something tender.

I narrow my gaze, forcing myself to forget the *everything* he's talking about. "Now I'm curious."

His mouth winds as he slips a hand into the pocket of his sweats and pulls out a black silk blindfold.

My brows shoot up. "Did you…conveniently have that there the whole time?"

A low laugh rumbles in his chest. "Yes. Now come on, get up. I want to take you somewhere."

"Mm, I don't know…" I scrunch my nose at him. "This is exactly what murderers say in horror movies before the girl gets chopped into pieces."

His grin widens. "If I wanted to chop you up, detka, I would have done it by now."

"Fine." I sigh dramatically. "But only because I'm curious."

He leans in and brushes a quick kiss to my lips. "Good enough for me.”

We walk out to the SUV together, and before I can climb in, he steps behind me, tying the blindfold around my eyes. The world goes dark, but his hands are there, steady at my waist, guiding me inside.

“Are you going to tell me where we’re going?” I ask as he buckles my seat belt.

“No.” There’s an unmistakable grin in his tone.

“Are you going to murder me in the woods?”

“Not today.”

“I’ll take it.”

The drive is short. Less than ten minutes. When the car slows and stops, I sense the door open and Aleksei’s hand guiding me out.

“Okay, walk slow. We are on grass now.”

He steadies me with a hand on my waist as we make it a short distance.

“You ready?” he asks.

“As ready as I’ll ever be.”

The blindfold comes off, and I blink against the golden light of the sun. We’re standing in a wide clearing at the edge of the estate, tucked behind a cluster of birch trees. There, in the center of the grass, is a laid-out picnic. Blanket, pillows, plates covered in silver domes, and a bottle of wine already chilling in a bucket.

“A picnic?” The laugh slips out of me before I can stop it, from sheer disbelief that this big, terrifying man planned something so nice for me.

Aleksei winces like I stabbed him. “Okay, this was stupid. I knew Konstantin was wrong. Never mind.” He starts reaching for my hand to pull me back toward the car. “We’ll go out to dinner instead. Something fancy. I don’t know why I thought—”

“Wait.” I catch his arm and tug him back, hating that I could’ve hurt his feelings. “Aleksei, stop.”

He looks down at me, bracing for the worst, and something in my chest squeezes. I lift one hand to his cheek, brushing my thumb over the rough stubble there.

"Hey. I didn't laugh because it was stupid." I tilt his face toward mine so he has to hear every word. "I just didn't know the extent of your soft side."

He huffs, low and rough. "I don't have a soft side."

But the way he presses into my hand betrays him completely.

"Then maybe I'm hallucinating." I rise onto my toes and kiss him. "But hallucination or not...I like it."

His gaze moves over my face, studying me, a flicker of uncertainty there. "You sure you like this?"

"This is the sweetest thing anyone has ever done for me. I just need time to get used to you being...less murderous and more romantic, that's all."

A sound that's half growl slips from him. "Which do you like more?"

"Both." I catch my bottom lip between my teeth, and the sound he makes in response sends a tremor through me.

Then he's kissing me, mouth fierce and hungry, pulling me under until we break apart in a breathless tangle.

"Come on." His eyes drag over me like a slow touch. "Let's eat. Before I get hungry for something else."

"Only if you promise to feed me."

A low chuckle rumbles out of him, and before I can blink, the world tilts and I'm tossed over his shoulder, his arm locked around my thighs. "We can arrange that."

He gives my ass a sharp smack, and I yelp.

"But only if you're tied up," he adds, far too pleased with himself.

"Maybe not," I shoot back, heat curling through me. "I want to use my hands this time. Maybe feed you too."

He stops mid-step, setting me down. And when he looks at me again, something inside him shifts, something possessive and warm all at once, like I've said the exact thing he didn't know he needed to hear.

"I like the sound of that." His fingers slide through mine, bringing the back of my hand to his lips, the kiss soft and lingering before he leads me toward the blanket.

We sink onto it together, our bodies entwined in a way that makes the food feel like an afterthought. My thighs straddle his lap, his hands resting possessively at my hips, and every time I reach for a piece of fruit, he leans in and steals it from my fingers, brushing his lips over them before feeding it to me himself.

I can't stop smiling. Can't stop laughing against his mouth when he kisses me between bites. For once, everything feels…easy. Light. Like the world outside doesn't exist. Like we're just two people trying to pretend we're normal.

His fingers tuck a strand of hair behind my ear, his attention fastened on me with something vulnerable flickering beneath the surface.

"I was raised to take what I wanted," he says with a fractured sigh. "But you…you make me want to be worthy of it."

"Aleksei…"

My eyes sting, and before I can push it away, his thumb sweeps away the tear that escapes. His vision locks with mine, and all I see is pure affection.

"Ya lyublyu tebya, moya ptichka," he whispers. "I love you."

My heart kicks harder, his confession plummeting deep, and the words rise out of me like they've been waiting for this moment.

"I love you too."

Because I do, and even though I've been afraid to say it out loud, afraid of what it will mean for us and our future, I can't keep it in anymore.

He freezes, like he needs to make sure he heard me right. Then his mouth crashes into mine, fingers sliding through my hair, pulling me closer until I'm pressed completely against him, every inch of me molded to every inch of him. When he finally pitches back, he leans in until our foreheads touch, neither of us willing to break the moment.

Moments pass before he reaches into his pocket and pulls out his phone. "I have something for you. The surprise."

I tilt my head. "Another one? Because the last one involved a blindfold, and I'm still traumatized."

"This is the one I wanted to give you." He grins, but it fades quickly as he scrolls on his screen, then turns it so I can see.

The text means nothing at first, just blocks of legal language, until the pieces click into place.

"Does this mean…"

My hand lands on my chest, finding this hard to believe. But the more of the contract I read, the more I see his signature on the bottom, the harder it is to deny what's in front of me.

"You're free," he says simply. "I signed the vineyard over to you. It's yours, Fiona, whether we are married or divorced. You have what you wanted now."

The words land slow. Did he really do this?

He picks up my hand and kisses the center of my palm. "You can leave. You can divorce me if that's what you want. I'm giving you your freedom."

A laugh bubbles up, filled with disbelief. "You're serious?"

He nods once.

I stare at this man who's terrified me, infuriated me, consumed me…and now, somehow, undone me. This is something I never expected.

"I can't believe I'm saying this," I whisper. "But what if I don't want to go? What if with you is where I was meant to be?"

He inhales sharply. "What are you saying?"

"That between all the hate and the insanity, somewhere in the middle of it all…" My throat thickens. "I fell in love with you completely, and I don't want to let you go."

He doesn't move at first, just watches me like he's afraid one wrong shift will shatter the moment. Then his hands rise to cradle the back of my neck.

"Thank God. Because I wasn't planning on letting you go anyway."

"I kind of figured that would be the case."

I rest my forehead against his chest, my mouth stretching into a grin as I listen to the steady beat beneath my ear.

For the first time since everything began, I don't feel trapped. I feel like I've ended up where I was always meant to be.

ALEKSEI

She sits on top of me, arms over my shoulders, legs curled around my waist, and I can't stop staring, like if I blink too long, I'll miss it. This moment. This feeling. This woman who was never supposed to be mine and somehow is.

My hands settle on her hips, thumbs tracing slow circles over the fabric of her dress. She tilts her head, a smile teasing the corners of her mouth, and those eyes… I could gaze into them for the rest of my life and never get tired of the view.

"I can't imagine my life without you," I tell her.

Her fingers toy with the hair at the nape of my neck. "You won't have to."

But I don't know how true that is. In my world, death is a bullet away. What if I'm not enough to protect her?

The thought shreds something in me until it's painful.

"You're my destiny, Fiona." The words scrape out low, rough-edged. "You always were. From the moment I saw you across that courtroom, fire in your eyes."

A soft laugh escapes her, and it makes my chest tighten.

"Even then, I think some part of me already knew."

"Did you, though?" A playful spark lights her expression. "Because I swear you wanted to kill me a few times."

"Just a few times?" I chuckle, and that lands me an elbow to my ribs.

"Blyat, woman, you're strong."

"That's right, I am."

Her arms cinch around my neck, and I draw her in, palms gliding up her back, gathering her close like I can shield her from the entire world if I just hold her tightly enough.

"I'll love you until the last breath leaves my body, moya zhena. Moya zhizn." *My wife. My life.*

There are moments when I could swear this is some cruel trick, or maybe some dream I haven't woken up from. That she's here with me, loving me back. That I haven't broken her too badly to reach this point. But here she is, peering back at me like she sees the man I'm trying to be. Like she believes in him.

It is why I had to give her the vineyard. I didn't want to chain her to me. I needed her choice, needed to know that when she stayed, it was because she wanted to, not because I backed her into a corner. I needed to know I was enough.

And right now, with her arms around me, her eyes glistening as she looks down at me, I start to believe that maybe I am.

Pulling back, she reaches for the strawberries, mischief dancing in those eyes I'd burn down the world for. One glides along her finger, crushed slightly at the edge, and she drags it across my mouth with a soft hum, smearing juice along my bottom lip.

I bite it straight from her fingers, eyes fastened on hers. Before the last of the berry is gone, I lean in and kiss her, letting her taste the sweetness on my tongue. She moans, her body writhing like she needs this just as badly as I do.

When I finally pull back, her lips are flushed, her hair a mess around her face, and I take her in like I'm starving.

How the hell did I ever live without this?

"What?" She watches me curiously.

"I am just wondering why it took me this long to realize how obsessed I am with you."

Her grin sparks, her fingers brushing the back of my neck. "Obsession's not very healthy, you know."

"That's right, Mrs. Marinova. It is quite the disease."

"For which there's no antidote?"

"I don't want an antidote." I brush my nose along hers. "I want you. Every minute of every day, until my very last breath."

"Aleksei…" Her voice frays.

I flip her onto her back in one fluid motion, her sundress riding up those soft thighs, her laughter breaking in her throat. The sunlight bounces across her skin, and I swear I've never seen anything more beautiful.

"I love you, detka."

Her fingers tug through my hair, massaging my scalp, and she lets out a low, lustful sound as she rolls her hips over my cock, slow enough to wreck me.

"You said that already."

My hand drifts to her thigh, gliding up that soft skin I can never get enough of. "What? A man can't tell you he loves you more than once?"

I tug her panties aside and let my fingers trace the slick warmth between her legs before sliding one inside, her body opening for me.

"You can say whatever you want," she breathes, her nails digging into my shoulders. "As long as you keep touching me like that."

My fingers thrust deeper, curling just right, coaxing the kind of sounds from her I want burned into my fucking soul. She moves against me with a slow, aching need that sets my nerves on fire.

I tear my mouth from hers only long enough to strip her dress off and toss it aside. She's already fumbling at my waist, pushing my pants down like she can't stand another second without me inside her. Her fingers curl around my cock, brushing the piercings, and a sharp bolt of pleasure shoots up my spine.

"Fuck." I shove her hand away so I can line myself up with her pussy, my grip tightening on her hip. "I need you. I need you so fucking much it hurts."

"Show me."

One hard, controlled thrust slides me inside her all the way. She clenches around me, pulling a broken sound from my lungs.

"Aleksei…harder," she gasps, head tipping back, legs locking around my waist. "Please."

My fingers dig into her hips as I start to move, driving into her with the kind of force she's begging for, every stroke deep and hungry.

"I love you," I tell her, and her sounds of pleasure come in gasping waves.

"Say it again," she pants.

I take her harder. "Ya tebya lyublyu."

My pace increases until she's trembling beneath me, her body going tight as the orgasm slams into her.

"Aleksei, oh God."

When she says my name like that, I lose whatever control I had left. I keep fucking her, pouring every vicious, desperate part of myself into her. Giving her everything I am and everything I'll ever be.

There will never be another man after me. I am making damn sure of it.

When I come, it's with a guttural growl, buried deep inside her, spilling everything I have into the woman who owns me.

FORTY-ONE

FIONA

My feet ache from standing in heels all morning, and the minute I close the door to my office and settle in my chair, I kick them off under the desk, sliding my toes along the carpet with a sigh.

Court was brutal. Three motions back-to-back, a judge with no patience, and opposing counsel who thinks "respectfully" means "condescendingly."

All I want is to go home. To Aleksei. To whatever sinful thing he's planning to cook for dinner tonight. Because the man doesn't just kill for a living. He makes a steak that should be illegal.

Of course, it doesn't hurt that he looks good doing it too. Sleeves rolled to his elbows, veins flexing as he chops herbs like they've personally offended him. I swear that man does things to me that shouldn't be allowed.

And usually, when the dishes are cleared, dessert follows in the form of his tongue between my thighs—and I sure as hell could use that right about now.

My core tightens at the memory of last night. The way he lifted me onto the counter and didn't let me off until I was trembling more times than I could count.

When my phone buzzes, I already know it's him before I swipe the screen.

ALEKSEI

Only a few more hours until you are mine, moya ptichka. I've been thinking about stripping off that tight little skirt you had on this morning, dragging you into the shower, and pressing you up against the tile. Mouth on your throat. Fingers inside your wet cunt until you're begging for my cock to take that throb away.

My throat goes dry and I bite my lip, warmth suddenly racing through my body.

Another message flashes across the screen.

ALEKSEI

Maybe I won't even let you undress. Maybe I'll bend you over the sink and fuck you with your heels still on.

Heat rushes up my neck so fast it's embarrassing. Jesus Christ. I can almost picture him smirking. He knows what he does to me when he talks like that.

FIONA

This is unfair.

ALEKSEI

Life is unfair, baby.

My hand snaps around the phone, and before I can stop myself, my mind flashes to last night. To the dirty things he was saying as he fucked me over the kitchen table, gripping my hair as he did.

"Hey," Dana's voice comes through, startling me.

The phone fumbles from my fingers, slipping onto the desk.

"Whoa." She grins. "Someone looks like they just got caught doing something naughty."

"Jesus, Dana. You scared the shit out of me."

She laughs, shutting the door behind her. "Mm-hmm. I wonder why. Is it that secret guy you've been hiding from me?"

"There's no secret guy."

Just a husband...

"So, what's up?" My back straightens as I regain my composure.

Dana lifts a white envelope from her folder. "The secretary handed me this on my way here. Said it was waiting for you at reception."

I glance at it. "What is it?"

She shrugs. "No idea. Doesn't say."

She hands it across the desk, and the second I see it, my stomach caves in. Every muscle goes rigid as a sharp, cold panic cuts through the warmth Aleksei's text left behind.

It's plain and unmarked. Just like the others.

For a moment, the office disappears, and all I'm left with is the familiar dread curling low in my gut.

"Fiona? You okay? You look like you've seen a ghost." Her voice sounds far away, like it's echoing down a tunnel.

I can't tear my vision off the paper. The edges blur. The pulse in my neck throbs so hard it's like the room is shrinking around me.

I was hoping the letters would stop. That whoever was sending them got bored. No such luck.

"Yeah, I'm fine." I force a smile and pick up the envelope, hoping I'm wrong and it isn't from whoever has been sending these notes.

But I can't open it now. Not in front of her.

"Are you sure you're okay?" Dana's gaze thins as she pulls up a chair and slowly settles onto it.

"Yeah, sorry. Just a long day." I force out a smile.

"Okay, if you're sure…"

"Yeah. How's your murder case going?" I'm hoping the change of topic distracts her from the letter on my desk. "Do you want to go over the argument?"

"No, I should be fine."

"Okay, sure."

She stays for a few minutes, rambling about her opening testimony and the witnesses she plans to call. I nod when I'm supposed to, but my mind's a million miles away. All I can think about is the envelope burning a hole on my desk.

As soon as she leaves, I pull it out and open it, adrenaline pumping through my veins. When I read the words, my entire world spins.

> Do you finally want to know the truth? It's in your parents' office.
>
> Look in the safe.

My attention stays fixed on the words, my heart knocking against my rib cage like it's trying to warn me of something I don't quite understand.

Maybe it's a joke. Another twisted game to mess with my head. That would make sense. But something settles in the pit of my stomach, and it won't let go.

I should toss it in the shredder and pretend I never saw it. That would be the sane thing to do. But my fingers fold the paper before I can think twice, slipping it into the front pocket of my purse.

Grabbing my coat, I smooth my expression into something neutral and tell my assistant I need to step out for the rest of the day.

If the safe is empty, if whatever this *thing* is turns out to be nothing, then it all ends there. But if it's not, if there's actually something inside, something my parents have been hiding from me…

I can't even let myself finish the thought. What could it possibly be?

God, this is insane.

I slide into the driver's seat, my bodyguards settling into the SUV behind me. The letter sits buried in my bag, but it might as well be burning a hole through the fabric. I can't stop thinking about it. What it means. What it could lead to.

I know I have to tell Aleksei. Not just because part of me is scared, but because I don't want to face this alone anymore. He'll help me figure it out and eliminate the threat if it comes to that.

A wry laugh slips out. Look at me, thinking like a goddamn Mob wife.

I don't know if that should terrify me…or make me proud.

The wheels crunch to a stop in the narrow dirt lot, but I barely register the sound. My eyes lift to the vineyard ahead, and even though I'm technically the owner now, I still feel like a trespasser, knowing I'm about to get into my parents' safe.

Do they even know he signed the majority share to me?

Doesn't matter. Right now, all I care about is whether there's any truth to the note.

As I climb out, I silently hope there's nothing to find. I'm seconds from reaching the door when it swings open, and I jolt back at the sight of one of the employees emerging with a clipboard tucked to her chest.

"Ms. Clark, how are you? Your parents are out walking the rows. Should I get them?"

"No," I answer too fast. "I just…need to grab something really quick. You don't have to bother them."

"Okay." She starts down the steps. "It's nice to see you. Have a good day."

"You too."

The second she's out of sight, I rush down the corridor and into the office, shutting the door behind me. My focus goes straight to the framed grape artwork on the wall. I lift it down carefully and set it aside, revealing the safe hidden behind it.

My fingers hover over the keypad for a heartbeat before I finally enter the code. My birthday. They have never used anything else.

A soft beep sounds, followed by the quiet click of the lock releasing.

My pulse spikes.

I pull the door open and start working fast, wanting to be done before my parents come in and wonder what I'm doing here.

Inside, the safe is packed tight. Manila envelopes. Thick file folders. Curled receipts. Stacks of documents that look like they have been building up for years.

Shit. There is a lot to go through.

I start pulling everything out, spreading the contents on the desk. Sifting through the documents in the folders reveals nothing but old contracts with various vendors. Once I start with the envelopes, it starts being much of the same.

Until I get to the second to last one.

At first, it seems like a simple contract, the one Aleksei signed with my parents.

Except this is different than the one I read after I agreed to marry him. This one was signed days before Aleksei presented me with the proposal.

What the hell…

My eyes scan the text, my heart rate escalating. Because in this contract…

Oh God, no. They wouldn't do this.

But no matter how many times I read it, the proof is there: they sold me to him.

I reread the paragraph so many times, my eyes bleed. This deal was made without me, and my signature was forged. The only person capable of doing that is my own mother.

A lump forms in my throat. This can't be real.

They did this. They all planned this, and Aleksei never said a thing. Even after things with us started to become good.

They sold me like property, and he went along with it.

Even if he's given me the vineyard now, even if he says he loves me, he kept this from me. How the fuck is that love?

The room tilts, the paper crumpling in my grip. I want to scream. Throw something. Break every bottle in this fucking building.

The door handle suddenly starts to turn, and when my parents step in, chatting with one another, they freeze the moment they see my expression.

But once they notice the opened safe, the contract in my hand, the silence crashes down like thunder. They know exactly what I found.

And now, so do I.

"Tesoro," Mom says gently, taking a few steps toward me. "What are you doing in here? Did you need something?"

A sting burns the backs of my eyes, blurring my vision as my fingers curl tighter around the contract.

"Don't," I snap, my tone so harsh, her eyes widen. "Don't stand there and lie to me. You both have done enough of that."

Her features sink, mirrored in the guilt tightening Dad's face.

I rise to my feet, the paper trembling in my grip. "Were you ever going to tell me?"

Her brows knit. "Tell you what?"

That only enrages me further, a bitter laugh scraping from my throat. "You're seriously going to pretend you have no idea what I'm talking about?"

My father runs a hand down his face, while my mother says nothing.

"You sold me to him!" The words fall like stones. "You gave me away like I meant nothing. To a man who kills for a living! A man I tried to put behind bars! Did you even consider what he could do to me?"

Dad closes his eyes and lowers himself slowly onto the desk chair behind him, as if the weight of everything has finally knocked him down. Mom starts to cry, wiping away her tears.

"Is that how much I meant to you?" I glance between the two of them, heart splintering with every word. "What's worse is I was willing to do it. For *you*. I married him because I loved you both that much. But you never gave me the chance. You just…did it. You were going to let him force me if I said no."

"We had no choice," she whimpers. "We did something terrible trying to save the vineyard. It cost us everything."

My head jerks back. "What did you do?"

When my father speaks, his voice is low and frayed. "We took a loan, stellina. For four hundred thousand. From a man we never should've gone to."

"A loan shark," my mom whispers, as though this asshole will just magically appear. "He threatened us. Said he would kill us. And you." She swallows hard, taking a seat beside my dad. "Then Aleksei came. He offered to pay off the debt. Help the vineyard. Said he could protect us. All he asked for was—"

"Me," I cut in, my stomach turning. "All he asked for was me. My life. My future."

"It wasn't easy," my mother cries, reaching for my hand, and I'm too numb to push her away. "We said no at first, I swear. But then Aleksei threatened us too, and we felt we had no choice."

"I'm sorry," Dad says softly. "Ogni giorno, mi maledico per averti tradita in quel modo." *Every day, I curse myself for betraying you like that.*

"You should've come to me. I would've helped you. But *this*?" I shove the contract forward. "This wasn't the way. I'm a human being."

"Please," my mother chokes out. "Forgive us. We did wrong. We know."

I shake my head. "I…I just need space right now, okay? Can you guys give me that? Because it's too hard to process it all right now."

"Of course." My father nods solemnly, while my mother silently cries.

I hate seeing them this way, and I feel guiltier for walking toward the door, but where do *I* matter in all this? Where does *my* hurt come into play?

Before I can stop myself, I rush out and get into the car, barely registering the slam of the door behind me. My fingers tremble as they grip the wheel, fury and heartbreak tangling in my chest like barbed wire.

I know exactly where I'm going next: to him.

To Aleksei.

He's going to look me in the eye and tell me why he stood there and pretended I had a choice when every move had already been made for me.

FORTY-TWO

FIONA

The drive is endless, though I don't remember the streets I take or the lights I run. Everything outside the windshield blurs into gray streaks of rain and motion, and my fingers grip the wheel until the leather creaks beneath them.

Every mile closer to Aleksei's building feels like another step toward detonating something that can't be undone. By the time I reach the glass tower, my stomach is twisted in knots. I sign in at security and mindlessly ride up the elevator to the top floor.

When the doors open, I spot his secretary behind a sleek white desk, phone pressed to her ear.

She looks up, smile automatic. "Good afternoon. Do you have an—"

"I'm here to see Aleksei. I'm his wife." My voice cuts through hers before she can finish. "Where is he?"

Her eyes widen. "Oh, Mrs. Marinova, of course. I'll let him know you're here."

"No." I shake my head. "Tell me where he is. I'll let him know myself."

The woman hesitates, glancing toward the corridor. "He's in the conference room at the end of the hall, but he's in a meeting. If you wait—"

"I won't be waiting."

I want the element of surprise.

My heels strike the floor in sharp, echoing beats as I move down the hallway. Each step seems to squeeze something tighter inside my chest, pressure building beneath my ribs. The contract burns against my palm, hot with betrayal.

When I reach the door, I don't stop. I push it open. As soon as I strut in, the room falls with a heavy silence.

Two dozen men sit around a long black table, every head swiveled toward me, Aleksei's brothers among them. When my gaze lands on Aleksei, his brows tug as he rises from the far end of the table.

"Fiona?" He advances, but something in my features holds him back. "Are you okay? What's wrong?"

The sound of my name shatters me. A cry tears out of me before I can stop it, and every man in that room stiffens.

Aleksei doesn't hesitate. "Everyone out. Now."

Chairs scrape, and the men file out quickly. Konstantin is the only one remaining, his attention flicking between us.

"Whatever this is, it will be all right."

He lays a hand on my shoulder, and I shake my head, swiping a tear away.

"No. It won't."

His gaze lingers on me for a beat. Then, with a firm nod, he's gone, the door closing quietly in his wake.

Aleksei moves toward me, but I edge back.

"Don't."

"Fiona, what's going on?"

My throat tightens so hard it hurts to breathe.

"I don't even know what I expected from you." I snicker. "Honesty? Maybe that was asking too much, considering who you are."

He frowns, confusion flashing across his features.

"Do you really love me, Aleksei? Or was this just part of the game?" A harsh, shaky laugh slips out of me. "That was the point, wasn't it? To hurt me? To see how far you could twist the knife before I broke?" I swipe at my face, angry at the tears. "Well, congratulations. You broke me."

He takes another cautious step, his tone firm but edged with tension. "Fiona, what are you talking about?"

"This." I throw the contract at his feet. "This is what I'm talking about."

He glances down, and the blood drains from his face.

"Yeah. That's right. I found it. The deal you made with my parents. The one where you bought me like one of your fucking cars."

His mouth opens, then closes again. For once, he has no words.

"Don't," I warn when he reaches out. "Don't touch me."

He freezes, and the silence between us roars.

"I can't believe I've been such an idiot," I choke out. "Thinking we had something real. That we were healing. But we have nothing, Aleksei. Nothing! We never have."

He shakes his head, eyes glassy. "That's not true, Fiona, I swear I—"

"Don't you dare say it. There's never been anything real between us. And thanks to whoever's been sending those cryptic messages, I finally see it. You and my parents, you're the same. You don't give a damn about me."

The change in his face is instant. "Someone is sending you messages? Why haven't you told me? Where is it? Show me."

"Don't worry about it." I look away. "It doesn't matter anymore."

"Of course it matters! Blyat! I love you, Fiona."

"Love? You have some way of showing it."

My fingers move to the chain around my neck, the one holding both my rings. I stare at the band on his hand, still there, gleaming under the harsh lights, and the pain inside me deepens until it's unbearable.

"You know…" I whisper, tears roving down my face. "I actually did love you too. More than you'll ever deserve."

I unclasp the chain and set it on the edge of the table. The tiny clink echoes like a gunshot.

He's on me in two strides, his hand buried in my hair as he presses me against the wall. His breath is ragged, his eyes wild.

"Did?" His voice is rough, broken glass scraping. "No. You *do* love me. You can't just erase that. I won't let you."

I place a palm against his cheek.

"You're right," I whisper. "I can't."

For a moment, we just breathe each other's air, the space between us trembling with everything unsaid before I lean forward and press a kiss to his lips. Soft. Fleeting. Final.

"It's why this hurts so much. You should've told me. You should've given me the truth. I would've been furious, but I would've respected you for it. Instead, you hid it. That's not love. And I can't live like that."

"Fiona…please. I'm begging you."

"I'm done, Aleksei. Whatever else you've been hiding, I don't even want to know."

His jaw locks, eyes burning with something broken. "I will never let you go."

The words sound like they're breaking him, like he won't survive losing me.

"Then kill me. Or let me walk away."

He shuts his eyes, forehead falling against mine. The tremor in his breaths snaps me in half.

"I don't know how to do that."

"You'll learn." My soul splinters, hating every second of this.

He takes a shuddering inhale. "Please. Please understand. I was a different man then. And your parents, they had no choice. Not with the debt they owed. Not when I threatened them."

"Yeah," I whisper. "They told me about that." Tears continue to stream down my cheeks. "And do you know what I told them? That I would've done anything to help them. I *did* do anything. I agreed to marry you. But they sold me to you like property. And you went along with it."

"I'm sorry," he says. "Fiona, please. I don't exist without you. I'll do anything you want. Anything. Don't walk away from me."

"I already have." The words leave me hollow and bleeding.

When I push off the wall, he grabs my wrist before I can move. "I'll leave the house. You don't have to go. Stay."

I shake my head, tears falling faster now. "It's not my home, Aleksei. It's yours."

His features twist with his anguish, his grip tightening. "You can't go back to your house. They're still after you. Do you understand that? I'd die before I let anything happen to you, ptichka."

"I'll go to a hotel."

His face flashes with anger. "The men will go with you."

"I don't need—"

He cuts me off sharply. "No. That's not negotiable. They will protect you. *I* will protect you. No matter what, you're still mine."

Still his…

God, what I wouldn't do to forget all of this and tell him how badly I want to be his again.

"Fine," I say instead, choking on too much pain.

He exhales harshly, the tension draining from him as his fingers slip from my wrist to my hand, weaving through my trembling ones. His words come out rough, unsteady, like they're being dragged from somewhere deep.

"I cannot watch you walk away. This is killing me."

"Then turn around," I whisper.

His thumb moves over my skin in slow circles. "I can never do that, detka. You are mine. And I will always be yours. I'll prove my worth to you. I'll fix this. I'll win you back." Every syllable is raw and desperate. "This is not the end for us."

I look at him one last time, memorizing the man I fell in love with…and the man who broke me. They're both standing in front of me, wearing the same face.

A sad smile ghosts across my lips. "You've already lost me, Aleksei."

I pull my hand free and turn toward the door. Each step is like walking barefoot across broken glass.

His gaze clings to me, scorching the space between us, but I don't look back. Not as I walk down the hall with my spine stiff, pretending I'm not falling apart.

Only when the elevator begins its slow descent do I break, coming apart at the seams as I leave him behind—leave *us* behind—and walk away from the lie I mistook for love.

ALEKSEI

The sound of the door closing behind her detonates something inside me.

For a long moment, I stand there, rooted and numb, staring at the space she left behind. Her scent still hangs in the air, and the silence swells around me until it splits me open.

A growl tears out of me before I can stop it. The nearest chair goes flying, crashing into the wall with a sound that rattles through my skull. Papers scatter. Glass shatters. The decanter of whiskey explodes across the floor.

None of it dulls the throbbing in my chest, but I need to break something else because I can't tear out the thing inside me that's already breaking.

The table is next. I sweep everything off it in one violent motion, folders and pens crashing across the floor, and in the dark window, I catch my reflection: bloodshot eyes, breath heaving, the hollow outline of a man who just lost the only woman he's ever loved.

I would give anything to go back and change that one decision. To never make her parents sign that contract. But it's too late now.

The door opens and Konstantin steps in, his gaze sweeping the wreckage before landing on me.

"Feel any better?"

"Not even a little."

He closes the door, walks over the broken glass, and stops a few feet away. "You'll fix it."

I shake my head. "I don't think I can. She found out about the contract, and there is the other thing she does not know about. And if I tell her…" My throat locks up. "If I tell her, it will be worse."

Konstantin exhales. "You will have to tell her anyway."

I drag a hand over my face. "I don't know how, brother. How do you do this?"

He knows what I mean. A marriage. Love.

He doesn't answer right away. He walks to the window, hands in his pockets, staring out at the buildings.

"When the woman is worth it, you find a way."

"I didn't want this." I slump into one of the leather chairs. "I fought against it. Against her. Against everything I felt. And now look at me." I gesture at the chaos around us. "Pathetic."

Konstantin turns, a faint smile ghosting his lips. "It's okay to love, Aleksei. It's okay to hurt. Not everything our father taught us was right. He made mistakes. A lot of them. With our mother. With us. We don't have to repeat them."

He comes closer. "You tried to hate her from the start. But the moment she entered your life, you lost that war. You can't kill what's real. You can bury it. You can deny it. But it will always claw its way back."

I stare at the floor, his words like truth and torture all at once.

"If you love her…" he continues. "You fight for her. Fight for your marriage, however it began. Because that does not matter anymore. What matters is now. What you do next."

I let his words hang between us before finally saying, "She's going to a hotel."

He just shrugs. "Then let her. Let her believe it is her idea. But you make sure it's the best one, and that she is protected every second she is there. Then you show her who you can be without demanding she come back. Give her space. Just not enough for her to think she can forget you."

A dry, humorless sound escapes me. "So now that you are married, you're the expert?"

"I think so." He flips his hands in the air. "Just look at me and Emilia. I'd say I'm more than qualified."

A smile dies before it can settle.

"I love her, Konstantin," I admit to someone else for the first time. "More than I thought I could love anything."

"I know," he says simply. "It will be all right."

But I don't believe him.

When he leaves, the silence returns, thicker than before. My mind won't let go of her face. It keeps replaying in brutal clarity. The way her chin trembled. The way she looked at me like every word I had ever said meant nothing. The sound of her voice when she said she loved me, like she could just erase it.

My fist slams into the wall. "Blyat!"

The thought of her somewhere crying, thinking I never loved her…it carves me open.

I'll love her until the day they put me in the ground. Even if she never forgives me, she will always be mine. My wife. My punishment. My salvation.

And I'll fight for her until my dying breath.

FORTY-THREE

FIONA

It's been a whole day since I walked out of that conference room, and every minute since, I've had to act like I'm fine. I've been going through the motions at work like my entire life hasn't been ripped from under me.

I swipe my cell against the doorknob of my new home, the penthouse suite Aleksei arranged for me, with the same two bodyguards following my every move.

Stepping out of my heels, I let them drop with a dull thud beside the door. My blouse clings uncomfortably to my skin, my slacks creased from hours of holding myself together. I don't even bother changing. Phone still in my hand, I move past the untouched minibar and sink onto the edge of the bed, the exhaustion settling in like gravity.

When the screen lights up, I think it's another text from him, but it isn't this time. I haven't bothered responding to his messages begging for my understanding or forgiveness. I don't have it in me. I'm completely drained from everything. My parents, Aleksei, all of it.

Still, I find myself opening the photo gallery and staring at photos of us. Him standing behind me in the mirror, his hands on my hips, my laughter caught mid-breath as he pressed a kiss to my temple. Another shot of us on his bike.

I scroll slowly, one photo to the next, like tracing a wound I can't stop picking at. Each image hurts more than the last. When the pain becomes unbearable, I open our messages, reading through some of the old ones he sent me like a masochist.

ALEKSEI

I missed you this morning. I'll be home early.

FIONA

Can't wait.

Then from just a few days ago:

ALEKSEI

I will burn that red dress you wore to court today. That is, after I fuck you out of it.

FIONA

I'll have you know my husband paid a lot of money for that dress.

ALEKSEI

I don't know what he was thinking. You look too good in it.

I love you.

And he does. I know he does. That's the part that won't stop echoing.

But I don't want this version of love. I want something more than he's capable of, and that's what hurts the most. Knowing he'll never be the man that I deserve.

I close my eyes, but instead of silence, I see his face again. That exact moment in the conference room when he realized I knew. The way the color drained from his skin, how his eyes shattered like glass. That broken look haunts me.

But I remind myself that it shouldn't matter. It shouldn't matter how destroyed he looked. Or that he reached for me like I was slipping through his fingers.

Because he let this happen. He signed that contract. He let my parents trade me and never told me what they all did.

How am I supposed to forgive any of them?

How could my own parents do this to me? I understand they were desperate, but when does that stop being an excuse to sell off your own daughter?

My fingers press into the mattress as if I can anchor myself, but it's useless. I'm floating through a mess I don't know how to escape.

How did it all fall apart so fast?

How can I ever trust Aleksei again? How can I look at him and not see the lies?

I curl onto my side, hugging a pillow that doesn't smell like him, and the loss hits hard. I long for him in a way that's all-consuming.

A sudden knock breaks the silence just as I sink deeper into the mattress.

At first, I don't bother getting up. It's probably the guards or housekeeping. I don't want to see either.

"It's me. Open up." Emilia's voice slips through the room.

Damn it, Konstantin must've told her.

But maybe talking to her would be good. I have no one else. Emilia is the only real friend I have left, and she's the kind of woman who shows up when you need her most, whether you realize it or not.

Dragging myself to the door, I unlock it and step aside. Her eyes widen the moment she sees me.

"Oh," she breathes dramatically, juggling two overstuffed shopping bags. "It's worse than I thought."

"Thanks, asshole," I mutter, managing a halfhearted smile.

She sets the bags down on the side table, then unzips her boots. "Don't worry. It's not nearly as bad as the way Aleksei looks."

For a second, something sick and twisted winds through my chest. Hope. Satisfaction.

"Is he really that miserable?"

Her brows pop. "Are you kidding? The man looks like he hasn't slept since you left. I don't think he's showered either." She scrunches her nose with disgust.

A laugh catches in my throat. "Is it bad if that makes me…happy?"

"Uh, no." She flops down onto the bed, her hair spilling across the pillow. "I'd be concerned if you weren't at least a little thrilled by his absolute spiral."

"This is why I love you." I sink beside her, exhaustion settling beneath my skin like a weighted blanket I can't shake off.

"I brought reinforcements," she announces, reaching into the bag like a magician.

First comes the bottle of Baileys. Then a gallon tub of coffee ice cream. My favorite. The sight of it makes something warm crack through the ice around my chest.

"You always know the way to my heart. Is it too late to get you to divorce Konstantin so you can marry me instead?"

She laughs, wiggling her brows. "As much as Konstantin adores you, I think he's done sharing me."

I jerk back. "Wait. What does that mean?"

"Never mind." She waves it off with a lazy flick of her wrist. "We're not talking about me. We're talking about you and lover boy."

There's definitely more there I want to unpack, but I don't have the energy right now.

Groaning, I tip my head back against the headboard. "I don't even know who I'm angrier at: him or my parents. I want to scream at both of them. Or maybe just crawl into a hole and never come out."

"It's not a competition. You're allowed to be mad at all of them. Frankly, I'm mad at them too."

I stare at the ceiling. "What would you do?"

"Punch something," she says without hesitation.

"I'm serious."

"So am I." Her grin widens. "Trust me, it helps."

Of course she'd say that. Emilia's obsessed with jiujitsu, with turning pain into power. I envy that. I've always carried mine until it rots me from the inside out.

"I don't know what to say to any of them," I whisper. "To my parents. To Aleksei. What am I supposed to do, pretend it's fine? Tell them I forgive them?"

"No," she says softly. "And no one expects you to. Least of all me."

A ragged sigh slips out. "I understand why they did it. I really do. They were desperate, scared. They thought they had no way out."

"But you're their daughter," she finishes for me.

I nod. "And Aleksei… I don't even know what to do with all these feelings. I hate what he did. I hate that he didn't tell me. But I miss him so much it physically hurts."

Emilia wraps an arm around my shoulders, pulling me in. "You don't have to figure it all out tonight. Or tomorrow. Take all the time you need. But, Fiona, he does love you, and you know I would never say that lightly."

"I know." The words break loose on a trembling exhale. "And that makes everything hurt even more."

ALEKSEI

It's been four fucking days.

Four days since she walked out. Four days since she touched me, looked at me, breathed the same air.

And somehow I'm still walking around like I'm alive when everything in me is dead.

I have returned to watching her on cameras, and I hate it now. I want her here. With me.

The house mocks me without her. Every hallway reeks of her perfume. Every room holds some ghost of her laughter or the sound of her footsteps. I've walked into our bedroom ten times only to turn around and march right back out, unable to stand one more reminder of what I've lost.

I haven't slept. I barely eat. I don't remember the last time I shaved, and judging by the state of my shirt, I haven't changed it in days.

What for? Nothing matters without her.

Today, I finally put something clean on because I had to. Konstantin called a meeting, and my presence is mandatory.

When I walk into his study, they're already there. Konstantin nods in greeting, seated behind his desk. Anton stands by the window like a hollow ghost, while Kirill is sprawled across the couch, foot bouncing.

Kirill looks up and mutters, "You look like shit."

I grunt and drop into a chair.

"Worse than shit, actually," he continues.

"Leave him," Konstantin cuts in. "We have bigger problems." He opens the folder on the desk. "We need to arrange a sit-down with the Italians and create an alliance. A marriage arrangement between us and them. It is the best avenue for lasting peace."

"No."

They all turn to me.

"Not after what that family did. They should be thanking us for not torching every last one of them."

Konstantin's eyes narrow. "We will handle that, Aleksei, but there is a bigger picture here."

"I don't give a shit about that." My hands fist against my thighs, the fury shaking loose through me. "And as far as the Volkovs, we need to kill them all, then take care of that Italian svolich before one of them tries something. I will not let that happen."

Blood roars in my ears as I get to my feet, untamed rage simmering in my veins. "If you don't want to start a war right now, fine. I will do it myself."

"Aleksei," Konstantin warns, but I keep going.

"They came into our city, threatened our blood, *touched my wife.* I will not let that stand. I'll take every last one of them apart with my bare hands if I have to."

Silence cuts through the room, then Konstantin leans forward.

"We will fight," he says. "In one week's time."

I stop pacing.

"That's why I called you all here," he continues. "To plan it. We need to be smart. I want every Volkov dead by the end of the month. We are not just going to retaliate. We are going to erase them."

A hard chill settles in my chest. "That's not soon enough."

Konstantin's mouth twitches. "Maybe you should go take a shower. Sleep. Eat. You'll need the strength."

Kirill snorts. "He will not unless she's the one feeding him."

He's not wrong. None of it matters without her. Not the power or the money, not if I'm doing it alone.

I settle back onto the chair and drag a hand down my face again, slower this time. "She won't even talk to me."

"Then you try harder," Konstantin says.

"I need to fix this. How do I fix it?"

"You start by telling her everything," he continues. "Even the things you think she will never forgive."

My jaw grinds. "And if she doesn't forgive me?"

He leans back, that faint ghost of a smirk pulling at the corner of his mouth. "Then you make her."

Kirill lets out a sharp bark of laughter, the sound cutting through the tension. "That's right."

Anton, though, says nothing, just watches us from his place by the window.

For a minute, I don't know if I envy him for not feeling this kind of pain or pity him for never knowing what it means to love someone so much it destroys you.

FORTY-FOUR

FIONA

My hands curl around the chamomile tea, letting the warmth of the mug settle into my palms while the TV hums in the background, nothing more than noise.

Every night in this hotel suite, it feels smaller. Maybe it's the loneliness, or maybe it's the way everything reminds me of him even when he isn't here.

It's been another two days, and I just want to go home. Back to my old life, away from the constant reminders of him. But the reality is, going back home wouldn't change any of it. He'd still be in every corner of my thoughts.

Finishing my tea, I change into an oversized T-shirt and leggings, pull my hair into a messy bun, and drop onto the bed, knowing what comes next. It's what I do every night, needing my fix.

I reach for my phone on the nightstand, unlock the screen, and stare at photos of us from when I actually let myself imagine a future with him. I gaze at the pictures until my chest twinges. Until I can almost sense the warmth of his breath against my neck, the sound of his laugh echoing in my ear.

It gets harder every day not to go back. Harder not to answer when he calls, not to fold under the weight of how much I miss him. But I can't seem to forgive him.

Love doesn't erase betrayal. It only makes it hurt more.

Just as I scroll to another photo, the phone buzzes, Mom's picture appearing on the screen, and I just don't have the energy to speak to her. A second later, a text pops up.

MOM

I know you need time, and Papa and I understand that, but we miss you so much and just want you to know we love you and we are sorry.

My eyes pinch shut and I text her back.

FIONA

I know. Good night, Ma.

MOM

Good night, tesoro.

Releasing a sigh, I drop the phone onto the comforter and stare up at the ceiling.

She's sorry. He's sorry. They're all sorry. But sorry doesn't undo what they did.

At least I know my parents are safe at Aleksei's. He'd never let anyone hurt them, no matter how angry I am with him. That's just who he is. The contradiction that is Aleksei Marinov: merciless to the world, but not to the people he loves.

I press a hand over my heart, the throbbing there deep and constant. It's been days, but it feels like years. Like I've been holding my breath since the moment I walked out of his office and haven't found the strength to exhale.

The room is colder all of a sudden, and I curl onto my side, pulling the blanket up to my chin while I flip through channels without really seeing any of them. No matter what's on the screen, all I can think about is him.

His voice. His hands. The way he looked at me before everything fell apart.

A movie plays in the background, something loud and dramatic, but it barely registers. I'm drifting, half numb, when a knock jolts me upright.

I glance at the clock beside the bed. Past eleven. Who would be here at this hour?

My bodyguards are on rotation, one always stationed right outside. If something was wrong, they would text me or just storm in.

The knock comes again, harder this time.

A groan slips out as I shove the comforter aside and pad across the floor. Pressing my eye to the peephole, I catch sight of who it is, and the air leaves my lungs in a rush.

Aleksei is there, running a hand through his disheveled hair, wearing gray sweats slung low on his hips and a wrinkled hoodie, like he pulled it on without thinking.

He looks visibly exhausted, dark spots under his eyes like he hasn't slept for days. I've never seen him this way. As though his entire world has imploded.

My fingers hesitate on the lock, a lump settling in my throat.

I want to see him. I don't want to see him.

God, I miss him.

Maybe I can just talk to him for a minute. I mean, the man looks like shit. It's the least I can do. It doesn't mean I have to forgive him, right?

Clearing my throat, I tug out my hair tie and rake my fingers through my hair, trying to look a little less like I'm falling apart on the inside.

As soon as I open the door, his brows pull in, emotions filling every line on his face. He doesn't move, and neither do I, even while I so badly want to jump into his arms and stay there.

"Hey," I manage, thin and brittle.

His jaw clenches, throat working like the words hurt before they even leave him.

"Privet, detka." Each syllable cracks around the edges.

And just like that, the ache I've been fighting all night shoves hard behind my eyes. Because even after everything, he's still the man I let into my heart, and now I can't seem to tear him out without bleeding.

I want to reach for him. I want to slam the door. I want a thousand things I can't have anymore.

"What do you want, Aleksei?"

The question tastes bitter, and he doesn't answer immediately. His eyes hold mine, so raw it's as though I'm sinking into them.

"You," he whispers, so broken it cuts into me.

My chin trembles. Just the sound of that word from his mouth threatens to undo me.

But I can't let it. I can't fall into the gravity of him again, not when I've barely learned how to stand without him.

"I told you we're over." But it's like I'm trying to convince myself. "I don't know what else to say."

"Then why…" He steps into the space between us. "Why does it not feel like we are?"

Before I can react, he's already inside, filling the room. Filling the air I've been trying not to breathe. Instinct kicks in and my feet retreat, carrying me backward as he moves forward until the door clicks shut behind him and I'm trapped again—by his orbit, by the power he's always held over me.

"I can't breathe without you, Fiona." His chest works with rough, uneven breaths, like he sprinted to get here. "Do you understand that?"

My tears threaten as I ache to bury my face in his neck and forget everything but the way his arms feel around me. The way his heart used to beat against mine. It hurts to see him so broken, his eyes bloodshot as they beg for my understanding.

It's like he's been stripped bare, and all that's left is his heartbreak.

"I want to be everything you need." His hand reaches for mine, and I can't seem to move.

His fingers lace with mine, and something inside my chest stirs, pain and longing tangled together until I don't even know what I'm feeling anymore.

"I've never felt more alive than when I am with you. I have spent my whole entire life avoiding this." He squeezes my hand. "Avoiding love. Calling it weakness. Saying that needing someone the way I need you made me less somehow." He draws closer, the heat of his body wafting over mine. "But then I met you. And you... You slit every lie I told myself. You are my destiny, and I destroyed it."

The tears come without warning, burning a hole through my heart.

"I hurt you." His words crack. "I betrayed the one person who ever saw me and accepted me anyway. If I could go back, I would. I would rewrite every second and make it right."

His knees hit the floor before the shock of it hits me.

I inhale sharply, hand still clutched in his. His head lowers, like he doesn't even deserve to look at me.

"I will do anything to earn your forgiveness. Anything. Just tell me how to fix it."

Seeing him like this, on his knees in front of me with a desperation that splits the room in half...it does something violent to me. I don't know what to do with the pressure in my chest that keeps growing, making it hard to speak, hard to think.

But I know this: words are just words. I need to be able to trust him and know he won't hurt me or lie to me. He has to prove it.

And if he truly loves me the way he says he does, he'll earn my trust back. He'll fight for it.

"I have never given this part of myself to any woman," he adds. "But every bit of me is yours, Ms. Prosecutor. You own me. And I swear I will do everything to prove I am the man you expect. I want to be more than my father taught me to be. I want to be the man you can depend on, the man you can trust."

Hearing him say what I needed overflows me with emotion.

"I cannot change what happened, I know that, but I can control what happens next. I want to be honest with you about everything. Just let me. Please, Fiona."

Do I believe he's capable of being the man he wants to be?

"If you don't want me after that…" he says, the words rasping through the silence. "Then at least I know I tried. I won't make you love me. I won't force you to stay. But you are so much more than I could ever be. You're not just my equal. You are a better version. And you always will be."

My vision blurs, full of hot and relentless tears that slip down my cheeks. He rises to his feet, brushing them away with the back of his hand, and that touch alone sends me spiraling.

"Just know, no matter what you decide…there will never be anyone else for me. I will die alone."

There's too much in my chest—anger, grief, yearning, all knotted so tightly I don't know where one ends and the other begins.

This man took my choices, twisted my life into something unrecognizable, and forced me to see a world I used to fight against. Still, with everything he's done, I want to fall into him, even if only for tonight.

Because God help me, I miss him.

I let my thumb brush his cheek, just to feel him beneath my skin. Just to remember what it's like to be whole.

"Aleksei…" His name breaks in my throat.

Tears slip down again, and I don't stop them. What's the point in fighting the ache when it's already taken root in every move I make?

"I miss you," he whispers, lifting my hand to his mouth. His lips brush my knuckles so tenderly, I have to shut my eyes just to hold the feeling. "I'm ill without you."

"Good," I whisper, a small laugh escaping.

A smile flickers through the devastation on his face while his fingers tilt my chin up, and the contact sends a rush of warmth shooting straight up my spine.

His eyes search mine—hungry, desperate, broken in all the ways I feel inside—and slowly, he leans in until his breath brushes my lips, the space between us tightening like a pull I can't resist. Then his hand shifts.

One moment, I'm standing in front of him; the next, my back hits the wall, his body crowding mine, heat rolling off him in waves. My stomach drops, my pulse surges, and his words grind out low against my cheek.

"I need you..."

I should stop this. We're supposed to be talking. I should be demanding answers, drawing lines, reminding myself why I left.

But every ounce of logic crumbles beneath the rush of wanting him. The feeling of his mouth, his hands, the way he touches me like I matter and like I belong to him all at once. I've missed the way he consumes me, the way he makes every cell in me feel awake, alive, wanted.

God, I've missed him too. And right now, wanting him drowns out everything else.

My mouth drifts toward his, pulled by a force I have no hope of resisting. When our lips meet, there's nothing soft about it. Everything else melts away. Every fight, every reason I walked away, every warning I've thrown at myself, until there's only him.

His hands are rough as they fist my hair, a growl ripping through him as his tongue invades my mouth, sucking my tongue before nipping on my bottom lip, like he's dying for every bit of me. I hold on to his biceps, muscles straining beneath my hands, and the feeling of him sends a sharp ache spiraling through my center.

His groan vibrates through both of us, a rough, wounded sound that drags a broken moan from my throat. Fingers hook into the waistband of my leggings, finding me burning and wet, slipping inside me with that familiar ease I've craved.

"You feel so fucking good."

Another hard thrust steals my breath, and I'm clawing at his shirt, yanking it up his torso. He tears it off himself, crashing his mouth to mine while I shove his sweats lower and curl my fingers around his cock, hot and solid in my hand.

My leggings are gone in an instant, peeled off with a single drag of his hands. I barely step out of them before he hauls me up, my back hitting the wall, my legs wrapping around him on instinct.

"I love you," he breathes, lining himself at my entrance, his cold piercings sliding over my clit and sending a shudder through me.

"I love you too."

The truth leaves me bare and exposed, but I don't care. I'll never stop loving him.

"Ti vsegda budesh moya." He growls, and the sound tears through me a split second before he drives into me in one brutal thrust.

The wall shakes. My breath breaks. My body clamps down around him so tight he groans against my neck.

His hands are rough as they tangle in my hair, his tongue driving into my mouth, sucking on mine before he nips at my bottom lip like he's starving for every inch of me. I reach for him, cupping his cheek, my cry swallowed by his mouth as he grinds into me, rolling his hips just right and dragging another ragged sound from my throat.

For a moment, nothing exists outside of us. Just this pull between us, a wild rhythm of need and pain and hope tangling together. The world narrows to this. To us. To the way we break and rebuild each other in the same moment.

When he kisses me again, it sinks through every inch of my skin. A violent pull. A homecoming. A plea.

A promise.

It's always been there between us. That unrelenting, beautiful force that drags us back to each other no matter how far we try to run.

He slams roughly, eyes on me, and the world stills. All the noise, all the doubt, all the bruised pieces of us fall away until only this remains: his body inside mine, my nails in his shoulders, our hearts pounding against everything that tried to tear us apart.

And even if I walk away tomorrow, even if we break again, this moment will stay.

A scar. A memory. Proof that for one moment in time, we burned so bright the world could've turned to ash around us and we still wouldn't have let go.

FORTY-FIVE

ALEKSEI

She's lying beside me, staring into my eyes, and I should feel relief. Maybe even some sense of victory. But I don't. I know what will happen when I tell her what I came to say. She will walk away for the second time, and I do not know if I can take it.

"What's wrong?" she asks, knowing me so well.

Two fingers press into my temple. "Fiona…" My hand moves gently across the curve of her bare back, fingers resting just beneath her shoulder blade. "There's something I have to tell you."

Her body stills as she lifts her head slightly, enough for our eyes to meet in the dim light of the room, and I see it. That flicker of dread. Like she already knows whatever I'm about to say will hurt.

"The reason I have always been one step ahead…" I begin, trying to convince myself that she will understand. "It's because I put a GPS tracker in you."

Her eyes grow, and she instantly pulls back as if I've struck her. "What?"

"I broke into your house after the trial and drugged your tea, just enough to make you sleep deeply, and I injected it in you."

She recoils like she can't stand the sight of me. "Where?"

My fingers brush the spot at the base of her neck.

Her hand flies to her mouth. "Oh my God…"

"It's small. Buried under the skin. You never felt it."

"Jesus Christ." Her whisper slices through the room. "You…you put something inside me?"

I sit up, reaching for her hand, but she yanks it away before I can make contact. There's nothing I can tell her that will make her see me as any less of a monster that I am.

"At first, it was because I wanted to know what you were planning for me after the trial. Then it became an obsession that turned into a need to keep you safe."

"That wasn't your choice," she fires back, trembling with something deeper than rage. "You had no right."

"No, I did not. I am a bastard, Fiona, but I'm a bastard who loves you." When I cup her cheek, she flinches, and it guts me. "We can go and get it removed tomorrow. I swear to you, I will not do that to you anymore."

She says nothing, just gapes at me like the walls of her world are tilting sideways. I'm tearing down everything she thought she knew.

"There is something else." I force the words out. "That night when you were attacked in your home. That man who broke in…"

Her head snaps toward me, a palm splaying over her chest. "Please tell me you didn't send him."

"No." I grab her hand in an instant, kissing the pads of her fingers with unflinching desperation. "I could never bring myself to do that."

A pause swells between us.

"I was the one who got rid of him."

Confusion flashes across her features. "What are you talking about?"

"The man who tried to take you. He wasn't random. He was an enforcer for a rival Russian Mafia family. I was following him because I did not trust him after a business meeting he had with my family. I didn't know it would lead to you, and I didn't even know who you were."

She shifts at that, her grip on my hand tightening just a fraction, a tremor running through her fingers.

"When I found you on the floor…" My jaw locks. "Something in me snapped. So I killed him."

Silence swallows the room whole for a few seconds.

"I…I don't know what to say." Her lips quiver, and she still lets me hold her hand.

"I know, detka. It's a lot." My arm winds around her. "Once we got together, I did not tell you because I didn't want to cause you more pain. I thought it would be easier this way, but I was wrong. I promised you honesty, and I plan to keep that promise."

She pinches the bridge of her nose. "I don't want to hear any more tonight. I, uh…this is too much."

"Alright." My arm tightens around her. "Tomorrow, next week, whenever you are ready. You tell me when. You tell me what you need. For now, just let me hold you."

I give her the chance to push me away, but she doesn't. Instead, she lies back down, pulling the blanket up, facing away from me.

I ease in behind her close enough to feel the warmth of her body, grateful that she's still here with me, which is less than I deserve.

FIONA

It's been hours, but sleep doesn't come. I stay on my back, staring at the ceiling like if I look long enough, it might change everything. Aleksei lies beside me, his breaths slow and steady, like he hasn't just shattered everything all over again.

And maybe that's the difference between us. He's learned how to live with the chaos, while I'm still drowning in it.

I can't stop thinking about everything he confessed. I wanted the truth. I thought I was ready. But now that I have it, I don't know what to do with it.

My fingers drift to the back of my neck. Even though I can't feel it, I know it's there, implanted in me without my consent.

Closing my eyes, I try to get some sleep, but it's impossible. I want to scream. To tear this room apart. To demand something from him, but I don't even know what.

The truth is, I've always known exactly who he is. He hasn't changed. I have.

And that's what makes this hurt even more. Because even now, after everything he's done, I still love him.

Maybe that makes me weak. Or foolish. Or worse…

Maybe it makes me just like him.

I hate him for what he did. But God, I still want him at the same time. And I don't know how to reconcile the two.

When I look over, his face is half shadowed by the moonlight slipping through the windows. His lashes rest against his cheeks, and a strand of dark hair falls across his forehead. That tattoo on his chest rises and falls with each breath, like he's finally at peace because I'm near.

But I don't feel peace. I'm unraveling.

Peeling back the covers, I swing my legs over the edge of the bed, the floor cold against my skin. Getting to my feet, I slide into my sneakers that are tucked neatly in the corner and grab my phone off the nightstand before throwing on his oversized hoodie.

Maybe a quiet walk and some fresh air will help me sleep.

As I give him one last glance, a part of me considers climbing back into bed and acting like none of this ever happened. Just losing myself in his warmth and the fragile illusion that love is enough.

But it isn't.

Without a word, I step out the door. The bodyguard is out cold on the chair, his head tilted back, completely unaware that I'm about to break Aleksei's rule. I only plan to be gone for ten minutes, just enough time to help clear my head.

When the elevator arrives, I step inside, and it descends with a quiet hum. By the time the doors open into the lobby, the massive clock on the far wall is the only thing that seems awake. It's barely five a.m., and the concierge doesn't even lift his head from the desk as I pass.

I push through the exit, and the salty air slams into me, seeping straight through the hoodie.

God, I've always loved being near water. There's something about it that never changes. Beautiful and terrifying in equal measure. It can calm you or pull you under without warning, and you never know which it's going to be until it's too late.

I follow the curve of the sidewalk toward the pier, the distant lights flickering through the dark like a trail of stars. The chill cuts through Aleksei's hoodie as I hug it tighter around myself.

I wonder if he woke up. If he's noticed I'm gone. If he thinks I ran.

I don't want to run. I just need to breathe. To think. To find space between the wreckage of us and the pieces of myself I'm still trying to hold together.

This thing between us, it's violent and beautiful, and some days I can't tell if it's love or war.

Is this what our life would be like? Him watching me all the time, under the guise of safety? Lying to me for my own good? Is that what it means to love a man who can destroy you and protect you with the same hands?

A woman jogs past, her shoulder brushing mine as she mumbles, "Excuse me."

I offer a faint smile. "It's okay."

And for a moment, it is. Until tires screech against the pavement behind me.

A black van cuts across the street, swerving too fast, slamming to a stop beside me.

My body stiffens, my heart tripping over itself.

The door slides open, and two men jump out. I spin on instinct, ready to run, but one of them grabs me, fingers crushing into my arm, the other palm clamping over my mouth.

"Scream and I kill you." His Russian accent makes the hairs on my arms stand up.

The rival Russian family Aleksei mentioned. Is this them?

Panic surges through me as I fight against his hold, but he's too strong, dragging me backward like I weigh nothing. The woman who jogged past me jumps into the van and speeds off, the tires screaming across the pavement.

She was part of it? Oh God.

The second man catches my legs, pulling me toward the pier.

I fight with everything I have left. I twist, kick, claw, anything to break free. My nails rake down the face of the man behind me, and he grunts but doesn't loosen his grip. When I bite the hand over my mouth, he smacks me hard across the face and stars burst behind my eyes.

"Let me go!"

"Zamalchi, suka."

His palm covers my mouth again, and I keep thrashing even as he drags me closer to the edge. My only thought is that Aleksei has to know I'm gone. He has to be tracking me. The same device I hated him for hours ago might be the only thing that saves me now.

The pier is only a few feet away, and panic floods every inch of me. They're going to kill me and throw me in the water.

Terror floods my veins, and all I can think about is my husband. The gentle way he touches me. The way his voice softens when he tells me he loves me. The way he promised to do better. The way I believe he can.

If this is how it ends, please let him know I tried to forgive him. That I wanted to stay.

I bite down again—harder this time, tasting blood—and kick the man in front of me. He growls, then slams his fist into my stomach so hard I can't breathe.

"You try again," he snarls, "and I tell boss you fall in water and drown."

Pain radiates through me, but I don't stop fighting. Not even when my vision blurs. Every second they yank me near the edge, fear builds like a scream stuck in my throat.

I'm not ready to die. Not without seeing him again.

Aleksei…

His name echoes in my head.

Please find me. Before it's too late.

FORTY-SIX

ALEKSEI

"Fiona!"

Her name tears from somewhere deep in my sleep. I bolt upright, heartbeats punching against my ribs like they know something I don't.

I swear I heard her. My hand reaches across the bed before my eyes even adjust to the dark, searching for the warmth of her body.

But all I find is emptiness, and it hits me like a bullet.

"Fiona? Where are you?"

I'm out of bed in seconds, phone in hand as I move through the penthouse, scanning every corner. Anywhere she could be sitting, thinking, hiding. I check the bathroom, the kitchen, and nothing. She's not here.

A weight drops onto my chest.

I open the GPS app, grateful for it now. The dot hovers near the pier.

Blyat! She's out there. Alone. What the hell was she thinking?

I throw on my clothes and fly out of the door only to find my useless guard sleeping when he should have been awake to follow her. My hand drops to my gun without hesitation, the barrel leveled at his skull.

"Padonok." *Scumbag.*

The silenced shot cracks through the hall and he collapses instantly, blood spreading across the expensive carpet like spilled ink.

I don't spare him another glance. He's lucky all he lost was his life. If I wasn't so consumed with getting back to her, I would take more.

I rush toward the elevator, pressing the button over and over. Each second is like a century, the blinking light above mocking me with its lazy ascent.

When the doors finally open, I run inside, chest tight. As I watch the floors blink, cursing for it to hurry, every bad thought flips through my mind.

My wife being shot. Killed. Taken.

"Nu davay!" I bang on the door.

If I don't get to her in time…

Fingers dig into my temple.

I won't just kill whoever touched her. I'll make sure there's nothing left.

The elevator doors slide open, and I'm already moving before they've finished. Every muscle in my body coils as I sprint toward the exit, phone clutched in my hand, eyes glued to the glowing dot on the screen.

Her signal flickers, steady but moving. I'm outside in seconds, the streets empty. I sprint toward the end of the pier, where she's supposed to be.

At first, I can't see her at all.

Then I do. And a violent crack shoots through me.

My legs move on autopilot, running faster than I've ever moved in my life, my gun pointing toward the two men in masks that she struggles against.

But I'm too far to make the shot. The wood of the pier groans beneath my boots as I barrel down the dock, the world narrowing until all that exists is her.

She fights like hell, and even from this distance, I can hear her muffled screams. Then her head turns.

"Aleksei!" Her hand reaches for me, fighting against them.

That one look, wild and desperate and full of fear, slices me open. She screams my name over and over, and I fire. One of the bastards drops, his body collapsing to the planks before rolling into the water with a hollow splash.

But three more appear, jumping from a boat. They plan to take her, but I will not let that happen.

The bastards shout to each other in Russian, gazes full of panic as I run closer.

"Davay. Bros yeyo." *Come on. Throw her in.*

I run faster, my lungs tearing with every breath, my finger tight on the trigger as I fire again. One bullet catches a shoulder; another hits the wood near their feet.

The engine of the speedboat roars to life as they shove her into it. Her hands scrape against the railing, hair flying in the wind.

"Fiona!"

She reaches for me across the dark stretch of water, her green eyes wide and pleading. "Aleksei! Please!"

Her fingers extend toward me—trembling, shaking, begging—and I know I'm not going to make it in time. As the boat jerks forward, one of the men grabs her, dragging her back by the hair.

I've already imagined all the ways I'll kill him. All of them.

"No!" I take another shot as the boat speeds away, dropping one of them at the bow.

But the others are already ducking for cover, shouting for the driver to go faster. The motor surges, the vessel cutting through the black water, throwing mist into the air as it pulls away.

The gun hits the ground as I sprint to the edge and dive. The ice-cold water is brutal, but I fight it, pushing upward until I break the surface, gasping, eyes glued on the retreating light of the boat. But I keep going, unable to give up and let her go.

"Fiona!" I shout, but the wind swallows her name.

Then I see her again at the edge, struggling free, arm reaching out toward me, mouth moving around my name.

"Aleksei!" Her voice hits me harder than the water ever could.

"I'll come for you!" I force strength into my lungs. "Hold on! Do you hear me? I will find you! I swear!"

I keep swimming, cutting through the waves until my arms ache, until my vision blurs with salt and rage.

But they're too far. The boat is faster.

I swear to whatever God is listening, I will find her. I'll burn every city, crush every man, and bring every empire to its knees.

The lion inside me will not rest until it's torn the wolves who took her to shreds.

FORTY-SEVEN

FIONA

The moment the boat surges forward, fear—sharper than anything I have ever felt—pours through me.

The engine thunders, the distance widens, and Aleksei becomes smaller and smaller until the darkness consumes him completely. I keep searching for one last glimpse, but he's gone, and something cold and heavy drops inside me like a stone.

"Sit down." A rough hand clamps around my arm and yanks me backward with no effort at all.

I hit the bench with a thud while another man steps in front of me with a sack hanging from his fist.

My pulse kicks up. "What the hell are you doing with that?"

He doesn't bother answering. The sack comes down over my head, thick fabric smothering the first bit of daybreak.

The boat slams against the waves, rocking hard enough to send my body to the side. I lock my fingers around the first solid thing I find until my knuckles burn. I don't know where they're taking me or what they want, but I know enough to realize nothing good waits on the other end.

Dread strengthens inside my chest, and even in the darkness, I can still see Aleksei sprinting down the pier the moment he realized I was being taken. The horror carved into his face as he dove into the water after me. How he cut through the waves like he would have rather drowned than let me slip away.

What if this is the end? What if I never see him again?

My mind races through all the things I didn't say, all the moments I thought we had more time for. I think about the look in his eyes when he begged me to forgive him, how much love I felt even when it hurt. I think about how badly I wanted him, how desperately I still do, and how unbearable it is to imagine a life that doesn't involve him.

I stay like that for what feels like forever, lost in my own thoughts and trying to convince myself this can't be how everything ends. The boat keeps moving beneath me, the sound of the water against the hull turning into a slow, relentless rhythm that makes it impossible to tell how much time has passed.

When the boat finally jerks to a stop, the sudden shift hits me hard enough to flip my stomach. Hands close around my arm before I can catch my balance, dragging me upward and pulling me toward solid ground.

With the sack still over my head, I can only guess what is actually happening. All I feel is the rough grip and the cold air brushing past my skin.

"Where are you taking me?"

A hard shove between my shoulder blades answers before any words do.

"Shut up and move," a man snaps, his Russian accent thick.

We walk for what might be a minute, maybe longer, and I sense the exact moment the ground beneath my feet shifts and the crunch of gravel is replaced by a hard, flat surface that echoes faintly under each step. A door creaks open somewhere ahead, like metal grinding against metal, and a faint generator hum vibrates through the air. The outdoor air disappears, and in its place is something musty.

Fingers stay locked around my arm, dragging me forward even as my knees threaten to buckle from fear and exhaustion. I consider trying to run, but I know it's pointless. I can't see. I can't fight. I can't even tell how many of them are surrounding me.

The only thing keeping me from losing all hope is knowing Aleksei can track me. Having a psycho husband does have its advantages.

Russian voices rise from somewhere to my right, and then I'm shoved again and forced to sit. Before I can brace myself, the hood is yanked off my head and the sudden light sears my eyes, blinding me with sharp, white pain. When my vision finally clears, I almost wish it hadn't.

Three masked men stand around me, each one dressed in black. One of them holds a small, thin handheld device while a steady beep slices through the air, and the sound alone makes shivers crawl over my arms.

Oh, fuck. No. Nononono…

If that's what I think it is, they're going to find it.

The man steps closer and begins to move the device along my body. It sweeps over my chest, down my arms, across my legs. I sit frozen, barely able to draw air. When he lifts the device to the back of my neck, everything inside me twists.

A sharp, shrill sound pierces the room, and my gut caves in.

Oh, God. No. If they figure it out, I might as well sign my own death warrant.

The man pauses, his dark eyes glaring, and when he presses a button, running the scanner again, it makes the same sound at the back of my neck. The blood instantly drains from my face.

He turns toward the others. "Uniyo shtota yest."

The second man flings a hand toward me, his tone cold and impatient. "Nu davay, vitishi."

Terror claws up my throat. *What the hell are they saying?*

The man with the scanner slips a hand into his pocket, and my heartbeat slams so hard against my ribs, it feels like it's trying to claw its way out. When he pulls out a small flip knife and snaps it open with a click, the room tilts, my stomach pitching as fear rushes through me so fast it makes my skin go cold.

"Wait." I scramble back as far as the chair allows. "Please. Don't."

Sudden footsteps echo from the hall, getting louder, and the men turn toward the sound as though waiting for whoever is coming to give them an order.

An older man appears in the doorway a moment later, tall and lean, black hair streaked with gray, a soft smile resting on his face as he takes me in. It should look kind, almost welcoming, but there's something menacing in his eyes that turns my stomach.

Is he their boss?

"It is so good to finally meet you," he says, his voice accented in Italian, maybe Sicilian.

"Who are you?"

But he ignores me when the Russian men approach.

"We found tracker in her." The man gestures toward me.

"*In* her? What do you mean?"

"In back of neck." He points to the back of his own.

The old man sighs, shaking his head. "Ah. That is very unfortunate."

As soon as he says that, my heart races.

He raises a single finger, and two of the men seize my arms, pressing me back against the chair.

"No, please, don't do this!"

Panic slices through me, and when the third moves forward with the knife, I fight them, kicking, screaming, trying to get their grip off.

But it's no use. They're too strong.

The older man pulls a chair across from me, lowering himself with unhurried ease, as though this is entertainment. When the blade lands at the back of my neck, his gaze stays locked on me, a small, satisfied grin tugging at his mouth.

White-hot pain bursts through me as soon as the knife slices into me, spreading like fire beneath my skin. I scream until my voice cracks, the sound almost animalistic.

"There, there," he says, almost like he's soothing a child. "You're fine."

Blood runs warm down my shoulder, the knife scraping, digging. When they're through, one shows him a small circular device, the size of a rice grain.

"It seems your husband enjoyed tracking you like you're his property. You should thank me for fixing that for you."

When he gets to his feet, stepping nearer, the scent of his woodsy cologne makes my stomach turn. I can't stop shaking. Tears stream down my face, my breaths coming in short broken gasps. One of the men presses gauze against my neck, so hard it hurts.

"What the hell do you want from me?" I spit out between clenched teeth.

The man's eyes soften. "Ah, so direct. I like that very much." He pulls his chair forward until it's right in front of me. "My name is Elio. But before we talk about what I want, perhaps I should tell you a story."

My vision swims as pain throbs in jagged waves at the base of my skull, but I force myself to look at him, to show him I'm unafraid.

"You see, my dear Fiona…" He folds his hands in his lap like a priest about to deliver last rites. "Our families have been connected for a very long time, and I was so happy when I finally found you." He shakes his head. "Then that pezzo di merda had to kill one of my men before he could deliver you to me properly. But what can we expect from a savage, right?" He tosses a hand in the air. "We're together now. So I choose to forget the past."

My world turns upside down.

The break-in. The man Aleksei killed…

Oh my God.

But why did this man send someone after me? What am I missing?

The room suffocates me, as if the walls themselves are creeping inward with every breath I take.

"Who are you?" I whisper, already afraid of the answer.

"I am not finished with my story." He tsks. "I have to get to the best part." When he realizes I'm not going to interrupt again, his smile sharpens. "A long time ago, a woman was told she had to marry a man she did not want."

He leans back, his features tightening like the memory of it is pissing him off.

"I did not blame her. The Russians can be…not very nice. But you should know all about that, no? Of course, you were in bed with the wrong Russians. History does love to repeat itself."

What the fuck is he talking about?

"Can you just tell me whatever it is you're dying to say and stop with this cryptic bullshit?"

He laughs. "I really like you. You've got that spunk, like someone I used to know."

The more he talks, the more I wish he'd just get to the damn point.

"Are you going to kill me or not?"

He clutches his chest like I wounded him. "Of course not. I am only here to tell you a story. To make you understand why I had to do this. It is necessary for you to listen. Then you can talk."

My God. I've dealt with men like him before. The ones who think charm is a weapon. Who smile while bleeding you dry.

And he has all of it. The charisma. The calm. The messiah complex woven into every syllable, like I should thank him for whatever horror comes next.

I dig my nails into my thighs, glancing around the large warehouse-type space, trying to find any chance of an exit. But there's none. If I run, I know they'll kill me.

"As I was saying, that foolish, reckless woman refused the path laid out for her. She did not want the marriage. So she did something unforgivable." He pauses, eyes dancing with sick anticipation. "She killed him."

Well, that's not good.

"She ran off with her bodyguard instead." He shakes his head. "Brought shame to my family. And I do not tolerate shame."

His tone is light, but there's something deadly curled beneath it. A rot in the foundation of his words.

"Her marriage would have ensured lasting peace between the Russians and my family. But instead, she set fire to all of it. And many men, good men, died because of her selfishness." His gaze hardens and the mask slips, giving me a glimpse of the madness in his eyes. "And for that, you must pay the price."

A tremor runs through me. "What do I have to do with any of that?"

His smile grows wider. Almost tender.

"Don't you see yet?" He leans forward, elbows on his knees, and for a moment, it's like time slows down. "Your mother's sins are now yours, my darling granddaughter."

A cold numbness floods my limbs. His words echo, rattling through my chest, ripping through everything I thought I knew.

Granddaughter?

No. This can't be.

"You're lying." A dizzy wave rolls through me, tilting the room for a split second. "That's not possible. My mother… She doesn't… She never said—"

"That she's a Scutari?" He tilts his head like I've just said something amusing. "Of course she didn't. She has been running away from her obligations her entire life."

My mother is…Mafia?

Oh God. I can't make sense of this.

He sits back in the chair, completely at ease, while my world cracks open like glass.

"Tony and Angelica thought they could hide you. Change their last names. Pretend the past was dead and buried. But nothing stays buried, Fiona. Not forever."

The bile rises in my throat.

Change their last names? My dad isn't a Clark? My mother isn't Ricci?

"But don't worry. I have a solution," he continues. "A way to make all our problems go away."

I barely hear him anymore. My ears are ringing, my fingers shaking against my thighs.

All I can think is *granddaughter*.

My parents lied to me for my entire life.

His smile widens, warm in a way that makes my skin crawl. "You must fix what your mother broke. You must unite the Volkovs and our family."

The Volkovs. I fucking knew it…

"That is the only way we erase the shame your mother left behind when she ran."

If this man thinks I'm going to marry anyone, he must be delusional.

"I'm already married. And as I'm sure you know…he tends to be a little possessive."

He scoffs. "Do not worry about him or that family. I have plans for all of them. There will be none of the Marinovs left to worry about soon."

A violent rage tears through me. He actually thinks he can talk about Aleksei, about Emilia, about *his family*, as if they're nothing?

He thinks he can threaten the people I love and we'll just bow our heads and accept it?

He has no idea what he's invited. And God, I hope Aleksei finds him soon and makes him pay for every word.

One of the masked men steps forward, holding out a phone. "A call for you."

The old man looks at the screen and rises, brushing imaginary dust from his slacks.

"Excuse me, my dear," he says before leaving the room without another word, two of the masked men following him out.

The door slams shut behind him, and suddenly it's just me and one masked guard. He's facing away from me, pacing slowly up ahead, talking in Russian to someone on the phone.

Glancing around, I spot a crowbar near the crate stacked inches behind me. My eyes lock on to it.

They didn't tie me up. Maybe they thought I wouldn't try anything, but they definitely underestimated my desire to get the hell out of here.

I shift my weight carefully, testing the ground beneath my feet and calculating the distance. I draw one shallow breath, then another, and then I lunge. My fingers wrap around the crowbar, cold metal biting into my skin as I rush behind the guard and swing it with everything I have. He turns just as I do.

A sickening crack splits the silence as it hits the back of his head. He stumbles forward, then drops like a stone, blood spilling beneath him in a widening pool.

I don't give myself time to panic. There's a gun holstered at his hip, and I fumble with the strap until it gives. It's heavier than I expect, but I don't let go even as the pistol shakes in my grip.

Across the room, there's a door. Not the one the old man exited through. Another one, half concealed behind a stack of more crates. A narrow window above it shows a sliver of the sky. If the door is unlocked, it means I might have a chance to get away…unless there's someone guarding it.

But I have to try. I can't stay here.

My body screams in protest with every step, but I move anyway, the gun heavy at my side, the crowbar in my other hand. I reach for the knob, and when I try it, it turns. The door creaks at first, and I slowly push it open.

And when I see who's standing there, I almost drop the pistol.

Every part of me grows numb, my mind refusing to believe what's in front of me. This can't be right. It doesn't make sense.

A smile twists across her face. "Hello, Fiona. Where do you think you're going?"

FORTY-EIGHT

ALEKSEI

I can still hear her screaming my name. That broken sound tears through every part of me, branded into my skull.

I see her face when I close my eyes. Her terror, her desperation, the way her hands clawed toward me as they dragged her away.

My tires screech as I speed, cutting through the streets, horn blaring as I fly through red lights and scream past traffic. I don't register the ache in my muscles or the cold from my soaked clothes. Just that choking fury swelling like a tide inside me.

She's gone. And I let it happen.

My fist slams into the steering wheel so hard my knuckles split, but it barely registers over the sound of her screams, like she's here in front of me.

But I will find her. She's close. The tracker lit up in Brooklyn, and then it was gone. Which means those bastards found it and either figured out a way to block the signal or took it out of her.

If they hurt my wife that way, they will wish they were dead before I get to them.

As soon as I arrive home, I tear the front door open, heading straight for the basement. Once there, I push a button, and the wall flips before I enter the hidden room. Lights flicker on, weapons lining the walls. An arsenal, enough to start a war, and that's exactly what I'm about to do. Duffel bags hit the floor with a thud, and I start filling them—handguns, rifles, knives, grenades. Every tool of destruction I've ever owned is coming with me.

Footsteps thunder above me until I register the creak of the stairs.

"Aleksei?" Kirill calls. "You down there?"

I don't look up as he walks into the room, just zip another bag and move to the next.

He stays there watching me silently for a few seconds before he asks, "Chto sluchilos?" *What happened?*

My blood simmers in my veins. "They took her."

"What?"

"They fucking took her. The Volkovs. Or the fucking Italians. I don't know exactly. But I saw it happen. I was there." I turn to face him, and the look I give could cut through bone. "I couldn't stop it. I just let them take her."

"That's bullshit. I know you did everything you could."

"Not good enough." I grab another duffel and fill it too.

"We will get her back, and we will raise hell to do it."

He's already dialing Konstantin and telling him what's happening. I don't hear the rest. I'm already gone, lost in the bloodlust of what's coming. Praying for the moment I finally have her back in my arms and never let go again.

I pack until the bags are full and heavy and the floor beneath me looks like an armory.

An hour later, the jet is fueled and waiting, my brothers and our men all with me. We board without words because there's nothing to say.

This isn't a rescue mission. It's the beginning of a massacre.

"How the fuck did you not know your wife is a Scutari?" Gio's question cuts through the heavy silence in the SUV as we tear through New York.

I'm in the backseat, one of my men behind the wheel, with my brothers and the rest of our convoy roaring close behind.

"I did know. She didn't." My jaw clenches so tight my molars ache.

I was going to tell her when she was ready to hear it, but last night wasn't the time. She couldn't handle any more. Maybe that was a damn mistake, but it's too late now.

Chyort. Damn it. *What the hell are they doing to you right now, moya ptichka?*

I don't even want to imagine.

"Did the Italians know about her?" Devlin cuts through my thoughts, heavy with his Irish brogue.

"No, not at first. From what we learned, Elio did this on his own."

Gio scoffs. "Elio's a fucking lunatic. You ever met him?"

I nod once. "Years ago. Did not like him. Now he will die."

Devlin grins, eyes flashing. "Bloody hell. I'll help you skin the bastard myself, and I don't even like your mug."

"Feeling is mutual."

Though deep down, I'm grateful they came without hesitation. As soon as Konstantin reached out about logistics, since they both live in New York, Gio and Devlin not only sent their men, but showed up themselves. That kind of loyalty means something in a world like ours. And I never forget a debt.

The SUV rolls to a stop about a block from the warehouse where her GPS last pinged. Maybe they've moved her by now, but this is the only trail we have left.

Industrial zone. Dead streets. Blocks of steel buildings and vacant lots. The kind of place people disappear into when no one is meant to hear their screams.

Grabbing the duffle with a few handguns and a rifle, I exit, the door slamming behind me, and we're heading toward the building. Every second she's out of my reach, it's like something inside me is tearing open.

I'm coming, detka.

And I'm bringing death with me. If she's in that building, I won't just walk out with her. I will level the place to the ground.

They have no idea what they've done.

I was born in blood. Raised in it. Shaped by it.

But Fiona? She was the one thing I never expected to need. And now that I've had her, touched her, tasted her, watched her fucking smile at me, there's nothing I won't do for her. No line I won't cross. No man I won't kill.

They don't know me, not yet. But they will.

Boots hammering over cracked concrete, I head for the entrance with everyone right behind. Once we arrive, I turn the knob slow, gun up and ready. The door gives an inch, then two, before I slip inside, eyes sweeping the room. There are metal stairs ahead and a single man off to the right, back to me, rifle hanging low at his side.

I slide the flip knife from my pocket and close in behind him just as he starts to turn, eyes going wide. His hand jerks toward the trigger, but I'm already there, faster than the fear hitting his face.

The blade slices clean across his throat. He lets out a wet, gurgling sound as his body goes slack. I catch him before he hits the concrete and lower him to the ground, leaving him there in silence.

Everyone's behind me now, guns drawn, while I replace the knife with the rifle from the duffle.

"Alyosha, ty tam?" someone calls from above the stairs. *Alyosha, are you there?*

When no one answers, he appears, and I greet him with a bullet between his eyes, killing him instantly.

Then chaos erupts.

We charge up the steps, my rifle kicking with every shot, bodies dropping like fucking dominoes. A man lunges for Devlin from behind, and I put a bullet through his skull before he even knows I'm there. Another dives low, so I shoot him in the leg, bone shattering. He howls as I close the distance, knife already in my hand, adjusting the rifle strap over my shoulder.

When I'm standing over him, I kneel for a moment, just long enough for him to see what's coming, then drive the blade into his eye. He drops with a strangled scream, and I step over him without slowing.

Someone charges from the left, and I twist, shooting into his chest, then drop another before the echo fades. Blood splashes the wall behind them in thick, dark strokes.

A scream rips through the carnage—ours, theirs, I don't fucking care. The only thing that matters is finding her.

The room dissolves into pure anarchy. I lose count of how many I put down, and with each body that falls, the fear that she isn't here claws a little deeper.

My elbow smashes into another man's ribs, and I slam him into the wall. He wheezes, gasping for air, and I pin him there with my forearm across his neck.

"Is she here?"

He grins, blood slicking his teeth and dripping from the corner of his mouth. "She cried your name like a little whore."

A low growl tears out of me. I picture her begging them to stop as my teeth sink into his throat. Flesh gives under my bite, hot blood flooding my mouth while he thrashes beneath me, choking, hands clawing at me.

Something slams into my left shoulder, burning straight through me, but it barely registers. I don't let go. Only when his body finally goes limp and the last breath rattles out of him do I shove him aside, wiping my mouth with the back of my hand, smearing blood everywhere I touch.

And then I move again. One of them is going to tell me where they're keeping her.

By the time the fighting slows, bodies lie on the ground, too many to count. But my brothers are still standing, and so are Devlin and Gio.

"You're shot." Konstantin glances at my arm, and I find a bullet graze there.

"Nothing that will slow me. We need to move. She has to be close."

Konstantin crouches down and rips the shirt of one of the dead. "But you're leaking like a stuck pig. If you lose more blood, you will pass out before you see her again."

"Hurry up."

I barely sense the pain as he wraps my arm tight enough to cut off circulation. Once he's done playing nurse, we start surveying the rest of the building.

Konstantin nods toward a man still breathing on the ground, bleeding from his mangled leg. "He might know something."

The bastard tries to crawl when he sees me coming. But I don't rush. I want him to feel every second of the inevitability closing in.

Konstantin crouches beside him. "Privet, you don't look so good." A cold grin bends his mouth. "So it would be in your best interest to tell us where the girl is. Otherwise, my brother here will turn what is left of your leg into soup before you bleed out. Painfully, of course. I assure you."

The man spits. "Edi na khuy. You kill me anyway."

Konstantin lifts both hands in the air. "I am a man of honor. You tell me where she is, you walk out of here alive. Or maybe not walk. Crawl. Same thing, right?"

The hesitation lasts all of two seconds before the man's gaze jerks to me.

"She…she is next door. Building there." He points toward his right. "They knew you had GPS, so they tricked you."

"How many men are inside?" I ask.

"Not many. Five, maybe." He looks nearly hopeful, like he'll actually survive this.

It's almost cute.

"Spasebo." Konstantin pats him on the arm before he straightens himself.

And with an icy grin, I point the weapon at him.

He backs away, his nostrils flaring. "Padonok! You said you wouldn't kill me."

"I am not."

The shot cracks through the silence, echoing off the concrete walls. His shriek follows a second later as the bullet tears through his other leg, leaving him rotting in a pool of his own blood.

I step over the spreading red. "You will still be alive when we walk out."

With that, we head for the exit.

Weapons drawn, I lead the way out, heading for my wife, my heart, my goddamn salvation, hoping that I'm not too late.

FORTY-NINE

FIONA

"Wh-what are you doing here?" The words leave me in a broken whisper as the figure before me slowly steps into the light.

Her smile is slow and cruel, the kind that makes my insides shrink with a quiet, dawning terror. My brain scrambles to catch up, to rationalize what I'm seeing, but there's no explanation that makes sense.

"Oh, sweetie," Marlene croons. "Elio and I go way back. Where he's the muscle..." She glides a finger along the steel beam beside her. "I'm the brains. Who do you think thought of those notes you kept getting?"

Holy shit.

I stagger back, my heart thundering in my chest. "Why? What do you have to do with this?"

"Everything."

Her expression hardens into something icier than I've ever seen. Like a layer has peeled back and I'm finally seeing what's always been underneath. She moves toward me until I'm cornered.

"I can't let you leave, Fiona," she coos. "If anything, you can blame your mother. Elio and I are only doing what is right for our families."

My lungs seize. "Your family? What the hell are you talking about?"

She tilts her head like I've asked a ridiculous question. "I'm a Volkov, darling."

I take another step back, my stomach dropping. How can this be?

Her smile widens, as if my confusion is the best entertainment she's had all day. "You must marry my brother. There is no other choice."

"I'm sorry, *what*?" A disbelieving laugh slips out before I can stop it.

She shrugs. "Yes. He's old. Probably has ten, maybe twenty years left, if we're lucky. You can deal with that. Consider it an investment in survival."

"Fuck off." My teeth grit, and she sighs, like I'm a child throwing a tantrum.

"The wedding will be tomorrow."

"I'd rather die." My nostrils flare, anger dragging through me.

Marlene's smile widens. "Suit yourself. But here's the thing, sweetheart. You don't have a choice. The Marinovs…we have plans for them. Big ones. So if you think they will save you, think again."

"I'm Aleksei's wife. He won't rest until all of you are dead."

Her eyes gleam. "Not for long, you're not."

"I swear to God…" I grit out. "When he finds me, when he—"

Her laugh ricochets through me. "Malinkaya durachka. When will you understand he's not coming for you? That precious little GPS chip? We planted it in the building next door. That's where he is now. If he's still alive, of course. But considering how many men are waiting for him…" She lets out a dramatic sigh. "The chances of your handsome man walking away from that are slim."

No way in hell. The Marinovs are smarter than that.

But the doubt crawls in anyway.

What if she's right? What if they got to him? What if he's gone?

I refuse to fall apart now. Aleksei would want me fighting. He'd want me doing everything I can to survive. And that's exactly what I'm going to do.

"If you think I'm going to walk out of here and play bride to some half-dead mobster, you really don't know me."

"Oh, I know you." Marlene steps toward me, too close, until I can smell her floral perfume, like she bathed in it to hide the stench of her rot. "But you'll come around."

I lift my chin. "Then I guess you've never seen what a woman does when she has nothing left to lose."

Marlene's hand twitches at her hip, and I don't think. I launch.

My body crashes into hers, tackling her mid-reach as her fingers brush the holster under her jacket. We slam into the floor, a tangled mess of limbs, and her gun skitters across the concrete, spinning once before clattering out of reach.

But there's no time to go after it. She's faster than I thought. Stronger too. Her age doesn't match the grip she has on me—fingers like claws, nails digging into my shoulder as she rolls me onto my stomach and pins me beneath her.

My breath punches out of my lungs as her knee slams into my back hard enough to make me see stars.

"I really hoped you'd be smarter than this." Her breath is hot against my ear. "I was going to make it easier for you."

I twist beneath her, elbow jabbing back blindly, but she grabs a fistful of my hair, forcing my head down again. Pain blooms across my cheekbone.

Clawing the ground, I search for anything I can use, and that's when I see it: a brick, mottled and chipped, half buried in leaves, just inches from my fingertips.

Come on.

She's dragging me, trying to flip me onto my back, but I stretch, nails scraping until I catch the edge.

"Stop fighting," she bites out.

My fingers lock around rough stone, and I swing with every ounce of panic and fury in my body. The brick cracks against her temple with a sickening thud. She lets out a grunt, body swaying sideways, and I roll out, chest heaving, the brick still in my hand.

She's stunned, blood trailing from her scalp, eyes wide with disbelief as she topples to the ground.

"I told you," I rasp, shaking with rage. "You don't know me."

My hand quivers around the bloody brick, chest still heaving, but she doesn't move. She lies sprawled on the concrete, head turned at a grotesque angle, blood pooling slowly beneath her.

I stare, waiting for a twitch. A breath. Anything. But there's nothing.

I did that. I killed her. I killed someone else.

My pulse jolts with the realization, and I drop the brick, the sound of it hitting the floor drowned out by the sudden echo of footsteps pounding the hallway.

Shit.

Fingers closing around her gun, my body moves on instinct, sprinting for the nearest cover. I dive behind a half-collapsed brick wall, heart pounding in my throat, hands scraped and shaking as I press myself flat to the rough stone.

Whoever it is, I can't let them see me. They need to think I escaped.

Boots thud closer, someone muttering in Russian.

Please, Aleksei. Please be alive. Please hurry.

I squeeze my eyes shut, tears burning hot behind them.

"Fiona!" Aleksei's voice cuts in. "Fiona, come on. Where are you?"

The sound slams into me, a rush of shock and desperate relief that lights up every nerve in my body all at once.

I push away from the wall, chest shattering open with a sob. "Aleksei!"

He turns, gun already half lowered, and the second his eyes land on me, everything stops. His whole body freezes, like his brain can't catch up to the sight of me standing there.

The gun instantly slips from his hand and clatters to the floor. "Fiona…"

I run, ignoring everyone else around us and throwing myself into his arms. He catches me in an instant, holding me with that unyielding strength.

"I was so afraid," he whispers.

"Me too."

My legs wrap around his waist, arms around his shoulders, sobs wracking my body as I bury my face in his neck and breathe him in. There's blood all over him, but I know it isn't his.

"I've got you." Every syllable splits him open as he grips me like he's afraid I'll disappear. "I've got you, moya ptichka. You're safe now. You're safe. I will never let you go again."

I pull back just enough to see him as I cradle his face in my palms. His eyes are glassy, a muscle in his chin twitching, but his mouth softens as he leans in and kisses me slow and deep, like he's trying to make up for every second we lost.

When we break apart, I press my forehead to his.

"I'm sorry," I whisper. "I'm so sorry I left."

His thumb brushes over the bruise blooming on my jaw, his other hand cupping the back of my head like he can't bear to let go. "You have nothing to apologize for. Not a goddamn thing. I should never have let you out of my sight."

Footsteps echo behind us, and Konstantin steps into the room, clearing his throat.

"Shto?" Aleksei doesn't look away from me.

"Elio got away."

"We'll find him." Tension cuts sharp across his features.

Konstantin leaves us, and I shake my head, tears spilling before I can stop them, everything I feel for Aleksei crashing through me.

"She said you could be dead."

He gathers me closer, words rough against my ear. "She lied."

I swallow past the knot in my throat, and that's when I notice the blood seeping through the cotton wrapped around his left arm.

"Oh my God. Aleksei, you're hurt."

"It's nothing." He tightens his hold on me. "Just a graze."

But it isn't nothing. He bled for me. Fought for me. Came for me.

And in this moment, nothing else matters. He's here. I'm alive. Those assholes couldn't do what they planned.

My fingers bury in his hair, fisting tight, because I can't breathe without him. His mouth crushes to mine, brutal and desperate this time, stealing whatever air I had left as heat explodes in my chest.

There's nothing gentle about this. It's claiming. It's punishment. It's him telling me without words that losing me nearly killed him.

His tongue devours mine like he's trying to take back every second we were apart, and I give it all right back, kissing him with every frantic beat of my heart, every fear that gutted me, every piece of love I never stopped feeling. My legs tighten around his waist as he presses me back against the nearest wall, his hand cradling the back of my skull so I don't hit it.

He groans low in his throat when I bite his bottom lip, his grip tightening like he can't get close enough. I can feel him shaking, barely holding it together, rage and relief bleeding through his touch.

When we finally pull apart, our breaths are tangled and shallow, lips swollen, foreheads pressed together.

"I thought I'd lost you," he says, thumb brushing a tear from my cheek. "If you were gone, I would've taken the world apart just to make them feel the hurt that I would've felt."

A sharp ache rises in my throat, splintering through me.

"You found me," I whisper. "I'm right here, baby."

My fingers trace the line of his jaw, brushing over the rough scrape of his stubble, and his eyes fall shut as he leans into the touch like he's been starved for it. Starved for *me*.

He kisses me again, gentler now, but no less consuming. There's something different in it, though. A promise. A vow. A new beginning forged out of everything we survived.

And in this kiss, the truth roots itself deep in my bones.

I'm his. I always have been.

And I always will be.

FIFTY

FIONA

Once we arrive back home, I change into clean clothes, the shower with Aleksei helping me feel a bit more human. With his hand in mine, we head downstairs and I know I'm going to have to face my parents. Konstantin had already told them what happened before Aleksei and I got home, and I'm sure they're nervous, as they should be.

"It will be okay," Aleksei says as we make it down the stairs, his lips pressing to my forehead right before we enter the den, where he said they'll be waiting.

My arms curl around him for a moment too long, and he grips me against his chest.

"You do not have to talk to them if you don't want to. They can wait."

"No." I pull back. "I want to get it over with."
Squeezing his hands, I draw in a long inhale.

"I will be nearby." He kisses the corner of my mouth before he turns and leaves.

Then I make my way to the two people I used to trust more than anyone in this world. They don't say anything at first. Neither do I. The silence between us is heavy, thick with everything that's happened, everything they never told me.

My mother tries to meet my gaze, but her eyes are already glistening with unshed tears, and my father won't even lift his head. They sit on the sofa like they've aged twenty years in the span of a few hours.

A part of me wants to scream at them and demand they explain how they could do this, how they could lie for so long. But no words come. It's like I have a million things to say, but I don't know where to start.

"I'm sorry, Fiona," Mom finally whispers, brows knitting tightly. "Please try to understand where we were coming from."

I look at her, and for the first time, I actually see the fear etched there.

"My father…" she starts and pauses like it's all so difficult. "He was a horrible man. He didn't care about me. All he wanted was money and power, and I was just a thing he could use to get more.

"Your father…" She takes his hand and kisses his knuckles. "He was my only love, and when he told me we could run together, that he knew people who could make us disappear, I took the chance. Because I was already pregnant with you, and we needed to protect you."

I swallow, throat thick as she continues.

"I didn't tell you because I knew how you felt. About people like my family." Her words falter. "Knowing where you came from, what you were tied to, it would've broken you."

She's right. Back then, it would have. I wouldn't have been able to handle it. But now that I'm married to Aleksei, nothing is the same.

My mother wipes her cheeks. "We are truly sorry, tesoro. I just did what I thought was right for you."

I close my eyes. "And selling me? Was that protecting me too?"

Her face crumples, and this time it's my father who speaks, finally lifting his gaze.

"That was wrong. We were wrong, stellina. We made a grave mistake, and for that, we will always pay the price."

I blink back the swell of tears trapped in my lower lashes.

"If you can't forgive us," he says, "I understand. Because I can't forgive myself either."

"I just…it's all too much right now. It's like I'm getting hit with one thing after another, and I don't know how much more I can take."

They sit there, this gaping chasm between us full of everything they'll never be able to take back. And still, some broken part of me wants to reach across it. Because they're my parents. Because no matter how much they lied, how much they failed me, they love me in the only way they know how.

"Is there *anything* else you've been keeping from me?" I ask. "Because now is the time to tell me."

My mother shakes her head. "There's nothing else, Fiona. I swear to you."

"She's right," Dad adds. "And you listen to me. We'll give you all the space you need. We'll move out. We shouldn't be here."

I shake my head. "No. Stay. Please. At least until Aleksei finds whoever's left and ends this. It's not safe yet."

Mom's gaze drops to her lap. "I'm so sorry. You don't know how sorry I am for all of it."

"I know." I walk to her and take her hand, squeezing it gently.

Her chin shakes, and something inside my chest gives way. I don't know who I'm comforting anymore: her, myself, or all of us at once.

A hollow silence settles over the room, stretching between us. None of us speak because there are no words left. Just the quiet, and everything we're trying so hard to hold together.

ALEKSEI

Konstantin leans over the counter, phone set to speaker as it rings, while my knuckles ache from clenching them too hard.

But I can't stop. Every image that flashes through my mind is Fiona. Her cheek scratched up, the bandage I put on the back of her neck where they ripped the damn tracker out of her like savages.

I cannot wait to tear Elio's throat out.

The line clicks, and then Adriano Scutari's voice fills the room. "Konstantin. To what do I owe the call?"

"We plan to kill your uncle, Elio, and everyone associated with him. He took Fiona and tried to marry her off to the Volkovs." His tone stays even and composed, like he's just listing what he plans to have for dinner. "If the Grazia family stands in our way, it will be taken as a declaration of war."

There's a pause, enough to hear Adriano thinking on the other end, calculating how to answer without appearing weak.

"We understand," he finally says. "As you already know, my uncle was acting on his own. Neither my father nor I are involved. Whatever you need to do, you have our permission."

Konstantin glances at me, his mouth curving into a faint, satisfied smile before he speaks again. "Very good. That is what we wanted to hear. Do you know where he and his men could be hiding?"

He sighs, like he knows he has no choice but to tell us. "He owns a shipping warehouse in Brooklyn. If I had to guess, that's where he'd be hiding."

Konstantin's satisfaction grows. "We appreciate this. Please tell your father we send our regards."

"Thank you."

"I think after this is over, we all need to talk and figure out how to better unite our families so this never happens again."

"We look forward to it."

"Us too. Speak soon." Konstantin ends the call and fixes his stare on me. "We end this tonight."

He doesn't need to tell me to get ready. I've been at war since the moment they took her, and I won't rest until I have their heads.

I hated leaving her, but this had to be done. We return to Brooklyn, our men stationed around the warehouse, mere miles from where they were keeping Fiona. Surveillance revealed that the Volkovs are definitely inside. And if they are there, so is Elio.

We fan out without a word, the click of safeties releasing the only warning this place will get. Kirill and Anton peel off toward the back with half the men, while Konstantin and I move in from the front.

Two guards by the entrance never make it to their radios. My silencer takes the first clean through the eye, while Konstantin drops the other with a single shot to the throat. They collapse like puppets with their strings cut, and we're already through the door, while Kirill and Anton shoot their way inside, surrounding them from all sides.

Gunfire cracks like thunder through the large space as men scramble, none of them prepared. We took most of their guys out already, and they barely have any here. Five, ten maybe.

One stumbles with a pistol raised, and I put three rounds in his chest before his weapon clears the doorway. Another tries to retreat, but Kirill intercepts him mid-turn, shooting him point-blank in the gut, then his head.

We clear the space body by body, the air thick with gunpowder and the scent of death. Screams echo while I scan the space for Elio, needing him alive.

Just as I head for the back door, I find him trying to escape with three men surrounding him. I let out a shot, dropping one of them, while Konstantin and Anton surround the others.

"Took you long enough," Elio drawls, a smug grin on his face.

I raise my gun, the muzzle aligned perfectly with the center of his skull. "Your own nephew gave you up. You must not be worth much."

He chuckles. "Neither is my nephew. Weak little bastard, like his father."

My temples pound so hard, the floor seems to vibrate beneath my boots as I think about how Fiona must have felt when they tore that tracker out of her.

"You're going to wish for death when I'm done with you." I step into his space, his men doing nothing about it.

He doesn't flinch. "We all die, my friend. I am not scared of anyone. Especially you."

The words barely leave his mouth before I slam the butt of my gun into his temple with a sickening crack.

A sudden thud echoes from the left, somewhere behind a stack of boxes. I meet Konstantin's eyes and jerk my chin, letting him know I'm going to check it out. Kirill falls in behind me, gun raised, covering my flank as I move forward.

When I round the corner and see who's crouched there, a laugh breaks out of me.

"Well, well. Daniil Volkov. We have been looking for you."

The Pakhan of the Volkovs looks nothing like he once did. The years have aged him poorly. He's, what? Sixty-five? Too bad he won't see to sixty-six.

"Ya tvayu mamu yibal," he curses, like I would even care what comes out of his mouth.

Konstantin answers without missing a beat. "That's not very polite."

"My brother's right." I fire a single round into his foot.

He howls, collapsing, and I grab him by the collar, dragging him out to the SUV, while our men take Elio and all the others who are still clinging to life. The bastard groans in the back next to Elio, head lolling.

Wait until they find out what I have planned for them.

Konstantin's estate rises as we make it down the private road, heading toward the barn, where his Calabrian pigs wait for their dessert.

All fifteen of them.

Once the vehicles stop, we haul them out of the SUVs one by one, forced to their knees in the dirt as zip ties cinch tight around their wrists.

Elio laughs. "Well, this is dramatic."

Konstantin steps forward, hands behind his back like he's about to give a lecture. "We like the entertainment. Life tends to be boring otherwise, don't you think?"

A slow, knowing grin curves across Elio's mouth, while Daniil's face twists with rage.

Elio lifts his shoulders in a lazy shrug. "Then let's not drag it out."

I move in, crouching down in front of the two of them, forcing their eyes to meet mine.

"You laid your hands on my wife." My tone is anything but calm. "You ripped her tracker out and left her bleeding like an animal. You enjoyed it when she screamed, didn't you, Elio?"

He doesn't deny it. "She's still alive, isn't she? Don't I get a thank-you for that?"

In an instant, I grab him by the collar and slam his head into the ground, the impact cracking through the dirt. The others flinch, but no one dares move.

Mud streaks his face, blood mixing with it, and I plant my boot on the back of his neck, grinding down until he groans.

"You're not dying quickly." I press harder. "You will feel every second of what you did to her. And you will die screaming."

He wheezes out something that might've been a laugh…until Konstantin places the bone saw in my hand. Then the color drains from his face.

"What…what are you going to do with that?" he whispers.

"Teach you a lesson you will never forget. Not even in hell."

Digging his face into the dirt, I let the rage take over as I slice through the length of his back, his screams adding to the beauty of the moment. I cut through flesh and grate against bone, just beside his spine.

When he cries, it doesn't slow me. It feeds something feral inside me. I carve down the other side, the earth drinking his blood as the crack of his ribs echoes, flesh splitting beneath my hands.

Dropping the saw, I reach inside him, fingers slick with blood, and rip out his lungs, setting them carefully on his back like butchered wings.

"You are not laughing now, are you?"

He shudders, twitching in the dirt, his body broken, but he's not dead yet.

"No, no, please!" Daniil breaks completely, sobbing like a coward.

I shove his body down, the saw slicing across his back. His scream tears through the air, and I leave him with his lungs on his back too, his face angled toward Elio so they can watch each other die.

When I straighten, my gaze drifts over to the rest of their men. The fear hits them all at once. Some beg. Others sit in silence, knowing there is no point. They will die today.

Lucky for them, I do not have time to drag this out. I want to get back to my wife, who needs me.

Picking up my gun, I level it at the first man's skull and pull the trigger. One by one, they fall, and I feel nothing but the cold clarity of vengeance.

When the last one collapses at my feet, I walk away. From the blood, the wreckage, from death itself.

Because I have something worth living for now. And she's the only thing that matters.

FIFTY-ONE

FIONA
ONE MONTH LATER

It's hard to let things go. Especially the things that once defined you. The things you clung to like lifelines because they made sense in a world that didn't.

But sometimes those very things—the beliefs, the convictions, the iron-clad rules you built your identity around—start to feel like chains instead of anchors. They stop fitting, and letting them go isn't weakness. It's growth.

Or at least that's what I tell myself when I think about how much my life has shifted in just a few short weeks.

A month ago, I thought I knew who I was. Now I sit behind a desk I never imagined would belong to me, in an office with my name on the glass, and it still doesn't feel real.

The sun spills across the polished surface—mine, all of it mine. I run my fingers along the edge, almost expecting it to vanish beneath my touch. Like I'll blink and find myself back in the DA's office. Back in my scratchy government-issued chair. Back to being a woman who thought justice was black and white.

But I'm not that woman anymore.

Quitting wasn't easy. I spent years carving a place for myself in that office, and walking away felt like cutting a piece out of my own chest.

My mother didn't help. She practically danced when I told her I was going to become a defense attorney and open up my own firm. Made a few comments about the irony, about me finally loosening the death grip I had on my moral compass. I let her have her fun. She deserved that moment, I suppose.

But this new life isn't about irony. It's about finally choosing for myself. Not out of fear or obligation, but because I want it.

Because I want *him.*

And maybe that makes me naïve or weak. But if loving Aleksei has taught me anything, it's that the world is never just one thing. People aren't either. Not even me.

I've made peace with my parents. I've forgiven them, not because what they did was small or easy to forget, but because I had to. For my own sake. For the sake of everything I still want from this life.

Forgiveness wasn't easy. But for me, it wasn't about condoning it. It was about survival. About letting go of the bitterness before it swallowed me whole.

My parents are not bad people. They just did a bad thing.

And maybe that's something we all have in common. Being flawed and scared and human. Making choices we think we can live with until we realize too late that we can't. The only thing that matters right now is that I'm okay and they're okay. The rest is in the past where it belongs.

A knock pulls me from my thoughts, and I lift my gaze toward the door just as it eases open, Dana leaning her head inside with a crooked smile tugging at her mouth.

"Well, well, counselor. You look damn good behind that desk."

I rise to my feet, giving her a quick hug. "Oh, shut up."

She struts inside, dropping a hand to her hip as she checks out the large space. "So, this is the famous office, huh? Swanky. Classy. Very you."

"How's the DA's office treating you without me?"

Dana raises a brow and drops into the chair across from mine. "Not nearly as well as your new firm's about to treat me. That is, if you'll have me."

I jerk back, leaning against the edge of the desk before her. "Wait…are you serious?"

"Absolutely. Did you think I'd let you leave without dragging me along?"

"Dana…" Emotion knots in my throat.

"Don't get mushy on me. Just say yes, because I already ordered new business cards."

"I was secretly hoping you'd come with me. I just didn't want to be selfish and ask."

She snorts. "Please. With what you'll be paying me? I'd be an idiot not to. Boss."

I shake my head, a grin tugging at my lips before it disappears. "So, there's something else we need to discuss…"

The discomfort grows; I don't know how she will process the news of the man I'm married to, but I won't hide it anymore.

"And what's that?" She leans closer, as though bracing for whatever I'm about to say.

"So…" I lift my left hand, and that's when she catches my rings.

"Holy shit." Her eyes grow. "Who? How? When? I have too many questions."

"That's the funny part." I nip at my bottom lip. "Or maybe the not-so-funny part, depends on how you take it."

"Okay, did you marry a serial killer or something?" She laughs.

My face twists in a grimace. "Well…"

"Wait, I was kidding. Did you?" she whispers. "Oh my God, just spill it out because there are too many things floating in my head right now."

I pinch the bridge of my nose. "Do you remember Aleksei Marinov?"

"The sexy Russian criminal you spent months trying to rail—I mean nail? Of course I do." Her mouth quirks up, and then her brows shoot up as realization hits. "No way! Are you fucking kidding me? And you kept it from me? Wait…" Her hand cups her mouth. "He's the secret guy, isn't he? He's the one who saved you that night you got drugged?"

I nod.

"Holy crap. For once in my life, I don't know what to say."

"Some days, neither do I."

The shock of it all still hasn't left her face. "But why would you marry him? I don't get it. You hate him."

"I did. But things got…well, complicated. It had a lot to do with saving my parents' vineyard, and he was the only one willing to help."

"Shit. He told you you'd have to marry him before he'd help, right? Wow. This is like a movie."

"Yeah. A movie. Sure." I let out a short chuckle. "I haven't told very many people. Well, actually, no one knows aside from our families. And Emilia, of course."

"Don't worry, I can keep your secret."

"That's the thing. I don't even know if I want it to be a secret anymore, because I'm actually happy."

"Well, that's great, then." She shrugs. "Life is too short. If marrying a sexy murderer makes you happy, I say good for you."

"You always know just what to say." I roll my eyes playfully.

"I know, right? Aren't you happy you're going to have me here with you?”

“You have no idea.”

I mean that, because knowing she’ll be by my side in this new beginning makes all the difference.

When I get home, the door opens before I can touch it, one of Aleksei’s men stepping aside as I walk in to find Aleksei already waiting.

His jacket’s off, shirtsleeves rolled, collar open just enough to expose the skin I ache to touch. And that smile—God, that wicked, knowing curve of his lips—is aimed at me like a weapon.

“Zdravstvuy, moya zhena.” *Hello, my wife.*

Thankfully, my Russian has been coming along in these last few weeks.

He closes the distance in a few long strides, arms wrapping around me before I can reply. His mouth brushes mine in a kiss that starts soft, then deepens, stealing the breath right out of me.

“I’m sorry I’m late.”

The words barely leave my lips before he’s backing me against the nearest wall, one hand sliding to the side of my neck, the other gripping my hip like he intends to leave his mark there.

“Never apologize.” The words ghost over my lips as he kisses me again, harder this time, his nose trailing up the line of my throat while he breathes me in like he has been starving for the scent of my skin. “I missed you,” he whispers as my fingers thread into his hair, tugging him closer.

“I missed you too.”

For a moment, neither of us moves as we breathe each other in, his forehead pressed to mine, our bodies flush, his thumb tracing circles at my waist like he can’t quite let go. And I don’t want him to.

"Is everyone here?"

His lips graze my temple as he answers, low enough for only me to hear. "Yes. But we waited for you."

He threads his fingers through mine and guides me toward the dining room, and the moment we step inside, a smile pulls at my mouth. Our family fills the room, voices weaving over one another, laughter warming every corner. For a moment, I just stand there taking it in, loving the sight of all of us together.

As soon as they see me, conversations fade and faces turn. Emilia rises immediately and wraps me in a hug before I go to my parents. My father kisses my cheek and reaches for the chair beside him, but Aleksei already steers me to the seat next to him with a gentle pressure at my back.

Across the table, my mother sits with Kirill, apparently teaching him Italian.

"No, no," she says, waving a finger at him like a schoolteacher. "It's *vorrei* del vino, not vo-ray de weeno."

Kirill raises an unimpressed brow, muttering something in Russian, and my mother gasps.

"Was that a curse word?" she demands, laughing even as she swats at him with a cloth napkin.

"I will try again." Kirill clears his throat and butchers it again. "That's it. I give up."

"Eh." My mother scoffs. "Giving up is for pussies."

"Mom!"

Kirill laughs, while my father looks mortified.

"Porca miseria, Angelica! Come on."

"What? I speak the truth."

They go on like this back and forth, Kirill teaching her some Russian, and her with Italian.

I stare at my dad for a bit as he sips on his wine, looking genuinely relaxed for the first time in forever. This is our life now, and they can finally breathe a little easier.

Across from Dad, Emilia rests her head on Konstantin's shoulder. When she catches my eyes, a smile spreads.

I love you, she mouths, and I give it right back.

My gaze then drifts to Lev, his small body curled over a thick book, fingertips gliding across the page as he reads to himself, completely absorbed, his headphones snug over his ears. He glances up briefly, his eyes scanning the room until they find mine.

He doesn't smile or wave, simply looking at me, and it's enough to make me wonder what it would feel like to have a son of our own. A child with Aleksei's eyes and my stubbornness, or maybe the other way around.

My hand drifts to my stomach before I catch myself, smoothing down my blouse instead.

As the table erupts in laughter again—this time at my father trying to pronounce "zdrastvuyte" and butchering it worse than Kirill did Italian—I lean into Aleksei's side, my head resting on his shoulder as he slides an arm around me.

It's not just love I feel. It's home.

But the thought that's been building in my chest for days won't stay down any longer. My pulse beats faster as I tilt my head toward him.

I'm terrified. I don't know what he'll do with this news, but I'll burst if I keep it to myself any longer.

"Can we talk? Privately?" I ask him.

His brows knit, that protective edge already sharpening behind his eyes. "Of course, lyubov moya. Come."

He stands, his palm warm against the small of my back as he leads me out of the dining room, the laughter and chatter fading behind us. The kitchen is quiet, and for a moment, I can't seem to find the right words. My palms are clammy, my throat dry.

"I know this is too soon." I glance down at the marble counter before meeting his curious stare. "And we've never really discussed it, but I think I forgot the pill a few days, and—"

He stiffens instantly. "What?"

My heart races as the words tumble out. "Ya beremenna."

His eyes widen, the Russian catching him off guard. "Did you just say…" He cradles my cheek. "Fiona, what are you saying?"

"I'm pregnant, Aleksei." My voice trembles, despite my best efforts to steady it. "You're going to be a daddy."

For a moment, there's only silence. The air between us is heavy enough to crush me. His expression shifts with shock, disbelief, maybe even fear, and my stomach recoils.

Shit. What if he never wanted this? What if this will ruin everything we've rebuilt?

Then suddenly, he grins, slow at first and then fully. Beautifully. And the sight knocks the air out of me.

He lets out a quiet, disbelieving laugh and shakes his head before lifting me clean off my feet, spinning me around. "You have just given me the best news of my life."

"Aleksei," I whisper through tears as he kisses me.

He pulls back just enough to see my face, his thumb sweeping along my jaw with a softness that makes my chest tighten. "I love you. You and this little one…you are everything to me."

"I love you too, Aleksei."

A low growl rumbles out of him before he lifts me off the floor in one smooth motion, spinning me as I laugh. "We have to tell the family."

"Okay," I manage between giggles as he sets me down, his hands firm at my hips.

Suddenly, he drops to his knees and rests his cheek against my stomach, whispering something in Russian I can't decipher, but feel everywhere. His fingers curl around the backs of my thighs, holding me there before he presses a kiss to my stomach.

My own emotions hit me, and when he rises, his stare is filled with affection he doesn't bother hiding.

The moment we reenter the dining room, conversation stops cold.

Kirill's attention moves to me, then to Aleksei with a flicker of curiosity. "Are you okay? You are smiling too much, brother. It is scaring me."

Aleksei ignores him entirely, his hand still firm on my waist. "I'm going to be a father."

For one long second, silence reigns. Then the room erupts all at once—shouts, laughter, congratulations.

Emilia reaches me first, wrapping me up so tightly I stumble back a step. "I can't believe we're pregnant together."

"I know," I laugh, the joy bubbling up in my chest.

My parents sweep in, both of them pulling me into a hug, my mom already tearing up. Across the table, Aleksei's brothers congratulate him too.

As I look around the room at what we've created, my heart feels too full for my body. Whatever came before, whatever darkness we walked through to get here, it led us to this.

Our future. Our family.

And for the first time, I truly believe we'll have it all.

FIFTY-TWO

ALEKSEI

I never thought I would have children.

It was never something I pictured for myself. Not because I didn't want it, but because I didn't believe I was capable of being any kind of father. Not after the one I had.

But then there's Fiona. When I look into her eyes, I start to believe maybe I could be more. Better than what I had.

She makes me want that. She makes me want everything.

The dining room is still loud, the table littered with empty plates and wineglasses, dessert only half eaten.

I lean toward her, mouth brushing her ear. "I'm done sharing you tonight."

She turns to me with a teasing smile. "Oh? And what do you have in mind?"

My palm grasps the side of her face. "Everything."

When she gazes at me like that—like she already knows exactly what I mean, like she wants this life with me just as badly—something cracks open in my chest. All the violence and ugliness that led us here, every lie and betrayal and fight we survived, it's worth it.

Because I have her. She's mine.

And somehow, after everything, I get this life with her as though I'm worthy.

My hand finds her thigh beneath the table, and she sucks in a quick breath, just enough for me to notice. She presses her knee against mine, almost like a dare.

That's all I need.

"Let's go."

She glances at me out of the corner of her eye, lips curving into something smug and sweet and wholly dangerous. "Yes, sir."

A growl rumbles out of me as I take her hand and guide her out of the dining room, past the echo of laughter and the clinking of glasses.

When we reach our bedroom, I shut the door behind us, needing her more than I ever have. She stands in the middle of the room watching me, like she's offering herself to me. And it's a gift every time, something I will always treasure.

I stalk toward her, taking my time, while her lips part, that perfect red lipstick just waiting for me to ruin it. When I reach her, I stop just shy of touching her, letting the anticipation burn between us. My knuckles graze her cheek, and she lets out a soft sound, leaning into my hand like she needs the touch as much as I do.

"I love you so much, Fiona. You've given me something I never thought I'd have."

"And what's that?"

"A future."

Her expression falters, just for a second. Like she didn't expect me to say that. But it's the truth. I am more than my father thought I would be. I'm a husband. A father. And I will carry that weight with pride for the rest of my life.

"You're going to be an incredible dad."

My jaw tics. "I don't know how."

She kisses my cheek, soft and certain. "You'll learn, just like you learned how to love me."

And somehow, looking into her eyes, I believe it.

"I never thought I'd be good at this. Marriage. Love. I didn't think I could be anything other than what I was built to become."

She leans in, her body fitting perfectly against mine, her gaze steady and unflinching. "You're more than that, Aleksei. You always have been. You just needed someone to remind you."

I exhale slowly, running a hand down her back, grounding myself in the feeling of her. "If we have a son, I don't want him to be like me. I don't want this life for him. I want him to be like you."

"He will be whatever he was meant to be. Our job is to lead him on that path. It's all we can do."

I look at her then, really look, and it hits me how much she has changed everything. How far I've come from the man I was.

"Tell me you want this," I tell her, brushing her hair away from her face. "Tell me you want me."

It's not enough to feel it. I need to hear it. I need her to say the words, to make them real.

She lifts her hand to my neck. "I want all of it. You. Us. This life. No matter the cost."

And that's it. That's all I need. Everything inside me stills.

Then I'm on her, my hand wrapping around her chin as I crush my mouth to hers like I've been starving for it. I kiss her with bruising intensity, claiming what's already mine. Her arms wind around my neck as I lift her effortlessly, her body melting into mine. I carry her to our bed, the rest of the world falling away.

We tumble onto the mattress, and I undress her slowly, like she's holy and I'm a sinner with no right to touch her, but with every intention of worshiping her anyway. She doesn't look away as I remove my clothes, her eyes on mine, carrying a trust I'll spend my whole life trying to earn.

I want her to see me. Truly see me. Not the man I once was, but the man standing before her now. The man she made.

I press my palm to the smooth, bare skin of her stomach. There's no bump yet. Just the faintest curve I imagine, even if I know it's too early. But I swear I feel it.

Right here. This is where our future begins.

"She, or he, is going to love their papa," she whispers, her hand sliding over mine, holding it there.

Her words echo through me, and I want so badly to believe them.

"I would die for you. For this child."

She lifts her head and kisses me. "I don't need you to die for us. I need you to live."

"I will."

Because for the first time in my life, I have something worth living for.

I lower my body between her thighs, my cock heavy and throbbing as I position it against her, the metal of my piercings dragging over her in a way that pulls a strangled moan from her throat. My mouth brushes hers as my hand slides down, forcing its way between her thighs. I stroke her once, then push deeper, just enough to make her gasp.

"Good girl. Always so wet for me," I growl against her lips, driving my fingers harder and adding a third, stretching her exactly the way she likes it. "You want more?"

"Yes…"

She grinds down on my hand and takes everything I give her. Her nails dig into my shoulders, her body squeezing tight around my fingers, right on the edge. And when she's seconds from coming, trembling for it, I pull my hand away.

She gasps from the shock, fingers sliding into my hair as she grips tight. "I swear if you stop now…"

"You'll what? Hmm?" With both hands, I open her legs up and stare at her glistening cunt. "What are you going to do, wife?" I spank her pussy, and her eyes roll back.

"Fuck, Aleksei, please."

"That's more like it." I give her another slap, rubbing my palm over her before I lower to her center and suck her into my mouth.

"Yes, yes, yes!" Her fingers dig into my scalp, her body writhing, chasing the orgasm she needs so badly that every tremor shudders through me. "I'm so close."

When I suck her clit and tease it with the tip of my tongue, she cries out.

"Aleksei! Oh God!"

She comes hard, spilling down my throat, and I drink every drop. Because it's all mine. Everything she is belongs to me. Her legs quiver, her body arched, and seeing her like this…it's like seeing heaven.

When I climb back up and kiss her, she laughs, blowing out a breath. "You're really good at that."

"Eating?" My lips trace her jaw. "Yes, I am a very hungry man."

My cock aches to be inside her; I rub it against her as she winces.

"Fuck me, please," she groans, her eyes heavy-lidded.

Without giving her a second to think, I line myself up and thrust into her in one hard stroke, burying every inch inside her. Her body tightens around me, a sound tearing from her throat that makes my grip on her hips tighten. My fingers find her clit, rubbing slow at first, just enough to make her tremble.

"Shit, I can't come again so fast."

"Of course you can. Show me what I can make you do."

Her breathing stutters, need overtaking every trace of hesitation. I speed up—my hips, my fingers—pushing her exactly where I want her. The tension in her body eases, and within seconds, she's shaking, pleading for more, begging for release.

And I give it to her. Pulling both legs up over my shoulders, I open her up and fill her the way she needs.

Who knew a man like me could ever have something so beautiful?

"You are everything to me." The words rip from my lungs as I take her harder, like I'm trying to carve the truth into her skin. "Moya zhizn. Moya sem'ya. Moya krov." *My life. My family. My blood.*

She drags me down to her, kissing me like she's choosing me all over again.

"Ya tebya lyublyu, Aleksei," she breathes, her pulse slamming against my heart, saying my name like it belongs to her alone.

And I'll spend the rest of my life earning the right to hear it.

THANKS FOR READING!

Want more Aleksei & Fiona? Scan the code below for a bonus scene!

I hope you're ready for possessive single daddy *Kirill* and his love, Sloane.

While you wait, jump into the *Savage Kings* series to get more of the Quinn family!

PLAYLIST

- "Enemies to Lovers" by Ruby Darkrose
- "Obsessed" by Henri Werner
- "Under My Skin – Soft Version" by Ash to Eden
- "Good Girl" by April Jai
- "Hate That I Love You" by Jonathan Roy
- "Come and Get It" by Austin Giorgio
- "Touchin' Me" by Chandler Leighton
- "Poison" by David Kushner
- "I Want It All" by Omido feat. Mandrazo and Rick Jansen
- "Never Ever" by Omido
- "Darling U Don't Make Me Wanna Stay" by Psylosia
- "Watch It Burn" by Oscen
- "Want Me" by Ex Habit
- "Cold Touch" by Psylosia
- "Raw" by Josh Alexander
- "Everything on Earth With You" by Allegra Jordyn
- "Masterpiece" by Sam Short
- "Y.O.U." by Raphael Lake
- "Love You Right" by Shaker feat. COBRA
- "Let Me Fall" by Ex Habit feat. BURY
- "Nasty Nasty" by Rumelis
- "Fantasy" by April Jai
- "Outta My Head" by Omido feat. Rick Jansen and Ordell
- "Love Me" by Ex Habit
- "Sweat On Your Skin" by Rumelis feat. Beneld and Omido
- "Not a Love Song" by Elvis Drew
- "Aphrodite" by Sam Short

- "All Mine – Remix" by Wavey Vayn feat. KAIT
- "Pay for You" by Psylosia
- "Don't U Cry" by Omido
- "Daydream" by Rob the Sun feat. Roby Fayer
- "Prey" by LIBERTO feat. Tara
- "The Wall" by PatrickReza
- "Porcelain" by Faouzia
- "Dancing With the Devil" by EMO
- "Sleep Through" by memyself&vi
- "Лилии" by MOT feat. JONY
- "Believe It" by Jared Benjamin
- "Play With Fire" by Sam Tinnesz feat. Yacht Money
- "Claim You Tonight" by Velvet Desires
- "Mine Tonight" by Velvet Desires
- "Lock & Key" by Velvet Desires

ALSO BY LILIAN HARRIS

Fragile Hearts Series

1. *Fragile Scars* (Damian & Lilah)
2. *Fragile Lies* (Jax & Lexi Part 1)
3. *Fragile Truths* (Jax & Lexi Part 2)
4. *Fragile Pieces* (Gabe & Mia)

Cavaleri Brothers Series

1. *The Devil's Deal* (Dominic & Chiara)
2. *The Devil's Pawn* (Dante & Raquel)
3. *The Devil's Secret* (Enzo & Jade)
4. *The Devil's Den* (Matteo & Aida)
5. *The Devil's Demise* (Extended Epilogue)

Messina Crime Family Series

1. *Sinful Vows* (Michael & Elsie)
2. *Cruel Lies* (Raph & Nicolette)
3. *Twisted Promises* (Gio & Iseult)
4. *Savage Wounds* (Adriel & Kayla)

Savage Kings Series

1. *Ruthless Savage* (Devlin & Eriu)

2. *Brutal Savage* (Tynan & Elara)
3. *Filthy Savage* (Fionn & Amara)
4. *Wicked Savage* (Cillian & Dinara)

Marinov Bratva Series

1. *Konstantin* (Konstantin & Emilia)
2. *Aleksei* (Aleksei & Fiona)
3. *Kirill* (Kirill & Sloane - Spring 2026)
4. *Anton* (Winter 2026)

Standalone

1. *Shattered Secrets* (Husdon & Hadleigh)

For Lilian, a love of writing began with a love of books. From Goosebumps to romance novels with sexy men on the cover, she loved them all. It's no surprise that at the age of eight she started writing poetry and lyrics and hasn't stopped writing since.

She was born in Azerbaijan, and currently resides on Long Island, N.Y. with her husband, three kids, and lots of animals. Even though she has a law degree, she isn't currently practicing. When she isn't writing or reading, Lilian is baking or cooking up a storm. And once the kids are in bed, there's usually a glass of red in her hand. Can't just survive on coffee alone!

FIND LILIAN ONLINE

www.ingramcontent.com/pod-product-compliance
Lightning Source LLC
Chambersburg PA
CBHW071752310726

48976CB00001BA/93